To Pam

GW01048763

Quarter Acre Block

by

Janet Gogerty

Best Wishes

Janet

Dedications

To Cyberspouse
my mother and sister
Lesley and Martin
Pat and Martin
in memory of Frank
and in memory of Beryl

By the same author

Novels

The Brief Encounters Trilogy

Brief Encounters of the Third Kind
Three Ages of Man
Lives of Anna Alsop

Collections

Dark and Milk
Hallows and Heretics
Times and Tides
Someone Somewhere

Table of Contents

Prologue   December 1963

As autumn brought dark evenings and the walls of their terraced house closed in, George began visiting Australia House in his lunch hour. The winter of '63 had been the last straw. George and Helen wanted to emigrate to Australia. They did not expect to make their fortune, but reasoned they would rather live on a tight budget somewhere warm. During the summer of 1963 they had faltered; to move to the other side of the world and never return seemed unthinkable; but late one December evening, alone in their small dining room, George and Helen whispered and pored over brochures and forms.

'One thing's for sure,' said Helen 'we've grown out of this house.'

Her third pregnancy had been a surprise and the arrival of twins a shock; owning their own house had been a dream come true until then.

'When they built these little houses in the thirties, people were thrilled to have an inside bathroom' laughed George.

'...and a garden' added Helen.

'Everyone lives in detached houses in Australia, with a laundry as well. By next Christmas we could be in a new house on a quarter acre block of land. Jennifer could have all those pets she wants and I could have my workshop.'

'Oh George, I don't think I could bear it if they turned us down.'

'They won't, it's an enormous country with hardly anybody in it; why else would they be paying our fares? Ten pounds to fly across the world.'

'Or voyage across the oceans.'

'Six weeks at sea with our lot, no thanks. Besides, I've looked into it; if we opt to fly, we should get our passage much quicker.' He gathered the attractive brochures into one pile and the forms into another. 'If we post these off, we're going to go, no turning back. But we can not tell anyone yet, not your mother, or your sister or Joyce and certainly not the children; it wouldn't be fair to get their hopes up until we're absolutely certain.'

She kissed his cheek and handed him the pen.

Chapter One   Jennifer

Jennifer remembered only the best parts of last winter; the beautiful patterns Jack Frost left on the bedroom windows overnight, the fun they had playing on crunchy, fresh white snow and the thrill of skating down their little road, where the old snow had compacted hard and smooth. She had forgotten the chilblains, frozen fingers, cold feet on the walk to school and the dash across the playground to the old toilet block.

She loved the exciting build up to Christmas; the deep reds and dark greens of winter, the cosy short days and the preparations for the nativity play. Now she was ten years old and in top juniors, she knew she would never play Mary or an angel. She was resigned to being in the chorus and helping others dress up in tea-towels, old curtains and dressing gowns, but she still loved the atmosphere and the Christmas carols thumped out on the piano.

Life in the Victorian buildings of Saint Stephen's Church of England school was safe, orderly and predictable. Four classes of forty children, one for each year, with the same teachers who had taught her older brother Simon. At morning assembly the headmaster spoke, Mrs. Jones played the piano and the fourth years sung a new hymn every Friday. Occasionally the vicar of Saint Stephen's visited.

On Monday mornings they paid their dinner money in, for the privilege of sitting at long benches toying with mounds of cabbage or staring at pink custard. If a child liked school dinners you knew their mother was a bad cook.

For the Christmas party the dining hall was transformed and the little glass bottles contained orange juice instead of milk.

Jennifer's parents and Simon came to watch her and the twins in the nativity play. The seven year old brothers made adorable shepherds and her performance in the back row of the choir went unnoticed.

Her big brother was fourteen, a grammar school boy and she regarded him with awe. As they walked back home up the hill after the play, he said to her, out of their parents' earshot, 'Nativity plays are stupid.'

She agreed with him, until he said none of it was true, she was shocked.

'Is Father Christmas true?' he whispered.

She was not a little kid, they pretended for the sake of Peter and Tony.

'Well nor is Jesus' declared Simon triumphantly.

'Of course he is' she replied defiantly.

The thought of not having Christmas was awful. In Scotland they had New Year instead, she felt sorry for Scottish children.

Indoors, the twins scuffled and protested about going to bed.

'Have you done your homework Simon?' asked their father.

'I could have finished it by now if you hadn't made me come to the play' he retorted.

Simon had to do his homework on the dining room table. Most evenings there was a rush to clear the table and push things through the hatch into the kitchen. When everyone was indoors, which was most of the time in winter; there was never enough room in their narrow 1930s mid-terrace house. They would squash together in the front room to watch television. If Simon had finished his homework he would want to put the record player on, while their father was settling to watch a documentary. On Friday evenings Simon was allowed to stay up to see 'That Was the Week That Was' while Jennifer lay resentfully wide awake listening to their laughter.

Upstairs, Simon had the tiny box room, with hardly room for a bed, her parents slept in the front bedroom and Jennifer shared the back bedroom with the twins. They swapped round regularly between the single bed and the bunks; the top bunk was most popular. Jennifer was promised the box room when she 'started growing up'. Simon grumbled continually that his room was too small, nor did he want to share with the twins.

On Palm Sunday St Stephen's was strewn with real palm leaves, bringing a scent of the Holy Land to the London suburbs. At school choir practice they had to sing 'There is a Green Hill' and keep their faces solemn. Jennifer only liked rousing hymns such as 'Hills of The North' and 'Guide Me Oh Thou Great Jehovah'. The vicar said Easter was even more important than Christmas, Jennifer felt guilty that she much preferred Christmas. On Easter Sunday the church was bright with fresh flowers and she wondered how many Easter eggs awaited them at home.

That evening she was allowed to stay up later, till the twins were safely asleep. The television was switched off and she and Simon were told to sit in the front room to hear important news.

'Australia,' exclaimed Simon 'why didn't you tell me?'

'We are telling you now' grinned his father. 'We haven't even told your grandparents yet, no point in getting everyone excited or upset till we know for sure.

'I'm excited,' said Jennifer 'going on an aeroplane to a hot country; I could learn to swim and we could have a dog.'

'I'm sure you can, when we're settled' smiled her mother.

'Or a horse... like those children on television.'

'What about my friends?' complained Simon.

'They can come on holiday to see you' said Jennifer.

'It's a bit further than the Isle of Wight' he sneered.

'You'll make new friends son' his father reassured him. 'Besides, the way things are going, you won't be the only boy at your school emigrating.'

She and Simon were sworn to secrecy; the twins must not know yet, they were sure to tell. No one must know, just in case; in case of what Jennifer wasn't sure. Perched on top of the concrete coal bunker, nibbling her Easter egg in the watery spring sunshine, she hugged the secret to her eleven year old self.

The summer term felt unreal. Everyone was talking about the eleven plus; the merits of the boys' and girls' grammar schools and the secondary modern were debated. It didn't matter to Jennifer, in Australia everyone went to the same school.

On sunny weekends they played 'down the rec' two roads away. Two roads filled with identical terraced houses, their ranks broken only by the narrow ways that led to the back lanes; access for the dustmen and those lucky enough to own a car and a little asbestos garage to put it in. Her friend Christine lived in an end terrace, next to the lane that led to the side gate of the recreation ground. Jennifer would call for her and they would pelt down the grassy slope to the tree lined ditch and jump over. In winter or on rainy days the steep banks were muddy, the sticky London clay clutching at their feet. In hot weather the clay was baked hard and grazed your knees if you fell. They clung to the leaning tree then raced up hill to the playground. Swinging high and whizzing round on the witch's hat roundabout, Jennifer gazed up at the sky, wondering how high an aeroplane would fly.

She and her mother went shopping for summer clothes; there was the school holiday to the Isle of Wight coming up and the clothes would get plenty of wear; they were going to have two summers in a row. She pleaded with her mother to go in the record shop; she was in love with Paul McCartney and Simon wanted to be John Lennon. At home she supported Simon when he wanted to watch 'Top of The Pops' and 'Ready, Steady Go'. He was impressed with her growing knowledge of the new pop groups bursting onto the scene.

The brotherly respect didn't last long, he was soon teasing her that she would be homesick and cry when she went to the Isle of Wight. She stuck her tongue out at him.

'I hope you two are going to behave when we go up for our interview' said their mother.

'The interview' was looming large in all their minds, Jennifer was getting nervous. Her father claimed the Australian officials would be more interested in the children than the adults; they were going to be the future Australian citizens. She knew she mustn't let her parents down.

On a Thursday afternoon, Mrs Wells gave the final instructions for the school holiday departure the next morning. They had already handed in their ten shillings pocket money to be kept safe by the headmaster. Jennifer remembered what time they had to be at the local station and the exhortations to good behaviour; somehow she didn't hear Mrs Wells say they could bring a small amount of money to spend on the journey.

Her father kissed her goodbye before he went off to the station. 'Ignore Simon, you've stayed away from home before, with Aunty and Grandma.'

'I won't be homesick at all' she replied. 'I'm looking forward to getting away from the boys.'

Her mother had to take the twins to school, she didn't trust them to go alone; they would have to dash off as soon as Alison's mother had picked Jennifer up. Alison was an only child and her mother owned a car, so she had offered Jennifer and Christine a lift.

The girls giggled excitedly on the way to the local station. Alison was embarrassed as her mother fretted and went through a list of all the things that could go wrong. Her family also had a telephone.

'Don't forget Jennifer and Christine, any problems, the headmaster can ring my house and I'll let your parents know.'

The two friends felt smugly grown up; they weren't expecting to have any problems and their parents weren't expecting to hear from them until their return next Friday.

When they arrived at Waterloo Station the headmaster, teacher and student helpers shepherded them onto the concourse and lined them up for the toilets, before recounting and heading them for the platform.

They boarded a steam train for Portsmouth and the children squealed with excitement as it built up steam and chugged out of the station. Jennifer felt the adventure was really beginning; if it was this exciting going by train to the Isle of Wight, the thought of taking off on an aeroplane to Australia was beyond imagining.

Some of the children had acquired sweets, she was puzzled.

'Didn't you bring any pocket money?' said Christine.

When they were safely on board the ferry Jennifer was disappointed how close the Isle of Wight looked, but as they leaned on the rail, feeling the wind and looking at the choppy water, she knew The Solent was real sea.

At Ryde everyone was buying ice creams and she was mortified to be the only child without money. She looked up to see Christine approaching with a cone in each hand.

'I just had enough money' she said kindly.

Suddenly Jennifer realised what Simon meant; she would miss her friends and her secret felt like a betrayal.

A coach took them across the island to their hotel; Christine, Jennifer, Alison and three other girls were soon exploring the room they were going to share. They'd had to help Alison carry her suitcase up the stairs; her mother had packed for every eventuality. Dinner wasn't a lot different from school dinners, except for being in the evening and cosy without the rest of the school. It turned out there was a catch to this holiday; after dinner the tables were cleared, new exercise books were handed out and they had to start a diary. Most of the boys did a lurid picture of Nicholas being sick on the coach. Jennifer drew a picture of the steam train and tried to write a poem. When the headmaster said stop, it didn't mean work was finished; they had to turn the book upside down and start from the back. Each evening they were going to do nature notes, starting with the tides of The Solent.

At bedtime the girls chatted, then whispered when Mrs Wells rapped on the door. Alison said they'd better go to sleep; her mother often told fellow parents that Alison needed eleven hours sleep every night. Sleep was the last thing on the minds of the other girls; they felt like their favourite characters in boarding school stories. There was so much to talk about; the Beatles, the young man from Germany who was one of their student helpers and which girls would pass the eleven plus.

'If I pass and you don't Jenny, I'm not going to the grammar school' said Christine loyally. 'I'm coming to the secondary modern with you.'

'If I pass, I'm going to get a new bike' said Alison, who had realised she didn't feel tired either.

'What if you don't pass?' asked Jennifer.

'I'm going to private school.'

'Then you'll be called a cherry' laughed Christine, reminding Alison the girls at the private school had green berets with a large red pom-pom in the middle.

Jennifer drifted off to sleep, thinking of everyone going to their new schools without her; were her family going to get on the aeroplane without telling anyone?

By the third night Alison was crying at bed time. Mrs Wells took her away to have another mug of hot chocolate, lest she upset the others. There was no chance of that; Alison's tears reminded the other girls they had not thought of home.

The first half of the week seemed to last for ever they did so many things, but the last few days sped by quickly. They visited Carisbrook castle, spent their precious pocket money on glass ornaments full of coloured sand at Alum Bay and paddled.

'No deeper than your waist' said the nervous headmaster, as they waded into the sea. Few of the class could actually swim. Jennifer thought smugly of how she would soon learn to swim in Australia; it wasn't the sea there, it was the ocean and she was going to go in it every day.

There were a few weeks left till the end of term and the end of Junior School. On Monday morning Jennifer's father was at home, he had taken the day off to visit the estate agents; their application to emigrate had been confirmed.

At school the headmaster came into the classroom to talk to her class. His visits made a welcome intrusion into lessons and he would chat about anything that came into his mind; geography, space rockets, the universe. Today he put his hand casually on the globe that sat on Mrs. Wells' desk.

'Who can tell me where Australia is?'

'Down under' quipped one boy.

Jennifer kept her arm down, hoping this was a coincidence; with her eyes lowered guiltily she didn't notice he was looking at her.

'Stand up Jennifer Palmer.'

She stood up nervously.

'Jennifer's parents came to see me today.'

The other children were losing interest.

'The Palmer family are moving to Australia…'

Now every child's attention was caught, there was a murmur as they turned to stare at her.

'…permanently. Does anyone know what that is called?'

No response.

'I'm sure Jennifer can tell us.'

Her mouth felt dry. 'Emigrating Sir.'

'Yes, I had a nice chat with your parents, can you tell us why you are going?'

For a moment her mind was blank, why were they going? So she could have a dog, because their house was too small? Then she remembered her parents' words.

'To start a new life Sir.'

At playtime, the girl who had spent her junior school years being fairly anonymous, was now surrounded by her whole class.

'Is it true... are you going to see kangaroos... will you live in Sydney... will you sail on a big ship?'

Christine and Alison had hung back, confused and silent.

Chapter Two   Summer 1964

George laughed at the silence of the house as they walked in at lunchtime.

'Strange being home on a weekday. Headmaster seems a nice chap. No going back now, time to tell everyone.'

'Time to get the house tidied up for the estate agent' said Helen. 'Such a lot to do now it's really happening.'

Upstairs they stood on the tiny landing wondering where to start.

'We'll clear the loft first and work our way downwards' he said, making it sound simple. He looked at his watch. 'Two hours till Jenny and the twins get home.'

'Is that enough time to tackle the loft?'

'No, I've got a better idea, let's celebrate.'

He swung her round through the bedroom door; giggling they fell on the bed.

'George, it's the middle of the day.'

'How often do we get the chance not to be disturbed? We can close the curtains if that will make you feel better.'

'No; then Mrs Watkins will definitely know what's going on, she was already peeping through her nets, wondering why you were home on a weekday.'

Within a few moments they had forgotten Mrs. Watkins.

'I hope you haven't run out' said Helen as he fumbled in the bedside drawer.

'A scout is always prepared, we don't want any more Palmers... well not till we get to Australia.'

'Not at all,' she laughed 'we're nearly forty.'

'Let's not waste any more time talking' he whispered as he rolled on top of her.

When he was inside her she tilted her face up and sought his lips. How long since they had kissed properly, passionately?

Afterwards she snuggled against him and he wrapped the crumpled counterpane around her.

They were woken suddenly by the door bell ringing; for a moment they forgot where they were, what day it was.

'The children' said Helen in a panic.

'Stay here and get dressed, better comb your hair' he smiled, as he hurriedly put his trousers on.

The twins burst through the door excitedly. 'Is it true Daddy, are we going to Australia?'

Jennifer stood sullenly behind them.

Over milk and biscuits they tried to calm the twins and pacify their daughter.

'I kept my promise, I wanted to tell my friends myself; now Christine's not talking to me.'

'I'm sorry love, we didn't know the headmaster was going to talk to your class, we thought it would be polite to tell him before everyone else knew. I think he's just pleased for the three of you.'

Helen was in the same position as her daughter; she had planned to pop round and see Christine's mother while George was busy, not spend the afternoon making love. She and Joyce had been friends since the girls started school.

'While Dad's here to look after the boys, we could go round to see Aunty Joyce and Christine.'

Jennifer brightened up. 'Mum, can you take dogs to Australia? Maybe her family would like to emigrate; their house is too small and their dog could have a nice big garden.'

When the eleven plus results came out Jennifer and Christine had both passed, Helen was pleased for Joyce. Nobody saw Alison's mother for a week; then they heard Alison had failed. When her mother finally emerged, Helen and Joyce were amused to hear her telling everyone how much better the private school was than the grammar.

Having reassured Jennifer, when Simon teased her, that it didn't matter if she failed, George and Helen were now at pains to tell her they were proud she had passed, but it was her brother's approval that pleased her most.

They now had a flight date for the end of September; it would not be worth Jennifer starting at the grammar school. The twins would start the autumn term to keep them safely out of the way while the house was packed up. Simon had realised that he would be fifteen by the time they arrived in Australia; the school leaving age. Leaving school was the last thing his parents wanted him to do. They had collected information on the education system and wanted him to complete fourth and fifth year high school and take his Leaving Exams. His form master, who had a cousin in Australia, had agreed to write reports for his future school, he was sure Simon could bypass the Junior Exams and get in to senior high school on merit.

But for now, George and Helen wanted the children to make the most of their last summer in England. They would not go away on holiday, the future seemed one long holiday, but George had outings planned. He had holiday owing and was working out when to hand in his resignation.

---o0o---

The night before the summer holidays felt as exciting as Christmas Eve. Six whole weeks of playing with her friends and then when everyone else was going back to school, Jennifer would be getting ready for the big adventure.

In a surprising show of brotherly affection Simon offered to take his sister to 'The Rex' to see 'A Hard Day's Night'; not with his friends of course, that would be embarrassing, but he figured his mother would pay for the visit and he would get to see it twice. From the opening chord that sent shivers down her spine, Jennifer loved the film and loved Paul McCartney more than ever. She too saw it twice; it was a continuous showing and Simon told her to sit quietly and watch it through again. It was probably the happiest day of her life, with the added pride of being taken out by her big brother.

Simon was going on a youth group camp at an empty boarding school, it included swimming lessons.

'It's a good opportunity Simon, all the kids in Australia can swim' said his father.

Jennifer was jealous, there was no pool locally and now it sounded as if she would be the only child in Australia who couldn't swim. But she was soon too busy to envy Simon. When they weren't whizzing down the road to the shops on their roller skates or bikes, they were taking Christine's boisterous dog to the 'rec'. It was the first summer Christine was trusted by herself with the dog.

Christine happily believed her family would emigrate also, though her parents had shown no inclination so far to venture across the world. Grammar School seemed a long way off as the two friends planned the first outing of the holidays. They were going with Christine's mother and older sister to the Natural History Museum; a trip involving the local train, the underground and a picnic. In return, Jennifer had volunteered her mother and the twins to take the dog out for his morning and afternoon walks.

Tony and Peter were already arguing over who was going to hold the dog's lead.

Jennifer loved the excitement of arriving at Waterloo Station with all its bustle and then finding their way down to the underground. Aunty Joyce let the girls plot the route on the map and find the correct platform. There was a thrill as the faint rumble grew louder and the lights of the train appeared around the bend just before it emerged from the mouth of the tunnel.

When they arrived at South Kensington Station they rode up the escalator, holding their breath to jump off at the top. Simon had told Jennifer that if you didn't step clear you could be sucked in; she didn't believe him but the girls decided it was best not to take any chances. A further air of excitement was added when they walked through the long tunnel to the museum, their voices echoing off the tiled walls.

Blinking in the sunlight they climbed the impressive stone steps to the main door. Walking into the huge hall they stood in awe; reaching out his long neck to stare back at them was the gigantic skeleton of a dinosaur. The three girls reverently walked the length of his body till they reached the tip of his tail, then back along the other side until they stared up at his vacant eyes again.

Later, eating their squashed cheese and tomato sandwiches in Kensington Gardens, they discussed all they had seen in the museum. How did they get the dinosaur in, who killed the polar bear, who stuffed the lion? Aunty Joyce was enjoying sitting in the sun admiring the beautiful flower beds, but the girls were set on popping back in the museum before they went to the station.

They set off home later than planned and the rush hour had already started. Aunty Joyce warned them to stick together, as they squeezed onto the underground train and stood wedged amongst grumpy commuters.

Chapter Three   Families

That evening George and Helen sat in the front room by themselves. With Simon away, the twins worn out from walking the dog and even Jennifer admitting she was tired after her trip to London, it was a rare chance for them to talk. With the television off they whispered, Helen suspected that her daughter would be trying to listen in. George had already been round to visit his mother by himself to break the news.

'It's not just the shock that we're going, but the realisation there's such a short time till we leave.'

'I know George, it's really beginning to sink in now, what we're doing. I don't think we could do this if either of us were only children. We'll go round on Sunday, we must see as much of her as possible.'

A short bus ride took the family to the house that George had grown up in; the road was identical to the one they lived in now, the terraced houses exactly the same layout. Privet hedges and creosoted fences were a feature of nearly every garden in the street; George and Helen stood at his mother's neatly painted narrow front gate and knew they were making the right decision.

He climbed up into the small loft at his mother's request; no one had been up there since his father died. Peter and Tony delved into the box he brought down.

'I should have passed it on to you ages ago, for your boys' said his mother.

Inside were books and toys he remembered, but had no idea his mother had kept.

'Sort out which ones were Dennis' then take the rest, they should go with you, don't forget the past.'

He opened a book and showed Helen the fly leaf.

To George on your tenth birthday,1935, with love from Mother and Father.

'How long ago that was, they were happy days weren't they Mum?'

'Yes indeed they were; your father and I were so proud to have our own house and be bringing up two fine sons.'

Helen hoped that was not a hint that she and George should be satisfied with what they had. Her thoughts were interrupted by Tony.

'Let me see, Daddy.'

When Simon came back he entertained them with tales of midnight feasts and his swimming prowess. He groaned at the plans for family outings, he wanted to go out exploring on his bike with his friends.

On George's last day at work Simon and Jennifer were to be left to look after the twins for the afternoon and evening; Joyce was coming round to make sure they had a proper meal. After a busy morning leaving the house clean, a stew in the oven and reiterating the instructions she had given her son and daughter, Helen finally stood on the platform waiting for the train to Waterloo. On a rare outing she was meeting George after work to go for a drink and a meal.

It felt strange to be by herself and she kept looking round to see what the twins were up to. On the train she tried to relax and read a book; not worry what the children were doing or if Tony had got hold of the matches. The idea was to get up to town early and enjoy a stroll in Oxford Street.

George and his two closest colleagues had gone for a quiet pint at lunch time, now he took Helen to the same pub, finding a cosy corner.

'I can't remember the last time we did this; missing the rush hour... no more rush hours. I'm not sorry to be leaving and I've vowed never to work in an office again.'

Over the next fortnight the family had outings to central London and the children were impressed at how well their father knew his way around. They walked miles and jumped on and off buses and tube trains. The children were surprised to see where Helen had once worked in a large store on Oxford Street; as if she had not had a life before they were born.

As the school holidays came to an end, there was a large family gathering at the home of George's younger brother, a rambling old house in the depths of Surrey. The children had always loved visiting; exploring the overgrown garden, playing with the rabbits and guinea pigs. Dennis had his own business, no one was sure what he did, but from his life style it seemed to be very successful.

Simon and his eldest cousin were popular with the younger children; helping them climb parts of the huge tree they had never reached before and swinging them round till they could not stand. George's cousins had young children they had not met and Jennifer was put in charge of making sure the rabbits and guinea pigs were kept safe from over enthusiastic hands.

The adults had a lot to talk about.

'Sit and relax Helen,' said Dennis 'the twins can't escape; the older ones will keep an eye on them.'

Great aunts and uncles had tales of cousins who had gone to Canada and a long lost relative in New Zealand. It made George and Helen's adventure seem quite tame.

By the time Tony appeared with a deep cut to his knee and varied accounts from the other children as to what had happened, it was time for tea. Elderly relatives exclaimed how the children had grown and wondered who they took after. As Tony limped around with his knee heavily bandaged, he enjoyed all the attention and the impressive tea.

Later, Dennis walked back to the station with them, more to avoid the big tidy up, Helen thought, than from brotherly love. As Tony limped and Peter skipped along, hanging on to their father's arms, Dennis walked beside Helen.

'It's not too late to change your mind you know, George doesn't have to go all the way to Australia just to change his job, I could probably find him something.'

Helen said nothing.

'You married the wrong brother' he chuckled.

She stiffened; she never knew how to take what Dennis said.

Helen invited her family round for their small get together. Her sister lived at home with their parents, who were hale and hearty; she had felt no qualms about leaving them, but now in the kitchen she tried to talk to her brother. In the future it wouldn't be fair for everything to rest on her sister's shoulders if their parents became frail. It was difficult; with his sick wife and five year old daughter, who had problems that were obliquely referred to, he was reluctant to discuss the future.

On the last day of the holidays Helen and Jennifer went round to Joyce's house and the girls giggled over Christine's bottle green school uniform. On the way home Jennifer was quiet and Helen felt flat. These last few weeks were going to be the hardest.

The house looked bare now; a removal company had taken away the contents that would be shipped on ahead. The children had kept their most precious possessions and given away other things to friends and the church crèche. They were not without furniture; most of it wasn't worth shipping and was being left for the buyers of the house.

Christine came round the next afternoon with tales of Bunsen burners and hockey sticks and Jennifer looked envious for a moment, but her friend had not enjoyed her first day. There was no one in her class from Saint Stephen's; she had naively assumed the half dozen girls would all stay together.

George and Helen were worried the sale of the house would not go through in time. Dennis had insisted they stay at his home in between moving out and flying out. More worryingly for George, he had offered to oversee things if the sale was not completed in time.

'What else can we do?' said Helen.

'We need the mortgage paid off and the capital in the bank before we go,' worried George 'we haven't got any other money.'

Helen knew that only too well. Unlike their parents, they had a joint account and managed the money together. They had no savings and lived from month to month on what was left after the mortgage and bills were paid.

'Perhaps Dennis could lend you a bit to tide us over till we get settled' she suggested tentatively.

'That's the last thing I want to do, admit defeat before we've even started.'

There was a final frantic round of activity, as Dennis and a friend arrived to pick the family up in two cars, four days before their departure. All the neighbours were at their front gates to watch or say goodbye as they filed out of the house with their suitcases. A large removal van heralded the arrival of the new family. Christine hovered by the gate and Simon's friends perched on their bikes on the other side of the road, trying to look nonchalant. As they drove off, Helen and Jennifer looked out the back window of Dennis' posh car, Christine was skipping up the road behind them, waving.

At London Airport there was a gathering of relatives and friends. The Palmers had arrived in plenty of time, too soon Helen felt. They all sat around drinking cups of tea and she and George explained their plans yet again, with interruptions from Simon.

'I wanted to go to Sydney.'

'The only Perth I've heard of is the one in Scotland' repeated Helen's old school friend.

'Perth, Western Australia, on the left hand side' said George. 'In a country of wide open spaces they have even more space. It's a small city, no commuting to work and a Mediterranean climate.'

Looking at the leaden grey sky outside the terminal windows, his friend laughed.

'You've got the right idea George.' He turned to the others. 'At least he's got the guts to try it.'

'We're not trying, we're doing it' George replied. 'We've burnt our boats; we can't afford to come back.'

Perth had another advantage. In the whole continent George only knew one person, John his old army friend, who had migrated ten years before. He had agreed to be their sponsor, so they would not need to stay in a migrant hostel.

Goerge looked at his watch with relief and stood up. The other men picked up the cases and they filed off to the check-in desk. Helen wished everyone would go now.

She was glad they had said goodbye to the close family at Dennis' house. He had invited her family to stay for tea and would be going home to report on their departure.

'Helen, it's time to say goodbye.' George had his arm round her shoulder.

There was a confusing huddle, with the boys trying to avoid being kissed by anybody.

'Don't forget Simon,' Dennis was saying 'finish your schooling first, then you'll be free to do what you want, they'll always be a job back here for you.'

George frowned at his brother, then approached him awkwardly.

'You will look after Mum?'

Dennis clapped his shoulder. 'Mum will be fine; anyway, you'll be back in two years. Come on everybody, we don't want them to miss the plane. He ushered them away with the other straggling, tearful families. It was a charted flight for migrants; for most of the passengers and those saying farewell it was the first time they had been to an airport.

The cases were weighed and disappeared on a conveyer belt, then each of the family were weighed.

'We're really on our way now' said George, as he marched the family off to join the others heading for the exit door.

Chapter Four   Flight

The excitement bubbled up in Jennifer's chest as her mother smiled reassuringly; at last they were really going on an aeroplane. As they crossed the tarmac everyone looked behind them, the balcony was full of waving people. Uncle Dennis had managed to be at the front of the crowd.

They climbed the steps to the Boeing 707 and were ushered in through the narrow door. Air hostesses tried to help the families find their seats in an orderly fashion.

Six was an ideal number, with three seats either side of the aisle. The children had already been instructed where they would sit to avoid arguing on board. Tony and Peter each had a window seat, separated so they couldn't fight. Jennifer and Simon had the middle seats and their parents sat either side of the aisle. Theoretically they would not disturb the other passengers. The aisle was thronged with parents loading bags into the overhead lockers. Helen slipped into her cramped seat beside Jennifer, who was trying to peer over Peter's head to look out of the window.

'Why are the windows so small?' complained Peter.

Jennifer could just make out Uncle Dennis, not waving now. It was unlikely he could see them. Their window looked out across the huge wing. She took out the card from the pocket on the back of the seat in front. Peter had already taken the sick bag out of his pocket and was waving it around. Jennifer read the boldly printed card; on one side were instructions how to put on your life jacket, the other side illustrated how to slide down the escape chute to the inflatable lifeboat.

She was suddenly afraid; it had never occurred to her that the plane could crash and she was sure she would not remember how to put her life jacket on, inflate it and find the emergency whistle. Mum and Dad would have to help the twins and Simon knew how to swim.

Her mother nudged her to do up her seat belt and the plane started moving slowly.

'We're not going very fast,' complained Peter 'when are we going to go up?'

Her father was answering the same question from Tony.

'We have to taxi first, get lined up on the runway.'

Jennifer realised she could no longer see the balcony; they would never see Uncle Dennis and the others again. The plane was rumbling faster, she looked over to the aisle and saw the floor was sloping upwards. She felt a thrill as they increased speed and began their ascent. Her mother looked nervous, but her father had a big grin on his face.

'Cotton wool' declared Peter as they climbed through the clouds.

It seemed they had not had a chance to see what England looked like from the air before they were floating above a heavenly snowy landscape.

The seat belt signs were switched off and stewardesses started rolling trolleys down the aisle, serving tea, coffee and fruit juice. Already some of the children wanted to go to the toilet and the aisle was becoming a busy thoroughfare. Not many families came in convenient numbers and had to sit next to strangers, there was much shuffling and apologising. Jennifer whispered to her mother that the wing seemed to be wobbling; her father had been avidly reading up on Boeing 707s and international flight, but she could not ask him if this was normal without drawing the attention of the twins.

The children had travel bags packed with books and colouring in, but Peter and Tony were more interested in going to the toilet. Half the visits were unnecessary, an excuse to get out of their seats or listen to the suction whoosh of the flush. When they were sitting, the eight year olds fiddled with the pull down trays and her mother worried the people in front would be annoyed. Simon tried to lose himself in his book and Jennifer was teaching Peter 'hangman'. The same scenes were being played over in close proximity by other families.

Dinner was a welcome diversion; the children were fascinated with the layout of their dinner in the segmented plastic tray, while the parents felt it didn't add up to a proper meal.

When the lights were dimmed and the hostesses brought round blankets, it seemed unlikely anyone would manage to sleep, those who were genuinely sleepy kept awake by those who weren't. The traffic up and down the aisle to the toilets hardly abated. All the children found it strange to be told to sleep in their clothes sitting up.

Tony and Peter had never been separated, they were not alike in looks or nature, but they still had a secret twin life that Jennifer envied. With a much older brother and a sister on the verge of adolescence, they were only close to each other. Now they were restless without their bedtime routine and their twin language chatter.

Dawn came as quickly as night, they were flying ahead in time, a concept that her father had been trying to explain to the twins. Down below were vast expanses of red earth, rippled like the beach. Fruit juice and moist wipes were brought round, a simple method of washing the twins approved of. Those who had just managed to get to sleep were rudely awakened.

The seatbelt light went on and everybody tried to catch a glimpse of Karachi Airport, where they were landing to refuel and have breakfast. Now they saw a deserted dry, red expanse with temporary looking buildings.

The landing was as exciting as take-off, as the wheels touched down the engines roared into reverse. Now the tedium of the night had passed, Jennifer felt a surge of excitement. They were abroad and they still had the thrill of two more take-offs and landings to come.

They filed obediently down the steps and onto several battered dusty blue buses which took them, a distance they could have walked, to a long hut.

'Like being back in the army' quipped her father. The other men laughed in agreement.

---o0o---

With no dinner to cook or dishes to wash, Helen had pictured herself sitting on the plane relaxing with a book; George had said they should treat the journey as a holiday. But the journey had been fraught and she had felt apart from George. The narrow aisle could have been a mile; conversation was impossible, leaning out into the aisle hazardous. She had not slept and as the children dozed had mused over the past few months; the excitement of change had not only brought a spark to their love life, but she and George were talking more. As their separate lives of home and work disappeared they had more to share.

Helen had imagined Pakistan to be very exotic and saw herself sitting in a cool white building writing postcards to her mother and Joyce. She was glad to get off the aeroplane, but was quickly disappointed.

'What a dump' grumbled Simon.

George frowned at him. 'You're a guest here, have some respect for the locals.'

They shuffled into a large dining hall and sat down at long tables to be served pineapple juice followed by a local interpretation of an

English cooked breakfast. Fried eggs swam in pools of grease.

'Thank you very much, that looks delicious' said Simon to the waiter, who appeared to miss his sarcastic tone and smiled back with a neat bow.

'See Dad, I'm getting on fine with the locals.'

Families began to chat now they were released from their serried rows. Helen and the other mothers giggled in relief as they exchanged tales of the dreadful night. Fathers chatted about their plans and reassured themselves they were doing the right thing.

When they landed in Singapore it did live up to Helen's expectations, everything seemed white and shiny. As they descended the steps a stultifying heat hit them, but the air-conditioned terminal provided instant relief. She did buy some post cards, but there was only time to have a cooling drink and a wash and brush up. As they filed outside again, huge drops of rain struck them, the air instantly refreshed.

After a light meal on board it was dark again, they were on their way to Perth. Helen was nervous, supposing John wasn't there to meet them?

As they stepped onto the tarmac there was not another plane in sight. Those carrying on to Sydney were ushered into a lounge; they followed other families to a desk. They had no passports, just their emigration papers. After coming so far they were ushered through in moments. Before them was a wood panelled wall showing clocks of the world. In Perth it was 1 am, in Sydney 4 am, Greenwich Meantime was 5pm.

'Remember we went to Greenwich, boys. Your mother would be cooking if she was at home now.'

The twins were now too tired to take an interest in clocks and international datelines; Helen wondered if George would recognise his friend.

'Hey Gip' a voice called.

A lined, tanned face appeared through the other straggling travellers.

'Charlie' George called back.

The two men clapped each others shoulders then the friend politely shook Helen's hand and turned to her daughter.

'You must be Jenny, lucky you take after your mother, not your father' he quipped. 'I've brought the station wagon, plenty of room.'

He picked up two suitcases and led them outside, in the dark, the light shed from the building picked out palm trees. The air was balmy and they heard crickets. A door at the back of the long car was opened and the cases thrown in. The children squashed into the back seat and Helen sat between the two men.

'Have you got a settee in the front of your car?' asked Tony.

'No mate, it's a bench seat; this is the sort of car you'll need Gip, with your brood.'

Helen could view nothing of their new country in the dark, they were on their way without seeing what happened to the other migrants. Would those going to hostels be bussed away like refugees? As they drove along they were given a running commentary which they couldn't take in. When the car finally drew up it was pitch dark.

'Street lights go out at 1am, better not disturb your new neighbours.'

They crept behind him as he opened a creaky door without a key, then unlocked another door. Inside it was gloomy; he showed them the bathroom then went to put the kettle on. Jennifer followed George into the kitchen.

Chapter Five   Western Australia

'Would you like 'milo' Jenny?'

'Yes please' she replied politely, without knowing what he meant.

'Sit down, make yourselves at home.'

Jennifer sat opposite her father. He had got on the plane in his suit, looking as if he was going to work. Now his tie was off and after not shaving for nearly two days, he looked like Fred Flintstone. He smiled at her.

'We're really here Jenny.'

'This place is rented for a month,' said his friend 'but you can extend, depends on your plans. Take a week off to have a holiday, settle in.'

'Thanks Charlie, for all you've done; point me in the direction of the Commonwealth Bank tomorrow and I'll settle what we owe you.'

'No hurry Gip.' He turned to Jennifer again 'I haven't seen your father since we got demobbed.'

'Why not?' she ventured to ask, pleased to be included in the conversation.

'I couldn't settle back into civvy street like your Dad, I went travelling, ended up here.'

'Private Jonathon Charles he was then' said her father, looking at her bemused face. 'We already had two Johnnies so we called him Charlie.'

'Uncle John to you love' he added.

'Gip sounds like the name of a dog Uncle John.'

"Initials on his kit bag, not very original; his mother embroidered them on…'

'George Ian Palmer… did Grandma really embroider…'

'Only joking, she did knit him some socks though.'

'What was it like…'she wanted to ask him about the war, all her father had told them was that he drove a truck.

George frowned at her and looked relieved when the twins burst into the kitchen.

'We'd better help your mother.'

'I'll get the chip heater going' said John 'run the bath, it's a bit primitive in there, but I expect you all want to freshen up.'

'Don't leave the kids unattended in that bathroom' said her father as he followed Jennifer into the bedroom, where her mother was sitting wearily on the bed. She looked up, alarmed.

'Don't worry, John's going to show me how everything works in the morning; he's supervising the twins, giving them army orders. We'll have to share that bath, not enough hot water for another, you and Jenny go in next, then Simon, I'll go last.'

'Dad, I like to have a bath by myself'' Jennifer protested.

'Not with that spluttering chip heater you won't' he grinned. 'Remember, this is just temporary, we're going to buy our own house soon, a brand new one, they're building all the time John says.'

He showed them to the twins' little bedroom; they were already tucked in looking pink and damp.

'Sorry about the sheets,' said John 'Yvonne went out and bought some cheap ones, we didn't have enough to lend, with only the four of us.'

'We have white sheets in England' said Peter, looking at the candy striped sheets.

'That's very kind of her, you must tell us how much we owe you' said Helen.

'No worries, Gip and I are going to settle up later, you'll meet Yvonne tomorrow, you're all coming round for tea. Come and see the rest of the house. We put Simon in the sleepout.'

They followed him to the back of the house, where he opened a creaky wrought iron door covered in mesh.

'Fly screens, you'll soon be nagging the children to keep them shut; they're bound to forget, so don't leave anything uncovered in the kitchen, blow flies.'

They walked out onto a veranda and he knocked on a flimsy door to the left.

'Sleepouts are just covered in verandas, handy extra space.'

Simon was stretched out on the narrow iron bedstead, fiddling with the transistor radio they had bought him in Singapore.

'I'm trying to find a pirate radio station.'

'We're civilised here, commercial radio stations are legal, plenty of pop music for you.

The radio in the kitchen's set on the ABC for your parents, I'm sure they'll want to listen to something more intelligent. Can I have a look?'

He turned the small rectangular radio over in his large palm.

'That's amazing, remember the radios we had in the army George?'

'I've got one as well' said Jennifer proudly. It was the most valuable possession she had ever owned. For the first time, she and Simon would be able to choose what they listened to.

Uncle John led them back inside to see her bedroom. 'I'm afraid you have the tiny room, but my girls have put a few of their things in for you, made it pretty. We'll leave you ladies in peace to get ready for bed, me and George will go in the lounge out of the way, have a smoke and a chat, gotta lot to catch up with. I'll be back in the morning to show you where the shops are. I've ordered the newspaper, so you can read about the locals over breakfast.'

In the gloomy, strange bathroom Helen and Jennifer looked nervously at the spluttering heater.

'Stay down the other end away from the heater Jenny, I'll unpack the sponge bags and put our things in the cupboard. At least it's bigger then our bathroom at home.'

Jennifer was still awake when her mother popped in to say goodnight. At home she would have to creep into bed in the dark, so as not to wake the boys. Now she was sitting up in bed reading.

'I wonder what Uncle John's daughters are like?'

Her mother followed her gaze to the little pile of ballet books and laughed. Jennifer and Christine had prided themselves on being tomboys and felt almost sorry for the few girls in their class who went to ballet lessons. She knew her parents' budget did not stretch to classes of any sort. Brownies only required a few pennies for subs and Explorers at the church was free. Simon went to Scouts and Pathfinders at the church and the twins had been in Cubs. All those activities were held at the church hall and most of the children were from their school. Now she wondered if she would join any clubs in Australia.

---o0o---

The men were still talking so Helen tried to finish unpacking, but she sat on the bed in a daze. For years she had run the house with necessary efficiency; washing, cooking and shopping every day. A small house with lots of people had to be run like a ship, she would joke to George. He agreed and called their kitchen the galley. In the past few months her domestic routine had been slowly unravelling. Now she was in a strange, dark house with no idea what food was in the cupboard.

Finally she got into bed and decided to browse through the Australian Woman's Weekly

Yvonne had left her. She felt a little thrill, it was large and colourful, different from the English version. When she turned the light off sleep seemed a long way off, so much to think about. She liked John, he seemed a straight forward sort of man and she could see why he and George had been friends.

She was startled when George came in, the room was so dark, but she must have been asleep.

'You're freezing cold.'

'The bath water was stone cold; I'll boil a kettle up in the morning to have a shave. Everyone's asleep, don't ask what the time is, we can have a lie in. I don't feel tired, seems like days since I had you to myself.'

'I don't care what this place is like, I'm just glad to be in a home of our own again, after being at your brother's.'

He snuggled up to her. 'I'm just glad to be able to stretch out in a proper bed next to you; I hope you're not feeling too tired.'

George and Helen were woken by the sound of doors banging and creaking. The twins were exploring the house.

'What time is it?' groaned George.

'Ten a.m., no wonder they're wide awake.'

'Did you enjoy your first night in Australia Mrs. Palmer?'

'The bed wasn't very comfortable,' she teased, as she stroked his rough face 'but I like your new rugged look.'

When they reluctantly got up, pop music was blaring from the back of the house, but not loud enough to drown the sound of Simon yelling at the twins. Jennifer's door was firmly shut.

'Close the fly screen door Peter' called George.

Helen laughed. They gathered their sons in the kitchen. It was dark, but they soon realised why; heavy metal venetian blinds covered the window above the sink.

'John says you need them in summer to keep out the heat.'

'It's spring and I want some light' protested Helen.

He pulled in both directions on grubby cords; finally the slats opened and sunshine streamed in, but she wanted to see the view properly. With more tugging the heavy bar at the bottom began to rise crookedly. Helen stepped back in revulsion as the dusty window sill was revealed; it was covered in large dead flies.

'That's what they make garibaldi biscuits with' laughed Tony.

'Up or down' said George.

Helen dithered then started opening cupboards. She emerged with a brush and dust pan.

'I'm still in my nightie, but we can't leave them there; the rest of the house seems clean.'

'John said Yvonne was rushing around dusting and polishing, they only had a couple of days. This blind probably hasn't been up in years.'

'Don't say anything George, they've been so kind to us; all this cleaning stuff looks new.'

'It might be worth us keeping our things in storage till we get our own place. We'd better check if our packing cases arrived safely in Fremantle; such a lot of things to do, we should make a list.'

'What are we going to have for breakfast?' pleaded Peter.

'There are plenty of eggs in the fridge' said his mother 'have some cereal first.'

Another cupboard revealed boxes of cereal with familiar pictures, but different names, rice pops and wheat flakes. The milk bottles in the fridge were a slightly elongated version of the English ones.

'I suppose this is what it will be like,' said Helen 'not a foreign country with a different language, just not the same.'

She was staring at the top of the cooker with its fat metal coils.

'No gas here, all electric' said George as he fiddled with the knobs and Helen looked for the kettle. 'That's electric as well.' He showed her a large, cream coloured, jug shaped appliance. 'I'll fill it up, see if there's enough for a cup of tea and my shave.'

'How will we know when it's boiled if it hasn't got a whistle?'

Nothing seemed to be happening with the cooker, but by the time they had eaten their cereal the rings were turning dull red.

'The eggs are going to take for ever to boil' complained Helen, as George turned the other rings off and the one under the egg saucepan brightened.

A furious spluttering announced the electric kettle was ready. By the time Simon and Jennifer emerged the eggs were ready and George produced some pale toast from under the grill. They squeezed in around the table, Simon with his transistor pressed to his ear.

'Not at the table' said George, wondering if they should have confined their duty free purchases to the cigarettes.

'Their DJs are rubbish anyway' retorted Simon.

'Have you looked in the mirror Simon' laughed Jennifer.

He rubbed his face smugly, she had been teasing him for weeks that he was only pretending to shave.

'We'd all better smarten up before we go round to meet John's family' said Helen.

'What are we going to do today' asked her daughter. 'Can we go to the beach?'

'Plenty of time, you've got the rest of your life.'

'But Dad, I can't wait to see it.'

'Half the day's gone and we haven't seen outside yet' he replied.

The kitchen window looked out over the house next door, but they could only see the trees that shaded it.

'I've been outside,' said Simon 'this house is made of asbestos, like next door's garage.'

'Weatherboard,' corrected his father 'it's cooler in the hot weather.'

'Uncle John said we mustn't crawl under the house,' piped up Tony 'otherwise red spiders will kill us.'

'Red-back spiders,' said Peter 'they don't kill grownups only eight year olds.'

'Uncle John didn't quite put it like that' said George as Helen looked alarmed.

When Simon led them outside, the children were fascinated with the back garden. The house was built on short stilts so you could crawl under it. The grass had blades that were thick and spiky and there were plants that looked as if they had come from the dessert, thick, dark green, stripy leaves with thorns on their sides. Around the garden was a fence of railings and wire mesh. Most fascinating for the twins was a heavy metal structure with struts and wires.

'That must be the rotary hoist for the washing' said George.

He turned a heavy handle to demonstrate how it went up and down, then ushered everyone to the front of the house before the twins started spinning it. They walked under a corrugated roof on posts, by the side of the house.

'Car port, don't need garages here.'

They inspected the post box by the metal gate, it was rusty and secured with a padlock.

"If letters go in here, where do they deliver the newspaper?' asked Helen.

There was a hollow thud as Tony hit Peter with something long. George whipped it out of his hand.

'Here's your paper, rolled up and fastened with brown tape, where did you find it Tony?'

'On the ground.'

Helen was leaning on the front gate staring across the quiet street, it was twice as wide as their road back home. Tall wooden poles looped with wires marched straight down the hill to their left and up the hill to their right. She looked at the painted number on the letter box, 536.

'How long is this road?'

At that moment John pulled up in his station wagon.

'You all look a bit better than you did last night.'

'What is the name of this road?' asked George 'We don't even know where we are.'

'Beach Road,' he winked at Jennifer and her eyes lit up. 'But you're a long way from the beach, 536 houses away; we're down the road and round the corner.'

'Do you go to the beach every day?' she asked.

'No, we do have to go to work and school. We'll take you down in a few days.' He looked at the disappointed expression on her face. 'The Indian Ocean will still be there.'

Helen was gazing up at the sky. 'It's so blue and it is still spring.'

'Yes, you came at the right time; give you a chance to get acclimatised before the hot weather.'

'Can you tell us where the shops are? I should get something for our dinner.'

John looked at his watch. 'A sarnie will do you, Yvonne's cooking us a baked dinner.'

'Oh… I thought we were coming round for tea, bread and butter and cake.'

'No, better save your appetites, tea is evening cooked meal here, baked dinner is a roast, I know it's Tuesday but she thought you should have a treat after those aeroplane meals.'

'We do need a decent meal after those child portions we got on the plane' agreed George. 'That'll give you another day to work out how to use the cooker, Helen.'

'In the country you'd be using a wood stove' said John.

'I think we'll have enough problems with the chip heater' said George.

'We've got a lot to get used to,' said Helen 'I don't know how we would have managed without you John, you must have taken time off work as well?'

'Always glad of an excuse, I had some days off owing. Now, do you want a quick tour of the neighbourhood, shops and school? Drive or walk?'

'Drive' the twins pleaded.

'Walk,' said Helen 'we need to stretch our legs after being cooped up on that plane.'

'Yes,' agreed her husband 'we need to reconnoitre on foot.'

'This is an old suburb, all the roads are laid out on a grid system; you can't get lost. I've brought a UBD round for you, map book.'

He marched them up the road with the twins jogging eagerly either side, asking about snakes and lizards. They stopped at a cross roads.

'Here's the main road for the bus into Perth.'

'Doesn't look very busy,' said George 'told you it would be nice and quiet here.'

'What are all those wooden poles?' asked Helen.

'Electricity, all overhead here.'

'Oh dear, isn't that rather dangerous?'

'Not if you don't climb up them.'

They arrived at a little corner shop.

'Tony's shop, good for bits and pieces' he turned to the twins 'and lollies'.

'You said we could have an ice-lolly when it's hot Mum,' cried Tony 'and it's my shop.' He poked his tongue out at his brother.

'Italian Tony, they keep their shops open all hours, work harder than the Pommies. Lollies are sweets here boys, if you want the frozen sort ask for an icy-pole. Better ask your parents first though.'

'Not today, save room for Aunty Yvonne's dinner' said Helen.

'Uncle John, what's a Pommie?' persisted Tony.

'That's what you are mate, English. Come on, turn right, a couple more blocks and we get to the primary school.'

Chapter Six   New Friends

Jennifer looked over the chain-link fence at the rows of low buildings with verandas set in a u shape around the playground. It was playtime and the sound of screams and laughter was familiar but louder; this was much bigger than her school. The jostling crowd was very colourful, no one was wearing school uniform. Her feeling of holiday euphoria was deflated; whatever the school was like, she knew no one there, at least the twins had each other. She realised Uncle John was talking and was anxious to find out her fate.

'The headmaster's expecting you to drop in by the end of the week, there are a few English kids; Terry's in grade 6 but hopefully they'll put Jenny in Grade 7, she won't want to spend another year in primary.'

Jennifer was filled with even more uncertainty.

'Don't worry, Trish is in first year high school, she'll fill you in.'

'Uncle John, have you got any boys?' asked Peter.

'No, I'm outnumbered, except for the dog, he's a boy.'

Jennifer's eyes lit up. 'What sort of dog?'

'A Kelpie, they're sheepdogs really, but he was too lazy and more stupid than the sheep. Right, time we went back for a cuppa and I'll show your dad how to work the chip heater.'

'Do you have to put real chips in?' asked Peter.

'Chips of wood and old newspaper to get it going.'

They sauntered back taking in their surroundings.

'All the bungalows are different' remarked her mother.

'Nobody calls them bungalows here, they're just houses; only rich people live in two storey houses.'

Later on they all piled into the station wagon and arrived at Uncle John's house. It was the same sort of house, but looked much smarter than the one they were staying in and had interesting creepers growing up the car port and around the windows. He swung open the fly screen door then pushed the front door.

'We're here Vonny' he yelled. 'Come in, don't stand on ceremony.'

Jennifer and the twins clustered shyly round Helen while Simon followed his father in. There was a delicious smell of roast lamb. Two girls hovered in a doorway, then a woman appeared ushering them in. She was the same height as her elder daughter, though it was her younger daughter who looked so much like her.

'Welcome to Australia, come through to the kitchen, do you kids want a cool drink, cordial?'

'Yes please' said Jennifer.

After discovering that Milo was like hot chocolate, she'd decided it was safe to politely accept whatever was offered.

Peter sipped carefully at his tall Tupperware beaker.

'Why has it got black bits in it?'

'Seeds, Passionfruit cordial, do you like it?'

'Not sure, tastes a bit funny.'

'Come out and see the back yard,' said Yvonne 'the boys can play with the dog, he loves everyone.'

A chocolate brown short haired dog, with alert ears, bounded up to them.

'What's his name Uncle John?' asked Jennifer.

'Drongo… called him that cos he's a right drongo.'

'Can we take him for a walk?'

'He doesn't need a walk, he gets enough exercise in the back yard and on the beach.'

'Your lawn is very nice,' said her mother 'the grass is rather strange at our house.'

'Took a lot of work; Vonny wanted an English lawn and Vonny gets what she wants' he winked.

'We've been in this house six years' she explained. 'Couch grass, you have to plant it in clumps, keep watering and hope it all joins up together. If you want a quick lawn you can use that tough stuff, but you wouldn't want to sit on it.'

Jennifer followed her parents as they strolled around admiring the orange and lemon trees and other unusual plants.

'The garden's not at it's best yet' said Uncle John's wife 'but you won't find one of these in England... Hibiscus, it's got a few flowers already, reminds me of when we were out East.'

'Why haven't you got any earth in your garden?' piped up Peter, as he scuffed his shoes in the grey sand.

'We're on the coastal plain, all sand till you get up in the hills, then it's red earth.'

'No mud, how wonderful' sighed her mother.

'Don't speak too soon,' said Uncle John 'when they get in that silver sand with their bare feet they end up black.'

'They'll have their shoes and socks on in the garden' she replied.

'No, they'll soon have bare feet like the locals; you'll all have to get thongs, you don't want to wear shoes in summer.'

Jennifer looked at her Clark's sandals and socks; they were all wearing their best summer clothes, her mother wore her Marks and Spencer dress and stockings and her father had a shirt and tie on. Uncle John was wearing shorts, she had never seen a grownup in shorts. His wife wore a shift dress and they both wore the same funny rubber things on their feet. No wonder he told them there was no need to dress up; she could have worn her shorts and tee shirt after all.

Back indoors Terri and Trish had put the television on. They and Jennifer had hardly exchanged two words. They motioned her to sit down.

'What are you watching?' she asked shyly.

'Children's Channel Seven' they replied without explanation.

Jennifer was soon bored; a group of irritating children pranced around singing a silly song and she wondered if this was the sort of programme ballet loving girls liked. She was spared any more when their mother marched into the room.

'We don't have television on when we have visitors, do we girls?'

Jennifer felt doubly guilty; worried Yvonne would think she had asked to watch and responsible for the girls being forced to switch off.

'Come and see my room' said Terri hastily, reading her mother's expression.

Jennifer followed obediently and was pleasantly surprised to see pictures of horses and dogs.

'Did you have a pony in England?' asked the younger sister.

Disappointed, Terri asked if she went to boarding school.

'No, it was a Church of England school.'

The girl showed her a book shelf, lots of the titles looked familiar.

'I thought you might be like the girls in the stories,' she explained 'my auntie sends them over from England.'

'Do you go to ballet lessons?" Jennifer ventured to ask.

'No, Trish does, I do Callisthenics.'

When Yvonne called them in for tea, Jennifer was still confused at all the strange expressions she was hearing, but she and Terri had struck up an easy exchange.

'Jenny's seen Buckingham Palace and she's been on an underground train' announced Terri, proud that she had got to know their new visitor before her sister.

'Why have I got two dinners?' asked Peter, as soon as his plate was put before him.

The Charles family looked puzzled, but Jennifer knew what he meant. Peter asked questions all the time and often embarrassed his parents, but sometimes they were the questions Jennifer was too polite to ask herself.

Their plates were full; thick slices of roast lamb and an assortment of vegetables, including a generous helping of cauliflower cheese.

'Just eat your dinner quietly boys' said their father.

There were disadvantages to being twins, both boys were always included in any admonition, Tony hadn't uttered a word and was tucking in heartily. Their mother started to apologise.

'Cauliflower cheese is one of our midweek favourites.'

'It's not my favourite, I hate it' persisted Peter.

'Well, your Mum will be able to afford meat every day here' said John.

Her mother looked embarrassed and Aunty Yvonne glared at her husband with one of those looks that mothers gave fathers.

'Rationing finished years ago' said her father. 'We often have a light supper on school nights; the children have their school dinners and I have the office canteen... did, funny to think that's all in the past.'

Her parents relaxed as family honour was restored, but Tony wanted his chance to speak.

'I hate school dinners.'

Uncle John winked at him 'You won't have to put up with them any more, here you take a packed lunch.'

'I'm sure Helen's a good cook' said Yvonne. 'Whatever she fed them on in England, they look well on it; Simon's nearly as tall as his father and Jenny hasn't got far to catch up with Helen. Girls grow up so quickly these days.'

Trish blushed, but Terri and Jennifer started giggling.

'This is what I have to put up with,' said Uncle John 'a house full of giggling women, sounds like the chook run sometimes.'

The girls couldn't share their joke. Jennifer had told Terri how she and Christine had examined her older sister's junior bras when she was out. Christine had secretly borrowed one to wear to school, but it had ridden up uncomfortably during P.E.

'This is a lovely meal Yvonne' said their mother.

'What's this orange stuff?' asked Tony.

'Baked pumpkin, love, it'll give you big muscles.'

'I'm stronger than Peter.'

'But I'm taller' Peter rose to the bait.

'You both look so much alike' Trish spoke for the first time.

'People often say that,' remarked their father 'but they look completely different to us.'

The twins didn't like being discussed; their mother turned the conversation back to the meal. 'Ten people to cook for, lucky you have a large table.'

'Yes, some of these older houses have the nice big country kitchens. Ten's nothing, I cooked for shearers when we lived in the country.'

'Did you like living there?' asked Jennifer's father.

'It was a great experience, when we first arrived, when the girls were tiny and we wanted an adventure. I think John would've liked to have stayed.'

'Yeah, we had to make a decision before Trish started school, Vonny didn't want her travelling miles on the school bus and if we'd settled there permanently, the girls would've had to board in high school.'

'Do many migrants go to the country? I assumed we'd live in Perth, but until I get a job and we buy a house I guess we're free to choose. That's what it's all about, for the first time in our lives we can do what we like.'

'You'd have to think carefully, it wouldn't be easy for Helen.'

Jennifer tried to picture her family in the countryside; they had no idea what the rest of Western Australia was like. They had only seen pictures of the Indian ocean and the sunny city with its wide river.

'I can't imagine the countryside,' said her mother 'but I guess hungry shearers would not be happy with cauliflower cheese.'

There was so much for the grown ups to talk about; Simon was listening eagerly to how they killed sheep on the farms and the twins were tucking into a second helping of Yvonne's legendary trifle. Jennifer had sneaked a look at her Timex watch, but didn't intend to draw her parents' attention to how late it was. The watch had been her tenth birthday present and she had carefully wound it up every bedtime since; it was her proudest possession until the acquisition of the transistor radio. Her father was offering round cigarettes, a good sign they would stay a while longer. He had two expertly balanced between his lips; he always lit her mother's for her. At home it was their after meal ritual; leaning back relaxing, as the first puff of smoke curled up into the air the children knew they could get down from the table.

'We'll call for you in the morning,' Uncle John was saying 'take you into Perth on the bus, you'll need to use the bus till you get a car. Do you drive Helen?'

'No, we've never had a car, Dennis would always lend us his for an emergency.'

'You'll want to learn to drive here,' added Aunty Yvonne 'but the buses are fine for going into Perth shopping.'

'I wish we could come,' grumbled Trish 'we'll be stuck at school while you're all enjoying yourselves.'

'It won't be much fun for the children,' Jennifer's mother reassured her 'visit to the bank and the post office, getting our bearings...'

'Can we take them to the beach at the weekend then Dad?'

'Yeah, I'll borrow the 'ute' from work and we can all pile down there. We've got some spare boards, can any of you swim?'

'Only me' said Simon.

'You'll soon learn' he turned to the other children. 'Trish is the best swimmer in the family.'

Jennifer began to warm to Trish.

'Good heavens, is it that late,' exclaimed her father 'past the twins' bed time.'

'Yes, but it's still afternoon in England' said Simon, grinning at his brothers.

'Yvonne, we haven't helped wash up' said their mother.

'Don't worry, you must be tired after that journey.'

'I'll give you a lift while the girls get in the kitchen' winked Uncle John.

'No, we'll walk back' said their father. 'I want to show the children the stars; I want to see for myself if they really are upside down.'

Chapter Seven   Perth

The next morning John and Yvonne appeared smartly dressed and led the family off to the bus stop.

'Which bus do we get?' asked Helen.

'There's only one, you can go to Perth and you can come back again' laughed John.

A few women waited at the bus stop, looking with interest at the newcomers. A cream and green single-decker bus soon came into view; John suddenly dashed to the rear end as it pulled up. A young mother was struggling to get her toddler out of his push chair; John helped her then expertly swung the pushchair up to hang on a rack fixed to the back of the bus.

'What a handy idea' said Helen

'Are you lot getting on?' called the driver.

John and Yvonne had stepped back to let the young mother on first, so George herded his family on behind the other passengers and urged them down the aisle. The driver, surprised to see so many passengers at this time of the morning, called out again.

'Fares please?'

'It's okay, my shout' said John as he clambered on board. 'Pommies… second day here.'

'I'd never have guessed' said the driver, looking at the fresh pink faces of the children. 'No clippies here, you have to pay me.'

'We haven't got any money' declared Tony.

'Yes we have,' said Peter 'it's in the bank getting changed into Australian money.'

'Come and sit by the windows boys' said Helen, embarrassed.

Simon was already sitting at the back of the bus, pretending he didn't belong to them. As they all shuffled into their seats, John and the driver finished working out the fares. A woman in front of Helen turned round smiling.

'I know what it's like, we've only been here a year.'

'The first ten years are the worst' came a cheerful voice behind her.

By the time John sat down all the women were chatting animatedly and cooing over the toddler. The young mother was equally fascinated with the twins and asked how Helen managed when they were babies.

'I certainly couldn't go on the bus by myself; if we were all going out George and I carried a baby each and Simon had strict instructions not to let go of Jenny's hand.'

'Another couple of years and Simon will have his own car, take you shopping Helen' John joined in.

'Goodness… we did promise to get him and Jenny bikes as soon as we're settled, we had to leave theirs behind, though it doesn't look as if he'll be doing a paper round.'

With all the chatter, they were surprised when the driver called out.

'Here we are, St. George's Terrace, welcome to Perth.'

John jumped off first to fetch the pushchair and the twins jostled as they waited for Simon to emerge. Helen looked around; everything seemed clean, wide and bright. She tucked her arm into George's and squeezed it; everything was going to work out.

'Can we find the bank first,' said George 'make sure the money's arrived from England.'

'You can't get lost in the city centre' said Yvonne 'it's so small, river to the south, railway line to the north…'

'Did you hear the one about the Pommies who asked where Hay Street was?' chipped in John. 'You want Hi Street? said the Aussi. No, not the high street replied the Pommies, we want Hay Street.'

'Come on John,' said Yvonne 'we're blocking the whole pavement. If we show them where the bank and post office are, we could maybe take the children down to the gardens and the river, then meet for a toasted sandwich at Coles.'

At each intersection George looked around to get his bearings.

'Yes we'll be fine Charlie, synchronise watches, regroup at thirteen hundred hours.'

Yvonne smiled at Helen. 'Back in the army.'

Torn between having a break from his parents or being included as a kid, Simon opted to stay with George and Helen.

---o0o---

The twins soon fell in with John, scurrying to keep up with his long strides. Jennifer walked behind with Yvonne; she felt suddenly shy, unused to being with adults by herself; usually she had the security of family or friends when talking to other people's parents.

Aunty Yvonne spoke first 'Supreme Court Gardens, just head for here when you want to catch the bus.'

Jennifer looked around; it was different from the 'Rec', quite exotic. Ahead the boys had discovered a new game, dodging the rotating sprinklers in the brief moment before they swept over the path again.

Yvonne laughed 'Don't worry if they get wet, they'll dry off in the sun before we meet up with your parents.'

'Oh that's nothing,' said Jennifer shyly 'you should have seen Tony when he fell in the muddy ditch in our park.'

'I can imagine, I had a younger brother. Uncle John's enjoying himself as much as your brothers; I'll tell you something, men never grow up.'

Jennifer looked at her, not sure if she was joking.

In no time at all they were at the other side of the gardens; she was a bit disappointed; Kensington Gardens had seemed to go on for ever and then you found yourself in Hyde Park with mounted soldiers riding by. She wondered if Aunty Yvonne could read her mind.

'We'll take you up to King's Park one day, three hundred acres of natural bush, have to keep an eye on the boys there.'

'Yup, if we lost the twins up there they'd have to send the mounted police out to search for them' added John. 'Now we're going down Barrack Street to The Esplanade.'

Soon they were on a wide expanse of grass.

'Is that the sea?' cried Peter excitedly.

'No, that's the Swan River on its way to Fremantle and the Indian Ocean.'

Jenny looked at the wide curving blue water as they reached the water's edge. It was hard to see which way it was going. They walked along to the Barrack Street jetty to see the ferry.

'You can go to Fremantle from here and on to Rottnest Island' explained Yvonne.

'Can we go there?' asked Peter 'We've never been on a boat.'

'I've been to the Isle of Wight' said Jennifer proudly.

'Well we haven't got time before lunch,' laughed Yvonne 'but you could go there for a day out, maybe see a quokka.'

'Is that a big fierce monster?' asked Tony hopefully.

'No, they're cuddly and harmless.'

'Not everyone enjoys that trip over to Rottnest,' said Uncle John 'I seem to remember your Dad was seasick the whole way over to France during the war.'

This was a new piece of information for the children.

'I thought he drove a truck' said Peter.

'He did, in France, but we had to get over there first.'

Jennifer felt uncomfortable; she knew her father didn't like questions about the war. She was relieved when Uncle John produced a tennis ball and changed the subject.

'Do you lot know how to play butterfingers?'

'Good idea,' said Yvonne 'let's get rid of some of the boys' energy before we go back into town.'

---o0o---

Helen spotted John and Yvonne first, George and Simon were busy chatting. From a distance she realised how grown up Jennifer looked talking to Yvonne; she had worried her daughter would feel shy, left so soon with new people in a strange place. She was glad Simon had opted to come with them. George had been able to make him feel more involved, explaining to him exactly what they were doing on the official and practical side; without revealing exactly how much, or rather how little capital they had, after selling the house and paying off the mortgage.

With six weeks to wait till they could claim employment benefits they would be living on that capital till George got a job.

The twins raced up excitedly, both talking at the same time about huge rivers, islands and 'crockers'.

'Didn't get lost then' said John.

Inside the large shop Helen was pleasantly surprised, the displays and counters looked different to the shops she was used to yet still felt homely. Yvonne took her and Jennifer up the escalator to the ladies rest room.

'How very civilised' Helen admired the wood panelling and comfy chairs.

'I guess Mr. Cole, or probably Mrs Cole, realised coming into the city was a big treat the country ladies deserved to enjoy.'

Back downstairs they enjoyed toasted ham sandwiches sitting at a curved bar; the twins tickled that they could eat their lunch in the middle of the shop.

Helen indulged in a daydream; she pictured herself coming here once a week when the children were at school and George at work. Perth was more interesting than their local town back home and a lot less hassle to get to than going up to London.

There would be lots of things to buy for their new life and until she knew what their income and her housekeeping money was going to be, she could fantasise about shopping. George's voice interrupted her thoughts.

'…is that alright with you Helen?'

John spoke up 'Simon will want to come as well, he's interested in motors.' He turned to Helen 'You can't go job and house hunting till you've got a car.'

'Good idea, as long as George gets the hot water going for me in the morning, so I can get the washing done. Jenny can help me with the jobs and the boys can play in the garden.'

Simon was smirking at Jennifer, who was about to poke her tongue out at him, till Helen gave a warning frown.

'No need to be smug Simon, they'll be plenty of chores for you while you're off school' said his father. 'We hadn't forgotten about school,' he winked at the twins 'Friday we'll go and see your new headmasters.'

Nightfall caught the Palmers by surprise that evening; Helen was trying to cope with the unfamiliar cooker and George was attempting to get the chip heater going so they could get the twins back to normal bath and bedtimes.

'We've missed the sunset again' said George after dinner.

Jennifer and Simon were more interested in the pop magazine he had managed to buy in Perth. It was American, but had articles about the Beatles. Their parents joined them in the little lounge room after they had tucked the twins in.

'No homework to do, but no television to watch' moaned Simon.

Helen produced a wad of pale blue paper and the postcards.

'Aerogrammes; we'll all sit at the kitchen table and write our letters back home, they don't even know we've arrived safely.'

'You can tell them' said Simon.

'I'm sure your friends will want to hear from you' said George 'and the school. I'll write to Grandma and Uncle Dennis and your mother can write to her family.'

'…and Joyce' added Helen. 'Jennifer will want to write to Christine and Alison…'

Jennifer started in large writing, but as she got near the bottom she looked up. 'I'm still on Singapore Airport and I haven't got enough room to tell Christine about Trish, Terri and Drongo.'

'I can't think what to write' said her brother.

'By next week we'll have lots more to tell them' said George as they all carefully folded, licked and stuck down the aerogrammes.

Chapter Eight Helen

On Thursday morning Helen turned the radio on to a fanfare of music which announced the ABC news and brought Jennifer out to the kitchen.

'What time did you turn your light off last night?' asked George.

'I couldn't get to sleep, I've read all the books Trish and Terri lent me.'

'Simon's still asleep' said Tony.

'I suppose it doesn't matter till they're back at school,' said Helen 'I don't think our bodies have adjusted to the different time yet, I was awake half the night.'

'We'd better wake him up, John will be round soon.'

By the middle of the morning Helen was bent over the trough in the little lean-to laundry at the back of the house and missing her spin drier. It had been passed on from Dennis and now had a new home with Joyce. Helen would have been happy to have her old ringer back and was glad of Jennifer's help carrying the dripping washing out to the rotary hoist. The boys' were in charge of winding it up and down. Looking up at the blue cloudless sky she soon cheered up, drying conditions were perfect.

'Don't look so glum Jenny, chores still have to be done, even in Australia.'

Her daughter's mood of excitement seemed to have evaporated.

'Let's have a picnic in the garden' suggested Helen 'I've only got a few more things to rinse out.'

'Where will we sit?' her daughter looked at the unyielding spiky grass.

'On the veranda steps?' They surveyed the splintered wooden steps that lay between Simon's sleepout and the laundry. 'We could sit on that funny old rag rug from his room' Helen tried to get a positive response.

The twins gobbled up their food, keen to get back to their game. John had been unable to resist buying them toys yesterday and a plastic bulldozer and dumper truck were busy excavating the silver sand at the bottom of the garden.

As predicted by Yvonne, the boys' feet were black; the children were trying out the rubber thongs she had bought them yesterday. Helen was enjoying the sun, but the uncomfortable steps encouraged her to get up and organise everyone for the afternoon expedition.

'You'd better all put your socks and sandals back on to go to the shops.'

Only the chance to put the hose on to wash their feet could drag the boys away from the growing hole. Yvonne had assured Helen that it didn't matter what happened to the children's feet, as long as you trained them to hose down before they came indoors. Jennifer's thongs had a thick red sole, white on top with red rubber straps plugged through holes either side of her heel and joining to part her big toe from its neighbour. Helen had never seen such footwear, but Jennifer declared them comfortable enough to wear to the shops.

At the shop Italian Tony shook hands solemnly with his namesake and gave each of the family a slice of salami to try. They were fascinated with the selection of sausages, cold meats and cheeses on display and Helen soon decided what dinner would be that evening. She asked Tony for some salad stuff and a couple of tins of soup. He put a shiny penny in the change and pointed out to the boys the kangaroo on the reverse side.

Following his directions they posted their aerogrammes, then made their way to the local library. Jennifer was lagging behind, but insisted her feet were fine. The library was in an old homely building and the children were soon ensconced in the junior section.

Helen asked for some recommendations on Australian books, fiction and non-fiction. She urged the children to take out as many as they were allowed, picturing television free evenings spent peacefully reading.

They set off in what Helen hoped was the right direction to complete their circular walk. Every road, at every intersection seemed to stretch in a straight line to the horizon. It wasn't long before the boys were complaining they were hot and thirsty and their books were too heavy. As Helen paused uncertainly at the next junction, Jennifer caught up with her, but stumbled and banged her toe. She assured her mother she was fine. With the bags of shopping and books Helen could not see Jennifer's feet and they carried on. At last they recognised John's car and realised it was parked outside their house.

As they stumped wearily up the steps of the little veranda to the front door, Peter put his books down to be first to yank open the fly screen.

'Oh yuk, look at Jenny's foot' he cried.

The front door opened and George emerged.

'We were just about to send out a search party, where have you been… what's happened to Jenny's foot?'

'I just stubbed my toe.'

Everyone looked down squeamishly at the skin flapping bloodily at the tip of her big toe.

'Oh dear, I suppose we haven't any Dettol or plasters?' said Helen.

'I'd better get the first aid kit out of the car' said John as he came out to see the drama. He was more worried than Helen and George; with three sons and a tom boy they were used to children falling out of trees, off bikes, over on roller skates and bleeding.

Once John had bandaged Jennifer's toe, the twins lost interest and wanted to know where their new car was.

'I don't want to rush into it,' said George 'we need something large and reliable, but suitable for Helen to learn on, preferably second hand…'

'He doesn't want much,' laughed John 'we saw a few possibilities.'

'I think I'll go back to that second place, look at that Holden again. Oh Yvonne wants to know if you'd like to go to the supermarket with her tomorrow afternoon. We'd better stock up with enough till we get our own car, you can't get everything from Tony's.'

'Remember the shops shut at midday on Saturday, that's why Vonny usually goes on Friday' added John.

'We don't want to starve at the weekend,' Helen agreed as she put the kettle on 'yes I would be grateful. Back home the milkman delivered a box of groceries every week, the butcher's boy came round on his bike and the greengrocer had his van.'

Bored with talk of shopping and their tiredness forgotten, the twins retreated to the back garden to run round and round the rotary. Suddenly the adults heard shrieks of pain.

Peter rushed in to the kitchen.

'Tony's been bitten by a redback spider!'

In the garden Tony was sitting on the grass holding his bare foot.

John lifted his foot up and sighed with relief, pulling something out with his finger nails.

'Yes I thought it might be that, double-gee, no danger.

He held aloft a tiny brown seed pod with sharp spikes.

'No creature would dare eat them, certainly painful if you tread on them.'

'The children better keep their socks and sandals on' said Helen.

'What did you say we're having for dinner?' said George an hour later.

'As it's so warm, I thought we'd have a nice salad and try the meat and cheese we bought. Soup first.'

'I only like tomato soup' said Peter as they sat around the kitchen table.

'Minestrone,' said George 'it's good to try new things, especially in a new country. We don't even know if they do Heinz tomato soup here.'

As they moved onto the salad, Helen couldn't remember what the various meats were called, George was suspicious, but the children agreed they were much nicer than the pink meat they had with salad at school. The cucumber wasn't so popular.

'This skin's very tough, I bet it's not real cucumber' said Simon.

'Tony's brother is a market gardener, the shop always has good fresh vegetables and I'm sure they know what cucumbers look like.'

On Friday morning George and Simon set off to find the High School and the rest of the family headed for the primary school. Helen felt nearly as nervous as the children.

The headmaster took them first to the grade three classroom; with a large school the twins had the choice of separate classes, but insisted they wanted to stay together. They agreed to stay and meet their new class while she and Jennifer went back to the headmaster's office. He solemnly perused the letter and reports Helen had taken out of her handbag. Jennifer looked nervous.

'Hmm, passed your eleven plus… your teacher's given you a good report… I hope she's telling the truth' he winked. 'I think you would be bored if you were kept back in grade seven next year. Lots of the English children start a year early and you'll be there at the start.' He paused '…but you'll have to work hard in the next couple of months, catch up with what the rest of the class are doing.' He turned to Helen. 'The end-of-year test results will determine which class she is put in next year, she should be in one of the upper classes, aim for a professional course. Is that what you and your husband want?'

'Oh yes…' said Helen, realising how little she knew about the education system here.

Jennifer hadn't said a word.

Suddenly he stood up and shook hands with both of them.

'Right, let's go and meet Mr. Gregson in grade seven.'

He marched them along a wooden veranda, rapped on a green door then entered. The class looked up from their maths books, glad of an interruption. Helen stood back in the doorway and Jennifer was reluctantly the centre of attention. Even sitting down the other children looked quite tall. Mr. Gregson was a man in his forties she guessed and seemed quite genial. He came over and shook Helen's hand then turned back to Jennifer.

'Monday week we'll see you then. Have a go at those work sheets, I'll be asking you where New Guinea is.'

'Jenny and I made a long list, but I can't seem to get my brain functioning, this lovely big shop and all these different makes.'

'I don't know how you manage with six mouths to feed' said Yvonne.

'When there was just the two of us I wasn't organised at all, but over the years I've had to learn to plan meals and budget. Ooh, three shillings for a whole bag of oranges or apples, that's cheap. I wonder if they've got any nice cucumbers, that one we got from Tony's yesterday had a really tough skin.'

'Didn't you peel it?'

"Oh, is that what you're supposed to do here?'

'I guess Australian cucumbers have to be tough to survive.'

'I wonder how Dad's getting on?' asked Jennifer as they finally reached the till.

'I hope he doesn't regret taking the twins.'

'Peter should be able to out talk any car dealer' said Yvonne.

When they arrived back at Helen's house, all was quiet.

'Shall I put the kettle on while we unload the shopping, are you going to have a cup of tea and wait for John?'

'Yes I certainly need one.'

The two women sat gratefully at the kitchen table while Jennifer offered to make the tea.

'Let's enjoy the peace, I'll be glad to get John back to work next week, return to routine.'

'I don't know what we'd have done without you and John helping us.'

'It's been fun, but you'll be on your own after the weekend, I've got some interviews on next week; I'm thinking of going back into nursing part time next year. I was going to wait until Terri was at high school, but they're both sensible... we could do with... well every bit helps and we should start saving to take the girls on holiday to England.'

'I didn't know you were a nurse, is that what you did in Malaya?'

'Yes, but during the war I was in England then France. What did you do?'

Helen sighed, she might have guessed Yvonne's war would have been more heroic than hers.

'It was nearly over by the time I got called up in the army. I thought it would be exciting, but it was all admin, logistics. I always wished I'd gone into something more romantic like nursing.'

'It wasn't that romantic or dramatic most of the time and the people on the front line couldn't have survived without your logistics and supplies.'

'Is that where you met John, in France?'

'No, he was in the Malay Police, a lot of English ex-army were. Getting married was the last thing on my mind. I'd already lost someone during the war, had my heart broken a couple of times; you know how it was back then.'

Helen didn't know what it was like; hadn't left England's shores, had not lost anybody or found anybody for that matter. There had been dates of course, but usually she was bored with the young soldier by the time his leave was over. With her mother's oblique warnings about the hazards of army life and the gossip of the other girls, Helen had been too terrified of 'getting into trouble' to be very adventurous.

Yvonne continued her story.

'I went out with his friend first and he dated a few of the nurses, there was a group of us hung around together. Then it was just me and Charlie, as everyone called him then; but I wasn't sure how he felt. So I decided it was time I went back to England and trained for promotion. I couldn't tell if he was bothered or not, so I booked my passage home. Charlie never talked about going home; he didn't want promotion, but nor did he want to go back to England. "Let's not think about the future, just enjoy our last few weeks" he said. So we did. No worries about what family would think and Charlie knew how to give a girl a good time.'

Jennifer was sitting quietly listening and Helen hoped Yvonne's descriptions wouldn't get too graphic She pictured Malaya as an exotic cross between Karachi and Singapore. Yvonne's life had definitely been more dramatic than hers.

'Did he follow you back to England?'

Yvonne laughed 'No, he followed me to the gangplank. It was crowded on the dockside, lots of ex-pats going back. We'd said our farewells the night before, I told him not to come and make it harder for me. I had just got on board, my cases had been taken down to my cabin, all the passengers were lining the railing. Then I saw him waving frantically, pushing to the front of the little crowd. "Vonny, stay here."

I wasn't sure if I heard him or just read his lips. There were still people boarding. I was angry, why had he waited till it was too late? Then he suddenly raced up the gangplank, he had his uniform on so people let him by. As soon as he reached me, he grabbed hold of my hands and said "Marry me". A little circle had gathered round us in anticipation.'

Helen had hardly breathed during this tale, now she exhaled in relief.

'Goodness, how romantic, did you say yes?'

'Of course, everybody cheered; then he told them to hold the gangplank while we raced down to find my cabin and retrieve my cases. It took me a few weeks to pluck up courage to write to my mother and tell her I wasn't coming back… and I'd just got married!' She sighed. 'Where did you and George meet then?'

Before Helen could answer, Jennifer butted in.

'On Waterloo Station, Dad said he missed his train and caught a wife.'

When the Palmers arrived at the Charles' house on Saturday morning, it seemed only Drongo was as excited as Jennifer about the outing to the beach. He raced around greeting all the visitors in turn, then tried to round up his own family, who were sauntering around in no hurry. Yvonne was in the kitchen, the girls had not emerged from their bedrooms and John was tossing mats and plastic boards into an open topped van with a small cab.

'Hi Palmers; do you twins want to go in the back of the 'ute' with the dog? Trish isn't ready yet, how can she take so long to decide what to wear to the beach? Have you kids remembered your bathers?'

'Swimming costumes,' Jennifer interpreted for the rest of the family 'yes, we've got them on under our clothes.'

'Have you got any real surfboards?' asked Simon.

The picture of the blonde, suntanned young man riding a brightly coloured surfboard on the crest of a wave, that had featured on the front of one of the shiny brochures, had helped persuade him going to Australia would be fun.

'You have to walk before you can run,' said John 'swim before you can surf.'

'Come and get the esky' called Yvonne.

Her husband soon returned with a large blue plastic box which he tossed into the back of the 'ute'. Then he swung the twins in. Drongo needed no bidding to jump and the back ramp was lifted and firmly shut.

Simon sat in the front cab with John, eager to inspect a different vehicle. Helen sat in the front of the station wagon with Yvonne, who was keen to give her an introductory driving lesson.

'The gear levers are on the steering column, not like English cars…'

Helen knew cars had gears, but that was the limit of her mechanical knowledge. She had never taken an interest in where they were located or what they were for. It was more interesting looking out of the window as they drove down Beach Road. Yvonne was a steady driver and slowed carefully at each intersection.

'The rule is give way to the right, that's all you have to remember.'

'Sounds logical and simple' said George from the back seat.

Jennifer peered over Helen's shoulder as they drove up rises and down dips; at last the horizon was no longer the next brow of the road, the ocean was in front of them. Yvonne turned right and parked alongside the beach, behind the 'ute'. Everyone clambered out and Drongo dashed to the edge of the water.

The sand was smooth and golden; George gazed around him.

'Nothing but sand; not a pebble in sight, not a deck chair to be seen, no pier, no amusements, nothing but beach… wonderful.'

'And the sky seems to be bluer each day' added Helen. 'I wonder why there aren't more people here?'

'Saturday morning, people are busy and it's not summer yet' said Yvonne.

'The waves aren't as big as I was expecting' said Simon.

'They look enormous to me' replied his mother.

'Yes, stick to the shallows,' warned John 'beware of rip tides, but even in shallow water the waves can knock you over.'

'The twins will only want to paddle and George and I will be happy to sit and soak in the sun.'

Jennifer looked nervous now she had seen the waves, but announced she only needed to get her toes wet to be the first Palmer in the Indian Ocean. She quickly discarded her shorts and T-shirt and jumped back as the cold water splashed her feet. Drongo dashed back and forth; he chased the waves, but knew when to retreat. Simon sauntered to the water's edge.

Helen and George watched the other couple expertly arrange mats and towels and described their last day out at the seaside; sitting on deck chairs at Bognor Regis with rugs over their laps and a flask of coffee.

'...so Jenny came hobbling over the pebbles, lips blue with cold, insisting she was enjoying herself and didn't want to get dried yet.'

'You two should get yourselves some bathers, no reason why you can't learn to swim, John and I didn't learn till we were in Malaya.'

The twins hadn't got as far as the water's edge, they were happily playing in the sand with the digger and dumper truck.

'Come on Vonny, let's go in for a dip. We'll take the boys for a paddle first.'

Yvonne took off her shift dress to reveal a blue one piece costume. Helen noticed she had kept her figure and wondered if she would ever feel bold enough to stroll on the beach.

When John stripped down to his swimming shorts his broad shoulders were as tanned as his legs. Helen was unused to seeing other men's bare legs, let alone their chests. She almost looked away, but as he turned she was shocked to see a livid, puckered scar which went round from his chest to his back. She looked to George for explanation, but he was looking past the couple to where Simon was.

The twins were happy to hold the adults' hands and venture in far enough for the waves to splash their legs, but they soon retreated back to the sand. Helen was impressed to see John dive straight under a wave, but she was relieved Jennifer was sitting with Terri where the waves petered out over the sand. She couldn't imagine she and George jumping in the waves and splashing each other, like John and Yvonne.

Simon had progressed to lying on the board and Trish was gliding elegantly on her red board behind a curling wave. Suddenly Simon was in front of the breaking white foam and disappeared inside it, his green board bobbed up empty.

John waded diagonally to where the boy had been somersaulted head first into the turbulent mix of sand and seawater. By the time she and George had stood up in alarm, John had pulled him to his feet, spluttering and choking.

'No panic,' said John as he led him up the beach 'he's had his baptism, happens to us all.'

Simon sat shakily on the mat, spitting out sand. All the children had gathered round to see the drama. Yvonne handed him a drink of water and a towel. John frowned at Trish.

'I told him not to go till the right moment' she said defensively.

'Thank goodness you were there to rescue him' said Helen.

John clapped him on the shoulders.

'Hardly a rescue, I just helped him get his footing, but that's why you should never go in the sea by yourself kids, you have to look out for each other.'

Yvonne decided it was time for lunch and the mysteries of the 'esky' were revealed; a large cool box filled with hearty sandwiches made with thick slabs of meat, bottles of Coca Cola, lemonade and cans of Swan Lager. The Palmer children were used to orange squash and cheese sandwiches on picnics.

Helen felt as if they had done nothing but eat since their arrival in Australia. She looked over at Simon, the feast had taken away the taste of sea water and the attention of the children; he had regained his equilibrium.

'How come you're the only one in your family who can swim?' Trish asked him.

He told her about his fortnight with the scouts at the empty boarding school.

'So you only learnt to swim two months ago?'

'There wasn't anywhere to learn locally' defended George 'and Helen and I couldn't teach them when we did get to the seaside.'

'I meant it was very brave to go in the sea when you've just learnt' said Trish, blushing.

'It was just a kid's pool where we stayed, the deep end only came up to my shoulders, you got a certificate if you swam one length' he laughed.

'Perhaps we should have taken you all to the river first,' said John 'but Jenny was so keen to see the ocean.'

'Tomorrow morning we'll take them to Crawley Beach,' decided Yvonne 'that's a lovely spot on the river. Then we could go up to King's Park.'

'Good idea,' agreed George 'I could treat you all to Sunday lunch in that restaurant you told us about.'

'Does Drongo like the river?' asked Jennifer.

'He loves any kind of water.'

'Let's go there then.'

'I'm sure I could learn to surf with a proper board,' said Simon 'but the river would be safer for the twins.'

That night Helen snuggled up to George.

'You've never told me much about the war, was that how John got his scar?'

'Yes, I was lucky, though I used to think an elegant scar on my face might help attract the girls.'

'But how did John get his, were you there?'

'Yes, that's what I mean I was lucky and John was luckier than the other bloke. Anyway that was a long time ago, at least Simon won't have to live through times like those. Let's talk about more cheerful things, are we going to get some bathers and venture into the water?'

'Do you think Yvonne's got a good figure?'

'Yes… nearly as good as yours.'

'Did John tell you how they met?'

'They were both in Malaya, neither of them wanted to go back home so they thought they might as well get hitched. What's so funny?'

'The way Yvonne described it was much more romantic.' She retold the story. 'I bet he was good looking then… still is.'

'You thought Waterloo station was romantic at the time.'

Helen fell in love with Crawley Beach; with the shady trees, pleasant beach and gently lapping river it felt an exotic but civilised way to spend a morning. The children were up to their waists in the water with the dog swimming round them in circles. John and Yvonne showed the twins how to lie and float while they provided a supporting hand under their backs. Trish and Terri helped

Jennifer, while Simon set out to prove he could swim further than the length of a pool. The pool that had been long and deep when he first came back from the scout holiday was becoming smaller every time he described it.

When the twins returned to play in the sand, Jennifer discovered Drongo never tired of retrieving sticks from the river. Trish inevitably beat her sister and Simon in a swimming race and he was glad to come ashore and prove he could throw sticks the furthest. Even John worried that Drongo had gone so far out he wasn't going to make it back.

'That dog is so stupid he'd swim over to South Perth or even down to Fremantle. I'll go and fetch him in, otherwise we'll never get to lunch.'

John struck out towards the dog, who was still circling looking for the stick and Simon looked relieved when they both returned safely.

Helen felt on top of the world as they admired the views from King's Park, looking down on the little white city and the wide curving river glinting in the sun.

'This was the first picture we saw of Perth.'

'It's the picture you always see of Perth,' laughed John 'we always bring visitors up here.'

Eating out was a treat for the Palmer family and John suggested they try the steaks. The children relished the crinkle cut chips that accompanied them. Simon demolished his steak and helped the twins finish theirs.

'Just what a growing lad needs' John teased Helen.

Conversation turned to cars and jobs.

'I'm just about set on going back to that first place we saw on Friday' said George. 'If I get the motor tomorrow we can go out and about next week; I'll find my way around ready for job hunting when the children start school.'

On Monday morning the twins raced in from the front garden with the 'Western Australian.' As Helen unrolled it she gasped at the headline.

'Look George, how awful.'

'What, what…' Peter nudged under his father's arm.

'Nothing son.'

But Simon was already looking over his shoulder and read it out loud.

Migrant Drowns on First Day in Australia.

'Poor man… his family back home…the sea really is dangerous, that could have been Simon.'

'Helen, Simon wasn't by himself and he didn't go out of his depth… sounds like this fellow went too far out and couldn't get back in, one of those rip tides.'

'It's lucky John was there to rescue him.'

'I didn't need rescuing, the water just got up my nose.'

The children helped with the chores while George and Simon set off on the long walk to the car sales yard.

They returned with a second-hand, green station wagon.

'Plenty of room in the back for a dog,' said Jennifer 'or even two.'

With no time for a long outing, the children pleaded to go to the river.

Jennifer waded straight in till the water came up to her chest.

Simon was not interested in helping the others to float; Helen was worried he was getting out of his depth till he started to swim swam parallel to the shore. The twins took it in turns to be towed along by their sister; when they finally came out to get dried they assured their parents they could swim.

As they packed up the car to go home, Helen was suddenly struck by the realisation they were on their own in a strange country. How would they find that little house amongst the long roads and wide intersections of Perth's northern suburbs?

It was Peter's turn to sit in the middle of the front bench seat and while he urged his father to go faster, Helen pored over the map book.

'You can close that,' said George 'I know the way, I memorised it when we were with John.'

But it was a feeling that stayed with her all that week as they went out and about. Shopping in Perth she felt at home, but each time they ventured out of the city she worried they would never find their way back to base.

The further they went, the more George enjoyed it. Each evening he thumbed through the map book looking for places John and Yvonne had mentioned.

Each morning the children impatiently waited for dishes to be done and washing hung on the line, while Helen enjoyed the novelty of knowing the clothes and towels would be dry by the time they got back.

George marvelled at how quickly the sun sank below the horizon, while his wife worried darkness would descend and they would drive in the wrong direction; heading for the vast empty space that lay between Perth and the rest of the country. John had talked of distances they couldn't comprehend, out in the wheatbelt, down south and up north. The suburbs had English and Italian names, but further out places had aboriginal names, all seeming to end in 'ups', 'oos' and 'ongs'.

For Simon the week with his family would be broken up by spending a day with John at work, having tea at their house and going with him to the boys' club he helped run. John had never claimed he could get George a job; he worked for someone who owned a garage and other businesses.

'I don't like to be tied down, cash in a brown envelope every week, handed straight over to Vonny' he had told them.

As the five of them set off that day, Helen and George could talk properly in the car, with the children in the back seat.

'I think Simon's hoping they'll give him a Saturday job, or even a holiday job, but of course we don't know how long we'll be in this area.'

Jennifer soon interrupted. 'Can we live near the sea? Trish is going to teach me to surf once I've learnt to swim.'

'We have to choose a suburb we can afford and near my job, but I'm sure we'll find a house Mum likes, with four bedrooms and a big garden.'

'Can we have a dog in the new house?' piped up the twins in unison.

The day's outing was a success; they had driven up into the Darling Ranges and found a waterfall. The children picked their way amongst large boulders set in the red earth and clambered beside the waterfall. She and George admired the view of the flat plain below.

'I think I would like to live here in the hills,' said Helen 'not in a suburb.'

Simon had enjoyed his day at the garage, sweeping floors and making endless mugs of tea, but with the chance to look at all the motors and ask the mechanics questions.

'What does Uncle John do?' asked Helen.

'Oh he can fix anything.'

'Always could,' said his father 'anything from a tank to a radio. I could find my way anywhere, so we made a good team.'

'No wonder you never worry about getting lost. It must be like Christmas come early to have your own car.'

'Yes, if it turns out to be reliable we can make trips into the country later on, maybe even cross the Nullabor Plain.'

Chapter Nine   School

The next day Simon wanted to visit Beatty Park swimming pools.

'The boys' club are going there next week, I need to practice. You can both try out your new bathers.'

The family were impressed with the building, built only a couple of years earlier for the Commonwealth games. As Jennifer walked with her mother into the shiny tiled changing rooms she relished the unique swimming pool smell. It was strange going into the changing rooms with her mother, like going to school with her. She enjoyed going somewhere her brothers couldn't come and being able to chat without being interrupted.

'Terri doesn't like surfing.'

'I don't blame her, I'm glad you stayed in the shallows.'

'She doesn't like going under the waves, but she likes diving in the swimming pool. You know Uncle John's scar?' Jennifer waited for a reaction from her mother.

'You didn't mention it did you, it's not polite to make personal remarks.'

'No…Terri asked me if my Dad had any scars. She said Gerry did it; that means the Germans, in the war.'

Her mother smiled 'Yes I know.'

'So Dad might have been there, shall I ask him what happened?'

'No, no, it was a long time ago and it isn't any of our business.'

When they stepped outside, the pool stretched out into the distance, the blue water twinkling in the sunshine. With two fifty yard pools and a diving pool to choose from they had never seen such a place. Around the pool were high tiers of seating.

'I'm glad we haven't got an audience' said her mother, as they walked to the shallow end to find the rest of the family.

'Bet you can't swim the whole length' Jennifer challenged her brother.

Her parents were hesitant to get in the water. It was not busy, but there were mothers and young children strolling by. The children were amused to see their father's tanned face and arms in contrast to his white chest and legs.

'Don't splash your mother,' he warned the twins 'we don't want to put her off, now we've got her in the water.'

'It's lovely now I'm in, warm and clean; this is the civilised way to learn to swim.'

Simon set off for the deep end while Jennifer clung to the rails kicking her feet, determined to train her legs to stay up. Her parents were happy to stand waist deep, supporting the twins in their efforts to float.

Peter pointed to Simon clinging on to the side further up the pool. No one was sure if he was on his way to the end or on the way back.

Their quiet morning didn't last long, suddenly there was a lot of activity; pool attendants laughing and swinging ropes of giant beads across the pool, shrill whistles being blown and lines of children marching towards them. Swimming lessons were starting.

Simon had chosen that moment to attempt a dive and had already launched off the side of the pool. As he landed in the water with a painful belly flop, a tanned middle aged man, in white shorts and t-shirt, marched over with three short blasts on his whistle. Jennifer had been clinging to the rail and edging nearer to the deep end.

'No messing around in my lesson and you do not enter the water till I give the say so.'

His class of a dozen teenagers had arrived at the side of the pool and Jennifer saw them giggle behind his back, but none of them ventured to tell the instructor Simon didn't belong with them. The teacher hadn't noticed her and he asked her brother why he wasn't in school. Simon was trying to explain, but avoided pointing out his family or looking at Jennifer.

'Only been here a week? Well members of the public should be in the other pool… and you'd better stay down the shallow end till you've learnt to swim.'

As Simon clambered up the ladder, she heard one of the boys mutter 'Bloody Pommie.'

As she waded back to the shallow end her parents were making a hasty exit before the pool filled with little children.

'Simon, why is your stomach all red' asked Peter as they made their way to the other pool.

He looked down at his chest and stomach, the landing flat in the water had stung more than just his pride.

'Glad I'm not in their swimming class.'

On Sunday they drove up the Great Eastern Highway into the hills to find Mundaring Weir. Uncle John had told them about the huge dam and the pipeline built to take water to the goldfields. He had warned them nobody was allowed to swim in it, but it was a popular outing to watch the overflowing water cascading down the wall and walk across admiring the long stretch of water that filled the valley. Her father recited the technical details with relish.

'Everything's on a grander scale here.'

Jennifer had never seen a dam before and she was thrilled. It made her dizzy to look down the sloping wall as the water dropped to the valley floor and flowed into a little river. It was the river that made the reservoir. The dam was so deep it filled the whole valley, before they built the wall there had just been one narrow river.

On Monday morning Jennifer was up very early, but her mother was already busy, making four packed lunches. If Simon was nervous he wasn't going to admit it. He had checked out the long walk to the high school, dropping loud hints about how handy a bicycle would be.

Her father planned to take the twins and meet the headmaster, but promised Jennifer he would not come to her classroom. After being officially greeted, she assured the headmaster she remembered which was her class and tiptoed along the wooden veranda. At the green door she knocked and opened it, but she had not tapped loud enough, no one noticed her hesitant entry. She recalled the rare occasions when a new child had started at St. Stephen's, the most sensible and amiable pupil was appointed to look after them.

Mr. Gregson looked up, beckoned a freckled girl to come to the front and introduced her as Meryl. He then declared a five minute break from arithmetic so Jennifer could introduce herself and answer any questions. She was the only English child in the class. There were just three questions; had she met the Beatles, had she been to The Cavern and had she seen snow.

She took the empty seat next to Meryl. In her leather satchel were the items Terri had advised her to take. Education was not free in Western Australia, pupils were expected to provide their own pens and pencils.

Meryl was already on the fourth question on the black board. Jennifer frowned, nothing looked familiar, though she was quite good at arithmetic and didn't want to put her hand up. Mr. Gregson beckoned her over to his desk, he was smiling. He asked her to show him how she would set out long multiplication, long division and fractions.

'Good, you can do the work, we just set it out a different way. By the time we do end of year tests you'll be fine.'

At playtime she trailed out with Meryl and her friends and they showed her where the water fountain and toilets were. The grade seven girls didn't play, they were content to sit in the shade of the wooden shelter. Perhaps that was what happened when you were twelve; Christine's sister had announced when she went to grammar school that she was too old to play. She sat listening to the other girls, but it was boring as she knew none of the people or places they were talking about.

There was no sign of her brothers among the boys and younger children rushing around the playground; then she heard Peter's voice.

'Jenny, Jenny, Tony's hurt his knee, the teacher's looking after him.'

If the teacher was involved it might be serious, but Tony appeared marching towards them with a bright purple knee.

The disappointment for her classmates of Jennifer not having met the Beatles was slightly compensated for by the discovery she had sweet twin brothers. They gathered sympathetically round Tony.

'Why is your knee purple?' asked Peter.

'It's stuff to kill the germs' his brother replied.

'Gentian Violet,' explained Meryl 'they always put that on; the boys like it to show off their battle scars.'

Jennifer felt more confident about composition. Mr. Gregson told her to write about an Australian adventure, if she preferred that to the title on the board. She chewed the end of her new biro, back at St. Stephen's she would have been dipping her pen nibs in the ink well. An idea came to her; Mr. Gregson was going to read this, not her big brother, she would write a dramatic account of how Simon was saved from drowning.

At lunchtime they were back in the wooden shelter with their lunch boxes. Jennifer had peanut paste sandwiches, a newly discovered delicacy for the Palmers, a piece of homemade cake, an apple and a plastic drinking bottle filled with cordial that was warm and tasted of new plastic.

In the geography lesson the teacher was impressed with her completed worksheet; she could not have done it without the visit to the library and her parents' help.

When they went out for sport the other girls were dressed in strange gingham tunics with different coloured cords around their waists. Jennifer had been placed in green faction, which she thought was something to do with arithmetic, but now realised was their name for teams.

They played softball, which was rounders with everything larger, plus gloves. She managed to wield the bat and hit the ball, but when her team were fielding she dropped the ball every time, the strange leather glove made her feel clumsy.

She hadn't spotted Terri all day, but she was there waiting for Jennifer at home time, beside her the twins hovered excitedly. Meryl and a friend came over to walk part of the way with them.

'Oh do you know Terri… and her sister?'

They asked Terri how Trish was getting on. It seemed that Terri's main claim to fame was being Trish's sister; otherwise they wouldn't have bothered to chat to a grade six. Now Jennifer was enjoying some of the kudos by connection. Whatever the reasons, at least she could tell her parents the other girls had been friendly.

Chapter Ten Home

Getting back into school routine was not easy, especially with four packed lunches to make. Helen rushed around to get a few chores done before George got back from the school. They were determined to enjoy their first day of freedom; it seemed months since the children had all been at school. When George arrived back he helped her hang dripping sheets on the line.

'Perhaps we should go into Boans and buy spare sheets?'

'It doesn't seem worth it when we have plenty of bedding in the packing cases. They'll be ready to go back on the beds this afternoon, no wonder they don't have airing cupboards here.'

'Okay, business first, then we'll treat ourselves to lunch, perhaps King's Park again. Let's enjoy this week and worry about budgets when we're tied up with a mortgage once more.'

At the bank they had a discussion with a manager obviously used to new immigrants who had no idea where they were going to live or what their salary would be. He could tell them only how much they might be able to borrow on their available deposit; the capital that was gradually going down with the purchase of the car, rent and shopping.

Helen couldn't see how George was going to find a job that was completely different, surely any company would want proof of experience, but her husband was full of the confidence that had not left him since they first had the idea to emigrate.

'This is a land of opportunity, they're not hide bound here, look how many jobs John has had.'

Helen smiled 'I think Yvonne would rather he stuck to one job.'

'I don't blame him, I was stuck in a rut for too long. It will be different for Simon, he can get a good education and have a proper career. Come on, let's walk down to the river and get a timetable for those ferries; we should have a proper outing each weekend and we've got the whole summer ahead.'

'I still feel like I'm on holiday, do you realise we've never been away by ourselves since our honeymoon?'

'All the more reason to make the most of it before I start work, I'll probably have to work long hours till we get established.'

They were glad of the cooler air by the river.

'I think it's getting hotter, still it is wonderful not having to cart jackets and raincoats around.'

George spent Monday evening perusing the job adverts in the paper and consulting the map book. The children helped with the dishes, as no one appeared to have any homework. Helen enjoyed the novelty of working in a larger kitchen, with room for everyone to help wipe up and put away.

On Tuesday Helen was in the kitchen early, the children had promised to leap out of bed as soon as they heard the ABC fanfare. George enjoyed the luxury of seeing the children off to school first, then hugged his wife before he set off for his first day of proper job hunting.

'Don't be disappointed if nothing turns up George, it could take a while…'

Helen felt strange in the empty house, but she was looking forward to a day by herself, a good spring clean was what she had in mind. With most of their possessions in storage, there wasn't much clutter to deal with, but it was surprising how quickly the children had spread their things around.

She felt she deserved a long lunch break and took a kitchen chair, sandwich and library book onto the veranda. It was then she realised they had still not seen any neighbours. All the houses were hidden by shady trees, but she had expected to see people coming in and out of their front doors.

When she walked down to Tony's shop in the afternoon she still did not see anyone else and was glad to talk to Tony and meet his wife Gina. At home she could never walk to the shops without meeting someone she knew, but it was bound to take time to get to know people and it would be best not to get too settled till they knew where they were going to live. There had been no post from home, but Helen had no idea how soon to expect letters.

When George came home after the children, it was hard to judge how his day had gone. There were a few companies he planned to phone back for news.

'We'll go for our swim tomorrow morning, then lunch in Perth before I visit some more places.'

'Good idea, I'll enjoy having a look round and come back by myself on the bus, I must get used to finding my way about.'

Jennifer had been given spare house keys and the usual instructions, in case her parents weren't home. The week fell into a pleasant routine.

Helen was looking forward to spending Saturday afternoon with the Charles' family and enjoying Yvonne's cooking. When John had come round with the invitation, she had tried to insist they should be guests at the Palmers, but he had assured her Yvonne would love to have them all round again.

'Why can't we go in the car Daddy?' piped up Tony.

'Have your legs stopped working since I bought the car?'

Even with their new casual clothes, the family were feeling hot by the time they arrived. When they turned the corner and saw the front of the house, Helen felt they were truly in an exotic country. The carport and half the house were covered in cascades of purple blossom. Yvonne opened the fly screen door.

'Bougainvillea, I thought you'd be impressed. One of my first memories of when we were out East, they're not native to Australia, but they love it here. Come and see the back yard, I think this is my favourite time of year.'

Drongo went wild when he heard the creak of the back fly screen door. He licked all the children's bare feet.

'I've just realised,' said Jennifer 'my thongs have been on my feet all day without me noticing.'

Helen looked down at the sensible sandals she had bought for herself in Coles.

'I don't know how you keep them on your feet, let alone walk and run in them.'

Yvonne told Drongo to go and lie down, then took Helen on a tour of the back yard. Another bougainvillea, deep pink, festooned the corner behind the rotary hoist and dark leaved shrubs with pretty pink flowers were dotted along the side fence.

'Oleander, I think they're Mediterranean, that is the type of climate we have here; hot and dry in summer, cool and wet in winter.'

'It's certainly hot today.'

'Yes, it doesn't usually get so hot this soon. Anyway, sit in the shade and I'll get cool drinks for everyone.'

George followed John out into the yard.

'…it's a long time since I went job hunting and of course I'm not sure what pay rates to expect.'

'No you don't want them to take advantage of you. Hey twins, how's school?'

Tony showed him his mauve knee and bright purple elbow.

'The teacher says she knows who is who, now Tony's purple' said Peter.

'How about the high school Simon?'

'Only two good things; they've got girls and one of the cricket team broke his arm, so I got on the team.'

John laughed. 'What other reasons would there be for going to school?'

'Jennifer got top mark for her composition' said George.

'Well done, Mr. Gregson doesn't give marks away. What was it about?'

Jennifer blushed. 'Our first week in Australia…'

As the twins played with the dog and Jennifer went off with Terri to see the latest pony book her aunt had sent, the conversation turned to the news. There was to be a hanging in a few days time.

'I can't see there being any reprieve' said John 'though hanging's too good for Eric Cooke.'

'Everyone will be glad when it's over,' said Yvonne 'such senseless killings, Perth wasn't the same after that, '63 was a bad year. Perth was a carefree country town when we first came.'

'No one knew who was doing it, or why and worse still, who would be next' her husband added.

'Where are they going to hang him?' asked Simon with relish.

'Some folks would love a public gallows, but we are civilised here, inside Fremantle Gaol.'

Helen shuddered; she hadn't expected Perth to be an innocent paradise, but nor could she imagine random murders taking place, certainly not shootings, that was what happened to gangsters in tough cities.

'My friend at school knew one of the people who got killed' said Trish.

'Yes, it affected a lot of people, but let's talk about something more cheerful' said her mother. 'How did you get on with the boys' club at Beatty Park Simon?'

'I volunteered to be the victim, they were doing life saving classes.'

'That was brave,' said John 'I wouldn't trust any of them. Have you got your mother in the water yet?'

'Helen and I have been to the pool a couple of times, but I think the best we can hope for is to paddle about in the shallows helping the twins. We're going to Crawley Beach tomorrow, I think we'll be glad to cool off in this heat.'

When they sat down at the big kitchen table, Yvonne served up lamb cutlets and bowls of delicious salads.

'Are there any more cutlets?'

George frowned at Simon.

'Yes, I cooked plenty, no shortage of sheep in Australia.'

'They are very tasty, you'll have to tell me how you do that breadcrumb coating' remarked Helen 'and the rice salad, the only rice we have is in a pudding.'

'I'm all for as many salads as possible,' said Yvonne 'you don't want to slave over a hot oven, especially in summer.'

'We haven't heard from home yet, how often do you hear from your sister, Yvonne?'

'Once in a blue moon, but she is very good sending the girls things, they've got a son so I guess she enjoys the chance to buy ballet and pony books.'

'Terri's got a "Kit Hunter, Show Jumper" I haven't read yet.'

'You can borrow it as soon as I've read it.'

'Terri will have read it by Monday' said her father.

'When we get our packing cases out of storage, Jenny can lend Terri all her pony books.'

Helen helped Yvonne wash up after tea. 'I can't believe we've been here nearly three weeks, sometimes it seems like three months and other times like three days. I think of things to tell Mum or my sister or Joyce, then remember I can't. I should write to them again, but I'm waiting till we have news of our plans.'

'Do you want to come to CWA with me next week, meet some other wives?'

'What's that?'

'Clucking Women's Association' said John, coming into the kitchen to get some beers out of the fridge.

'Don't let Mable hear you say that, Country Women's Association, but you don't have to have lived in the outback to join. If you're interested in sewing and crafts and having a good gossip…'

'I did go to dressmaking evening classes with Joyce, more of an excuse to get out of the house. I didn't do much at home, there never seemed to be enough time or room, but I'm thinking of getting a new machine when we're settled, get Jenny interested, it's so useful if you can make your own clothes.'

She wasn't surprised when Yvonne said 'Yes, I made all the girls clothes when they were younger. Jenny will do dressmaking at High School.'

Trish came into the kitchen to fetch cool drinks from the fridge. Helen had noticed there was a pathway beaten to the large fridge, which contained an endless supply of cold water, fruit juice, fizzy drinks and beer.

'Dressmaking is boring, I've only made an apron for cooking.'

'Next year will be better' said her mother.

'Yeah, a nightie…'

'Once you learn, you can make your own clothes, can't be difficult these days, all the dresses are straight and you don't need much material for those short skirts.'

As the Palmers stepped out onto the veranda, ready to go home, Helen commented on the welcome cool air.

'It smells wonderful after dark.'

'Eucalyptus, next door have got that gum tree in their front yard' said Yvonne.

'You'll welcome the evenings when we get the real hot weather' added her husband.

Over the next couple of weeks family life for the Palmers began to take on a routine. Letters from home appeared at intervals, until they had heard from everyone. Helen found some of the letters stilted and formal; friends and family were used to talking to her not writing. She endeavoured to reply to each of them straight away.

Her mother seemed to have written on behalf of her father and sister; she would write separately to her sister next time. They would have even less in common now they were so far apart, but she would miss her sister's stories about work and their occasional Saturday trips to Oxford Street. Her longest letter was to Joyce, describing their floundering around in the river and swimming pool and the Country Women's Association.

Yvonne said I should take 'a plate', which meant a plate with something on it! I took flapjacks, but some of the ladies had gone overboard, I think they vie with each other. Yvonne said we don't want to slave over hot stoves in summer, but there must be a lot of slaving and hot stoves for all that baking. We're having a 'lamington drive' next time, that involves baking as well. I shall have to watch my weight, we seem to be eating all the time here. Anyway, the ladies were very nice; the older ones loved my stories of Mum's mending and make do during the war, it reminded them of managing with what they had in 'The Bush'. A couple of them looked really ancient, but it turned out they were the same age as Mum; I think the rugged life and hot sun gives them a sort of leathery look.

Simon has a Saturday job where John works, so at least he has a bit of pocket money; they don't have paper boys here, the roads are too long and the houses too spaced out (they're all detached). A chap in a van drives slowly, hurling rolled up papers onto the front lawn. I think Simon likes school, he doesn't tell us much. He should be more settled when he starts studying for his Leaving exams.

George has a couple of job possibilities, but he wants to make sure he settles for something he will enjoy and that's secure. John says he should 'grab anything short term and keep looking for something better'. In the meantime we are enjoying spending time together as a family, it's like being on holiday all the time here (except for the cooking, cleaning and washing! Though even that's easier, it's really hot already so we have lots of salads and the washing dries so easily). George and I make sure we have some time to ourselves while the children are at school...

'though our second honeymoon nearly came to a halt when George came home with a roll of cellotape instead of…' no I'd better not write that, thought Helen.

Lots of things have different names here, you'll never guess what they call cellotape - Durex!

Jennifer likes her new teacher and he is very pleased with her work. The twins' teacher said they should go in separate classes next year as Tony is 'carried' by Peter. We don't know what to do for the best, I feel guilty we have been so busy in the past year we haven't given them enough individual attention.

We had some drama last week, a man was hung at Fremantle Gaol, they still have hanging here. It passed without protest, only one woman kept vigil outside the gaol overnight; he had shot innocent people he didn't even know, but I wonder what it must be like for his wife and all their children…

Anyway back to more cheerful things. Mum and Dad are fine, they enjoyed their tea at Dennis's the day we left, though I was rather miffed. Apparently he regaled them with exaggerated tales of weeping emigrants and relatives at London Airport and assured them we would be back in two years. We certainly won't, we know we made the right decision to come here.

Well must finish so I can post this tomorrow…

Helen sat with pen poised, the end of letters was the hardest part to write, when you knew you were never going to see the recipient again.

Hope you are all well and the dog isn't getting up to mischief, Jennifer and the twins all want a dog now, they love John and Yvonne's. Everyone sends their love…

'Jenny, do you want me to post your letter to Christine tomorrow?'

Jennifer had half the aerogramme left and was staring into space.

'I don't know what to say, Christine's letter is all about hockey matches and experiments with Bunsen burners.'

By the beginning of November the temperature was regularly reaching a 'century' and the family were excited by the sight of their new thermometer showing one hundred degrees Fahrenheit. Though Simon came home from school after his long walk with his shirt un-tucked and his face bright red, shining with sweat, the sheer novelty of the heat stopped any of the children complaining. Beach Road had been transformed with masses of azure blossom; the jacaranda trees were in bloom.

When George came home one afternoon with a big grin on his face, Helen knew their new life was about to begin properly.

'Victoria Park, where's that?'

The family were gathered round the kitchen table having their evening meal.

'The other side of the river, where we come off the causeway, it's an older suburb.'

'Are you going to drive a big lorry Dad?' asked Tony.

'I'm going to be driver's mate to start with, they need two blokes for each vehicle, with all the loading and unloading.'

'What will you actually be loading?' said Helen, wondering if he was cut out for this sort of work.

'All sorts; it's only a small company. They deliver to the little shops like Tony's, he gave me their name. I'll be going all over the place. The pay's not that great, but he offered me the job straight away. Once I've found my way around I'll be driving as well.' George laughed 'He assured me he'd need help in the office when he expands, he couldn't believe I was trying to avoid offices.'

'What's your new boss like then Dad, how much is he going to pay you?' Simon was an expert on the world of real work since having his Saturday job.

'Same name as me, that's what they call him, but it's Georgiou really, he's Greek. He was glad to get someone who speaks perfect English and can speak politely to the suppliers. My driver is Joe, he's Italian.'

'But will we live in Victoria Park?' said Jennifer.

'I don't think so; we're more likely to get a new house in the suburbs further out.'

When they were on their own in the kitchen, George admitted that it wouldn't be a well paid job, nor was there any guarantee it would be secure.

'That's probably why he hasn't any Australians working for him, he's got another English bloke though, Tom from Lancashire.'

'How big is the company' asked Helen, wondering if she should sound enthusiastic or cautious.

'Three lorries and looking to buy a fourth. He's got business sense, other migrants are opening more shops in the new suburbs, he knows where the houses are going up. I just hope the bank manager looks on the positive side, impressed I've got work quickly and we can offer a good deposit before we spend any more of it.

Wednesday tomorrow, that gives us three days to look properly without the kids, then I start on Monday. Or if I'm on an early shift, we could house hunt in the afternoons.'

'Shifts' said Helen in dismay.

'These shopkeepers start work very early and we need to deliver the perishables while it's still cool.'

Despite her misgivings Helen was thrilled at the prospect of looking around at new houses, George's optimism was catching.

'We can tell the landlord we'll be out of this house by the end of the year, let the children finish the term, then we'll have seven weeks school holiday to settle in ready for their new schools.'

On Wednesday morning the river twinkled in the sunshine as they crossed the causeway. George pointed out shops and named roads, as they drove through Victoria Park to meet his new boss. Helen was still enjoying the novelty of being driven everywhere and looked out of the window with interest at the various shops; there was more of a buzz here than where they lived.

At the chaotic offices of 'Swan Supplies' Helen was greeted enthusiastically by a short stocky man with dark olive skin and a large black moustache. He was dressed in khaki shorts and shirt; she had expected the boss to be in a suit, not dressed the same as his drivers. Georgiou extended a hand the size of a plate and his short sleeve revealed a muscular forearm smothered in black hair. His smile revealed a set of very white teeth. A man who seemed larger than life in every way, she mused.

'Welcome to Australia, I been here five years, old hand eh?'

Greek George's accent was strong but easy to understand. He reassured her she would be able to get buses from the new house to Victoria Park and Perth, as if they had already moved in. 'Good shopping and plenty of office if you want job.'

'Oh my wife won't be working, she's got the family to look after.'

'How many children you got? Three sons and a daughter? Well done.'

He slapped George on the back.

'I did have a bit of help from Helen' laughed her husband.

Helen wasn't sure how to take this banter, she couldn't imagine a conversation like this with Mr. Cummings, George's old boss.

Later, in the café Georgiou had recommended, owned by his sister, George and Helen looked through the paperwork the estate agents had given them.

'I'll miss our lunches out when you're back at work.'

'Maybe I'll have some weekdays off, I expect I'll work weekends occasionally.'

'Do you think this is going to work out?'

'Of course, you like my new boss don't you.'

Helen laughed. 'Why did he assume I would want to work in an office? I might want to try something different, if I had to get a job.'

'You won't need to go to work.'

'The Greek and Italian ladies seem to work.'

'Only the ones who are helping in family businesses. I certainly wouldn't want us to work with Dennis, could you imagine?'

'Do you think he would ever want to come out here?'

'I don't think so, he's pretty well set up as he is, but I'd better not make it sound too good in my letters in case he does!'

'I wonder if my sister would? Think of all those years she's spent commuting up to London on the train, in winter…'

'She has an easy life, your mother always has dinner ready for her, no mortgage, only herself to worry about.'

'Yes she does do a lot of things we can't do, she's out a lot, she might still meet someone…'

'Of course, she's hardly over the hill.'

'I must write to her; it's funny we never thought that much about the lives of the rest of the family, just took it for granted we were all in our little set grooves, but now we're away from everything we knew, I feel we're on the outside looking in.'

'Come on, that's enough philosophising; let's look at all this paperwork.'

They looked with delight at plans showing large gardens, laundries, verandas, then consulted the map book as George worked out a route.

As they drove out, the mature roads with their chain link fences, weatherboard houses and trees gave way to wide empty roads. New houses were interspersed with stretches of shrubby open land. Even with the windows wide open, they were getting hot. Helen had stopped wearing stockings and they both wore sunglasses.

'I bet it's a hundred again today' said George.

'We'd better choose a house with schools nearby, the children can't walk too far in this heat.'

'At least they won't have to walk in the freezing cold and get chilblains.'

'I hope Jenny's remembered we might be home late.'

'She and Terri will have a good time playing mother, all your cakes will be eaten and the boys won't want their dinner.'

By the time they drove home Helen wondered if they had too much choice, but George was happy they now had a better idea of what to expect. He was already planning the next day's expedition.

That night they made love, but it was so hot sweat made their bodies slip awkwardly; they laughed.

'I don't know how people in hot countries have so many babies' said George.

'Shsh, the children will hear you, these walls are so thin.'

'I hope they're asleep.'

'It's hard for them to sleep in this heat. I could almost wish for our cold bedroom back home, snuggling under the eiderdown, not daring to let an arm or shoulder be exposed to the cold air outside.'

'Yes, with you accusing me of pulling all the blankets over to my side' George teased.

'Now we only need a sheet.'

'We could go camping out in the bush, like John and Yvonne; sleep outside, make love under the stars.'

Helen stifled a giggle 'What if someone came along?'

'I think that's the point, there is no one else around.'

'What about the children?'

'Hopefully they'd be fast asleep in their tents.'

George seemed set on doing as many things as possible that they would never have done back home; she admired him for that, but she could not imagine what it was like 'out in the bush', let alone the logistics of taking the family camping there.

On Thursday they were better organised, their new 'esky' was packed with a picnic to take to the river. After viewing a few completed houses and many with barely the foundations laid, they drove to Bayswater and found the beach where John claimed Rolf Harris had taken children's swimming lessons. Close to the bridge and with two wooden jetties it was a good spot for families. Feeling a little self conscious, having a picnic without children, they found a shady spot and discussed what they had seen so far.

'I like the bathrooms with the separate shower cubicles and the laundries; washing children and clothes is going to be a lot easier' said Helen.

'There's a lot less choice if we want four bedrooms, but we can't manage with three.'

'That last house looked nice, but it was so far from anything.'

'Hmm, you don't want to be stuck without a bus stop, even if you learn to drive Simon and Jenny will need to get the bus if they want to go into Perth.'

'I didn't like that bloke from the first building company, I don't want to buy a house that's only reached our waist, it might not be ready in time and I want to see what it looks like properly.'

'Yes, he was all flashy brochures and flashy smiles. We won't be rushed into anything, if necessary we'll rent in Victoria Park.'

As they drove to the next area on their list they already felt like seasoned house hunters, but they both fell in love with the third house, even before the agent arrived with the keys. There was just one vacant house next to it on the corner; empty bushland lay on the other side and across the road. The front of the house was bland with a concrete veranda and grey sand stretching between the road and the house, but when they went round the back they were delighted to see natural bush and gum trees in the long yard.

'Before my wife gets too excited, can you tell us where the high school, primary school, shops and bus stop are' said George, as the agent stepped out of his car.

He answered with a strong Yorkshire accent.

'I wish all my clients were as sensible, how many weeks have you been doing this?'

'It's only our second day,' said Helen proudly 'how long have you been out here?'

'Two years, we love it; but I think my wife is only just settling.' He turned to George. 'If you want my advice, choose a house the wife is going to love, it's harder for them. The first year they think they're on holiday, then the second year they realise how much they miss their mothers and sisters and friends.'

He took them up on the veranda and unlocked the fly screen then the front door. The smell of new wood greeted them.

'Solid jarrah floors, lounge, main bedroom at the front, kitchen large enough to eat in. The house isn't big, but you've got your four bedrooms and you can extend later on if you want a hobbies room. The local area fulfils your criteria, think carefully, but don't hesitate, we've got other buyers interested.'

'Let's have a proper look out the back' said George.

'It's got a garden path already,' said Helen 'what's that concrete thing at the end?'

'Air vent, that's your septic tank,' grinned the agent 'no deep sewerage here, everything goes into the soak-away.'

'Oh dear, sounds a bit primitive.'

After one more look round the house they shook the agent's hand and drove away.

'First phone box we come to, we'll make an appointment with the bank manager, tomorrow hopefully. We won't say anything to the kids yet, wait till we know for sure if we can get the finance.'

'So we're definitely going for it?'

'I'm sure that's the one, don't worry about the drains, he said they all have those septic tanks, so they must work okay.'

When they arrived home an old lady appeared in the front garden next door.

'Hello, how are you getting on?'

'Oh hello, I don't think we've met…'

'Your little boy's been telling me all about you, it's nice having a family next door again, but sounds like you won't be here for long.'

'How strange,' said Helen when they got indoors 'just when we're getting ready to leave we start meeting the neighbours.'

Chapter Eleven   November 1964

Jennifer lay awake that night, trying to hear what her parents were saying; bank managers, wages, trees, gardens and schools were all mentioned, but didn't join together to make sense. She drifted onto other thoughts. It was her fourth week at school and she was no longer the new girl; Meryl saw no need to shepherd her around. The twins were trusted to go home by themselves and Terri usually waited for her after school. Her own group of friends seemed happy to include Jennifer; she was a little embarrassed to be a Grade 7 hanging around with Grade 6s, but it was Terri who had become her best friend. The girls in her class were friendly, but she didn't belong to any particular group, as she had at St. Stephen's. So she had fallen into the routine of walking home with Terri and her two friends who went the same way and going to each other's houses after school. The disadvantage of not having a television set was offset by having a big brother who they thought looked like John Lennon; Simon had avoided the barbers since their arrival in Australia. The girls also liked her mother's homemade cakes.

School was stranger than she had expected; from being in a little school with four classes and knowing exactly what was going on, she had felt lost at first. The large school with seven grades and lots of classrooms, had no hall, no piano and no morning assembly. Singing took place in the classroom, the pounding piano of Mrs. Jones replaced by Mr. Gregson blowing a flat plastic instrument with keys like a piano. It was called a melodica and his favourite song was the Maori Farewell. The Maoris said farewell a lot; they lived on small islands in the Pacific Ocean and often set off in their little boats, exploring.

Inspired perhaps by the presence of Jennifer, who knew nothing of the southern hemisphere, Mr Gregson would tell them fantastic tales. A few hundred years ago the Maoris found two new islands far away, where no people lived. For thousands and thousands of years New Zealand had no human history; exotic creatures were safe from hunters. There were giant flightless birds, taller than an elephant, but their size was no defence against clever human beings; they didn't know they should run away to avoid being a tasty meal and were hunted to extinction.

Australia was the opposite; the Aborigines had lived there for ever, longer than anyone else had lived anywhere. While civilisations rose and fell, they wandered around the huge continent thinking they were the only people in the world. Jennifer loved these stories.

She had enjoyed English history at junior school; they started in Class One with woolly rhinoceros and mammoths, by the time they finished Class Four, they had reached the Second World War. Important things happened in other parts of the world, such as Ancient Egyptians, Jesus being born and America being discovered, but she had pictured world history neatly fitted into less than four thousand years. Now she struggled to imagine a time before that, whole continents not knowing about each other.

Mr. Gregson's stories meant a break from work and she had decided her new class worked less hard than at St. Stephen's, the atmosphere was lighter; perhaps it was the prospect of Christmas and the summer holidays coming together.

Today the teacher had told them a different story, she couldn't remember how the subject had turned to war. Mr. Gregson had been in a different war to her father, in the jungle fighting Japs; she could never understand how or why the Germans and Japanese had decided to link up and start a world war. One of the few things her father had told them was that the German soldiers were exactly the same as the young Englishmen; they didn't want to be fighting either.

The Japanese soldiers were not the same; one day the Australian medics were carrying a wounded prisoner, when they stopped for a break they just dropped the stretcher from shoulder height. The Japanese and the Australians did not regard each other as human.

Something bad happened to Mr. Gregson and his mates; one of them had his face sliced off by a shell. Jennifer pictured a giant sea shell whizzing through the air, like the petrol sign, only black instead of yellow. The soldier begged them to shoot him in the head and put him out of his misery; it was hard for them to hear what he was saying, with his face destroyed, though they understood what he meant. But they were too scared; they couldn't bear to look at him, they wound bandages round and round his face, ran away and left him to suffocate. Lying in the safety and comfort of her bed, she pulled the sheet over her face, trying to imagine what it would be like to suffocate. She regularly related Mr. Gregson's stories to her parents, but she would never tell them this one.

She didn't even tell Terri at home time, but she told her about the other girls at lunchtime. Sitting in the shelter there had been whispers and glances, Jennifer had no clue what they were talking about, but it sounded serious. Later on, Meryl swore her to secrecy and finally told her. After the anticipation it was an anti-climax; they thought one of the other girls was away from school because she had started her periods.

Now she had the privacy of her own room, Jennifer's mother had started talking to her at bedtime about growing up. She was still hazy about the connection between bleeding every month and having babies and now she knew how babies came out, she was scared of having one, but babies and periods seemed a long way off. She preferred to think about having a dog or learning to ride a horse, like Terri was going to do in the holidays.

But if Jennifer thought she could avoid thinking about growing up, she had reckoned without Terri's mother. When they arrived at her house on Friday, to celebrate the end of the week, Trish was flouncing off to her room with a face like thunder. As Terri raided the fridge for cool drinks Yvonne explained.

'She's just grumpy because she was looking forward to going to the beach with her friends tomorrow and now her period's started.'

Terri sympathised, while Jennifer was puzzled.

'Has your mother explained everything to you love?'

Jennifer blushed. Wanting to appear grown up, she assured Yvonne she knew everything, but just wondered how periods could stop you going to the beach.

Yvonne laughed 'Of course you can go to the beach, but you can't go swimming.'

Jennifer was dismayed, she hadn't anticipated such practical problems. She was still hoping they would have a new house by the river and go swimming every day.

'When's your birthday?'

"March the seventh, I'm going to be twelve, Mum said she didn't start her periods till she was fifteen.'

'It was different during the war, we didn't go hungry, but there was rationing. Girls have a good diet these days, grow up quicker. My mother never told me anything; I woke up one morning, saw the blood and thought I was dying…'

Terri giggled, she had obviously heard the story before.

When Jennifer arrived home later that afternoon, the twins rushed to tell her they were all going on a boat.

'I thought we should have an outing to celebrate my new job,' said her father 'so we're off to Rottnest in the morning. Catch the ferry in Perth, voyage down the Swan River to Fremantle then out on the Indian Ocean.'

On Saturday morning the excitement of travel was recaptured by the prospect of going on the ferry. The cool of the river was welcome, the hot spell was unbroken. Jennifer looked out for Crawley beach and gazed up at King's Park. The river meandered slowly to Fremantle and the twins kept asking when they were going to see the sea. As they finally edged out of the harbour the sea looked calmer than it had from the beach; she forgot about Simon's predictions that they would all be sea sick. The brown of the river merged into the green sea, further out the water was deep turquoise. As the island came closer a few people were hanging over the side being sick, while others retreated below deck to throw up in the toilets. Regular passengers told them they would feel better staying up on deck. Simon was the only one to feel sick and clung to the rails taking deep breaths. The twins were delighted to report to their parents when he did start vomiting over the side.

Jennifer steered clear of the boys and went to watch the island jetty approaching; the sea journey had been much quicker than the river trip.

As they pulled up she was delighted, this was a real island of sun and sand.

'Come and help your mother children' called their father.

They had bags full of swimming gear and picnic food. Simon looked white underneath his tan and was stepping shakily down the gangplank. Her parents had got chatting with another couple who gave directions then waved farewell.

'What country were they from Dad?' she asked.

He laughed. 'England, they're Geordies, been out here for years.'

'What's a Geordie?" asked Peter.

'From the north east, they come from Newcastle-upon-Tyne. It reminds me of the army, we met people from all over the country. We'll meet people in Perth from all over Britain that we would never have met back home.'

'They suggested a nice sheltered beach we could go to,' said her mother 'they were off to hire bikes and cycle around the island, takes about three and a half hours apparently.'

As they found the beach Jennifer knew this was going to be their best day since they arrived in Australia. She persuaded her parents to paddle and Simon had soon recovered enough to plunge into the sea.

Unsure what they would find on the island, her mother had packed a grand picnic with a varied selection of sandwiches. Simon demolished a lot of them, starving now his stomach had recovered. To round off were the lamingtons

Helen had brought back from the lamington drive the evening before.

She described how all the women had brought slabs of sponge cake, which were cut into cubes and dipped in runny chocolate icing then coconut. The dozens they made were laid out to dry, ready to sell the next morning for club funds. Made even gooier in the hot sun, the children made muffled cries of approval as they bit into the cakes.

They all stretched out on the beach towels after lunch. Jennifer was longing to cool off in the water, but the one thing her mother knew about swimming was that you mustn't go in the water for an hour after eating. The children giggled as their father started snoring and their mother dozed. Simon had his transistor earphones plugged in and tried to ignore the twins covering his legs with sand. Jennifer read the boarding school adventure Terri had leant her; smug that she was having a better time than the girls in the book. When exactly sixty minutes had passed she roused her parents. The children had a quick dip, but it was too hot to stay on the beach and they set off to explore.

The little square with its old ochre buildings was very pleasant, then they strolled under the shady trees, coming across a camping site. A new plan formed in Jennifer's mind, they had to come to Rottnest for a camping holiday, not just a day out. Simon had the same idea and promised she could cycle all round the island with him.

They had not explored much of the island or seen a quokka, as it was soon time to get back on the ferry, but they all pleaded with their parents to bring them back soon.

Chapter Twelve   Money

George woke up every hour on Sunday night and Helen didn't sleep much better, worried they wouldn't hear the early alarm for work. When they finally drifted into a deep sleep the alarm startled them. They had tried to put aside their worries and enjoy the weekend with the children and it had given George time to regain his confidence.

'Even if I don't get to a phone box this morning I'm going to the bank as soon as I've finished work. No point in giving up at the first hurdle, anyone would think it was his money.'

Helen tried to sound bright, despite her worries. 'Whatever happens we've still got somewhere to live, you've got the car to get to work and the boys wouldn't even have to change schools.'

'I'll still be gutted if we lose that house.'

'They'll be other houses, maybe we could save for a bigger deposit.'

'Helen, I'll be forty in January, we have to get signed up now so we can get a twenty five year mortgage.'

'Go and enjoy your first day at work, don't think any more about money till this afternoon.'

She hugged him then laughed. 'This is just like sending the children off on the first day of term.'

By the time the children had gone to school Helen felt as if she had been up for hours, she had been up for hours, but if she stopped at nine o'clock for elevenses she would never get any work done. She put the radio on for company; the dial had remained on the ABC, they heard enough of the commercial stations with Simon's transistor. A busy day wasn't the same without the regular BBC programmes that had marked her domestic days at home; Mrs Dale's Diary, Woman's Hour… she gave herself a mental shake and went to strip the beds. The chores were catching up with her after being out last week and there was no need to look in the food cupboards to know they were empty. They had popped into shops when they were out and about last week, but that food had all disappeared over the weekend. She wondered if her brother had been hungry during the war, teenage boys seemed to eat so much. Simon probably ate a week's rations in a day, she smiled to herself. It was a good thing the food was cheap in Australia, the food bill when the twins reached Simon's age didn't bear thinking of.

When she at last sat down for coffee it was indoors, she was beginning to realise the benefits of keeping the house shaded and cool. She browsed through the 'Western Australian'; there never seemed to be much international news in it. George had bought 'The Australian' a couple of times, but that hardly mentioned W.A. She made a shopping list; the milkman only delivered milk and bread as far as she knew. He came so early she had never seen him; he left the bill each week and she left the money. The problem of not buying more than she could carry was solved when she checked her purse, they should have got more cash out of the bank on Friday. She liked Tony's shop, but when he started slicing ham on the machine and cutting chunks of cheese, you were never sure how much it would come to.

When she arrived perspiring at Tony's shop, he and Rosa laughed.

'It's too hot to come out, you didn't walk all the way?'

'I don't know what to have for tea tonight, George should have a good meal after his first day at work, we can't keep having salads.'

'Pies,' suggested Rosa 'Aussie tradition, pie and tomato sauce.'

The route home was getting shorter with familiarity, but longer with the heat. When she arrived, hot and tired, the old lady next door was in her front yard.

'Your husband was off early this morning?'

'Early shift' replied Helen. She didn't have the energy to tell her more and was glad to shuffle her bags through the two doors and get into the cool. She felt a little unkind, but wondered how the lady knew anything that was going on with her blinds permanently down and the house surrounded by large shrubs.

She sank down gratefully with a cup of tea after putting the food in the fridge. Surprisingly, hot tea was a good thirst quencher, the cordials and fizzy drinks the children craved held no appeal for her. The next thing Helen knew the twins were rattling the locked flyscreen door. They liked to race home and beat Jennifer. Their faces were red and their foreheads damp.

'Is Dad going to bring his lorry home?'

George was last to arrive home, his new khaki shirt soaked with sweat. He went straight for the fridge where they now kept bottles of cold water. The twins were interested in his new job, in England they had never asked what he did at the office; now they wanted to know what the lorry was like, if he delivered ice cream and Pepsi Cola.

'I'll tell you the rest after dinner Helen.' He turned to the boys 'Good thing I wasn't driving, we went here there and everywhere, vegetables, meat, boxes and boxes of tins; so heavy you boys wouldn't be able to pick them up.'

'Could Simon pick them up?' asked Peter.

'Maybe.'

When Helen went to round everyone up for the meal George was fast asleep in the armchair.

'Not salad again' groaned Simon.

'Pies as well, one each for you and Dad.'

'Everyone has chips with pies.'

'It's too hot to cook chips, besides I couldn't manage a bag of potatoes with all the other stuff' she snapped back. 'We need to stock up on Saturday morning George.'

'I might be working, you children will have to help your mother carry the shopping at the weekend, you're happy to eat it so you should help fetch it.'

'Mr. Gregson said people only used to eat what they could kill or pick' put in Jennifer.

'So I'd better get a boomerang and kill a kangaroo' retorted Simon.

Helen smiled to herself, Jennifer had a 'Mr. Gregson said...' for every situation.

In the kitchen later, George helped Helen dry the dishes. Simon had retreated to the sleep-out with his transistor, Jennifer was reading and the twins were playing in the lounge, waiting for their father to tackle the evening ritual of the chip heater.

'I'll be glad when we've got a civilised bathroom.'

'George, just tell me what happened at the bank.'

'Do you remember how I always put on my best suit to see the bank manager in England? Today I had to go like this.'

'But what did he say?'

'I told him I was going to move my account to another bank, he said we could go over the figures again.'

'So can we have the mortgage?'

'Basically... no.'

Helen's head was going round in circles. 'We'll just have to budget carefully, like we always have done. The bills should be cheaper; no coal to buy, no winter coats for the children. Outings are cheap, picnics by the river don't cost anything.'

'I'm sorry love, we know we can do it, but if he doesn't believe us…We'll have to sit down with the figures when the children are in bed. I'll meet you in Perth tomorrow. Once the children have gone to school you can get to the phone box and call the agents, play for time, we don't want to lose the house. You would have thought he was giving his own money away, we can't let him turn us away, just like that.'

The next morning Helen stood nervously in the telephone box listening to the ringing tone, she pictured the agent showing another starry eyed couple their dream home. She looked at her watch and decided to dash for the bus stop and phone again when she got to Perth. The years of being at home had left her unused to dealing with business matters and business people. She realised how much she depended on George, assuming it came easily to him, by virtue of working in an office.

At the third attempt in the post office phone box a man's voice answered. Their offer was safe as long as no other offer came along, but he had more important advice; the Home Building Society was worth trying.

Sitting at the sandwich bar in Coles twenty minutes later, she began to relax. She had found the office of the building society and had made an appointment. George would not be impressed with the office, it was just one room, but they had nothing to lose. Now she had two hours to fill in till she met George; she could browse in the shops, though it was nearly as hot inside as it was outside.

Helen hovered uncertainly at the corner where they planned to meet, there was no sign of George as she looked back up the road. Swan Supplies was not like an office, he couldn't leave at a certain time, maybe they hadn't even got back to the depot. Suddenly he came rushing up, large patches of sweat round his armpits. She explained quickly and whisked him along to the offices of the Home Building Society.

The manager stood up to shake their hands and Helen suppressed a smile; she still found it strange to see businessmen dressed in shorts. It was sensible of course, in this heat; wandering around Perth she had noticed there was a dress code; short sleeved shirt with a tie, smart dress shorts and long socks with lace up shoes.

'Well done, you've only been in Australia eight weeks' said John.

'Thanks to Helen and the building society, I was resigned to losing that house, there would have been other chances, but we had a good feeling about this house.'

'Perfect birthday present' added Yvonne.

'Having a birthday near the end of November in England, it was always cold and getting dark early; I'd never have imagined this time last year I would be sweltering under a hundred degrees Fahrenheit. George brought home the leaflets from Australia House as a birthday surprise.'

'We don't usually have such a long hot spell before Christmas' said John.

'We'll be like real colonials, I'm looking forward to my proper English tea' said Yvonne.

'I thought of having a garden party, but we reckoned without the flies.'

'Tony ate a fly when he took his lamington outside' said Peter.

'The flies are the only ones who would eat Tony's lamingtons' teased Simon.

'Mum liked them.' Tony turned to the adults 'I made them for her thirty ninth birthday treat.'

'No chance of hiding your age' laughed Yvonne.

Helen looked at her watch. 'I invited the old lady next door to come in.'

'The one who never talked to you?' said Yvonne.

'She doesn't stop talking now' said George.

'When do you actually get the keys to the house?'

'Next week hopefully, when the electricity is on and they've made the final inspection. We won't move in till term's finished, but we can get our packing cases out of storage and order some furniture, that's the part Helen's looking forward to.'

'Helen, we should have a girl's lunch out in Perth, have a 'recky' round the furniture shops before you drag George out.'

'That would be lovely, I need your advice on what type of fridge to buy.'

'That's easy,' said John 'the biggest they make. When you move out of here I could borrow the 'ute', I bet you've accumulated more stuff than you realise. There'll just be time before we go away.'

'Where are you going?' asked George.

'Down near Albany, staying on a friend's farm. We usually go South for Christmas, nice and cool. This time we're going to stay six weeks, working holiday for me; fix all the machinery, help Steve build a new shed, generally earn our keep.'

'I'm going to have a holiday,' said Yvonne 'apart from washing and helping with the cooking. They've got a couple of horses, that's what Terri's looking forward to.'

Helen felt a hollow disappointment; of course she should have realised that even without relatives, the Charles' family would have their own plans for Christmas. Until now she hadn't thought beyond getting the keys to the house. In England they started planning Christmas after her birthday, although they inevitably did the same each year; her parents and sister over on Christmas Day, then over to Dennis' for his big family get together on Boxing Day. Trish interrupted her thoughts.

'I don't want to go away.'

'But you love going down to the farm' said John, looking bewildered.

'When I was a kid. All my friends will be going to the beach every day.'

'I'm sure some of them will be going on holiday or visiting.'

'No.'

Yvonne sighed and turned to George and Helen. 'People here don't make a big deal over holidays, they've got the sea and the sun.'

'I want to go to Rottnest in a tent' piped up Peter.

'Going to our new house will be a holiday,' said George 'I won't be able to take any time off now I've started a new job.'

'What's the name of the place?' asked Trish.

'Glendale, sounds more like the name of an English hotel.'

'Never heard of it' replied the girl.

'I looked on the map' sneered Simon 'and everywhere is called dale or vale; Aussievale, Perthdale.'

'Tonydale and Petervale' added the twins in unison.

'The street name is Smith' Helen raised her eyes to heaven.

'Could've been worse,' said her husband 'there's a Palmer Street and a Charles Road nearby.'

'Have the kids seen it yet?' asked Yvonne.

'No, George has been so busy, but we've put their names down at the high school and the primary.'

'I don't want to go back to school,' said Simon suddenly 'what's the point? I want to be a car mechanic or I could come and work for Dad's boss.'

'Of course you're staying on son, you need qualifications, you won't even have a Junior certificate.'

'I will, I'm going to do all the exams; Maths, English, French and Science easier than I was doing at the grammar. The only stupid subjects are Social Studies A and B, why don't they just call them History and Geography? I'll pass Geography, you just need to know 'factors affecting climate' and where Canberra is.'

Simon's outburst put a grin on Trish's face for the first time that afternoon.

'I'm not going to do fourth and fifth year either, two more years and I can leave and get a job.'

'You certainly will not be leaving,' said her mother 'you put down for the professional course next year.'

'Only because typing and shorthand are boring.'

'And what sort of job would you get without them?'

Any further discussion of the future was interrupted by the rattle of the flyscreen door. Helen went to answer it.

'Everyone, this is Effie from next door. Effie, this is Yvonne. Effie's coming with us to CWA next week.'

'How's work George, what's your driver like?' asked the old lady.

'Joe, he's a good bloke, calls me the old man. He only came out here three years ago and didn't speak a word of English, amazing.'

Once Effie got into her stride she kept everyone entertained with her stories, in between complimenting Helen on her scones and Tony on the squashed lamingtons. Widowed the year before, her only son lived in Sydney and she hardly ever saw her grandchildren. Helen realised what a huge country this was; people talked as if 'The Eastern States' was another country.

Chapter Thirteen   Glendale

Jennifer plunged into the river, glad to cool off after the long drive in the hot car. Her parents did not venture into the water; Bayswater was less sedate than Crawley and they had not spotted any other adults in the river. Boys Simon's age were jumping, diving or being pushed off the two wooden jetties that marked the large swimming area. She wondered if her brother would dare climb up the wooden ladders; the jetties looked higher from the water than they had from the beach. A teenage girl was challenging her friend to race across the river, while some lads were disappearing beneath the surface and coming up with handfuls of slimy black mud to throw at their friends. Younger children were splashing and wrestling, with no fear of the water. Jennifer waded deep enough for no one to notice she could not swim, whilst trying to keep a firm footing and avoid being splashed or pushed over.

Trying to move away from one boisterous group she plunged deeper, felt the cold water in her ears and nose and saw the sun filtered through the brown cloudy water. For a moment she was suspended calmly, the shouts and screams of the other children muffled. She imagined her parents' Australian dream dashed, pictured them writing letters to all the relatives, explaining what had happened. Her mouth was no longer tightly closed; she spluttered and in panic kicked her legs and flailed her arms. Something hard bumped her head and her hands grasped a slimy surface; she was clinging on to the wooden ladder.

In the few seconds Jennifer had been under the water no one had noticed anything was wrong. Tentative steps down the ladder revealed she was out of her depth; as she had not sunk she must have swum. An older girl was coming down the steps, Jennifer had no choice but to let go and swim back to the shallows.

When she padded back up the beach her mother said 'Oh good, are you ready for your picnic?'

'Mum, Dad, I really swam just now.'

She decided not to mention the drowning.

'Well done dear… oh what is Tony doing…go and fetch your brother.'

Jennifer returned to the water's edge to see Simon towing Peter in like a beached whale and Tony splashing some other boys.

As they ate their sandwiches, she realised she had told her parents so often that she could nearly swim, they would not realise the significance of today. She resolved not to tell Simon and surprise him next time.

With the picnic packed away and everyone dried and dressed, it was time at last to go and see the new house. They drove over the bridge, passed a race course then crossed the Great Eastern Highway. Jennifer felt a hollow disappointment; the further they drove the more obvious it became that they were not going to live near the river. Squashed between her brothers, her resentment grew; there had been no point in learning to swim, nobody had noticed anyway. Her father was giving a running commentary.

'This is Smith Street we're turning into now, but it's a long way down.'

She couldn't see properly, stuck in the middle, another cause for resentment. Then at last they stopped.

The road had a cowboy feel about it; no pavements, no trees.

'Here we are, number 146.'

Her father triumphantly held the shiny new keys aloft.

The twins were kicking up the grey sand and Simon was up on the concrete veranda peering in the front window. Silently Jennifer helped her mother get the brand new electric kettle out of the back of the car and the milk out of the 'esky'. She wondered why grownups were always desperate for a cup of tea.

After the gloomy interior of the rented house, the whiteness struck her, then the lovely smell of new wood. She had never seen an empty house before. Her mother switched on the lights and plugged in the kettle; relieved that the electricity was turned on. Her father led them out into the back yard. They stood on a small brick terrace slippery with sand; surrounding it was more sand strewn with builders' planks and odd bricks, but beyond that the rest of the garden looked as if no human had ever walked there.

George put his arm round his daughter.

'Do you like it?'

She nodded and put her arms round his waist, taking in the familiar, comforting scent of tobacco and mild sweat. His enthusiasm was infectious and she suggested they make a tour of inspection.

'You know we're very proud of you Jenny, doing well at school, teaching yourself to swim and helping with the twins.'

Indoors, the twins had discovered that empty rooms echo. Simon offered to let Jennifer choose which of the two smaller bedrooms she wanted; they were both the same size, so she opted for the one at the back with a view of the garden.

'Come out and see Petervale' the twins pleaded with her.

Already they had christened the back yard Petervale and the empty land beyond the boundaries, Tonydale. They marched along the concrete slabs to the air vent for the septic tank.

'No grownups beyond this point' announced Peter.

'Now we have to ride the boundaries' added Tony. 'Uncle John said stockmen must do that to check the fences.'

The three children inspected each gum tree and discovered other strange plants; stubby black trunks sprouting green spikes that were easily snapped off by small boys to use for sword fights.

'Time to go exploring' called their father.

'But I don't want to see the school,' complained Tony 'we need to explore Tonydale.'

'You'll have seven weeks to do that' said their mother 'and Jenny and Simon want to see where their school is.'

'Jennifer's school' Simon reminded them.

His parents refused to rise to the bait.

The road was empty, with bushland either side and only the wooden electricity poles to show a new suburb was springing up. They turned off onto a wide track of levelled sand marked with wooden stakes.

'The primary school is brand new, they haven't even finished the road yet' said George.

Glendale Primary stood on a large, unfenced square of tarmac, the grey brick building was u-shaped with verandas running around the inside. On the other side of the building was the sign for Glendale Senior High School, but between this and the spread of buildings was a huge playing field.

'Do you want to walk over and have a closer look?'

'No Dad, it's too far' complained Tony 'can we have an ice-cream?'

'The shops are in the opposite direction.'

'I'm thirsty' said Peter.

'Let's go back to the house and have a drink of water, then set off for home' said Helen.

'Yes, but which is our home now?' said Peter.

That evening Jennifer wrote to Christine.

...only two weeks and a bit till the end of term. Next week we all get our test results and Mr. Gregson will tell me if I can go to High School. We have also got our school outing to Yanchep Park where they have real caves with dead aborigines in, a lake and a swimming pool. We can wear what we like that day, which is funny because nobody wears school uniform anyway.

I have learnt to swim, but not in the sea yet.

Yesterday we went to see our new house, you will see the address on the back of this aerogramme. It is quite big and the garden is very big, your dog would love it, but he might get his nose scratched with all the strange plants. We are going to get a dog or maybe even three as the twins want one each as well. The garden is called a yard and has lots of gum trees. Next to our house is an empty house, but the rest of the street is wild bush; there are Christmas trees, but not like ours, they are covered in yellow flowers. Our new house is quite near the river and if we get bikes, Simon has promised he will come swimming with me.

Simon has done his exams and says they were easy and he is going to get all distinctions. He is not going back to school, he wants to become a car mechanic and earn lots of money to buy an electric guitar.

Terri and Trish are going to the country for the whole of the holidays; Terri asked if I could come, but her parents said I should be with my family for our first Christmas here. I can go camping with them another time.

It is really hot here and we don't even need jumpers or socks. Dad is brown now from not working in an office and Simon was brown but it all peeled off. Mum and Dad told him not to sunbathe too much. Tony is brown and Peter is sort of brown because he's got lots more freckles and they have all joined up!

I hope you get my homemade Christmas card. Have you persuaded your mum and dad to emigrate yet? You could come and live in Glendale because they are building lots of new houses and they are all bigger than yours.

Love from Jenny

---o0o---

On Tuesday morning Yvonne picked up Helen in the car for their trip into Perth.

'Didn't John need the car?'

'I dropped him off at work, it's more than his life's worth not to let me have the car when I want it, besides, it means he doesn't have to get involved in shopping.'

They were there in half the time it took on the bus and parked in a shady road near the Esplanade.

'Did the kids like the house then?'

'The twins loved it, all that space to play, it's a big adventure for them. Jennifer loved the garden, but she was very quiet, I think she's worried about starting at high school. She did very well in her tests and Mr. Gregson wrote a nice letter for her new headmaster.'

153

'What about Simon?'

'Be thankful you've got girls.'

'You must be joking, wait till Jenny hits adolescence, it's a nightmare.'

'George told him we will discuss it when he gets his exam results, but of course Simon replied that if he failed he wouldn't be allowed to start fourth year. They've got a fifteen year old lad working at George's depot, but that's because his family have just arrived from Italy and he doesn't speak a word of English, poor boy.'

'John says education is wasted on the young. Tell Simon if he wants to go out to work he will have to study at evening classes, that should put him off.'

'George is going to look out at the local shops; if Simon had a holiday job he might realise what full time work is like. Is Trish any happier about the holiday? How far away is Albany?'

'Three hundred miles, a long way from her friends, but I'm sure she'll enjoy it once we're there, well that's what I've reassured John…This is a nice shop, it must be good to have an excuse to buy modern stuff.'

'We're just going to get the basics; sitting, eating and sleeping. When the packing cases arrive we'll have the smaller things, coffee table and cabinets.'

Helen wanted to ask the store manager about methods of payment, but with Yvonne there she produced a notebook and made a note of prices and measurements.

'Very wise madam, let your husband measure up the rooms first, you'd be surprised how often our delivery men have to bring the furniture back.'

They ate lunch in Boans Department Store.

'This is very pleasant. We could still meet up in Perth, after I've moved. It's nice to have a chat without the men and the children around.'

'Does George ever talk about the war?'

'Hardly, I did ask him if he was there when…well, how John got his scar, but he wouldn't tell me what happened, just said the other bloke wasn't so lucky.'

'He didn't tell you he saved John's life? I used to hear the story when I first knew him and asked why he didn't keep in touch. Then not that long ago, when we were doing the Christmas cards, he said he ought to have a go at tracking George down, while his parents were hopefully still alive.'

'Yes George's mother got the Christmas card and George was really chuffed. He'd often talked about Charlie, but had no idea where he was. Do you know what happened when he got hurt?'

'Shrapnel, messy wounds, not fatal if you got medical care straight away, but loss of blood, infections, lots of men died that way. With their truck blown up and chaos all around, John had to patch him up the best he could and start carrying him back to the field station. The sort of thing you get a medal for, but not if no one else was around to notice.'

'I'm sure that happened a lot. Do you think they ever talk about it?'

'No, men don't, they want to leave it in the past. Their best mate was killed, there had always been the three of them since they trained together.'

The next day George had the day off to drive over to Smith Street and wait for the delivery of the packing cases.

'This will be like Christmas,' Helen laughed 'pity the children are going to miss it.'

'We can leave them to unpack their own boxes at the weekend. I just hope everything arrives in one piece. Tom at work said his brother's stuff was in a container that was dropped by the crane, family heirloom dining table smashed into matchsticks.'

'Goodness, lucky we haven't got a grand piano or any valuables, though I would be upset if my favourite vase got broken… Oh look at those trees, such a vivid scarlet. I'll ask Yvonne what they are; I wish we had trees in Smith Street.'

By the time the delivery lorry arrived, the sun was high in the sky and beating down onto the front of the house. With no fridge and nowhere to sit, all they could offer the two men was a cup of tea. The younger man looked quite smart in his bottle green uniform, but Helen was worried about the older one, though it was hard to tell with the more weather-beaten men just how old they were. He perched on a small packing case and

156

drank a glass of warm water and mug of tea down in one go. It was the first time she had seen the sweat literally pouring off someone, large droplets were dripping onto their new wooden floor.

'There's more tea in the pot and I've put the kettle on again.'

She felt guilty that he had to work at all in this weather, let alone hump packing cases around; although George and the young man had actually done most of the carrying.

The older man finally spoke after downing his third cup. 'Looks like you've landed yourself in a heat wave. You'd better get a big awning to go over that veranda. These new houses… brick boxes, no good for this climate.'

After they had gone George laughed 'He was a little ray of sunshine.'

'I think rays of sunshine are going to be a problem, this room is so hot.'

'I was thinking; if I'm working Saturday, Simon can help me unpack this lot on Sunday. If we go to Perth now we can get the furniture and fridge ordered. It would be nice if John and Yvonne saw this place looking like a home before they go away.'

In the car they wound all the windows down, hoping soon to feel the 'Fremantle Doctor', the cool breeze from the sea that came in the afternoon.

'We're doing pretty well, by Christmas we'll be sorted' said George. 'Yvonne thinks you're amazing.'

'Does she?' said Helen, surprised.

'Of course, so does John. Leaving everything behind, bringing up four children, coping with the twins…'

'George… you never told me you saved John's life.'

'Is that what Yvonne told you? It wasn't like that, not like the films, anyway how would John know, he was unconscious. Everything was chaos, perhaps it was just an excuse to save my own skin; it was lucky I had a fair idea how to cut back towards the field station, if I hadn't come across one of our lorries with more wounded we wouldn't have got there at all. But the worst thing was leaving Billy behind, there's nothing dignified about dying in battle, I couldn't even cover him up, let alone bury him.'

Helen put her hand on his knee.

'I didn't even know you had a friend called Billy.'

'Going to see his parents when I was on leave was the hardest thing I've ever had to do.'

At the furniture store it was not easy to make a decision.

'Settee looks as if will collapse the moment Simon throws himself on it.'

'Shsh the man will hear you. I like the modern stuff, I was glad to see the back of your aunt's three piece suite.'

'That could have lasted us another sixteen years' he teased.

'This is the sixties, not the thirties.'

'We do a very good hire purchase scheme, most of our migrant buyers organise it that way… with an empty house to fill.'

They hadn't noticed the assistant creeping up behind them.

'Goodness knows what my mother would say' Helen said, as they drove home.

'Your mother's not here; everyone does hire purchase these days, nothing wrong with it as long as we keep up the payments… we don't want them coming to take it all back again.'

That night Helen wrote to her sister.

...so for a few weeks we'll have two homes. I will have to make my way by bus from Victoria Park when George goes to work on Friday and wait in for the furniture and fridge to be delivered, everyone has a fridge here. On Sunday Simon can help George unpack cases and arrange the furniture. I'm sure Simon's grown a couple of inches since you saw him.

The house has two large bedrooms and two medium size - no box rooms! The back yard is very long with several big gum trees and some prehistoric looking plants called blackboys. Next to our house and across the road is wild bush full of beautiful yellow trees called Christmas Trees.

We wish we had bought a duty free camera in Singapore, instead of transistor radios for Simon and Jenny, they have them on all the time. So we are going to buy a camera for our Xmas present to each other, then we will be able to send you and Mum and Dad pictures of the new house.

If you go up Smith Street, the road that crosses it is called Palmer Street! On the corner is 'Tom the Cheap Grocer' a bit like Fine Fare and opposite is a little Greek shop, open all hours. George will take me to Victoria Park when we want to get lots of shopping, which is all the time!

The money you and M&D gave us for the children's Christmas presents we will put with the money Dennis gave us ditto and buy the children bikes.

Helen didn't add that all the money family had given them to spend on the children, had long since been spent.

That was kind of Dennis to invite you all for Christmas, tell Mum and Dad of course you should go. Who's this Reg from the office you went to the theatre with? Sorry to hear about old Mrs. Howes, Mum's going to miss her. We haven't got around to finding a church yet, much to Simon's delight. When we're settled in Glendale we'll look for one with a nice Sunday School.

The next time I write will be on the Xmas cards.

George and the children send their love, PS...

...

Helen couldn't decide what else to say.

Chapter Fourteen   December 1964

On Sunday morning Jennifer woke up with a Christmassy feeling. She put the kettle on and made her parents a cup of tea in bed, much to their surprise; Simon was even more surprised and not at all grateful. She wanted everyone to hurry and get up so they could drive to the new house, see the furniture and unpack the crates. It was over two months since she had seen her books and toys.

She was not disappointed when they arrived at the house; in her bedroom was a bed called a divan, no springs, just a wooden base and mattress. There was a wardrobe she didn't have to share and a desk and chair. Simon's room was identically furnished. Her parents expected them to sit in their bedrooms and do their homework, though Simon was still insisting he wasn't going back to school.

Her parents had a big wardrobe with a mirror and for her mother there was a modern dressing table. In the lounge was a long settee with two matching arm chairs, in light colours with wooden legs. All the furniture had a wonderful new smell.

Simon was relieved the record player had survived the voyage and delighted that his Beatles records had not been broken. Jennifer had forgotten which books she had given to Christine

161

and which she had kept, so she was pleased to find 'Black Beauty' and 'Kit Hunter Show Jumper'. Then there were the games; Monopoly, Chinese Chequers and spin the wheel. Another box was full of the plastic farm animals they all shared.

From the kitchen came the delicious smell of roast beef, they were going to have their first proper Sunday lunch in the house, at the kitchen table with its six aluminium and vinyl chairs.

Her parents ceremoniously switched on the new radio; their Australian Sunday lunches had become exactly the same as their English ones. The ABC even broadcast their favourite English radio comedies. Now on Sundays they also listened to 'Two Way Family Favourites', wondering if anyone would request a record for them. The programme was full of letters from relatives who would not be spending Christmas together, some who had not seen their families for years and years.

After lunch Jennifer played with the twins in the back yard while her mother continued unpacking china, linen and ornaments and Simon helped his father measure up for the list of jobs that was evolving. She helped them set out the toy farm animals in the sand, under the shade of the tree nearest the house. The spikes from the black boys made ideal fences for the paddocks; Terri had told her they were never called fields in Australia.

When it was time to go back to the other house the twins did not want to be parted again so soon from their toys and pleaded that they should sleep at the house and not go to school.

The last full week at school seemed to rush by with plenty to look forward to at the weekend. Even Simon was excited on Friday evening; the Palmers were having their first visit to the drive-in cinema. The main film was deemed suitable for all the family. Jennifer had already seen it in England with Christine and her sister and she couldn't wait to see it again.

When they arrived they could see the advantages of having a station wagon. Younger children were wearing their pyjamas and sitting in the back with pillows and sheets.

'What a good idea,' said her mother 'no worries about babysitters, we could do that with the twins.'

'I don't want to wear my pyjamas to the cinema' protested Peter.

There was disagreement as to where they should park, but finally they edged near a speaker stand and parked on a little slope. People trekked back and forth past them and they realised they were near the toilet block. Her father hung the heavy metal speaker on the open side window and after much twiddling with knobs managed to get the sound at a level her mother approved of.

By the time the main feature started it was pitch dark and the children had changed seats several times during the B movie. Jennifer now sat between her parents, Simon had the back seat to himself and the twins were playing in the back.

Jennifer loved films and soon forgot she was sitting in a car. 'The Moonspinners' featured Haley Mills' first screen kiss and Jennifer was also in love with the hero.

When the film ended, her reverie was interrupted by beeping of horns and revving engines as everyone raced for the exit.

'I don't know what the hurry is,' said Helen 'let's wait till everyone else has gone.'

'We might get locked in' said Simon 'and have to stay here all night in the dark.'

The next morning Jennifer was up early packing; she had to leave only enough stuff for the last few days of school, everything else was going in the car or Uncle John's ute. The kitchen was nearly as empty of food as when they first arrived and her mother was worried she wouldn't get the house cleaned in time for the renting agent to inspect.

There was more than just suitcases to load up; Uncle John's ute was full of rolls of fly screen wire and pieces of wood, wedged in between an assortment of tools. On top of that was a second hand awning he had managed to get hold of.

When they all arrived in Smith Street John and Yvonne were impressed with the house and block of land. Indoors they admired the new furniture.

'It feels homely already' said Yvonne.

'The twins must have unpacked every toy they possess' laughed John.

In the back yard Jennifer helped the twins dismantle their obstacle course made with builders' planks and bricks. Once the stuff was unloaded, her father used the planks to construct a temporary work bench. With a few nails and hammer blows, Uncle John made a wooden gun each for the boys, from wood found lying around.

The men tackled the awning first, before it got too hot to work at the front of the house. Simon helped hold it in place while Jennifer was sent back and forth for drinks of water and plasters.

In the kitchen her mother and Aunty Yvonne sat at the kitchen table with a cup of tea.

'That'll keep John happy for a few hours, he likes something to get his teeth into.'

'I'll be glad to get those screens up and have all the windows open,' said Helen 'I thought with a new house there wouldn't be any jobs.'

'Did you see all those lovely flame trees when we were coming out of Vic. Park?'

'Ah, is that what they're called.'

'I think they come from Africa.'

'Thank you for bringing the Jacaranda and Oleander, you'd better suggest the best places to plant them.'

'Just a little house warming present. Does it feel like home yet Jenny?'

'Yes, I've got my Beatles pictures stuck on my bedroom wall, but Paul's got a crease right through him. Dad's going to put up a gate at the side so we can have a dog.'

Aunty Yvonne laughed. 'I don't think they'll get that done today.'

---o0o---

On Sunday afternoon the Palmers walked round to the Charles' home for their first barbeque. There were quite a few neighbours and friends in the garden and Helen recognised a couple of the wives from CWA. Drongo was tied up in the corner sulking.

'Has he been naughty?' asked Jennifer.

'Not yet,' said John 'if we let him loose he'll eat all the steaks and burn his nose. He's been to the beach this morning so he's knackered.'

John slapped George on the back and put his arm round Helen.

'Here are the new Pommies, George is my old army mate and this is his lovely wife Helen... Simon who's going to be a pop star, Jenny who's going to be a vet and the twins who run rings round everybody.'

The men were gathered round the smoking barbeque with beers in their hands, while the wives popped in and out of the kitchen. Simon found a girl from school to chat up and Jennifer disappeared with Terri into her bedroom.

For a moment Helen stood uncertainly till John gave her a plate of food; then she felt even more awkward. Holding the plate, eating the hot food and waving the flies away seemed an impossible task. The steak was charred black on the outside, but red and too tough to bite on the inside; she wondered if she could slip the meat to Drongo and just eat the salad. Looking for the twins would be a good excuse to retreat. Tony was washing a sausage under the tap.

'I dropped it in the sand, Peter dropped his, but Drongo ate it.'

'Never mind, come and have some trifle.'

'How's it going,' said John 'ready for a chop?'

'No… I'm full up thanks.'

'Hope you've got room for some of Yvonne's pavlova.'

'Yes it's legendry' said one of the wives, handing her a dish piled with meringue, strawberries and ice-cream.'

'Another recipe I'll have to write down.'

'Do you get the Woman's Weekly? They have good Australian recipes in.'

'Yvonne's been passing hers on, but I'm going to get it regularly when we've moved, when life gets a bit less hectic; I always enjoy a good magazine with my elevenses.'

When Simon said he was going to walk the girl from school home Helen wondered if they could make a move as well. She was tired after their busy week and a little bored. The men were on the veranda chatting over their beers and the women had helped Yvonne tidy up the kitchen. She tried to catch George's eye.

'I think it's time we took the boys home, they have got school tomorrow.'

'They don't look tired' said John 'I told them they could untie Drongo; he's on duty tidying up the garden.'

Helen spotted Trish, who was giggling with a couple of her friends.

'Could you go and tell Jennifer we're leaving.'

'Do we have to go,' said Peter 'we're training Drongo.'

'Yes, your father has to get up early tomorrow.'

'Hey George, she who must be obeyed has spoken' called John.

To Helen's relief the other wives started rounding up husbands and families. She just wanted to get home and put her feet up with a cup of tea. They ended up being last to leave and stood on the front veranda enjoying the cool night air and the scent of the frangipanis.

'Thank you for a lovely evening, have a good holiday.'

John kissed Helen's cheek. 'Enjoy your first Christmas.'

On Christmas morning Helen felt strangely empty; there had been no run up to Christmas, they had not found a church yet in Glendale and had done none of the usual seasonal things; carols by candlelight or hearing church bells. Other migrants had said it never felt like Christmas and Helen realised it wasn't just the different weather. George was still asleep, exhausted after making extra deliveries. She kept her eyes closed, hoping

the twins were still asleep and pictured all the
family back home, still in the middle of the night.
Ironically they now had a house big enough for
visitors, but no one to invite. Her mother would
have loved this house and would have enjoyed
sitting at the kitchen table doing the sprouts;
although it wouldn't be sprouts, you couldn't get
them here. She had taken Yvonne's advice and
cooked the turkey yesterday so they could have it
cold with salad.

They had put by some little toys and trinkets
for the twins' stockings and explained to Simon
and Jennifer that they were getting a bike each
from all the family; there were no parcels from
England.

The children had made paper decorations
and the snowy scenes on the Christmas cards
looked incongruous, but at least the lounge looked
jolly. She could now here the twins chatting
excitedly, they were no doubt swapping their
gifts, but at least they were keeping each other
occupied.

Finally Jennifer tapped on the door and
came in with two cups of tea, George stirred. She
presented them with a homemade Christmas card.

'Careful you don't smudge it, I made it with
my oil pastels.'

It was beautiful and they were genuinely
impressed; a picture of their house surrounded by
yellow Christmas trees and scarlet flame trees.

'I didn't put us in it, because I can't do
people.'

'Plenty of famous painters only did scenery' said George.

After breakfast the bikes were unveiled. Simon had helped George choose them, they knew he would rather choose for himself than have a surprise. They had settled on a lady's bike for Jennifer, not wanting to waste money on a bike she would grow out of; with the saddle at its lowest, her toes just touched the ground. There was a blue bike and a red bike for the twins and they immediately swapped over.

Outside, the air felt cooler. Simon and Jennifer disappeared up the road, glad to be on wheels again.

Tony was ahead of Helen and George as they walked up the road and Peter wobbled beside them. The light seemed different and there were a few clouds in the sky, but they were surprised when it spattered with rain.

'I thought it didn't rain till winter' said Helen.

'At least it's broken the heat wave. I'm really going to enjoy today and tomorrow, no visitors, no wrapping up in coats and scarves and trekking off to the station on Boxing Day. We can do exactly as we like.'

'I will miss seeing Mum and Dad and it will be strange not hearing Denis' stories about his National Service or being organised to play games by his sister-in-law.'

'Precisely and it will be wonderful for you not being stuck in the kitchen all day, with me trying to keep your mother out of the way.'

A tinkling bell startled them and Simon and Jennifer appeared behind.

'Do you know how long Smith Street is?' said Simon.

'We've been all round a great big block' said Jennifer.

'And we didn't see a soul,' added Simon 'anyway what are we going to do now and when's lunch?'

'What would you like to do?' said George, breaking his own rule of never giving children a choice.

'Let's go out in the car,' said his daughter 'somewhere we haven't been before.'

'No, your father needs a rest from driving.'

'That's okay, Joe's still doing most of the driving. Good idea love, let's chop a few bits off the turkey and throw it in the esky.'

'And the Pepsi Cola' added Tony.

There were four bottles sitting in the fridge for a Christmas treat.

'I know where we'll go, up into the hills, John Forrest National Park, Joe says there's a natural pool you can swim in.'

Helen was glad they had come out. The trees, huge boulders and the rocky pool delighted them all. Already she was writing a letter home in her head.

...So we just threw Christmas dinner in the back of the car and ate our picnic under a shady gum tree. George and Simon made short work of the turkey legs. After lunch the children played in the pool and we dangled our feet in. We tried out the new camera, so let's hope the pictures come out.

When they got home George suddenly said 'I forgot, John gave me a bag of presis for the children.'

'Oh dear, we only gave them a little gift each' said Helen.

Inside the bag were several presents each for the children and books for Helen and George.

'They couldn't have chosen a better present for me; I haven't missed the Christmas pudding, but I do miss getting books from Mum and Dad and other people.'

Chapter Fifteen   January 1965

The New Year slipped in unnoticed by the Palmers, though Helen had bought the biggest calendar she could find. She was worried they would forget the times and days George was working; with the school holidays it was hard to keep track of what day it was.

They usually went out on his days off; the children's favourites were the river or the national park, but on George's fortieth birthday the children were delighted he chose Rottnest Island. They headed straight for the bicycle hire this time; but didn't attempt to go around the whole island. On their leisurely ride they saw some quokkas, but the children were just as excited at seeing their parents cycling; their father had been right, you never forget how to ride a bike.

When George was at work they settled into a routine, the children helping with the shopping and chores in the morning before they went out. A holiday job had not materialised for Simon; at the little corner shops the owners had their own children to help them out and other holiday jobs had already been taken by local teenagers. George gave Simon and Jennifer pocket money, on the understanding they did their chores willingly and didn't ask Helen for money; the housekeeping was stretched to the limit.

Simon's pocket money was also stretched to the limit; he wanted to buy records and magazines. When he was out in the heat he wanted cool drinks and ice creams. George and Helen did not want him to get a full time job merely out of boredom or to have money in his pocket. If he was lured into a permanent job it would be even harder to persuade him to go back to school.

One of Simon's first holiday explorations was to see how long it took to cycle to Bayswater. He was gone for ages and Helen worried he had been knocked off his bike or drowned. He arrived home the same time as George, red faced and sweating.

'Of course I'm alright' he said, downing several glasses of cold water. 'You cool off swimming, then as soon as you start cycling home you're boiling hot again.'

'Can I come next time?' asked Jennifer.

'Maybe, if you can keep up.'

'You just want to look at the girls in their bikinis.'

He ignored her remark. 'I met a couple of boys who go to Glendale.'

'Oh good' said Helen.

'Yeah, they said it was a rubbish school.'

'No teenager is going to admit to liking his school' replied his father. 'What year will they be in?'

'Fourth year… if they pass the Junior. Jenny, one of them had his sister with him, she's starting Glendale this year.'

'That's nice,' said Helen 'you won't be the only one to take his little sister swimming.'

'She's a real pain.'

'I won't be. Anyway, I could go by myself.'

'You certainly can not,' said George 'it's a long way and you've only just learned to swim. Besides, some of those lads down there can be a bit rough.'

Simon snorted. 'Dad, they're only having fun.'

'Well it won't hurt you to look after your sister.'

'It won't be tomorrow, remember I arranged to meet some friends from the old school at Beatty Park. Can I borrow some money? I'll have to get two buses.'

The next day Jennifer mooched around resentfully and Helen tried to placate her.

'Dad will give Simon plenty of jobs to do at the weekend, there'll be days when you go out with your friends and he stays at home.'

'I haven't got anyone to go out with.'

To Helen's relief there was a distraction when George and Joe turned up for a break. The twins were thrilled to meet the young Italian driver and he swung them up into the cab. George was glad to sit in the kitchen and cool off.

'Joe seems nice, what would he like to drink?'

'Anything cold; it's handy living here, all our deliveries are going to be south of the river now the boss has got that new lorry.'

After lunch Jennifer said 'Where shall I go on my bike?'

'Isn't it too hot? Wait till it cools down a bit. Let's look in the paper and see what's on the cinema in Perth. We could go out tomorrow, have a picnic in the gardens.'

At dinner when they asked Simon if he wanted to come to the cinema he looked worried.

'I'm already going with my friends. What are you going to see?'

George laughed. 'I suppose you don't want to bump into this lot tomorrow.'

'I bet you're going with that girl from the barbeque' said Jennifer.

'Mind your own business.'

That night in bed Helen and George whispered, even in this bigger house they knew Simon and Jennifer had sharp ears.

'I'll give Simon a bit of change in the morning; it's good he's going out with his friends, but it's difficult if the others have got more money in their pockets. John says you wouldn't believe how much pocket money some of the kids at that school get.'

'If we take sandwiches we can just about afford an outing tomorrow, Jennifer's looking forward to it. The twins aren't bothered, they'd rather stay and play in Tonydale and Petervale. I think all this is easiest for them; they're having a great time. If it's too hot outside they've got their toys from England. I'm glad we packed their paints and felt pens; this afternoon they were painting outside on the terrace, it's in the shade and I get no mess indoors. They painted wanted posters for Ned Kelly.'

'Yes, they love that book John and Yvonne gave them. It's good they can amuse themselves, we certainly can't afford a television yet.'

Despite the heat, Helen had drifted off to sleep, but it wasn't long before she was awake again. She could hear a whining sound near her head and suddenly felt a prick on her bare arm. The whining noise seemed to multiply. She whispered to George, not wanting to wake him, but hoping he was awake.

'I don't believe it, mosquitoes,' he mumbled 'I thought you only got them in the tropics.'

The next morning Helen's arms and neck were covered in red itchy bumps and Jennifer was also complaining of her disturbed night. Peter was rubbing his arms and Tony was claiming he had the plague. George, Tony and Simon had not been bitten.

'Your blood must be more tasty' said George.

In Perth that afternoon the cinema was full of excitable children and Helen remembered wistfully the occasional outings to 'The Rex' on Saturday nights with George. They should try to go out occasionally; Perth was so easy to get to and Simon and Jennifer were old enough to stay with the twins.

That evening at dinner George asked how the day out had been.

'We went to Perth museum in the morning' said Jennifer 'and it was tiny, they didn't have any dinosaurs. We thought we were lost because we couldn't find the rest of the museum.'

'I asked someone,' said Helen 'described where we'd been and it turned out we'd seen it all. So we had plenty of time for our picnic.'

'Perth's a new city, they probably haven't got much history. Did your friend enjoy the film Simon?'

'Girlfriend' giggled Jennifer.

'She's not my girlfriend. Anyway she's invited me to her family's barbeque next week. Can you give me a lift Dad?'

'We met a family who live nearby when we were coming home on the bus' said Helen. 'They're from oop north and they only moved into their house a few months ago. The older girl's starting at the high school. We're going round for a cup of tea next week.'

---o0o---

Jennifer had been timing her bike rides and thought she was getting faster. She was secretly worried Simon would leave her behind when they went to Bayswater. He seemed to get taller and stronger each day and faster on his bike, though she reasoned he was unlikely to leave her behind on the way back. If she couldn't find her way back to Smith Street he would have to explain to their parents; her father had been full of instructions yesterday evening.

The further they cycled, the more she got into a rhythm, though it still seemed a very long way. Their bicycle bags were filled up with sandwiches and bottles of water; Uncle John said you went mad before you died of thirst.

When they arrived she obediently put her stuff down on the little sandy beach and they sat and rested for a moment, drinking their water. A tall boy came up to them, a girl trailing behind him.

'Hey Si, is this your little sister?' Simon nodded without introducing Jennifer.

'Oh good, she can play with mine. This is Maiya.'

'You okay Jenny?' asked Simon before dashing off with the other boy.

The girl was quiet, but Jennifer was relieved. She was several inches shorter, thin and freckled and it seemed unlikely she would be the Trish type who could do anything. Jennifer had been worried Simon would leave her to play with someone who would expect her to dive off the jetty or plunge under the water.

The two girls paddled into the shallow water and watched the boys running to the end of the jetty and leaping into the air. Simon went last so the others could not see his more cautious entry into the river. After that first time in the sea and her drowning experience, she was scared each time that he would not resurface.

'I'm not allowed out of my depth' said the girl.

'When did you learn to swim?'

'A couple of years ago.'

'Aren't you Australian?'

'No, Dutch.'

She didn't look Dutch, but then the only Dutch children Jennifer had seen were in books; dressed in hats, coats and mufflers skating on canals.

As they chatted she discovered the girl didn't like horses or The Beatles and went to ballet classes, but she did like the river, they came nearly every day. At least she now knew two girls going to her school.

The others had brought sandwiches. George had given Jennifer enough change to buy her and Simon an ice cream; her brother said ice cream was for kids, he was going to have a Pepsi.

The Australian ice cream was strange; it had chips of ice in and was not smooth like Mr. Whippy. The other girl accepted when Jennifer offered to buy her an ice cream. The boys were sitting a couple of yards away. She listened to them talking; Simon sounded different when he was with other teenagers.

'You haven't got a television?' marvelled one of the boys.

'We're going to get one soon, I've seen colour television.'

They didn't believe him, but Jennifer knew it was true. She had been envious when Uncle Dennis had taken him on an outing to Kingston to see a colour television on display in Bentalls.

'…yes it was nearly as big as a cinema screen and the picture was 3D.'

She knew that wasn't true, they had both come back disappointed that it was a small screen with a fuzzy picture.

Later, Simon checked his watch and they left exactly on time. The ride home was long, even when they turned into Smith Street there was still a way to go, but Simon was quite impressed. 'It doesn't seem so far the second time' he encouraged her.

With the twins circling on their bikes in front of them, Jennifer and her mother walked up the road. With no pavement, the quiet bitumen road was easier to walk on than the sandy verge. They were following the directions Valerie had given them when they met on the bus. After rounding two corners they spotted the number and saw a white house with a dark green lawn; her family had gone for the instant lawn, on closer inspection it was covered in dense, thick spikes. They were greeted enthusiastically.

'Hello Helen, glad you found it okay, I was saying to Mike, it's nice to meet soomebody else from the old country. Caroline, your little friend is here.'

Caroline emerged reluctantly from the dark depths of the house into the little lounge.

'Orange cordial Jenny? I bet you Mum would like a nice coop of tea, though I don't think it tastes the same here, different water I suppose. It's our second anniversary on Saturday, we always said if we didn't like it we could go back hoom.'

'And do you like it?' asked Helen.

'Mike does, I think we'll wait and see if Caroline settles at the high school. It will be hard for her, she's shy and there are fourteen hundred children.'

'Mr. Gregson said it's the same for everyone' Jennifer shyly butted in. 'We'll all be new and we'll all be the youngest again, instead of the biggest in the school.'

Her mother smiled. 'I'm sure Caroline will be fine and she and Jennifer can go together on the first morning.'

'Another cup of tea? I always put the kettle straight back on in this hot weather.'

Jennifer had been hoping they could go after the first cup of tea. Caroline had not spoken a word and trailed out to the kitchen with Valerie. Jennifer and her mother exchanged amused glances.

Caroline came back in with a plate of plain biscuits.

'What wouldn't I give for a real English digestive biscuit' said her mother.

Jenifer's mother laughed 'I would love a chocolate digestive, I always used to have one with my elevenses. I haven't seen any chocolate biscuits to buy.'

'They take them all off the shelves in the summer, otherwise they melt. Sometimes I crave a jaffa cake, no six jaffa cakes' she went off into gales of laughter.

'At least it's good for our figures... I wonder if I should check on the twins?'

'They're fine, playing with the hose.'

'Oh dear…'

'I'll check them' said Jennifer, glad of an excuse to get outside.

'Go on Caroline, take Jenny outside.'

Outside the back door was a small lawn of the same spiky grass, with a blanket spread out. The rest of the long yard was scattered with metal drums, planks of wood and other unidentified objects. The abandoned hose was making a river and the boys were constructing an obstacle course for the little sister. The girls sat on the blanket, but Jennifer could feel the uncomfortable grass underneath.

'How old is your sister?'

'Eight.'

'Same age as my brothers; are they allowed to play with that stuff?'

'Yeah, Dad collects anything that might come in handy, he's thinking of keeping chickens.'

'We're going to get a dog.'

'I don't like dogs.'

'I need someone on my team' called the younger girl.

Jennifer readily volunteered.

When they walked back home half an hour later, the little girl trailed after them.

'Aunty Helen, can I come and see Petervale and Tonydale?'

'Yes, of course you can dear, does your mother know where you are?'

She ran to catch up with the boys and Peter let her have a go on his bike.

'What's her name Jenny?'

'Patricia, but she only answers if you call her Pat, you know like George in the Famous Five.'

'I hope Valerie's husband doesn't mind all that mess in the garden.'

'Caroline says they're allowed to do what they like in the yard. Her dad's going to make a chook run. We could keep chickens, then you wouldn't need to buy eggs.'

'We would have to buy chicken food.'

'No, you feed them on scraps.'

'We never have any scraps, Simon eats them all. Besides, if you want a dog he would be chasing them all the time.'

'We could train him not to... when can we get a dog?'

'When we've settled in properly and put a fence and gate at the side, you know how busy Dad is. Perhaps when Uncle John is back, they could do it one weekend.'

Jennifer sighed; she had hoped they would get a puppy soon, so she could train him during the holidays.

Chapter Sixteen   Holidays

George was busy; sometimes he worked his days off to help out if another man was away. For Helen the holidays seemed to be going on for ever, but Simon took Jennifer swimming quite often and she enjoyed the company of the little Dutch girl. At home alone with the twins, Helen appreciated their company, they weren't little boys any more. She marvelled that they were so different from each other and neither was like Simon at the same age.

Pat often came round to play with the twins. Usually they dismissed girls as 'yuck', but perhaps they didn't think of her as a girl; she was always dressed in T-shirt and shorts and enjoyed their roughest games. But Helen couldn't relax when Pat was playing with the boys. It was one thing to have your own children ripping their clothes in the bush, scratching their legs or cutting their bare feet; someone else's child was a big responsibility. Thankfully the nimble child had so far avoided any accidents.

Sometimes Caroline mooched round as well; if Jennifer was out with Simon she didn't seem bothered and mooched home again. If Jenny was home she didn't want to do anything her daughter suggested and her ennui seemed to pervade the whole house leaving Jennifer listless.

Early one afternoon all the children were home; they had trailed round 'Tom the Cheap' with Helen in the morning and there had been a lot to carry home; George had been too busy to take her shopping. Now they were trying to cool off after lunch. Helen had read all her Christmas books and was starting on one of the books she had brought from England; after only one page she dozed off in the armchair. She was startled by the rattling of the fly screen door. Simon was there first and she got up to find Joe and George in the hall.

'He's feeling crook' said Joe.

Her husband looked so dreadful there was no need for Joe to explain why he had brought him home. He rushed through to the toilet in the laundry and was violently sick.

'Oh dear, I said he didn't look well this morning, it must be food poisoning.' Helen recalled Yvonne's warnings of the dangers of flies, but was sure she had left no food uncovered.

Joe looked relieved that he had delivered George home safely.

'Reckon he's got sun stroke.'

'Do you think I should call a doctor?'

'Nah; he just needs to lie down in the cool and drink plenty of water; you Pommies can't take the heat. I've only got a few more calls to do.'

'Have a drink before you go, Simon will get you one.'

George was leaning on the laundry trough his head under the tap. Helen thought he was going to collapse and persuaded him to get to the bedroom and lie down. Simon brought in a glass of water.

'Heat stroke, we did it in first aid at the boy's club.'

'Tell Joe I'll be ready in a moment.'

'Don't be ridiculous George, you can't go out like this. Simon can go to the phone box and call the doctor.'

'Okay I'll rest, but I don't need the doctor, remember we have to pay for them here.'

The children had appeared anxiously at the bedroom door, not used to seeing their father ill.

'Hey Dad, I could be driver's mate' said Simon. 'When we get back to the depot I'll get the bus home. Give me some money Mum and I'll get you those things we couldn't find at Tom The Cheap's… and some cool drinks.'

Joe agreed 'Boss won't mind, Simon can see how hard we work.'

George slept the rest of the afternoon and ate nothing in the evening. Simon reassured him the deliveries had gone well and claimed Greek George had offered him a job.

That night George couldn't stop shivering and neither of them got much sleep. When they did doze off the mosquitoes started again, Helen was sure they always waited till they were asleep. A month ago Helen could have popped down the road to ask Yvonne's advice. She even wondered if she ought to wake Simon and send him to phone for an ambulance, hopefully he would remember the number, she knew it wasn't 999.

187

But George insisted he couldn't have heat stroke if he was shivering.

By the morning George was sleeping and Helen tried to remember where he had put the phone number for work. Would anyone even hear the phone in that noisy depot? In England, on the rare occasions when George had suffered from flue, she had wrapped up, checked she had the right change, told Simon to get the twins ready for school and gone to the phone box; hoping to call after his boss had arrived, but before he became annoyed at George's absence.

She was still searching for the number when Simon came out.

'What time's Dad due at work?'

'Not early thank goodness; do you know where Dad put the number for the depot?'

'I could do his shift, it'll be fun… Dad can pay me what he would have earned.'

'Let's discuss money later; but at least we wouldn't be leaving Joe and the boss in the lurch. If you're serious I'd better cook you some breakfast now, so you can get off to the bus stop. Don't let the others make a noise, it's best if he sleeps on.'

The other children co-operated in the new game of creeping round the house. When George woke up at eleven o'clock he was shocked at the time. Helen sat by the bed with a cup of tea.

'You don't think you're too old for this sort of work?'

'No, it's the heat, it will be cooler next month or March. I feel terrible I've let them down.'

'Simon's enjoying the drama, perhaps it will make him realise school might be an easier option.' She kissed his brow, relieved that the drama hadn't turned into an emergency.

Simon and Joe turned up for their lunch break. The boy's knuckles were grazed and bleeding.

'There's a knack to getting boxes in and out when they're crammed together' laughed Joe. 'You can lose fingers if you're not careful. George, you look terrible; good thing it's our day off tomorrow.'

When Simon returned in the evening he was exhausted and didn't talk till Helen was serving up the pudding.

'It was okay, Greek George used to do all the work by himself when he first started, you have to if you want to own your own business, like Uncle Dennis.'

'I know,' said Helen 'he never ceased to tell us.'

'You need more than that,' said George 'the right idea at the right time, business brains and a big dose of luck. Do you see yourself as a businessman son?'

'No way, too much hard work. I think I'll be a teacher, they get lots of holidays and who wants to work in the summer? Joe says I should stay on

189

at school and go to uni, then I can choose any job I like. His son's going to go to uni.'

'...and how old is he?' asked Helen.

'Three.'

'Well tomorrow's decision day,' said George 'you get your results.

'I wonder what time the evening paper will be in the shop?' asked Helen the next morning.

'They might forget to print your name in the paper' teased Jennifer.

Simon claimed not to be nervous, but decided to go off swimming by himself and fetch the newspaper on the way back.

'I don't blame him,' said George 'he won't want the five of us hovering round him all morning.'

'Do you think you'll be alright for work tomorrow?'

'Yes, I feel fine today, there're a few jobs I could be getting on with.'

'Just sit and relax, you've got four people to wait on you hand and foot.'

When Simon returned he held the newspaper behind his back.

'I failed them all so I'm off job hunting tomorrow.'

'You can't have failed them all surely…' said Helen.

'Only joking, I failed Social Studies B, but I got distinctions in English, French and Maths.'

'Well done son,' said George clapping him on the back 'so you'll be off to Glendale High.'

'I'll try it, if I don't like it I can still leave and get a job…'

'No, you have to be positive, work hard; you need good results to get into university.' George looked at the expression on his son's face. 'Okay, no lectures today; enjoy the rest of the holidays and thanks for helping me out.'

That evening George sat on the edge of the veranda watching Helen watering the wiry clumps of grass that clung tenuously to the silvery sand. If the pressure of the hose was too great there was the risk of washing them away, but the gentle stream took a long time to give the ground a good soak.

'I can't imagine these clumps ever joining up, let alone making a lawn like Yvonne's' sighed Helen.

'She said it would take time, though how anything survives in their garden with Drongo racing around is beyond me.'

They had decided to make a nice front lawn and just a small lawn out the back in the shade by the terrace.

'Oh look, the kookaburra's back again.'

It was Peter with his bird book who had been teaching his parents the different birds and Helen who had taught him the song they used to sing at Girl Guides.

Kookaburra sits on the old gum tree,

Merry, merry king of the bush is he,
Laugh kookaburra, laugh kookaburra,
Gay your life must be.

None of the guides had had any idea what a kookaburra or gum tree looked like, but Helen had been thrilled that he really did laugh. Tony had declared that he could be king of Tonydale and a member of their gang; a great privilege, Pat was the only other member. The other gang in the neighbourhood were the magpies; smaller than English magpies, their only similarity was to be black and white. Caroline had told the twins they didn't like little boys and dived on their heads during the nesting season.

One afternoon when Helen popped out to the shops by herself she noticed white hazy smoke coming from the small patch of bush next to one of the half built houses. She wondered if anyone else had noticed; by the time she reached the phone box at the shops it could be out of control; John had told them frightening stories of wild fire and all the scrub was tinder dry. To her relief, as she drew closer she could see the builders playing their hoses on the small circle of flames.

'Bloody kids' said one to the other and Helen was relieved the twins were not in the vicinity.

When she got home she was surprised to find Peter and Tony playing in their bedroom.

'I thought you were out playing with Wayne?'

'We got too hot so we thought we'd come home' said Peter.

The start of the new term was approaching; George and Helen had been trying to put by money for school uniforms. Greek George had paid George in full for the day he had been taken ill, but not for the day he had taken off. Simon received a day's wages at the same rate he paid the Italian boy in the depot. The children were not looking forward to shopping for uniforms.

'Do we have to go with them?' moaned Jennifer. 'Can't we go with Dad, Caroline's so boring.'

'I know, but I can hardly say that to Valerie when she's been kind enough to offer us a lift to Victoria Park and show us where the shop is. We'll only have time to get the boys' on Saturday and it's nice for me to have another mother to chat to.'

---oOo---

Jennifer took an instant dislike to the school uniform. The dress material was covered in thin horizontal and vertical stripes of red, blue and grey, that reminded her of her father's handkerchiefs.

In the changing room Caroline said 'If you fail your junior exams, you have to repeat the whole three years.'

A feeling of hollow depression descended upon Jennifer; she would not tell her parents, they would be very worried. Mr. Gregson had told the class they would not know what work was until they got to high school.

The two mothers returned to the changing room. Aunty Valerie had arms full of clothes and her reluctant younger daughter in tow.

'Perhaps you should have the next size up Caroline? Patricia, you can't wear shorts to school, try this nice blue dress on.'

Her mother was holding a white hat for Jennifer to try on.

'Mum, I can't wear that, Simon will say it's square.'

'Even though it's round?' her mother smiled and turned to Aunty Valerie. 'Everything is square according to Simon.'

Aunty Valerie talked non-stop as she led them off to a store that had a little tea bar in the corner. The two mothers were inevitably dying for a cup of tea. Pat skipped along, hanging on to Jennifer's hand and Caroline plodded beside her mother.

'Mike's thinking of working oop North.'

'Oh, I thought he had a good job in Perth?'

'Up North is where the money's to be made, mining and stuff; lots of men do it for a short while, if they don't mind being away from home.'

'I wouldn't want George to work away.'

'We need to save money for our fares home.'

'Have you decided to go?'

194

'Not yet, but it would be good to know we could if we wanted.'

Jennifer tried to listen with one ear, while Pat was talking non-stop in her other ear. Her father had instilled in them the idea there was no going back, but Aunty Valerie seemed to treat the whole thing so casually.

'It's the spring I miss... and the autumn, what wouldn't I do for some drizzly rain... of course Mike always said *Think of it as a two year holiday, an adventure, then if you really want to go back*. This tea's not very nice, we used to have a lovely little restaurant in 'Bradley and Wilkins', wonderful afternoon teas, I used to take Mum there every Wednesday, do you remember Caroline, Grannie's treat?'

Jennifer saw her mother glance surreptitiously at her watch and hoped she would suggest going home, but when people gave you a lift in their car it was rude to want to leave before they did. She wondered if her mother would start to feel homesick if Aunty Valerie didn't stop talking about the 'Old Country.'

'How did your day go?' asked George at teatime. 'What's so funny?'

'Aunty Valerie didn't stop talking.'

'If the shops hadn't closed we would probably still be there' said her mother.

'Is that why we've got salad tonight' moaned Simon.

'I bought a nice joint of meat at that butcher's, perhaps we should invite Valerie and Mike round for tea one evening.'

'Do we have to?' replied her husband. 'Have you met this Mike yet?'

'No, he wants to work up North so they can go back to England.'

'Yes, some of Joe's mates do that, it's so hot you get a beer allowance. What does Mike do in Perth?'

'No idea, he worked in a factory in England, I can't think why he would want to go back, when they've just bought that nice house.'

'Strange no one's moved in next door yet.'

'Yes, if it's a family who've bought it you'd think they would want to be settled before school starts.'

'I hope it won't be an elderly couple who hate children' laughed George.

'Perhaps it will be a family with some girls and a dog' said Jennifer hopefully.

'I've got a couple of days off so we can enjoy the last week of the holidays and have a surprise outing.'

Jennifer was looking forward to the last week and even getting a little excited about school, despite Caroline's dire warnings of strict teachers and mountains of homework. She and Simon might go swimming a couple more times and on Saturday the Charles family were coming over to visit.

The surprise trip was to Fremantle, the sea port where they would have arrived if they had sailed. George had heard an ocean liner was docking for one day. After exploring the lovely yellow stone buildings of the old town and imagining being a convict in Fremantle gaol, they went to the docks. Her father had timed it so they would see the ship set sail for England. She had come from Sydney and this was her last stop in Australia before crossing the world. Young Australians leaving home for the first time and rich retired folk going on holiday had friends and relatives at the dockside to bid them farewell. There was an air of excitement and bustle as the passengers walked up the gang planks, then gathered at the railings of the decks to wave and throw ticker tape. Tanned, bare armed men moved thick ropes and chains and the huge ship sounded its deep horns, sending a shiver down her spine.

At that moment Jennifer realised that sailing was even more exciting than flying and felt a pang of regret that her family had not experienced the long holiday on board that Aunty Valerie had described; deck games, children's parties and the crew dressing up to cross the equator.

'It will be five or six weeks before they see Southampton' said her father.

'I'm going to work on a ship' announced Simon.

'In the navy?' asked his sister.

'No, whatever those blokes in the white uniform do; I bet it's like being on holiday all the time.'

197

That evening Jennifer felt tired and queasy after tea. When she went to have her shower she noticed blood on her pants, she was more annoyed than scared. She peeped out of the bathroom door and called for her mother, but with all the noise going on in the house she didn't hear her from the kitchen.

She had been shown the pads she would have to wear, but they were not in the bathroom. Under the shower she remembered that she and Simon were going to the river tomorrow, the rest of the holiday was going to be ruined. There was a knock on the door. Her mother had come to see why she was so long, she wanted the twins to get in the bathroom and clean their teeth.

Jennifer woke up and remembered; she checked her pyjamas and the sheet with relief. Caroline had known someone whose sister's friend had started her period and didn't stop bleeding. She was home alone and there was no telephone in the house; when her family arrived back she had bled to death.

She opened her underwear drawer where she had hidden the paper packet of 'Modess' sanitary towels; 'STs' her mother called them. Each pad had a loop at either end, which you had to fix to metal clips on straps, which in turn were attached to an elastic belt. The whole contraption was uncomfortable and she wondered if she would be able to ride her bike or climb the stubby trees with the twins. Not that there was any point riding her bike when there was nowhere to go. Her mother had promised to explain to Simon she couldn't go swimming, but what would he say to her Dutch friend? She had hoped Maiya would suggest they meet up at school on the first day, though the other girl had a whole class full of people and her best friend back from Sydney to be reunited with.

There was a knock on the door; she closed the drawer quickly in case the twins burst in. It was her mother.

'Everything okay? There's nothing to worry about, it's just something we women have to put up with.'

'But don't you stop having periods when you've had your children?'

'No unfortunately, they carry on till you're about fifty.'

Jennifer was confused.

'You can ask me anything you're not sure about.'

She related Caroline's story and her mother laughed.

'Don't believe everything that girl tells you, old head on young shoulders, I don't know where she gets her ideas from.'

'So it's not true they're going to Sydney?'

'Sydney? I thought her father wanted to work up north.'

The rest of the week dragged by; Jennifer was fed up with her brothers and irritated by her parents. She couldn't wait for Terri and her family to arrive on Saturday and hoped they would bring Drongo.

She raced out when they turned into the driveway; Drongo was hanging out of the open window.

'He won't run away will he?'

Uncle John stepped out of the car. 'No, he won't want to miss anything going on here, but if he's a nuisance we'll tie him up, don't want him ripping up your Mum's new lawn.'

Drongo leapt out of the car and bounded into Jennifer, putting his nose straight between her legs. She pushed him away, embarrassed and irritated, remembering dogs had an amazing sense of smell, they could smell blood.

Luckily he was soon more interested in the twins, who called him to see Petervale. She whisked Terri into the bedroom and shut the door so she could shyly tell her the new secret. Then they admired the wall where Jennifer had stuck up some new pictures of the Beatles Simon had given her from his magazine.

'If we ask Simon nicely he'll play his Beatles records. It's Mum and Dad's record player, but he doesn't let anyone else touch his records.'

'I'm going to live in the country when I'm grown up,' said Terri 'if I had my own horse I could ride it every day.'

'Did you do lots of riding?'

'Me and Trish had to share the horse and he was rather old and slow. Trish says she's going to be a surfer and live by Bondi Beach when she leaves school.'

'Jennifer, come and help lay the table' called her mother.

Drongo was shut out of the house, he wasn't allowed indoors at home; Jennifer was relieved she could avoid him. Her mother was laying out a big buffet, so everyone could spread out in the kitchen or lounge. She heard her name mentioned.

'…so Jennifer was right, they are going to Sydney. The only family we've got to know and now they're leaving Perth, they'd bought Caroline her school uniform and everything.'

'We haven't even met the husband, but they sound a feckless lot' said her father.

'Valerie said there's nothing to do in Glendale and they'd always said they would try Sydney if they didn't like it here.'

'How are they getting there?' asked Uncle John.

'Driving across.'

'Do they know how far it is?'

Her mother laughed. 'I asked her that and she said they'd pack a few sandwiches.'

'Good heavens, not very responsible when you've got young kids. It's three days drive even when you're used to it and it's only gravel road across the Nullabor Plain. Does she drive? It's tiring for one driver, you fall asleep on those long straight stretches of road.'

'I bet they'll never be heard of again' said Simon.

'I don't understand why they want to go when they have just bought that nice house,' said her father 'wonder how much they'll get renting it out?'

'Next door's still empty then?' said Aunty Yvonne.

'Yes, the agent said it's sold, but they can't move in yet' said her mother. 'We're enjoying being the only house in the street, not having to worry about annoying the neighbours.'

The twins begged to go outside again while the adults were still eating.

'We have to swear Drongo into our gang,' said Peter 'he can replace Pat.'

They soon rushed in again. 'Drongo's found a snake.'

'Stay inside boys' said their mother.

Their father followed Uncle John out to the end of the back yard then returned.

'Come and have a look before he disappears.'

The snake's head had been identified as a goanna, disturbed when the dog was ferreting around in the dry undergrowth. The lizard surveyed them for a moment then disappeared. Their parents' relief was short lived.

'Of course it could have been a snake,' said Uncle John 'Dugites are six feet long when they're fully grown. If they start building on that land next door or if they do any burning off, that's when you'll have to watch it, when they get disturbed.' He changed the subject. 'Thought you'd have a puppy by now Jenny.'

Aunty Yvonne shot him a warning glance.

Before Jennifer could open her mouth to speak her father said 'I'm going to build a fence and gate behind the car port first, we won't want him wandering around loose like the Aussie dogs.'

'If the puppy went wandering up Smith Street or into the bush, we'd never see him again' added Helen. 'Jenny's happy to wait.'

'Yes, she's been busy going out cycling and swimming with Simon' said her father.

Jennifer blushed.

'Yeah, she's quite a good swimmer now' said Simon 'she can even dive... off the bottom rung of the ladder.'

'Been to the ocean again?' asked John.

'Only that nice little bay on Rottnest island' said her mother, 'but they love the river and that pool at the national park, even George and I have had a dip in there.'

'Go and put the kettle on Jenny' said her father, as they arrived back at the shady terrace.

She tried to carry on hearing what the adults were talking about.

'Has that old Greek given you a pay rise yet?' asked John.

'Yup, he's a fair boss. I share the driving with Joe now and help in the office occasionally.'

'Oh I got my nursing job,' said Aunty Yvonne 'the letter was waiting for me when we got back.'

'She reckons she'll save enough to take us to England for Christmas.'

Her father laughed. 'You're welcome to it, we had a great Christmas, lovely and relaxed, no relatives, picnic up in the hills.'

Chapter Seventeen   Glendale Senior High School

On the first day of school the twins insisted they would go by themselves, even though their brother and sister were going the same way. Jennifer could hardly swallow the scrambled eggs on toast their mother insisted they needed. Even going with Caroline would have been better than going on her own. Simon claimed not to be nervous, though at the last moment he offered to walk with her.

'Do you realise, I'll only be three years ahead of you now, not four like I was in England.'

'In March, when I'm twelve you will only be three years older than me' she pointed out.

The road to the school was still a sandy track and there were only a few other teenagers shuffling along in front of them. Her school dress felt scratchy and her hat uncomfortable. As they walked across the playing fields, boys and girls of all shapes and sizes were converging on the sprawl of buildings. Simon was quiet. She noticed that none of the other girls were wearing hats.

'Stuff it in your bag' said Simon.

She wasn't sure if he was being sympathetic or didn't want to be seen with her wearing a hat, but she did as he said; there was plenty of room in the new bag with its wide shoulder strap.

The school had a public address system and they strained to decipher what the man's booming voice was saying.

'First years assemble by the outside veranda, they must be your lot Jenny, they look like little kids.' He spotted one of the boys from the river. 'Right, I'll see you at home later.'

He slowed to a casual saunter and disappeared round the corner with the other boy.

There was no sign of Maiya, but in the sea of uniforms it would be hard to spot her. She plucked up courage to ask a couple of girls if they were first years; they were, but also had no idea if they were in the right place.

A middle aged man in smart shorts and shirt appeared on the veranda with a loud hailer.

'If you are NOT a first year, make your way to your own quadrangles.' After a pause he continued. 'I will call each class number and introduce you to your form teacher who will call out the class register. Each name will only be called once. If we have three John Smiths and four Linda Browns, then your middle names will be used. When you hear your name, line up in front of your teacher without talking. Anyone left at the end, report to me immediately.'

Jennifer imagined herself being left at the end.

'One nine, Mr. Pearson.'

The names rolled out and children giggled with relief or parted from their friends disappointed.

'One eight, Mr. Reynolds.'

Mr. Reynolds looked less severe than Mr. Palmer.

'Susan Anderson, Catherine Leticia Brown.'

A red haired girl blushed and edged forward as others giggled.

'…Linda Coates, Maria Da Costa…'

Jennifer sighed, it would take a long time to get to the letter P and a long time to listen to every class.

'Patricia O'Brian, Jennifer Palmer…'

For a moment her legs wouldn't move, then she shyly stood in line.

'Christine Rogers, Melissa Sands…'

The girls stood and listened to the boys being called out. A hand tapped her shoulder and she turned to see a girl with masses of black curly hair and a jolly face.

'Do you know anyone?'

Jennifer shook her head.

'Nor do I.'

'Stay in your lines and follow me to the classroom' Mr. Reynolds was saying.

At the end of the veranda was an open entrance to a large quadrangle which they walked across; then through another passage to shuffle along a concrete veranda, turning right into yet another quadrangle. Behind her, Melissa giggled.

'This is like a prison, we'll never find our way out again and our parents will wonder why we haven't come home.'

They halted outside a classroom that was identical to the others they had passed.

'Line up neatly, never enter a classroom until your teacher arrives.'

Mr. Reynolds opened the door. 'Sit down quietly, any desk will do, you don't have to sit next to your friends.'

Melissa slipped quickly behind a desk at the back and plonked her bag on the desk next to it, motioning Jennifer to sit down. There was much shuffling and giggling till Mr. Reynolds rapped on his desk with the wooden blackboard rubber.

'I'm going to call the register again, when you hear your name answer 'present' and raise your hand.

Good, everyone seems to have found their way to the right place. This is your form room, where you will come every morning for the register and also the lessons I am taking you for, English and Social Studies A. Outside on the veranda are the girls' lockers and that is the quadrangle for first year girls only.

Boys do not set foot there except for lessons, otherwise you will have the Headmistress Miss Higgins to deal with. Look out the window boys; that is first year boys' quadrangle and your lockers are there. You may only leave that area for lessons or to go to the canteen at recess and lunchtime. This is not primary school, do not run around or act like idiots in the quadrangle; the oval is for racing around letting off steam in Phys. Ed.'

Jennifer was beginning to get confused, but Mr. Reynolds had not finished.

'Lockers; your packed lunch stays in there so do all your books, take out only what you need for each lesson or homework. You will see why when you have finished collecting all your books, only Wayne here could carry that lot around.'

They all turned to see the broad-shouldered boy who was a head above the other boys.

'Locker keys; when I call your name come and collect your key, do not swap lockers, you are responsible for that locker and if you lose the key Mr. Jones the caretaker will have to come and break it open.'

There was giggling and fussing around as they collected keys and fixed them to the chains that had been on the uniform list. There was a leather tab to attach the chain to the button on the uniform belt.

'The chain is so you don't lose your key, not for swinging round and taking someone's eye out. Keys stay in your pocket unless you are opening your locker… Timetable for class one eight; there is a copy for everyone, do not lose it otherwise you will not know where you are meant to be or what lesson you are doing.

At recess you will hear the announcements over the PA system, listen carefully. When the siren goes you may leave the classroom when the teacher tells you, not before. Then you may go to the canteen and buy drinks that rot your teeth and cakes that make you fat.'

It had not occurred to Jennifer that she would need money, what if she was the only one who couldn't buy things? She looked at her watch and looked up to see Mr. Reynolds grinning.

'Only fifteen minutes to go Jennifer. Wayne, you can hand round the homework diaries; these will be your bibles. Write down all your homework and when it has to be done by, plus any other important messages.'

Jennifer wrote her name neatly on the front of the blue-grey exercise book, then opened it to a lovely smell of new paper. On the first page went her first task; all exercise books and text books borrowed from the school shop to be covered in brown paper and clear plastic.

'Our class's turn tomorrow to collect books; any books lost or damaged will have to be replaced at your parents' expense. The bookshop is there so they don't have to go out and buy you new books each year, so don't abuse the system.'

They were all startled when the loudspeaker above the blackboard suddenly burst into life. The headmaster spoke first to welcome everyone, then the gruffer deputy head reeled off boring notices followed by a list of pupils to report to the office. Jennifer wondered what they had done wrong or if they had gone missing.

As they filed out, Melissa asked her if she had any money. Jennifer shook her head wondering if the girl wanted to borrow some.

She was relieved when she said 'Adam's Ale then.'

The girl led her to the water fountain, then they sat on the bench exchanging details about their lives. The next lesson was back in the form room for English, so they did not have to worry about getting lost. Some of the girls returned with glass bottles of bright green or cherry red cool drinks and a few were biting into thick, squelchy custard slices.

'You're still eleven?'

'Nearly twelve, how old are you?'

'Nearly thirteen.'

'Do you live in Glendale?'

'In Glenmount, it's not far. Dad just got a new job in Glendale and we bought a new house. Mum said I'd be bound to meet someone else who didn't know anyone' she smiled.

Jennifer's house seemed to have shrunk when she arrived back from her first day at school; it was as if she had lived in a bubble for the past two months. On the kitchen table were three glasses of milk and home made cake, the twins were already tucking in. Her mother hovered expectantly.

'Did you see Simon?'

'Not till we were coming out of school, he was going to the shops with those boys from the river and two others I don't know, he said he'd be home later.'

'Sounds as if he's settled in, so how was your first day?'

She told them all about Mr. Reynolds and Melissa.

'We've got a new friend' announced Peter 'he's called Wine.'

'That's an unusual name, is he a migrant?'

'No, he's Australian.'

'Here's Dad back, I'll put the kettle on.'

'One good thing about early shift, I get home the same time as you.'

'Dad, we're not in the same class, Tony's in Grade Four and I'm in Grade Four and Five, so that means I'm higher than him.'

'No it doesn't, it just means they didn't have room for you in my class.'

'Mr. Reynolds says 1-9 and 1-8 are the top classes so we have to work hard and set a good example. We're the only ones doing French.'

'Well done love, but I don't know why they study French, it's the only language I haven't heard spoken in Perth.'

'I've got homework already, English.'

'What I did in the holidays? That's what we always had to do' said Helen.

'No, we have to introduce ourselves, so Mr. Reynolds gets to know us.'

'That's just the teacher being nosy' said Simon as he walked into the kitchen.

'Also, I have to get all my books covered in brown paper and plastic by the end of the week or sooner, otherwise I'll get into trouble.'

'I'll have to get some in Vic Park tomorrow' said her mother.

At school the next morning Melissa was waiting for her in their quadrangle. In the classroom Mr. Reynolds collected up their homework; three pupils had not done it.

'If you can't manage one small piece of homework, how are you going to cope when you start doing lessons properly? You'll be expected to do revision and studying every night, as well as your homework. Handy tip, do the homework as soon as you get it, not the night before it's due.'

Jennifer's heart sank, it had taken her a long time to do one piece.

Everything was in blocks, class 1-8 headed for the science block. When they went in, the smell of the classroom was a delicious mix of gas and other unidentified substances. Jennifer was looking forward to using the Bunsen burners, but she was disappointed. Half the lesson was taken up by Mr. Holloway regaling them with tales of burns and fingers lost by pupils who had not listened to instructions; the remainder they spent writing out safety rules in their red exercise books.

At lunchtime the girls found their way to the canteen, which lay between two quadrangles. It had no tables and chairs or walls, just windows at which the pupils queued to buy meat pies with tomato sauce and more cool drinks. They had both brought sandwiches and Jennifer decided she wouldn't bother to ask her parents for money in the future, the queues looked too daunting. Melissa agreed and Jennifer was relieved she would have someone to sit with and eat her sandwiches.

That evening there was much family discussion as to the best technique for covering the books. You had to remember to write your name, class and subject on the brown paper before putting the plastic on. Jennifer had already written on the back of her science book by mistake. To put the polythene on you had to hold it in place then quickly stick it down with the durex on the inside of the cover. If it was too tight you couldn't close the book and paper covers would curl up. If it was too loose it looked messy.

'I'm sure it doesn't have to be perfect' said her exasperated mother.

'I'm not going to cover my books,' said Simon 'the kitchen table looks like something out of Blue Peter.

The next day Jennifer was embarrassed to discover she was the only one with plain brown books, the other girls had stuck pictures of animals and pop stars or even decorated them with intricate patterns in felt pen, so they would be easily identified.

'I didn't think we were allowed to do that' she whispered to Melissa.

'Never mind, you can decorate your English book when you get it back.'

In the girls' changing room they put on their blue gingham sports dresses with matching bloomers. Jennifer had always coveted the light blue airtex T-shirt and navy hockey skirt that Christine had for the grammar school. She looked at the thin cotton garments in dismay.

'These are like the romper suits my cousin wore when she was a baby.'

Melissa got a fit of the giggles and they were last out of the changing rooms.

Miss Thompson the sports teacher was already standing on the veranda telling the girls to 'gather in'. She was young and sporty and wore a bottle green tracksuit and a whistle on a ribbon round her neck.

'Girls, if you take this long to get ready, we'll never have time to do any sport. At the end of the lesson you need to be even quicker. You'll be sweating a lot in my lessons, so you need to shower afterwards. You are young ladies now and we expect you to keep clean and smart.'

Jennifer couldn't imagine having a shower at school and tried not to start giggling again. She had no towel or soap. Beside her Melissa whispered 'I take half an hour at home.'

The boys were over on the other side of the field and had already started playing cricket.1-8 and 1-9 girls would do their lessons together, so they had two ready-made teams for softball. More by luck than judgement, Jennifer managed to hit the ball and make a round, but the game went downhill for her after that; when her team was fielding she never got near the ball. When they were in to bat again, the team captain put she and Melissa at the end and the siren went before it was their turn.

In the changing room it was chaos; girls had lost locker keys and socks, others were complaining the water was cold. Melissa and

Jennifer stood politely waiting for a shower. Miss Thompson came in and blew her whistle.

'Come along, get dressed quickly, my next class are coming in.'

The class were already going in for French when the two girls rushed to the end of the line.

'No running on the verandas' came a man's voice from the other side of the quadrangle.

The young French teacher had a fashionably short skirt and some of the boys were nudging each other. The children were told to get into pairs. By the time they had told each other what their names were and how old they were, the lesson seemed to be over.

The two girls walked out of school giggling.

'Je m'appelle Melissa, J'ai douze ans et J'habite… Glenmount...how do you say that in French?'

'I'm going to practise on Simon and Dad.'

The boys were dodging the huge sprinklers, rusty pipes laid across the field, as pupils poured out of school.

'That water smells like rotten eggs' said Jennifer.

'It's bore water, that's why the walls of the school are brown. They pump it from underground. My Dad's going to sink a bore in the back yard, Mum wants a green lawn.'

Jennifer had visions of a well in the middle of their garden, it sounded like a good idea; their parents were always telling them not to waste water as they had to pay for it.

That evening she wrote to Christine.

...everything is different from primary school. We have to work hard and the teachers are quite stern. I'm never going to learn all the rules. I have a new friend called Melissa Sands, you would like her, she is good fun. I am going to cycle round to her house at the weekend.

The school is enormous, I never see Simon. It has playing fields on two sides, but they are called 'the oval' even though it is L-shape. The sports teachers all dress in tracksuits and they are called Phys Ed teachers. Tomorrow we are going to do Home Science, which means cooking.

The home science block was the newest part of the school and boasted a real flat, but the girls of 1-8 would never see inside it.

'Only 1-S goes in there' said Christine Rogers. With two older sisters in the school, she was the self appointed expert on Glendale High and Home Science.

'What is 1-S?' asked Jennifer.

Near the top of the roll call on the first morning, she had not noticed what happened to the remaining two hundred first years.

'One Special, that means you're too thick even for 1-1. They learn how to look after the flat instead of doing maths; so they know how to run a home when they get married.'

'Lucky things' said Melissa.

'Yes, but who would want to marry them?' said Linda, genuinely puzzled.

'I wouldn't want to come to school to do housework' exclaimed Susan.

'We are going to do housework, we have to do laundry first term' said Christine.

Jennifer didn't believe her. 'I know how to do washing, I've helped Mum.'

Christine wasn't joking; Mrs. Butcher marched them past the cooking room, past the sewing room and into the laundry room.

'Term one, laundry, term two sewing and term three cooking, any questions girls?'

'Is it true we have to wash the cricket team's whites?' asked Susan.

Everyone giggled.

'No, next week we will do washing and ironing handkerchiefs. Today you learn how to make soap jelly.'

'I told my brothers I was going to bring cakes home' Jennifer whispered to Melissa.

'You two girls, are you planning to marry very rich men and have servants?'

The others laughed and Jennifer blushed.

'…because if not you will need to learn how to run a household on a budget.'

The soap jelly was made by boiling up left over bits of soap.

'Looks like snot' complained Maria.

At recess Christine was collecting empty cool drink bottles. 'If you take them back to the canteen you get money for them.'

Jennifer and Melissa thought that sounded a good idea and wondered how many they would have to collect for a doughnut or custard slice.

At home that evening she told the rest of the family about the scheme.

'They call you a scab if you do that' said Simon.

'Can I have some money for school then?' said his sister. 'One of the girls in our class has a custard slice every morning.'

'No, you have plenty to eat in your lunch box and I'm sure those cool drinks are bad for your teeth' said her mother.

'If you put a penny in coca cola, it comes out all shiny the next day' said Simon.

'Don't either of you bother your mother for money, it's more important for her to spend money for good food at home.'

'I'm not even going to do any cooking till third term' Jennifer described the Home Science lesson.

'It sounds Victorian' said her mother.

'Mrs. Butcher is very old, Melissa said she probably lived out in the bush and we'll have to use flat irons.'

'And how were your lessons today Simon?'

'Okay, we did biology, but we don't get to dissect mice yet. There's these fifth years who go in the labs at lunchtime and dissect animals; they found a stray cat and killed it with chloroform, then boiled it till only the skeleton was left.'

'Yuk' said Tony with delight.

Jennifer didn't believe him.

'You can see it in science room three, or look through the window.'

'I'm going to look tomorrow then.'

Melissa would think it a good laugh if they went hunting for a skeleton.

Chapter Eighteen   February 1965

On Thursday evening Helen wrote a long letter to her parents, she would have it weighed and mailed at the post office when she went to Perth in the morning.

Sorry it's taken so long to reply to your nice newsy letter. I loved the hilarious account of Xmas Day with Dennis and his family, but as you say, they put on a good 'do' and it was nice of him to drive you home. So Reg came to dinner on Boxing Day, does that mean my fussy sister might be serious about him?

I have enclosed our first photographs; the garden (back yard), the Swan River and some views up in the Darling Ranges, but you can't really tell the scale from little pictures. Also the twins' thankyou letters, hopefully you have already received Simon's and Jenny's. Getting them all bikes was the best idea, Simon and Jenny go miles on theirs and Peter is keeping up with Tony now. There have been a few minor injuries, as they insist on cycling in their thongs, or even with bare feet!

The holidays were long, but suddenly we were in a panic to get ready for school. Kitting the boys up was easy; all the school boys seem to wear the same grey cotton shorts and shirts. Jennifer did not like her uniform, but she's getting used to it. We had to go to the primary school before term started and buy a pack of things the twins would need; pencils, exercise books etc. and at the high school they have a book shop.

We were very proud of Simon's exam results and pleased that he has ambitions to be a teacher. He has at last been to the barbers, but only for a trim, he still looks like John Lennon.

Jennifer has made friends at school already…

On Friday morning at the bus stop, Helen felt childishly excited; she had not left Glendale all week and had hardly spoken to another adult; she deserved her lunch out in Perth with Yvonne. The children seemed to have settled into their new schools better than they had dared hope and she had relaxed as the week progressed, getting back into a routine that was familiar yet utterly different.

At the post office she bought aerogrammes, anticipating more time to write properly. With no library in Glendale she looked in the book shop, but could not afford to buy. The weather was still very hot and it was not much cooler inside the shops.

Yvonne was waiting at Boans restaurant for her. 'Have you been enjoying the peace and quiet?'

'Yes, though it's been strange; I keep looking out to the back yard or over the fence to see if the twins are okay, then remembering. I seem to have spent all week hanging over the trough in the laundry, heaving sheets onto the rotary hoist or sweeping up sand indoors. I think I deserve every Friday off. George is going to meet me in Vic. Park to get the shopping, then we're taking fish and chips home for tea.'

'Well this will be my last day out for a while.'

'How did your first day at the hospital go?'

'Like being the new girl at school, a lot has changed since I was nursing, but I enjoyed working with the patients. The girls didn't even notice I wasn't at home.'

'What does John think?'

'He was happy for me to do two days a week, but I've already volunteered to do extra next week, someone's on holiday. He thinks they're going to take advantage of me being new, but I bet he won't say no to the money.'

'Have you had to do anything too ghastly?'

'Plenty of the basic stuff, they only trust me on the general ward.'

'We got a postcard from that Valerie; they arrived safely in Sydney, she said she didn't realise Australia was so big. They much prefer Sydney and Mike's got a brilliant job lined up.'

'Have you met any other neighbours yet?'

'No, I've only talked to the couple in the Greek shop this week, I don't know where everyone else hides, with that big school there must be other mothers around. There's no library in Glendale; I've never lived in a new suburb before, things I took for granted at home don't exist. I must make an effort to join something; George thinks he has found the nearest church, we haven't broken the news yet to Simon, that's where we're going on Sunday.'

'Terri's in Mr. Gregson's class now, he asked after Jenny.'

'Oh that's nice, he is a good teacher. We keep hearing about Mr. Reynolds; he's Jenny's form teacher and he takes them for English. He was pleased with her homework, not much doesn't know about our family now; it started

One day when I was three years and three months old I got a big surprise, or rather two little surprises; Mum came home with two tiny babies. When I was eleven I had another big surprise when Dad came home with six tickets for Australia.

Yvonne laughed 'Has she made any friends yet?'

'Yes, this Melissa seems to have taken her under her wing, though they've already been told off for giggling. The little Dutch girl she went swimming with is in another class, but she's seen her a couple of times. How's Trish getting on?'

'Everything's boring; I told her it's only the first week, once the lessons get going properly they'll be doing interesting things. She says all the teachers are old and grumpy. Oh guess what, Lynne down my road had twins, she thought she was having a big baby, then the midwife heard two heartbeats. She was already nervous about having her first baby.'

'What did she have?'

'One of each, both healthy; I told her she was jolly lucky, won't have to bother having any more.'

'We were only planning to have two, in fact Jenny was my only planned pregnancy.'

'Did you have to get married?'

Helen blushed, 'No, but we didn't want to wait; it was so difficult after the war for couples to find anywhere to live. There was no room for us to stay with either set of parents. We imagined it would be romantic to get married soon and live in digs, at least we'd be together; then we could save up and have children in the future, we thought we knew it all.'

'What was it like?'

'Cosy and fun to start with, washing hanging above the sink in the corner, shared bathroom. When I discovered I was pregnant we were still naively positive; how much room does a tiny baby take up? But my mother was not pleased, said she thought George was more responsible than that. The landlady was not pleased either; she didn't take in families, we had to find somewhere else. The next place was dreadful, like one of those gritty black and white films, a real eye opener; I tried to put Mum off coming to visit.

Then the four parents had a council of war, after all Simon was the first grandchild on both sides; they lent us the money for a deposit, we'd hardly saved a penny. Years later Dad told me he'd had some money put by for a rainy day; he wasn't expecting the rainy day would come so soon.

From Simon's first birthday my mother-in-law kept dropping hints about looking forward to a granddaughter, Denis' first baby was a boy too. Ironically nothing happened for a while, I thought I'd never have another baby.'

Yvonne was enjoying the story and Helen laughed, but suddenly there was a cold feeling in the pit of her stomach.

'What's the matter?'

'I've lost track, with the moving and Christmas, I didn't put my dates on the new calendar, surely this couldn't happen to me again, at my age?'

'You're not overdue are you?' Yvonne looked as worried as Helen felt.

'I'm certain I haven't had a period since Christmas.'

Yvonne went into nursing mode and put an arm round her shoulder. 'You're probably just late, all the upheaval you've had in the past five months.'

Helen felt reassured 'Unlikely at my age I expect.'

'No, quite likely, look at all those women whose husbands came back after the war, the baby boom, women in their late thirties and forties. I should be alright, I persuaded my doctor to put me on the pill.'

Helen was shocked 'Is that safe, they don't know the long term effects, are they allowed to?'

'GPs are allowed to prescribe it to healthy married women, it's safer than an unwanted pregnancy or major surgery to get sterilised.'

'I don't think George would like me to risk the pill.'

'It's been great for both of us, all the fun without the worry.'

'My parents only had sex three times.'

I don't think my parents did it at all,' laughed Yvonne 'and certainly not with their clothes off.'

Helen looked around the restaurant nervously 'I hope nobody's listening.'

'It's the sixties, people talk about things these days, but seriously, you know the signs, go and see your doctor as soon as possible, he could make sure everything's okay.'

'I haven't even met our new doctor yet, what could he do?'

'Sometimes there's a way round things…'

On Sunday morning Simon did not want to get out of bed, let alone put his best clothes on and go to church. Helen left George to sort him out, she felt sick with worry and in no mood for worship or meeting new people; she had not said anything, no point in worrying him for a few days yet.

The church was tiny, an older building near the river in an area settled earlier. Inside it was dark and cool; a little old lady in a strange hat sat pedalling at a wheezing harmonium, producing a squeaky tune. Most of the pews were empty. The little congregation could hardly fail to notice their numbers swelled by six. The vicar stood up and spoke in a flat tone.

Helen thought longingly of the sun filtering through the ancient stained glass windows of Saint Stephen's and the stirring sound of Mr. Rogers playing the organ. On this Sunday the congregation of the lovely Norman church were still in bed, but in a few hours time they would be getting up to prepare for the recording of 'Songs of Praise'; Joyce had written excitedly of the news in her last letter.

Worshipping God did not depend on the building, Helen knew that, but she began to question her own religion, which she had always taken for granted. A friendly neighbour had whisked them off to St. Stephen's when they had arrived at their new home with baby Simon. The 'Young Wives' had been a Godsend with their weekly coffee mornings and monthly second hand clothes swaps. The vicar was an ageless and genial man who had made it a family church. His sermons were uplifting and he avoided the sort of 'big questions' her brother-in-law brought up when he'd had a few drinks; 'where was God when six million Jews were killed, why does He let babies suffer.'

At St. Stephen's the family service was popular and the children filed out to Sunday school before the sermon. There had been a few people she didn't like, but generally the congregation were warm and friendly, rallying round when the twins were born. Helen and

George in turn had helped other families. Now she realised how much she missed them all.

She looked around and realised she had not heard a word the vicar had said in his sermon. Her husband's expression was inscrutable, Simon's face was a picture of sheer boredom and Jennifer was trying to ignore the restless twins. It was a relief when the old lady squeezed the harmonium into life again and people began filing out.

The sun was blinding after the dark interior of the church and Helen found it hard to see the expressions of the other people.

'Nice to see new faces' said the vicar, shaking her hand.

'Yes, we've just…'

But he had turned to the family behind before she could introduce herself. George was telling off the twins for skidding in the dust by the car, Simon was leaning on the other side, trying to be invisible and Jennifer hovered uncertainly by her side. A middle aged lady appeared at her elbow.

'Mother's Union meets on the first Tuesday afternoon of each month, what a pity you've just missed it.'

'I'm hungry.'

'Can we go to the river?'

The boys distracted her before she could reply politely to the woman.

In the car Simon said 'Dad, if I'm old enough to go to work and I'm an agnostic, does that mean I don't have to go to church with you next week?'

'What's a Nogstic?' said Peter.

'Better than being an atheist, it means you hedge your bets' his brother replied.

'We haven't decided which church to attend' said his mother.

'Haven't we?' said George 'I thought you wanted to go to that one.'

'Perhaps we needn't stick to the Church of England; there might be a different church nearer to us.'

'Tony and I are Roman Catholics' piped up Peter.

'No you aren't' said Jennifer.

'Yes we are, we went to Father O'Connor's lessons at the other school.'

'You were supposed to do scripture with the Anglican vicar.'

'We didn't know we were Anglians so we went with our friend.'

'Melissa's Roman Catholic and she got confirmed when she was seven and wore a lovely white dress.'

'You don't like wearing dresses,' said Helen 'but I did want us to find a nice church, so you could start going to confirmation classes.'

Back at home the house was hot and Helen was glad she had cooked the beef the evening before. George came into the kitchen as she washed the lettuce.

'I forgot we were having cold, I was just looking forward to a roast.'

'You're the one who wanted to live in a hot country' she snapped at him.

He put his arms round her. 'Salad's fine, I wasn't complaining; gives us more time to go out this afternoon. Where would you like to go?'

When the alarm went off on Monday morning Helen woke with a start; for a moment she couldn't place the nameless fear that was weighing her down.

'Five more minutes' said George wrapping his arms round her. 'Is everything alright, you didn't seem yourself at the weekend.'

'I'm fine' she lied. If he hadn't guessed yet she wasn't going to mention it.

She roused herself to sound cheerful, it wasn't fair for her husband to start a busy week on a flat note. 'I don't know which is worse, trying to get Tony out of bed or Peter leaping out of bed and talking non-stop before my brain's started working.'

'I'd better hurry and shave before the children start hogging the bathroom.'

Ten minutes later he sat at the kitchen table eating scrambled eggs while Helen put more toast on and they tried to ignore the bangs and shouts coming from the bedrooms. She felt a dragging feeling and her head was throbbing.

'I don't think I could cope with another member of the family' said George.

'What do you mean?' said Helen in alarm.

'A puppy; I was thinking Jenny's birthday would be the ideal time to get her a dog, but that's not far off.'

'Don't mention dogs, perhaps we could delay it for a while, till it's cooler and you've got the gate done.'

'We'll talk about it tonight, remember I'll be home later, we've got that new shop on the round… Bye kids, enjoy your second week at school.'

Jennifer was happy going to school, she was going to meet Melissa on the way, Simon set off on time, but the twins played up.

'Why can't we be in the same class?'

'You see each other at play time, come on you'll be late.'

'No we won't,' said Peter we like running all the way.'

When they had gone Helen made a cup of coffee and promised herself a sit down before she tackled the dishes and the washing. Again she tried to recall her last period and put a date to it, desperate to reassure herself it was a late period, not a missed one. After eight years it was hard to remember what it felt like being pregnant. She had always been thankful not to suffer from morning sickness, but it did mean there were no early warning signs.

She looked out of the laundry window as she pounded the washing in the trough; the back yard seemed alien today, usually she delighted in looking out at trees instead of the upstairs back windows and roofs of other houses. When she carried the washing basket out to the rotary hoist, the garden was silent except for the strange bird calls. An overwhelming feeling of loneliness swept over her.

A busy round of housework did nothing to dispel her strange mood nor could she put the thoughts of pregnancy out of her mind. She and Joyce had laughed about the aunt who had declared so proudly that her husband had never seen her naked. At CWA there had been the older woman who recalled in hushed tones that her late husband had been a good man who 'never bothered her' after her youngest child had been born. George had been understanding after the twins were born, she gathered from other mothers not all men were so kind. The pregnancy had gone well till the midwife revealed her suspicion there were two babies, after the initial shock George and the rest of the family had gone overboard to make sure she rested as much as possible. But nobody else could go through the labour for her and afterwards she was left with internal bruising and stitches. When she came home she could not imagine being able to walk properly again, let alone run a large family or enjoy making love.

Her mother had come round saying 'They let you young mothers get up much too soon these days, we used to stay in bed for a fortnight.'

Usually nervous of babies, her sister had discovered she could change nappies and comfort one baby, while Helen fed the other. Since then she had always been especially proud of her twin nephews and Helen realised with a twinge of guilt that her sister must miss them.

As the kettle boiled, her thoughts went round in circles. What did she dread the most? Giving birth again, the embarrassment for Simon of everyone knowing his parents had sex or coping without her family to help? Only the man from Australia House would be pleased. At the interview he had beamed at the children and said just what they needed, lots of new Australians. If it was a girl Jenny would be glad, though not as excited as having a puppy…

George walked in the door just as Helen was serving up lamb cutlets, he was tired but cheerful. Simon entertained them with accounts of his German lesson, boasting to Jennifer that it was much harder than French as there were three sexes, male, female and neutral.

'I've learnt the verb 'to be' already' she countered. 'Je suis, Tu et…'

'There's a bloke at work,' said George 'who speaks perfect Australian, but can't read or write a word of it.'

Helen served up pudding glad to let everyone chat. Tomorrow she would walk round to the doctors and make an appointment; as soon as she had been to the doctors she would talk to George.

---o0o---

On Tuesday afternoon Jennifer brought Melissa back after school. They couldn't wait to tell Simon that they had seen the cat's skeleton through the window; it had become an adventure when the deputy head told them off for being in the third year boys' quadrangle. Simon laughed as Melissa did an imitation.

What class are you in? Well you should be bright enough not to get lost after two weeks at the school.

Simon deemed them deserving enough to hear whichever of his Beatles' records they chose; after Melissa had thanked Helen for the homemade cake they went into the lounge to watch the boy reverentially take charge of the record player. The room was hot, even with the windows wide open.

After a few moments their mother came in looking irritated. 'Can't you turn it down a bit Simon?'

'We can't disturb the non-existent neighbours, anyway, I thought you loved the Beatles?'

'I do, just not so loud; thank goodness you don't like the Rolling Stones.'

'Jenny loves Mick Jagger.'

'No I don't.'

'All these new groups will never last' said their mother.

Simon turned to Melissa, 'I was going to start my own group, but then we came to Australia.'

'You could start one here, maybe you'd become famous.'

'Yeah… we could be called the 'Red-back Spiders'.

Jennifer was proud she had a big brother, her usual annoyances forgotten when she saw how impressed her new friend was. When the twins bounced in Melissa thought they were great fun and agreed to swear the secret oath and be taken to see Petervale.

When her father arrived home Jennifer introduced him; Melissa said goodbye politely to both parents and asked if Jennifer could come round to her house the next day.

Melissa's house was more exciting than Jennifer's; as she was an only child they had a large spare bedroom where her mother did dressmaking and Melissa did her art work. The room smelt delightfully of new fabric and poster paints. Her mother did sewing for other people and trusted her daughter to keep paint and glue well away from the material.

The whole house was decorated in a way Jennifer had never seen before. Paintings by Mr. Sands, of lonely ghost gums in red landscapes, adorned the walls, but in the hall there was a scary print in an ornate frame. It was Jesus' familiar gentle face, but his hands were ripping open his chest, revealing a lurid, red bulbous heart with light radiating from it. On the opposite wall hung a bejewelled cross, Jennifer was too polite to ask or comment.

Melissa's parents were out; that was one of the excitements of her house, she never knew if they would be home. Jennifer's mother was usually home and if there was a possibility she may be still out after school, plans were made and instructions given several times the evening before and in the morning.

Giggling, her friend led her into her parents' bedroom. On the wall above the bed was a painting of a young woman reclining on a beach. Her long dark hair was tied back in a pony tail and there was nothing covering her large breasts. She was smiling and not at all worried that someone might come along and see her naked.

'That's Mum when she was young, Dad painted her; he says the human body is beautiful, nothing to be ashamed of.'

When Jennifer got home and walked round to the back door, her brothers were digging in the yard. The kitchen was empty; puzzled, Jennifer looked in the lounge. Her mother was asleep in the arm chair; sometimes she dozed off after lunch, but never when it was time to cook tea.

'…Jenny, I thought you were going round to Melissa's?'

'I did, you told me to be back in time for tea.'

'Heavens, is it that time already, I just sat down to have a cup of tea.'

Her mother looked flustered.

'I'll make it; if Melissa's parents are back late she starts getting tea ready.'

'Goodness, I wouldn't expect you to do that love; no chores on school night when you've got homework. Are the boys alright?'

By the time her father came home the potatoes were on and Jennifer was squelching mince and breadcrumbs together to make rissoles. George hugged and kissed both of them.

'My favourite dinner, I'm starving.'

'I should have made you more sandwiches.'

'No, we were so busy we hardly had time to eat. Where's Simon?'

'He said her was going round to Paul's house and he'd be back in time for tea' reported Jennifer.

'And I am.' Simon banged the fly screen door and came into the kitchen.

'Good, on school nights tea on time, so you can get your homework done afterwards.'

The twins appeared at the door with black hands and feet and Helen handed them the old towel she now kept in the laundry. 'Wash your feet.'

At the table their father always asked them what they had been doing at school. The twins usually answered in unison 'nothing.'

His daughter was happy to fill him in. 'We had Health Education and Mr. Roland the Phys. Ed. teacher takes us. We're doing the digestive system first; he says there's nothing rude about that, as everyone works the same way. Do you want to know what happens to your food after it leaves your stomach?'

'Not while we're eating, how was PE?'

'Stupid, make up a sequence using five different movements. I wish we had a gym with ropes and climbing frames on the wall like Christine has at the grammar school.'

As her parents washed and dried the dishes Jennifer went reluctantly into her bedroom to do her homework. She had brought home the books for Social Studies A and B; dispiriting paperbacks, wodges of typewritten pages with no pictures, glued together. One had a blue/grey cover, the other a green colour that reminded her of paper towels. Australia did not have beheadings and battles sort of history and she thought she was going to be bored.

She opened her homework diary with good intentions, wrote out her French homework, then looked at the science questions. From Simon's room came the sounds of his transistor radio.

Mrs. Thompson the Home Science teacher, started and finished the lessons with instructions. Do all your homework every evening, plus one hour's study; two hours in second year, then three hours a night when you are studying for your junior exam. All girls should be in bed by eight pm on school nights as they need their sleep.

At recess Melissa had moaned. 'How is it her business what time we go to bed, is she going to come round to our house and check?'

There was a knock on the bedroom door. 'Don't work too long Jenny, come out and have a glass of milk before you get ready for bed.'

Jennifer snapped shut her books, she had been gazing into space and hadn't done much work at all.

In the kitchen Simon was making himself a cheese sandwich. '…so why can't we have a television, I'm the only one at school who hasn't got one.'

'I find that hard to believe,' said his father 'it's only a few years since TV started in Western Australia; from what programmes I've seen, we're not missing much.'

'You've only seen 'Children's Channel Seven' with that bloke dressed as a lion' laughed Simon.

'Your mother and I don't miss the television at all.'

'Well, only Z Cars,' said Helen 'but I do miss having a library, I wish we hadn't given so many of our books away.'

'We've got a library at school' said her son.

'You never mentioned that.'

'I haven't visited it yet.'

'Nor have I, Mr. Reynolds says we should read, read, read if we want to do well in English.'

'You and Simon could bring books home for me' mused Helen.

'Pony books' said Simon.

'I wonder what they have? Jenny you could get out historical romances, you'd enjoy them as well.'

'Simon, see if they have books on gold mining or explorers' said George.

At school the next day, Jennifer was surprised to find the library looked like a real one, they even had a grumpy librarian. But Miss Sims cheered up when the girl appeared at her desk with the maximum number of books.

'Quite a selection, are you new?'

'Yes, Mr. Reynolds told us to read, read, read and broaden our horizons.' She did not want to reveal the secret plan.

'He tells his class that every year, but not many of his pupils are so keen.'

Coming out of school Jennifer could hardly carry her bag, when they got to the road a horn beeped and Melissa's parents appeared in a battered Volkswagen to take her off on one of their spontaneous outings. Simon was walking out with several girls. She had noticed when he was talking to girls he was always much nicer to her. If he was with the other boys, he gave her a barely perceptible nod of recognition.

'Hey Sis, I'll carry your bag, you haven't got any muscles.' He turned to the older girls. 'I'll show you where we live. This is Jenny, she's the youngest in her class, still eleven, but she's got brains like me.'

The girls giggled, they seemed to find everything Simon said funny. They all trailed along the sandy track and one of the girls asked her about England.

'Simon says he's seen The Beatles.'

Jennifer wanted to add 'only on TV', but kept silent out of family loyalty. That was the strange thing about lies; one could tell people any lie about England and they wouldn't know. If you told some girls you had lived in a castle, they would believe you.

When they got home, their mother was sitting at the kitchen table and was startled when they all came in.

'Mum, I told them how nice your cake is' said Simon.

She roused herself and managed to cut just enough slices, giving Jennifer the last crumbly piece with an apologetic look. Her daughter knew guests must always have the best and made no comment.

Chapter Nineteen   Weekend

The week dragged on; the only appointment Helen could get was two thirty pm on Friday, she should have insisted it was urgent. She did not feel well, perhaps it was the worry; the dragging feeling was still present and even doing the basic chores felt beyond her; washing, cleaning, baking and thinking what to have for dinner.

Jennifer had brought a good selection of books from the school library and Helen lost herself in an historical novel as she ate lunch on Thursday. There had been no letters from home, but at least that absolved her from replying. Next door there was some activity, a car had drawn up, but disappeared after half an hour.

She had got into the habit of bringing the washing in early, otherwise the twins managed to get it wet with the hose. Playing with the hose had the advantage of watering the so called back lawn, but she and George had restricted hose play to feet washing time, conscious of the water metre. Still the grass clumps had not spread and they were pinning their hopes on winter.

Mechanically she served up dinner, but everyone enjoyed it, a new recipe from her magazine. Regular meals that had required no thought in England, had to be discarded because the weather was too hot or she could not get the right vegetables or the same cuts of meat.

This evening the enjoyment of the food put the rest of the family in a good mood; or perhaps a good day had predisposed them to appreciate her cooking. As her mood mellowed she pictured a high chair squeezed into the corner and a Drongo lookalike hoovering up the scraps tossed by a lively toddler, a little girl.

By the time the toddler had outgrown her high chair, perhaps they would have moved to a bigger house or built an extension.

'Mum, can we have our pudding now?'

Helen pulled herself back to reality.

'I don't like fruit salad' said Tony.

'I hate all these funny bits' complained Peter.

'Fruit salad is nice after a big dinner' said Helen.

'Paul's allowed to eat what he likes,' said Simon 'he makes himself something when he's hungry.'

Helen shuddered at the thought of Simon rummaging round the kitchen, helping himself. The previous evening he had devoured the contents of the next day's lunch boxes in a homework snack.

'You're welcome to cook dinner,' said George 'as long as you make enough for six.'

'I think his mother's not well.'

'What's wrong with her?'

'I dunno' he shrugged.

That night Helen was glad was glad to get into bed. George set the alarm early.

'Second week nearly over, they seem to be settling in well.'

'You don't have to get the twins off to school, I do wonder how they're getting on.'

'I'm sure we'd hear if anything was wrong, it's bound to take them a while to settle in.'

'Jenny seems to like school, especially having Melissa as a friend, though she hasn't said much about her family; at least with friends like Christine and Terri we knew the home she was visiting.'

'Melissa's a nice polite girl, I'm sure her family are okay.'

Helen closed her eyes, she wouldn't be able to sleep, but she was tired of talking. George was restless.

'Why didn't you tell me you were worried?'

'About what?' her eyes snapped open.

'Your period being late.'

'How did you know?'

'We've talked about everything else and you haven't been yourself. I should have guessed sooner, it must be ages since we couldn't make love because you had your period and the last week or so you've used every other excuse.'

'I have felt tired and not well' she whispered, motioning him to keep his voice down. 'I didn't want to worry you, with work and the money problems. I was going to tell you after I'd been to the doctors tomorrow.'

'Doctors, you don't think you're pregnant!'

'Ssh, I knew you'd be upset.'

He held her hand. 'I'm not upset, I wouldn't mind six kids, it's your health I'm worried about.'

'It's probably the start of the change, you men are so lucky…'

'If we did have a little Australian we'd manage, what's one more and you are healthy. I reckon the blokes at work would be pretty impressed.'

George, I don't think my mother would be impressed or my friends.

'Who cares what others think, the kids would be tickled pink and Jenny would love to have a sister; they would all help.'

'I think they would rather have a puppy.'

'I should be home before the children, we can talk properly.'

George crept out early without disturbing anyone. Helen reset the alarm hoping to doze for half an hour, but her back ached and she had cramps in her stomach. When she sat up and felt the first warm wetness she pulled off the top sheet relieved to see blood on her nightie, but the amount scared her; she felt so bad she wondered if it was an early miscarriage. She wrapped her dressing gown around her and crept to the bathroom toilet, hoping not to be disturbed, it felt as if her insides were pouring out.

Back in the bedroom she put a towel on the bed, there was more blood on the sheet than she had realised and she could not put it to soak until the children were safely off to school. In twenty minutes she would have to get up, despite the warm weather all she wanted to do was curl up with a hot water bottle.

Somehow she cooked breakfast and persuaded the twins going to school early would be fun, especially with the prospect of the weekend to lighten their mood. She should cancel the doctor's appointment, but was worried about going out as the heavy bleeding continued. If George popped in at lunchtime he could go to the phone box, but she couldn't ask with Joe sitting at the table. She pounded the sheet in the trough and shakily put it out to dry.

George did not come home and after a quick sandwich she roused herself to go to the phone box. Looking out of the kitchen window she saw a woman coming out of the house next door. On any other day she would have left the house and hoped to say hello, now she just wanted to avoid seeing anyone. She felt ridiculous keeping watch, the other woman stood on the sandy kerb looking lost. A man drew up in a car, she greeted him and they went inside, Helen took the opportunity to scurry past.

The doctor's receptionist didn't sound pleased to have a cancellation at such short notice. George was already home when she arrived back.

'Shouldn't you have kept the appointment, supposing it is a miscarriage?'

'Nothing the doctor could do, all I need is another shower and a sit down.'

'Go and lie down, I'll make you a cup of tea and tell the children you're not well. We can have fish and chips for tea. If you're still bad tomorrow perhaps we should call the doctor.'

She hadn't realised how tired she was, till the banging of the fly screen door awoke her and she heard the twins' exclamations of surprise to find their father in the kitchen. They crept in melodramatically to see how she was. Peter showed her his English book with a gold star for his story which he read to her; a lyrical description of Sir Peter fighting off a giant snake in the wild bush. Tony had brought home a letter from his teacher.

'What does it say?'

'I don't know, Dad's reading it.'

Jennifer brought her in a new library book; Helen perused the back. It was a 'heartwarming story' about a rescued puppy and his new family.

George brought her aspirins, the only medicine they had in the house.

'I couldn't face fish and chips, you have yours.'

'I'll make you vegemite on toast,' said her daughter 'that's what Melissa gets her Mum when she's got a migraine. If she gets home from school and her mother's in bed, she has to tip-toe around.'

Helen wouldn't wish ill health upon anyone, but was comforted to think of other mothers not coping.

George insisted she spend Saturday in bed.

'Don't be ridiculous, I'm not ill.'

'Jenny and Simon have offered to go to Tom the Cheap and cook tea tonight, make the most of it, may never happen again.'

George was tidying up the kitchen when John turned up unexpectedly in the 'ute'. Helen could hear the men talking on the veranda.

'Vonny's working today and the girls have gone into Perth, ideal opportunity to bring this lot round.'

She wondered what he had brought.

'Lucky I've got a free day, Helen's in bed not well.'

'That's not like her, what's the matter?'

'Women's trouble.'

'Ahh'.

It seemed she would have to stay in bed to avoid explanations. There was much clanking around, then George tiptoed in and started rummaging around in his drawer.

'John's brought round some timber he picked up cheap, I was hoping we had enough cash in the house so I could pay him back, before he has a chance to refuse. We're going to make a start on the side gate; when they get back from the shops Simon can help and Jenny can put the kettle on.'

Jennifer brought her in a cup of tea and a sandwich.

'Can I go round Melissa's now? I've made everyone a picnic.'

'Yes of course, did you get on alright at the shops?'

249

'Yes, we bought loads of stuff, you'll get a surprise at teatime.'

When the twins came in they announced they were 'goffas'.

'Uncle John says we have to go for this and go for that.'

Everyone was coping fine without Helen and she felt slightly miffed, but it was nice to have nothing to do except lie in bed. She was still bleeding heavily and crept back and forth to the bathroom.

When she heard loud voices floating through the window, she realised she must have slept all afternoon.

'I put my foot down and said no working on Sundays, that's a family day. So if we have a barbeque, they won't have to cook Sunday dinner.'

'Is Drongo coming' said Tony.

'Of course, one of his favourite places.'

She wondered what they were planning, the last thing she felt like doing tomorrow was going out and having a barbeque.

George came in and sat on the edge of the bed. 'Nice surprise for you, we're going to meet John and Yvonne for a barbeque and swim tomorrow, Lake Leschenaultia. It's up in the hills so I knew you'd like that; we'll take the picnic chairs so all you have to do is sit in the shade and you can talk about women's things with Yvonne.'

'The children will enjoy that, how did you get on with the carpentry?'

'All done, except a few finishing touches such as hinges and bolts. We didn't work that hard, too hot. Simon's turning out to be quite a carpenter. Sorry, I forgot to ask you if you were feeling better.'

'Yes.' She had heard tales of menopausal women 'flooding' and needing to go to hospital for a blood transfusion, how would she know if she was okay?

The lake was serene and the setting pretty; for the first time Helen yearned to go in the water and wished she knew how to swim. She resolved to learn by next summer.

With so much going on the twins left her in peace to read her book, the shade and just being near water brought relief from the heat. January and February were the hottest months of the year John said.

Yvonne came over to wrap a towel around herself.

'I'm getting too old for all this stuff.'

'Nonsense, I'm determined to be swimming by next summer, though I don't think I'll ever enjoy being splashed.'

'Is your not going in the water today a good sign?'

'Very good sign, yesterday morning; I didn't feel too good but it's a great weight off our minds.'

'What did the doctor say?'

She had to admit she hadn't seen him.

'You left that a bit late.'

Helen felt irritated and wanted to change the subject, luckily the men came out to get dried and start the barbeque. Drongo was getting over-excited and running around shaking the water off his fur; another picnicking family looked at her accusingly. Simon was showing off to the girls and they were all trying to do handstands in the water, she didn't know how they could bear to put their heads under the water.

The Charles' family 'esky' was bottomless as usual and Helen worried their contribution was very paltry. The kitchen had been in disarray when she entered this morning and her meal plans for the week would have to be re-arranged.

This time she resolved to enjoy the meal. She could understand why Australian wives liked barbeques; men who wouldn't dream of going in the kitchen to cook, loved presiding over blackened racks and smoky fires. John whistled to Drongo, who ignored him. He was lured with a piece of meat and tied up so everyone could eat in peace, including other families.

The children sat on rugs and Tony declared it was their camp.

'This is an artificial lake, you know' said John. Helen felt slightly cheated, she had imagined early settlers trekking up in the heat and coming upon the lovely expanse of water unexpectedly. 'They needed it to water their steam engines... Hey boys, don't feed that greedy mutt any more.' Helen looked up to see the twins feeding the dog what would have been tomorrow's dinner, she wondered if they had eaten anything themselves. 'What sort of dog are you going to get Jenny then?'

'If,' said Helen 'we haven't decided to get one yet.'

'But she has been good not mentioning it,' said George 'she just brings home lots of books like 'Training Your New Puppy' and 'Keeping a Great Dane.'

'You want to get a Bitzer said Yvonne.

Helen was having trouble eating and talking; another barbeque problem had revealed itself, they were plagued with flies. You had to wave them away as the food approached your mouth.

'The West Australian salute' laughed John. 'That's where the Aussie accent comes from, have to speak with your mouth closed so the flies don't get in.' Helen thought wistfully of roast dinners on a cold winter's day after church. The outing had deferred the decision of where to go to church.

---o0o---

Jennifer was enjoying their Sunday out; that was the fun thing about Terri's family, they always had good ideas for outings; days out that turned into an adventure. Terri's family did not worry about should they go to church, did they have enough food for a picnic, would it be too far to drive or too hot when they got there; they just went.

She and Terri had lots to talk about. Jennifer's days at the primary school seemed as remote as her four years at St. Stephen's junior school, but she enjoyed hearing Mr. Gregson's latest stories. Trish treated her more like an equal now she was at high school and was amused to hear of the things that happened to her and Melissa. Jennifer was also trying to hear what the adults were saying, especially when she heard dogs being mentioned.

Her steak in a bread roll was not easy to eat, the bread black and soggy and the meat tough, she wondered how Trish ate hers so daintily. Terri had tomato sauce running down her wrists and the twins had it all round their faces; they sneaked the meat over to Drongo and just ate the bread. Simon was already putting more sausages on to cook.

After eating, the adults sat dozing, but her parents were alert enough to look at their watches and say 'One hour's not up yet' if they tried to sneak into the water.

'Can't we just paddle?' asked Jennifer.

Simon was in the twins' and parents' good book today. He made the boys rafts out of twigs. Uncle John had an endless supply of useful things in the car; balls of string and pen knives.

When they got back in the water Trish helped Tony to swim and Simon was holding Peter up; it was more a competition with each other. Trish held both arms in the air, with the water up to her neck, to show she was not supporting Tony. He was splashing along by himself. When Simon took his arm from under

Peter his legs dropped and he grabbed his brother in panic. Both boys' pride was bruised.

Jennifer felt suddenly defensive. 'It will happen soon Peter, when you're not expecting it, like riding your bike.'

Simon had already started a new game which sent Drongo paddling furiously in circles; swinging Tony round then throwing him in the water. Jennifer and Peter gasped as he went under, but he emerged laughing.

'That boy's got no fear' said Uncle John, who had waded in to reassure their mother fratricide wasn't being committed.

Simon ducked under the water and rose up with Tony on his shoulders.

'Uncle John, can I go on your shoulders' Peter pleaded. When he was up he begged not to be thrown off.

'Hang on tight and we can defeat them, just wait for my signal.'

After lots of splashing they caught Tony unawares and Peter knocked him into the water.

'Okay boys, you're even now, ten minutes and we have to pack up.'

Jennifer was relieved when her mother came in to paddle. With all the drama of Friday and Saturday, she had wondered if there was something seriously wrong. In their class was a girl called Nicola whose mother had died a year ago. Everyone knew about it, though the girl never talked of it and there were several versions of how she met her untimely demise. Jennifer thought mothers only died young in the olden days; she couldn't imagine her mother not being there.

She took her daughter's hand. 'I'd better stay in the shallows, I just wanted to cool off before we get back in the hot car. Has Tony really learnt to swim?'

'Mum, Mum watch' Tony waded out deep then kicked his legs; paddling furiously to where Simon was cupping his hands and providing a diving platform for Trish and Terri.

Jenny was not sure she trusted her big brother, but her mother hadn't seen her dive yet. It was more of a plunge, but her mother seemed impressed by anything that involved going under the water.

Monday of week three and all the teachers were on a hard work campaign, especially the Social Studies B teacher, Mr. Tonkin, who was old and stern. Their lessons often started with a lecture on behaviour and the responsibility of being a top class.

As they wrote notes and copied diagrams from the blackboard, he paced up and down between the desks making comments.

'How do you expect anyone to read that writing?... Have you never heard of a ruler?'

It was a ruler that Melissa was looking for in her bag, which was still on her desk. Suddenly the bag went flying as Mr. Tonkin swept it off the desk.

'Bags go under the desk and you have everything out ready before the lesson starts.'

At lunchtime the girls giggled about the incident. Jennifer and Melissa were often in a small group now; other girls who didn't go to the canteen, girls who didn't like sport or who went the same way home.

Jennifer had to go straight home to supervise the twins; her parents were going to the primary school to see Tony's teacher. Melissa came with her as she thought it would be fun. The two girls walked through the gap in the new fence, past the gate propped up waiting for its hinges; they were surprised to hear a dog barking. There was no sign of the twins.

When she called out they emerged from behind the tree at the end of the yard; jumping up excitedly round them was a black shaggy dog.

'Jenny, Jenny we found a dog.'

The dog wagged its tail and bounced up to Jennifer and licked her hands. Melissa was giggling.

'He must belong to someone,' said Jennifer 'we'll have to take him home.'

'But we don't know where he lives, he's lost and he likes it here.'

The dog licked their faces in acknowledgement. It had no collar, he could leave voluntarily, but that seemed unlikely.

She wondered what her parents' reaction would be. That might depend on how her mother was feeling, what sort of day her father had had at work and what Tony's teacher wanted to see them about. On the good side they could keep him and they would save money not buying a puppy.

'Just tell your parents he walked into the garden' suggested Melissa. 'He'll probably wander back home soon.'

'But if he doesn't want to go we can keep him' said Tony.

'We haven't got any dog food' said Peter.

'Water is what he needs.' said Melissa 'his tongue's hanging out.'

'We need a drink' pleaded the boys.

'Don't let the dog in, you get your drinks and I'll find a bowl to put some water in.'

The dog stood whining and pawing at the fly screen door so Jennifer put the bowl out and sent the boys out with their milk and biscuits to keep him happy.

The girls sat at the kitchen table with glasses of cordial and ice cubes.

'He doesn't look like a sheep dog or a guard dog' said Melissa.

They went in the bedroom to look at Jennifer's 'Observer's Book of Dogs'. He did not resemble any breed illustrated.

When they went outside to see if the dog had gone the boys were sitting on the terrace watching the dog licking out the bowl.

'We gave him some dinner.'

'What?' asked their sister.

'We found some raw meat in the fridge, that's what dogs eat. Uncle John said all dogs are descended from wolves.'

Jennifer was very worried. 'Mum will be furious, that was probably our dinner.'

'You could buy some more' said her friend hopefully.

'We haven't got any money and she buys the meat at the butcher's in Victoria Park.'

'I've got an idea,' said Melissa 'we'll take the dog out and he can lead us back to where he lives. The owners will be pleased and you can tell your parents you've done a good turn.'

'I expect we'll get a reward' Peter said excitedly.

'Then we could give it to Mum to pay for the meat' announced his sister.

'He doesn't look a very valuable dog,' warned Melissa 'I don't suppose they'll give us anything.'

The dog bounded round them happily as the boys led the party back to the spot in the bush where they found him.

'Now stand still quietly and give him a chance to use his homing instinct.'

The dog lay down contentedly at their feet.

'Let's walk towards Palmer Street,' suggested Jennifer 'that's where the nearest houses are.'

'We could knock on the doors and ask people.'

'No Peter, we're not allowed to knock on strangers' doors, but if we walk slowly up the road his owners might be out looking for him.'

The dog walked contentedly behind them and showed no sign of recognising any houses. Jennifer looked worriedly at her watch.

'Mum and Dad might be back soon.'

'We'll go back and hope he doesn't follow us, but if he does we'll make some lost dog posters.'

Melissa always had good ideas and made everything sound simple and logical. It was also helpful to have a friend present when parents were likely to get cross; they would be too polite to tell Jennifer off in front of her friend.

They tried telling the dog to go home, but he stuck to their legs like glue until he heard a sharp whistle.

Chapter Twenty   Twins

George dashed into the shower as soon as he got home from work.

'Do you think I should wear a suit?'

'Not in this weather, you're not going for a job interview. All the teachers wear shorts according to the children.'

'Perhaps you should take me shopping, I need some smart dress shorts.'

Tony's teacher looked as if he had just left school, but it didn't stop Helen feeling nervous at being summoned to the school. He shook their hands and offered Helen the teacher's chair. He and George had to perch on the children's desks.

'Tony's quite a character, I've never taught twins, but I gather from Peter's teacher they are very different.'

'Yes and different again from how their older brother was.'

'You've not had problems with your older son?'

'No, he's done very well at school, grammar school, then he took his junior exams when we'd just arrived' said George. 'He wants to be a teacher.'

'More fool him' laughed the teacher. George frowned and the teacher cleared his throat. 'Peter's teacher is very pleased with him, quiet, but works hard.'

'So what is the problem with Tony' asked Helen.

'Very bright, answers all the questions before anyone else gets a chance, but at the end of the lesson his page is blank, he has trouble putting pen to paper.'

'That's why we liked them being in the same class, Peter spurred Tony on to do his work' said George.

'Is there a possibility Peter did the work for him?'

'Oh no, they wouldn't cheat' said Helen.

'I wouldn't call it cheating, they're little kids; team work, Tony provided the answers and Peter wrote them down, twice. In England was it suggested they be in separate classes?'

'There was only one class for each year, forty children; it was a very good school, Church of England.'

He didn't seem impressed.

'Large class, the teacher couldn't watch everyone... his reading age is above average, I thought we should sort this problem out early, we need to know if he can't or won't write.'

Helen felt the honour of St. Stephen's was at stake, not to mention their reputation as parents. Why did she feel like a naughty school girl in front of someone young enough to be her son?

He must have read her thoughts. 'We've got some good English kids in this school, including your sons. I'm going to set a small task for each lesson, one paragraph, a page of sums. If I give him one homework exercise each evening, you could make sure he does it by himself.'

'I'm sure once he settles in to his new school he'll be fine' said George.

'No I think Mr. Reed is right, when was the last time we saw Tony write? He draws and Peter writes. Thank you for taking the trouble.'

'That's okay, it would be a shame for him to waste his potential.'

'He's only known Tony for two weeks' said George, as they trekked down the sandy tracks of the unmade road.

'Sometimes it takes an outsider to see things clearly, we'll give Tony the benefit of the doubt and see how he gets on. I suppose Mr. Reed is new and enthusiastic.'

As they turned into Smith Street an old battered Holden screeched by.

'Young drivers, there're too many of them here' said George.

'I could have sworn that was Simon in the back seat' said Helen.

'What would he be doing in a car, anyway he's got cricket practice today.'

'Yes, he'll be disappointed if he doesn't make it on the team.'

'You don't suppose it's because he's English?'

'Simon?'

'No, Tony, perhaps the teacher's biased.'

'No, he said the English children got on well; I expect Australian parents get letters as well.'

When they walked round to the back yard there was no sign of any children.

'That's strange, what's my kitchen bowl doing on the terrace?'

Unlocking the back door, the empty glasses and bags thrown on the floor were evidence the children had been home.

'I'm sure they'll be back by teatime,' said George 'maybe Jenny's taken them round to Melissa's house.'

'No Jenny said she was coming round here, she loves playing with the twins.'

George peered over the fence, there was no sign of them in the bush; he gave the family whistle, a piercing sound the children always obeyed and which Simon had only just learnt to imitate. Within seconds a streak of black flew into the garden and a shaggy dog jumped up to greet them.

'Where on earth did he come from, good thing the children aren't here, they'd want to keep him' said George.

'Maybe he's from next door, I'm not sure if anyone's moved in.'

'Shall we take him round there?"

'Supposing he's not theirs and they don't like dogs? We haven't introduced ourselves properly.'

The dog was sitting at their feet wagging his tail, but jumped up as soon as the children appeared.

'Liquorice knew your whistle' said Peter excitedly.

'Liquorice?'

'Yes, that's what we decided to call him; we rescued him, can we keep him?'

The children explained their attempts to return him.

'I'm sure he's got a home, the Australian dogs are allowed out to wander, he'll go home this evening as long as we don't feed him. It's a good thing I bought the hinges and bolts for the gate.'

'So he can't run away?' said Tony hopefully.

'No, so he can't get in.'

'He's so friendly,' said Helen 'he must be a family dog, there might be another little boy wondering where he is.'

'What have we got for tea Mum' asked Peter.

'Macaroni cheese, I thought we'd better have something quick as Dad and I have been out.'

'Oh, that's good.'

Helen was surprised, she thought it was Peter who didn't like cheese.

Jennifer and Melissa disappeared into the bedroom to make the 'Lost' posters and George sent the boys to stay at the front of the house, in the hope that the dog would walk off up the road.

'I'll measure the gate and start fixing the hinges, Simon can help me hang it when he comes home.'

Helen was already busy grating cheese. '...and we thought Drongo was boisterous, I don't think I could cope with a dog. Though I always wanted one when I was young, I'd nearly talked Mum and Dad round when the war started.'

'When Jenny gets her puppy we'll train it to be obedient.'

Helen wondered with a smile if Tony and Liquorice had concocted a plan to divert attention from his school work. Jenny wanted Melissa to stay for tea.

'Won't your mother wonder where you are?'

'No, she knows I'm coming round here.'

Simon had still not arrived home. George opened the fly screen door ajar and made the boys slip through before the dog could get in. When they peeped out of the lounge window he was sitting to attention on the veranda.

George brought the stool from Helen's dressing table to make up seven seats and the twins fought over who was going to sit on it. Helen felt an unexpected pang; they could have made room for another child.

When Simon rushed in the back door, the dog was even quicker and slipped under the kitchen table.

'Simon, we found a dog' said Tony triumphantly.

'Do you know anyone with a dog like that?' asked Helen hopefully.

'No… he's an ugly old mongrel.'

The other children leapt to the defence of Liquorice.

'Can't he stay just one night?' pleaded Peter.

'It wouldn't be fair for him to get used to us,' said his father 'he'll be gone by morning.'

The only way to get him out of the house was for the boys to race into the back yard and hope he followed. The boys were slipped back in and the back door locked. They could hear him whining pitifully. When Melissa was ready to go home he appeared at the front door seconds before they opened it.

'I hope he doesn't follow you dear.'

'I've always wanted a dog, I could ask if I could have him… only if you don't want to keep him.'

She set off up the road, but Liquorice remained at the front door, scratching at the fly screen.

George and Simon sneaked out of the back door to try and hang the gate before the light failed; the dog was at their side, trying to help. When they tested the bolt he was locked inside the back yard with them. The dog was quickly pushed out and the gate closed again.

Indoors Jennifer and the twins were gathered at the lounge window.

'Come away from the window, close the curtains now and don't on any account open the front door. If we ignore him he'll get bored and wander home.'

'This is like being under siege,' laughed Simon 'I wonder if he'll send for reinforcements.'

'Imagine if he went off to fetch the 101 Dalmations' said Jennifer.

---oOo---

When Jennifer woke up she could hear her father talking in the hall.

'How does he know I'm going out? He's sitting waiting by the car.'

Jennifer got up.

'You're up early, your dog kept us awake half the night, whining.'

'He's not mine, the twins found him, or rather he found us; he's decided we're his family.'

'We don't even know what they do with stray dogs here' said her mother. 'Can we take him to a police station? Where is the police station?'

'Don't worry, once the children have gone to school he'll get bored and wander home.'

'What if he follows us to school?'

'I can't take him to work, sorry to leave you with all the trouble Helen.'

'Don't run him over when you go out Dad.'

At breakfast the twins asked if they should take one of Jennifer's 'Lost' posters to school.

'Yes and I could take the other one; I wonder where we'd be allowed to put it up, perhaps Melissa could ask, she's good at asking things.'

'If Liquorice follows us to school,' said Tony 'we can ask if he belongs to anyone.'

'I hope he doesn't follow me' said Simon. 'If he does, he might get stuffed and put in the science lab.'

'Simon!' frowned Helen.

'But I have seen a stuffed dog, at a railway station.'

'I thought you would be too young to remember that, you are right.' She turned to the boys. 'He was a lovely dog that died of old age; all the passengers loved him, he used to collect money in a box for charity. When he died they thought that would be a good way to remember him.'

'Taxidermy' said Simon.

'Taxiwhat?' asked Peter.

'I've seen a stuffed tiger in the natural history museum' added Jennifer.

'But Liquorice won't really be stuffed will he?' pleaded Tony.

Jennifer looked at the clock. 'I'm going to be late, bags the bathroom first.'

But Simon beat her to it. She wandered into the lounge. The windowsill was low and the dog was on the veranda with his paws on the window ledge and his nose pressed against the glass. If he followed her to school she could pretend she had never seen him before. Mr. Reynolds hadn't said there was a rule about not taking dogs to school, but there probably was.

'Do you think Dad would be cross if I gave him some scraps,' said her mother 'he must be very hungry by now.'

'Good idea,' said her daughter 'feed him when we're ready to go and he will want to stay here.'

They had reckoned without the speed at which he ate. As the children walked up the road, he soon caught them up and when he saw Melissa at the corner he rushed to greet her like a long lost friend.

There was no fence or wall to stop Liquorice roaming around either school. Jennifer knew dogs could follow your scent trail, there was no way of hiding from him. She sent the twins into their playground and called the dog away from the primary school. Other children stared; the dog circled the girls delightedly as they crossed the oval. Jennifer wished he would follow someone else.

'Have you got the poster?' said Melissa. 'If we put it up by the canteen, lots of people will see it.'

'We'd better ask first.'

'No, it doesn't have your name on, only your address. I brought durex so we can stick it up.'

The dog's nose twitched as he smelt meat pies. While he was busy sniffing the litter bins, they dashed to their classroom. By the time they were lined up, he had joined them.

'Just look straight ahead' whispered Melissa.

Mr. Reynolds arrived at the classroom door. 'Hmm, a new class member; anyone know who he belongs to?'

There was silence. Jennifer felt herself turning red.

'Wayne, you're big enough to block the door, stand guard and make sure he doesn't get in, then you can go and fetch the caretaker.'

The class filed in, giggling.

'Okay, settle down, he's probably got more brains than most of you.'

When Wayne came back, Mr. Reynolds told him to get out his books. There was no sound of Liquorice.

At morning recess the notices on the PA system made no mention of dogs and outside in the quadrangle there was no sign of him.

Melissa and Jennifer walked home, debating what the caretaker might have done with him. Simon came over with Paul; tall and skinny, his face was quite scarred with acne and he always looked a bit scary to Jennifer.

'Paul liked your poster, but the deputy head took it down at lunchtime.'

Paul spoke. 'We had a good laugh this morning, the caretaker was trying to catch the dog with a rope, but he ran off.'

'So he'll be lost again?'

'We're going to hunt for him, Paul knows someone who wants to buy a dog.'

'You can't sell him, he's not yours.'

'If he hasn't got a collar and a licence he can't be anybody's' said the other boy. 'We're doing him a favour, finding him a good home.'

'If Liquorice is back at our house, keep him there, Paul knows where he can borrow a collar and lead.'

Melissa had to go to her aunt's for tea, sorry to miss the dog hunt.

When Jennifer arrived home she was relieved to see the dog sitting in front of the house chewing a bone and the twins on the veranda watching him. Her mother came out, quickly closing the fly screen behind her.

'Did he follow you to school? He was back here by 9.15, he came with me to the Greek shop; they didn't know anyone who'd lost him, but they gave him a ham bone, he carried it all the way home.'

Jennifer told her about Simon's plan. When he arrived back by himself, he had his arm behind his back. When the dog rushed to greet him he slipped the collar on.

'Don't forget to tell them his owner might be looking for him and certainly don't take any money' said Helen.

'Don't worry, it's Paul's aunty and she's got plenty of money. Her dog just died, so she's going to be pleased.'

Liquorice walked trustingly by Simon's side up the road. Jennifer was envious he was taking him for a proper walk. Their father pulled up in the car at that moment.

'I'm sure it's for the best, we'll get a dog of our own soon, a puppy.'

'Really, really?' said Tony.

'Perhaps at Easter' added their mother.

Jennifer thought the time for getting a dog kept moving further away, they had the gate up, so they were ready.

'Half an hour till tea.'

Jennifer mooched in her bedroom; when she was sent to see where the boys were, they emerged from the bush carrying something.

'We're detectives' said Tony, holding aloft a dog collar. 'It was hanging on a bush.'

The collar was fastened and had two metal discs attached. Their father examined it.

'He must have got his collar snagged and managed to pull out of it.' He read the tags. 'Shire of Glendale, dog licence and a medal with an address, 35, King Street, that's quite a long way, especially if it's the other end. I could drive up and find the house.'

'…and tell them we've given their dog away?' said Helen.

'We don't know this belonged to Liqu…that dog.'

'We could go searching to see if there's another lost dog' said Tony hopefully.

'After tea I'll go and see them, he must be well cared for and they will be worried. When Simon gets back he can tell us the address he took him to.'

They finished eating with no sign of Simon.

'Perhaps he went to Paul's house for tea' suggested Jennifer.

'Do you know where he lives?'

'Near the Great Eastern Highway I think, he's one of the boys Simon met at Bayswater.'

'We'll put Simon's in the oven. I'll clear the table so Tony can sit and do his homework.'

'What do you have to do?' asked his sister.

'A little story about something that happened at home.'

'You can write about Liquorice.'

'I don't know the end of that story' he sighed.

'Just start it and see how you get on,' said his father 'Jennifer's going to do her homework. Mum and I are going to sit in the lounge and have our cigarettes, Peter can sit with us and read his book.'

Jennifer felt as disinclined to do homework as Tony; after ten minutes she rushed out when she heard voices and joined her parents at the window.

Simon was trailing wearily down the driveway with Liquorice happily at his side. With his lead on it was safe to open the front door. The dog greeted them as if he had been away for weeks.

'Turn's out Paul's Auntie's dog that died was a stupid Pekingese. She said she's not ready for another dog yet and certainly not a boisterous mongrel.'

'That's understandable, it's not your fault; Paul should have asked her first.'

'I thought you'd be annoyed, what's the joke?'

'We're detectives' said Tony, telling the story.

'Come on, let's go' said his father. 'If the dog wanted to get in the car yesterday I reckon he'll happily jump in the back.'

'Can I come' said Jennifer.

'We've got to come' pleaded the twins.

'Yes… boys make sure the dog behaves and Jenny look out for the street numbers.'

Liquorice was enjoying the new adventure. Jennifer showed him the collar to see if he recognised it, but as he wagged his tail at any attention, it was hard to tell. Number thirty five was at the other end of the street; a neat new house with a chain link fence at the front and a letter box by the little gate.

'Boys stay with the dog, Jennifer come with me. We don't want to worry them with a strange man on the doorstep.'

'Why would they be worried?'

'I might be a travelling salesman trying to part them with their money.'

'Or a burglar?'

'Yes, so if we're not home you should always look out the window and don't open the door to strangers.'

When a woman opened the door she was surprised; her face fell when she saw the empty collar, but before George had finished explaining, she had looked past him to see the dog sticking his head out of the front window.

'Rover!' she called in an English accent.

She kissed Jennifer and nearly kissed George before dashing out to the car. When George opened the car door, the dog ignored the twins and leapt out to lick her face.

'Come inside and meet the boys, my poor husband's out searching for him this very moment.' Two boys, older than the twins, appeared. 'We brought him out from England, he had to stay in quarantine for six months, like a prisoner. We felt so guilty, but he never blamed us at all. I suppose everything's still strange for him… no idea how he got out of the back yard.'

'We called him Liquorice' said Peter.

'Can you guess why my son wanted to name him Rover?'

'After the boring reading books?' suggested Jennifer.

She nodded. 'Boys, go and get the lollies out.' She handed them round to the children, the sort they weren't usually allowed to have, because they were bad for their teeth. 'A little reward for finding Rover.'

Jennifer hoped Peter wouldn't ask why they weren't getting a proper reward. Her father was obviously thinking the same and quickly started talking before Peter could.

'Which part of England are you from?'

'Buckinghamshire.'

'Is that where the Queen lives' asked Tony.

276

'No that's Buckingham Palace' his brother dug him in the ribs.

'The Queen has lots of houses, but she didn't live near us' laughed the woman. 'One year exactly we've been here. You must write down your address and I'll write and thank your wife.'

With the address written, George started backing the children out of the house.

'Homework to be done…'

'We should have got a real reward' said Tony, as they drove off.

'You shouldn't expect money for helping people son, just be pleased Rover' is back with his family and you have an end for your story.'

Chapter Twenty One   Dogs

Won day we fond a dog.

That was all Tony had written in his book. It had been a hopeless evening for homework, but how could Mr. Reed understand life in the Palmer household? Likewise Helen could not imagine having Tony and a whole class to teach. She resolved future evenings would be better organised and devoted to her son.

George came into the kitchen.

'Are the twins asleep?' she asked.

'Yes, Jenny's reading in bed and Simon's in the shower. Come and sit outside; at least we're not under siege any more, well only from the mosquitoes. Let's have a cigarette before I start the mossie hunt.'

George had taken to hunting and swatting the mosquitoes before bedtime. Sometimes when he scored a direct hit the bloody mark left on the white plaster wall proved the insects had been feeding on some poor person.

'We should do this more often, it's cool out here and quiet… There's a light on next door.'

'I should go and knock, just say hello, without being pushy… I rather miss Liquorice, it was company having him around, he settled down when we were by ourselves. I was beginning to think it would be easier to keep him than work out what to do.'

'So we'd better start looking out for a puppy.'

'A puppy would be a lot more work.'

'Are you still feeling off colour?'

'I think things are returning to normal, but I feel so washed out.'

'I've got Thursday off; we'll go into Perth, wander round the gardens, have a leisurely lunch at Boans.'

'That would be lovely; I'll still have to go to Vic Park tomorrow. I know I was only out of the kitchen for a couple of days and we had the barbeque, but I was sure I had enough meat in the fridge for this week.'

On Wednesday morning there was no one waiting at the bus stop. Helen had made a resolution to talk to someone each day, get to know who lived locally. The house next door had the blinds pulled down with no sign of life. Perhaps if anyone was living there they had gone to work early.

On the bus she listened to people chatting; they were either going to Victoria Park or Perth, there wasn't really anywhere else to go. She got out her notebook; she hadn't had a chance to make a shopping list and she needed to work out how much money to take out of the bank, the minimum they could manage with. They were now passing older houses; streets with trees and pavements. With only two houses in their section of the street, they were unlikely to see improvements, but if they built more houses it would spoil the outlook and the twins would be devastated to loose their wild playground.

Suddenly her notebook and pen went flying and there was a loud thud; the driver had slammed on his brakes. There was a disgruntled murmur.

'Sorry folks, someone didn't give way to the right.' He was already out of his seat. 'I'll go and have a look.'

There were more murmurings as everyone looked out of the windows. Two cars had collided at the intersection, one was upside down. Neighbours were already coming out of their houses and one was heading for the phone box.

'Stay on board everybody, looks like there's enough help.'

Helen felt quite shaky and was amazed when a young man climbed out of the upside down car laughing; the other driver approached him looking relieved. The bus driver climbed back on board.

'Nothing broken, young idiots, they were very lucky.'

Helen shuddered; a year or so and Simon would want to learn to drive.

That evening at tea they all wondered how Liquorice/Rover was getting on and had suggestions for Tony's story. Mr. Reed had enjoyed the boy telling him about the dog and was determined that Tony should get it down on paper. But the twins were more interested in their next project.

'We're going to be private detectives,' said Peter 'we can put posters up at the shops and if anyone loses their dog, or purse or bike we can go and look for evidence.'

When the table was cleared Helen sat down to write a letter, hoping to encourage Tony to write alongside.

Dear Joyce,

> *The weather is still hot, so easy to get the washing dry and there are not many clothes to wash, the children don't even need to wear a jumper. Do you remember that time my washing line broke and all George's shirts ended up in the mud? I don't have any whites to wash; Jennifer has her school dress, the boys wear grey and George has his uniform.*

Why did she always end up writing about washing?

> *Jennifer still wants a dog, we had a bit of an adventure this week...*

She looked up from her letter; Tony was sitting with his pencil poised in the air.

'I can't think what to write next.'

Helen looked at the page, he had added four more words.

We cold him Licrish

On Thursday morning Helen stood at the sink washing up and looking at the house next door. The milkman came early, before the temperature rose and people took their milk in the moment they got up; it was impossible to tell by milk bottles if anyone was living at a house.

George came up behind her and hugged her.

'Can't remember the last time we were by ourselves. We don't have to rush into Perth, we could have a leisurely morning.'

'Oh George, it's not… I haven't finished bleeding.'

'I know, that doesn't mean we can't have a cuddle. As long as you're feeling okay, I wish you had been to the doctors to make sure.'

'We've been lucky no one's needed the doctor yet, one less bill to worry about.'

'I suppose it's just as well you're not pregnant, I don't think we could cope with a new baby and Tony's homework… right, no more talk about children, this is our day off.'

As George backed the car out of the driveway Helen thought she saw someone step back inside next door.

'Not another mystery neighbour' he laughed. 'If someone's moved in they can come and knock at our door. Right, shall we park down by the river today?'

'We mustn't ever take this for granted' said Helen as they stood looking out across the wide water. 'Do you remember our first visit to Perth? The sky seems bigger here. It would have been nice to live by the river.'

'You do like our house don't you?'

'Of course, it's just sometimes…'

'What?'

'Oh nothing… I never ask you if you're still enjoying your job. I worry you work too hard; if you've had enough you could look around for something else.'

'You mean something better paid.'

'No I don't mean that; things are bound to get easier later on, when we've paid off the HP.'

'I am still enjoying it except when it gets too hot in the middle of the day or we get the grumpy shopkeeper... yesterday when we went to Gianni's he started talking to Joe in Italian, so I knew he had a complaint. They both stood there waving their arms around getting angry, then they slapped each other on the back all smiles again. I wonder what everyone at the office would say if they could see me humping out boxes full of vegetables? Remember wrapping up to leave the office in the dark to walk to Waterloo? No regrets.'

'I didn't get a chance to tell you; we had some drama on the bus yesterday.' She described the accident.

'They were jolly lucky, that's what I mean about these young drivers; they all seem to get cars as soon as they've got their licences. We saw a nasty accident the other day.'

'You didn't tell me.'

'Didn't want to say in front of the children and you didn't notice I'd had to get a new shirt from the depot. Joe was quite impressed with my first aid. You don't forget, even after twenty years; it almost looked like a battle scene, but it was a shock when you're not expecting it. There wasn't much I could do and the ambulance was soon there. I think one of them must have died; it was on the front page of the newspaper, he was only nineteen.'

'Oh George, that's dreadful; even if you're driving safely, if someone shoots across without looking…'

'Come on, let's talk about more cheerful things. Jenny's looking forward to her weekend with Terri.'

'Yes, quite an adventure going into Perth on the bus by herself; it will be strange without her and you working on Saturday.'

Friday would be busy, catching up on housework and washing after the day out. Saturday would be the rush to Tom the Cheap before it closed at midday, but Saturday afternoon, what was there to do in Glendale by herself at the weekend? She would be at home anyway; the twins had invited their friend round to play. Since seeing his name written on his school book, they had realised it was Wayne not Wine, though they still called him Wine as a joke.

'What are you worrying about now?' asked George.

'Nothing… the twins.'

'Perhaps we worry about Tony too much. You see immigrants arriving who don't even speak English, let alone write it, but they work hard and get on well.'

'Yes, but as Tony is English, won't employers expect him to be able to write it?'

'Perhaps he and Peter will go into business together. Tony could do the hard work. Or he could be a brickie, there's always plenty of work in the building trade, earn good money apparently. Come on, I'm hungry, let's head for the big city.'

'We haven't heard from your mother lately George, you did write to her?'

'Yes, posted it last week or was it the week before, I'll drop a line to Dennis, ask him if everything's okay.'

'Maybe it's beginning to sink in, not seeing us at Christmas, realising she's never going to see us again. It's that time of year in England; February is such a depressing month, grey and dreary. Once we had Jenny's birthday I used to feel spring was on the way.'

'Doesn't sound as if your Mum and Dad have the winter blues.'

'No, their last letter was very perky, I think my sister's love life has given them something new to think about; Reginald this and Reg that, I just hope they aren't reading too much into it, sounds as if he's very fond of them, taking them to restaurants and outings in his car.'

'He must be keen on your sister.'

'It's hard to tell from her few letters how keen she is on him, but then she never was the sort for girly chats. Isn't it strange to think of life going on without us. Joyce is going to start doing Tupperware parties.'

'Joyce doing Tupperware! Will Clive mind her going out in the evenings?'

'I don't think he believed she'd pass her driving test, but he doesn't need the car in the evenings. She reckons all the money she earns will go straight into saving for a holiday, not into the housekeeping.'

'Will you mind much if we don't go away at Easter? If we've got a new puppy we'll be busy and there are plenty of places we haven't been to for days out.'

'As long as you have some time off I'll be happy.'

---o0o---

Jennifer was up early on Saturday morning, checking her duffel bag yet again.

'You're only staying one night' said her mother.

'I don't want to forget my bathers.'

'You will be careful in the sea won't you?'

When the bus pulled up at St. George's Terrace she was relieved to see Terri, Trish and another girl waiting for her; they were planning to see 'Mary Poppins' at the cinema, then go back to their house on the bus. Trish had a new outfit and her friend was dressed almost identically.

'It's their 'Mod' look' whispered Terri, giggling. 'We have to walk ten yards behind them as we haven't got the right clothes.'

Jennifer thought Trish looked like a model.

When they came out of the cinema, blinking in the sunshine, the other girls wanted to know if London was really like that.

'Mary Poppins was in the olden days and we certainly didn't have a big house…'

Sitting at the back of the bus Trish's friend had a fit of the giggles and set them all off; an old lady turned round and frowned.

'I'm going to ask Mr. Gregson if he can spell 'Supercalafragilisticexpialodocious' said Terri.

'I bet Mr. Reynolds can spell it.'

Trish was looking at the Beach Boys LP she had bought and couldn't resist slipping it out of the cover to make sure it was the right one; when the bus pulled up at the traffic lights it suddenly fell and started rolling down the aisle, to Trish's horror. She made a grab for it and ended up bumping into the old lady, producing more tuts of disapproval.

'Simon would cry if he saw that happen to one of his records.'

As Trish scrutinised the disc for scratches, Jennifer wondered if she would ever be able to buy her own records. The record player didn't belong to Simon, though anyone would think it did; she could hear her favourite pop songs on his singles and LPs, but it would be nice to play her own. Melissa's parents were going to buy her a portable record player for her birthday; she would keep it in her bedroom.

When they arrived at the house it was strangely quiet; they walked round the back to find Uncle John and Aunty Yvonne sitting on the veranda with a glass of beer each.

'Where's Drongo?' asked Jennifer.

'He's gone AWOL' said John 'absent without leave' he added, seeing her puzzled face. 'Must be a bitch on heat somewhere, he's been whining to get out all night; dogs can always find an escape route if they're determined enough.'

'Will he be alright?'

'He'll come back when he's ready, as long as he doesn't get in a fight with another dog. They come from miles around to find the bitch.'

Jennifer wasn't sure what they were talking about.

'You'd best get a male puppy Jenny,' said Yvonne 'your mother won't want all the dogs in the neighbourhood round and unwanted puppies two months later.'

'Females make good pets and it's only twice a year they want to mate,' said her husband 'not like female humans.'

'John…' she gave him a warning frown.

'I would like my dog to have puppies; we've got plenty of room, the twins could have one each and Melissa would like a puppy.'

She wanted to know more about the mysteries of breeding, but was too embarrassed to ask. According to her dog books all that seemed to be required was the bitch to be 'ready' and the male dog 'introduced'; she couldn't see how all the dogs in the neighbourhood would be involved.

'Terri, you and Jenny get your room ready while I start on tea. Do you like fish mournay?'

'Yes please' replied Jennifer. She had no idea what it was, but liked most things Terri's mother cooked.

Trish's friend was staying the night as well, not because she lived far but just for fun. Jennifer wondered if she could have Terri or Melissa to stay one weekend, but she imagined her father saying her mother had enough to do already or her mother saying perhaps 'later on' when it was cooler, after her birthday or when they were 'settled in properly'. She couldn't see why things like getting a puppy or a television or a guitar for Simon would be easier in this mythical future.

As Jennifer and Terri wandered into the kitchen to get a drink, the older girls were poring over the newspaper and muttering in hushed tones.

'What are you reading?' Terri asked her sister.

'Nothing, you're too young.'

'Mr. Gregson said we should read the newspaper to see what's going on in the world.'

'Gang Rape on Beach' Trish read out the headline. 'That's not far from where we go.'

'That's bad' said her mother, leaning over her shoulder. 'I bet those boys had been drinking and what was that girl doing out by herself so late?'

'What's gang rape Mum?' said Terri.

'A gang of blokes attacking a woman.'

'But why?'

Her sister giggled.

'It's not funny Trish. Tell your father to stay out of the kitchen while we have a girls' chat. Jenny love, has your mother told you the facts of life? I wouldn't want to tread on her toes, but with your periods started I'm sure she's told you where babies come from and I believe in being straight forward. People used to tell girls nothing and they were completely unprepared for the world.'

Jennifer nodded, embarrassed.

'And how women get pregnant? You don't sound too sure.'

Jennifer was comforted to see that Trish's friend looked equally embarrassed.

Aunty Yvonne pulled across Terri's drawing pad that was lying on the table.

'Girls need to know the mechanics so they don't get in situations they can't handle.'

Jennifer was confused, what were these 'situations'?

Yvonne drew a picture of a man and woman in profile. 'You have brothers Jenny, so at least you know what boys look like and there's nothing wrong with using the correct anatomical names for body parts.

'Mum, you've told me this already…'said Trish blushing, as her mother went on to explain what went where and how.

Jennifer was intrigued, relieved and appalled at the same time. Realisation dawned that her mother thought she had understood about the neighbours' guinea pigs in England and husbands and wives.

The idea of a baby growing from a tiny egg was so amazing that it was easy to believe God could start the baby growing. All that was required was for male and female animals to be present in the same cage or field and for a man and woman to be married and live in a house together. She never dreamt it involved such squeamishly physical things, but she wasn't going to let on to the others that she was so ignorant.

'Yuk,' said Terri 'I don't want babies anyway, I'd rather have a horse.'

'You might change your mind when you grow up and fall in love with a nice bloke.'

Jennifer was trying to come to terms with the fact that her parents had had to do that three times, or perhaps you had to do it twice to get twins.

Aunty Yvonne was still talking. 'If a man and a woman both want to do that together, it's called making love. If a stranger or even a man she knows forces a woman to do that, it's called rape and worst of all if a group of blokes attack one girl, that's called gang rape. The girl could be affected for life, not be able to have normal relations with her husband. So when your parents want to know who you're going out with or don't let you stay out late, they're not spoiling your fun, just want to make sure you're safe. Don't look so worried Jenny, most boys are decent, you just have to be aware.'

At last Jennifer had an inkling why she wasn't allowed to go to the recreation ground by herself, why Aunty Joyce and her mother made veiled references to 'nasty' and 'peculiar' men. Growing up seemed to be fraught with even more dangers than the recreation ground; all she wanted to do was play with her friends and have a puppy.

But at the same time she felt guiltily curious, no wonder Simon didn't let her in his bedroom, or didn't wander round naked like the twins. Aunty Yvonne said boys got 'bigger' when they were teenagers, how big? It was a bit scary.

'I'm definitely not getting married' Terri was saying.

'When you're teenagers it's more fun to go out in groups, boys and girls together; you don't want to get serious with a boy too young.'

'That's what my Mum says' added Trish's friend, who had been silent till then.

'Right, smells like tea's nearly cooked, your father will be getting hungry.'

Terri and Jennifer escaped from the kitchen to have a look outside for Drongo, but there was still no sign of him.

At the table Uncle John said 'You girls are quiet. Don't worry about the dog, if he's not back tomorrow I'll call the dog pound.'

Fish Mournay turned out to be like macaroni cheese; with fish instead of macaroni. It was one of the nicest dinners she had ever tasted.

'Aunty Yvonne, can you write the recipe down for me, I could surprise Mum by making it.'

'Good idea, do you like cooking?'

'Simon and I made tea when she wasn't well, he just made it up; we called it Scout Goulash.'

That night she and Terri were late getting to sleep as they chatted and giggled, though neither of them mentioned the 'girls' talk' round the table. Terri was trying to persuade her parents to buy her a pony, but it seemed unlikely as they had nowhere to put it and Terri confided they had no money to buy one; she knew this from listening to her parents talking when they thought she was asleep.

Even after her friend had dropped off, Jennifer was wide awake thinking. Terri had a dog and lived near the sea, just what Jennifer had always desired, but Terri was not satisfied with that. Jennifer had a transistor radio, it was the best thing she'd ever owned, but now she longed to have her own record player.

In the morning the dog had still not returned.

'He'll probably be waiting for us when we get back from the beach' Uncle John reassured them.

Trish and her friend wore bikinis and laid their towels down to sunbathe away from the rest of the family. The sand was hot and the beach smelt different from the river. Large turquoise waves were rolling and the sky was a deep cloudless blue. Sitting in the hot sun made Jennifer long to dash in the water, but she felt more nervous than on their first visit to the Indian Ocean. If the waves would just roll like hills, you could lie on the plastic surf board and have fun; but the way they reared up and collapsed in furious foaming surf scared her.

Before anyone could suggest it was time to go in the water, a familiar brown shape came hurtling towards them and halted in a shower of sand.

'Drongo, you stupid old mutt' said Uncle John grabbing his collar. He looked the most relieved to see him again.

'Clever boy to know where we were' said Aunty Yvonne.

Drongo greeted everyone as if it was they who had abandoned him. As they all looked up to see where he might have come from, Uncle John stood and shielded his eyes. They heard a man call out.

'Charlie, you old bugger, what the hell are you doing here.'

A man with a leathery face, faded shorts and what looked to Jennifer like a navy vest, but what the Australians called a singlet, came marching up.

'Bill Murphy,' laughed John 'thought you were in Queensland.'

Aunty Yvonne didn't look as pleased as her husband to see him.

'Language Bill, young ladies present.'

'Not all yours are they? Last time I saw you they were puking babies.' He turned back to John. 'Bet you have to keep them under lock and key.'

'No, they're good girls, mother hen here keeps a close eye on them.'

'Is that your dog? Might have guessed, he's been creating havoc at my place. Missus told me to take him for a long walk and come back without him or not come back at all.'

'We didn't even know you lived here and my dog manages to find your house, how's that for a coincidence Vonny.'

His wife sighed and opened the esky, handing both men a beer and making room for Bill on the beach mat.

'I'm married now, nice rich widow, breeds Labradors, thought that would be easier than kids, but I'm beginning to wonder. She's got this lovely yellow bitch, Sheba; first time she's going to mate her. Friday her friend brings round the stud, black Labrador called Prince something or other. Well he doesn't have a clue what to do; owner embarrassed, missus annoyed and me laughing my head off.

Yesterday she's on the phone round all the breeders, trying to find another stud before the moment passes. Looks out the front window and there's Sheba, got out somehow and your dog's doing the honours on the front lawn for all the neighbours to see. I'm laughing and she's screeching for me to get him off. *Too late love* I said *better let nature take its course*. Then she turns on me as if it's my fault.'

'Good old Drongo, got more brains than we gave him credit for.'

'Got more something' laughed Bill.

'John, we'll have to go round and apologise. I'm so sorry Bill.'

'It's hardly our fault, but I guess pedigree puppies would have fetched a good amount' said her husband.

'You must bring her round for dinner Bill.'

'The dog or the wife?'

'I see you haven't lost your sense of humour Bill Murphy.'

'Tell you what mate,' said John 'let your long suffering wife know, I'll buy the whole litter when they're ready, not at the pedigree rate of course, but it'll take them off her hands.'

'John, what are we going to do with a pack of puppies?' his wife protested.

'We could take one of Drongo's sons, keep the line going and Jenny could have the pick of the litter. They'll have Drongo's good looks and Labrador brains. Hey Bill, this is Jenny, a very special person. Remember Gip, my old army mate I told you about, the one who saved my life? This is his daughter. They just migrated; he's got three sons… Trish go to the car and get Drongo's rope and a pen and paper… You'd better go home and sweet talk your wife; take notice of someone who's been married a lot longer than you. I'll write our address, we're not on the phone.'

When Bill had strolled off, the family chattered excitedly.

'Who was that weird bloke?' asked Trish.

'I didn't think we'd ever see him again' said her mother.

'He's a good bloke, showed us the ropes when we first arrived out in the country.'

'He hasn't got an unkind bone in his body,' added his wife 'but he always managed to create havoc around him. He always expected your father to come out with him spending money like a bachelor.'

'Out,' laughed John 'I seem to remember he was always in our house enjoying your cooking.'

'Anyway, don't get Jenny's hopes up, we don't even know if this Sheba the wonder dog has fallen pregnant or what Mrs. Murphy will want to do with the puppies.'

But Jennifer wasn't thinking about puppies at that moment; she was pondering on Uncle John's throwaway remark that her father had saved his life. Was she the only person who didn't know about it? She was too shy to ask what happened. It might explain why he had scars and her father didn't.

The others were still talking about dogs.

'They would be Kelpidors' said Trish's friend.

'Or Labradrongs' said Terri.

'Bill won't let us down, but I'll have a word with your Dad when we take you back this evening. They might have a puppy lined up already.'

Jennifer thought that was unlikely and hastily added that she would like one of Drongo's.

'Let's have a swim before we get baked' said Aunty Yvonne.

Jennifer felt the hottest she had ever been. They had fetched the dog bowl they kept in the car and filled it with cold water, but Drongo was still panting.

'That leaves fruit juice and coca cola for the humans. We'd better get him in the sea.'

'Don't you let him off that rope John, he'll head straight back to Bill's.'

'I'll hold onto him,' volunteered Jennifer 'play with him in the shallows.'

It was an honourable way to avoid trying to swim and Drongo thought it was a new game.

For lunch Yvonne handed out plastic plates dolloped with salad, pieces of chicken and cold sausages.

'Good as a proper Sunday lunch' said John, as trifle emerged from the bottom of the esky. 'We could do with Simon being here to help polish this lot off.'

When they went for a paddle to cool off after lunch, the sand burnt their feet. Trish and her friend sauntered off to the friend's house and they all got ready to drive to Glendale. Even with the windows wide open it was too hot and Jennifer felt quite queasy after the large meal and coca cola. It was a long drive back and her face felt stiff from the sun.

The twins appeared from the bush across the road as they drew up in the driveway. With them was a little red haired boy who edged back when the dog jumped out of the car.

'Jenny, your face is all red' said Tony.

'This is Wayne, but we call him Wine,' said Peter 'he's going to be a detective as well, but we haven't found anything yet.'

Jennifer's mother appeared on the veranda.

'I've got the kettle on. You all look very hot. Boys, isn't it time Wayne was going home?'

'No, he doesn't have to go yet.'

The adults sat around the kitchen table; it was too hot in the lounge. Jenny got drinks for all the children, as slowly as possible so she could hear what the grownups were saying.

'Who's the little lad then?'

'He's in Tony's class, very shy, he hasn't uttered a word; he just appears.'

That evening Jennifer looked in the mirror at her bright red face while her mother examined her shoulders.

'I hope you haven't caught too much sun. I'll get the calamine lotion, if we can get in the bathroom.'

It was the usual evening chaos of getting the twins ready for bed and stuff ready for school and work. Her father came out of the bedroom holding aloft something white.

'What on earth has happened to my handkerchiefs?'

'We had to iron them in laundry, it's called a waterfall.'

'Can you imagine what the blokes at work would say if I took that out of my pocket?'

Jennifer tried to get comfortable in bed, even though she was smothered in lotion her back still felt uncomfortable and then a mosquito started buzzing around. She had half wanted to tell her mother about all she had heard at the weekend, but somehow the moment passed and they had ended up talking about laundry and school.

Chapter Twenty Two   March 1965

Helen looked at the clock; it was ten past three; she couldn't believe she had gone to bed after lunch and fallen asleep. She told herself it was to catch up before the busy time; everyone coming home, getting tea on time, supervising homework and bedtimes. Next week was Jennifer's birthday and they had not decided on a present or whether they would do anything special.

Jennifer was now set on having a puppy from John's friend and had read up on gestation periods and separating puppies from their mothers. Helen was happy to go along with this, but hoped her daughter wouldn't be disappointed if the bitch wasn't pregnant or they had other plans for the puppies.

Helen was thankful to postpone plans for anything that required effort. She kept setting herself targets for when she might feel differently, less tired, more positive. There was no reason to feel like this; everyone felt fed up sometimes, you had to pull yourself together. Her mother had the war to worry about when her children were growing up.

Everything was going better than they could have hoped. George still enjoyed his job and his boss gave him a small monthly bonus for helping him at the depot once a week, while Joe trained the young lad on the road. George didn't regard this as office work as they were checking stock, doing physical things, but it still involved lots of paper work and telephone calls.

Simon hadn't moaned about school lately and still claimed he wanted to be a teacher. Jennifer declared she liked school most of the time and the twins were sturdy and healthy. What more could a wife and mother want? Why did she feel so empty? Everyone had entered fully into their new life except her.

She put the kettle on hoping a cup of tea would revive her; once she was busy she would feel better or at least would not have time to think. Soon the evening would be rolling by in half hour spans. Eventually the twins would be in bed and Jennifer would bring her drink of milk and sit with them. Simon would emerge from his bedroom and raid the kitchen for a snack; complain that he wasn't a child when George pointed out the time; then grumble that as there was no television to watch, he might as well go to bed and listen to his transistor.

Helen would make her and George a cup of coffee, half milk and water boiled in the milk pan, the same as they always had in England. He would read her snippets from a school library book, often one of Simon's reference books for Australian geography or history. Sometimes it was interesting, as they tried to imagine a vast barren hinterland or men with horses following creek beds. Other times she would have given anything to sit by the fire watching 'Doctor Finlay's Case Book' or 'Compact'.

Her thoughts were interrupted when the twins burst in, followed by Jennifer and Melissa.

'Mum, Simon's going to be a disc jockey' said Tony.

'We haven't asked him yet' added his sister. 'Mum, you know you said we could do something I liked the weekend after my birthday…'

'Yes, Dad thought we could all go out somewhere nice.'

'But we do that most weekends; we've got a better idea. As that will be the weekend before Melissa's thirteenth birthday, we could have a joint party for our school friends and Simon could play his records.'

'Melissa, won't you're parents want to celebrate at home; becoming a teenager is quite an important event these days.' According to Jennifer, Melissa's family was much more interesting than theirs and Helen imagined the girl having a big party with lots of cousins.

'Oh no, they won't mind; we'll probably go out to dinner with my aunties and uncles. Mum's too busy to organise a party' she said disarmingly 'and a noisy party might trigger one of her migraines.'

Helen now pictured Melissa's mother with wild hair like her daughter's, but greying, sitting bent over her sewing machine surrounded by bales of material, while her husband painted and earned little money.

'We'll ask Dad tonight; how many girls are you going to invite?'

'Just a few and it will be easier than in England, we can go outside.'

'Yes, we can have a barbeque' said Melissa.

Building a barbeque had been one of John's suggestions, but to Helen's relief George had not got around to it.

When Simon got home he didn't sound keen on his part in the celebrations.

'It's only for a couple of hours' said Helen. She knew from experience with children's parties it was wise to set a time limit.

'I suppose Paul could bring his new guitar round.'

Melissa was nudging Jennifer. 'Tell your Mum about the other thing.'

'Melissa got two forms from the office, we have to fill them in and take them back tomorrow in case there are no places left.'

'Places for what?'

'It isn't as far away as the Isle of Wight and Melissa's mother will let her. It's a Phys Ed. Camp, up in the hills.'

Helen laughed. 'You don't like P.E.'

'But this is different, trampolining and bush walks. Melissa needs to know if I can go before she asks her Mum.'

Helen skimmed through the form; it looked interesting and she could understand the hurry to book, but didn't want to discuss money in front of the other girl. Jennifer must have read the expression on her face.

'Mum, I could have it as my birthday present.'

'I'm not going to give an answer till we've discussed it with your father. Don't mention it the moment he walks in the door, let him have a shower and eat his tea first.'

'Are you all plotting something?' said George over tea. 'The twins said Jennifer had two important secrets.'

After Jennifer had relayed all the information he told her to wait till morning for the answers. 'You won't get there any quicker by knowing tonight.'

When everyone was in bed and the mosquito hunt was over, George lit two cigarettes, passed one to Helen and sunk into the arm chair.

'What do you think?' she asked.

'About what?' he teased.

'You're hardly likely to have forgotten; Jenny dropped enough hints.'

'Whatever we do for her, we have to do for the others when their birthdays come along, but a little party would be okay, a few sandwiches, homemade cakes and coca cola.'

'What about the camp?'

'Of course she must go, it's just the sort of opportunity we came out here for. I know we can't afford it; let's see if we can scrape up enough change for the deposit and worry about the rest later.'

The next morning George handed Jennifer a sealed envelope. She hugged him gratefully.

'You do understand we can't afford to get you anything else for your birthday?'

Helen sat down with a cup of coffee as soon as everyone had gone. Jennifer was so excited she hoped for her daughter's sake Melissa's family had also agreed. It was not a large amount of money; it was just that they had no spare money. The occasional nights out with George, while Simon and Jennifer babysat, had not materialised, but as George pointed out, they had their nice new home to enjoy. She sipped her coffee slowly, reluctant to get up and start on chores. Last night they had made love; it was the first time they had made love properly since her bleeding. Helen had encouraged George; she needed to feel things were back to normal and she had wanted it too. But as he became more ardent, she felt herself loosing interest; pretending she was enjoying it and hoping it would be over quickly.

Afterwards she clung to him affectionately; he would be upset if he knew she had felt so distant from the event. They had always joked about 'Victorian husbands' and he prided himself on being an attentive lover. It was not his fault and now she felt more depressed than if they had not tried at all.

This morning she must go to Victoria Park. There had just been enough money left after Jennifer's deposit for George to have some change in his pocket and for her bus fare. The bank, butchers and several other shops were on her list and she was glad of an excuse to get out of the house.

Washing the dishes, she saw a car leave from next door's driveway; by now she was convinced someone must be living there permanently, perhaps a man living by himself, although she had seen that woman the other week.

She put the radio on to take away the silence as she bent over the laundry trough; only shirts, socks and underwear today, they would soon be hanging up. Outside she tried to appreciate the garden; the air was fresh in the morning and March had brought slightly cooler weather. It was quiet as usual, but if you really listened you could hear raucous birds or a car driving by; but never the distant rumble of a train. She realised now that had been a comforting sound. Strange, you didn't appreciate little things till you no longer had them.

Helen locked the front door and shut the fly screen, then walked in the road to avoid the sandy verge. Round the corner there was still no footpath, but other new houses, with gardens gradually taking form. There was nobody around; one car passed her. At the next corner she turned into the main road and made her way to the empty bus stop, enjoying walking on pavement and past mature trees.

On board the bus a woman got on at the next stop, but sat further back. Helen heard her talking to someone, asking advice in an Australian accent; new in the area, another missed opportunity for Helen to talk to someone. When they were driving into Victoria Park, she heard the other passenger offering to get off at the same stop and show the new woman the way to the bank. Helen almost laughed as she pictured herself following them, asking if she could join in, like the lonely new child at school. She sighed, being new never got easier with age; first day in the army, first day at the Oxford Street store, first months as a new mother.

Walking round the shops she felt she was just pretending to be a participant in real life; trying to look purposeful as other housewives greeted friends and shopkeepers. At the bank she took out the minimum amount they could manage on, almost too embarrassed to ask what the balance was. She had thought of investigating things she could join in Victoria Park, after all it was easy to get here and there was nothing much in Glendale. But even with time to spare, she was now as keen to get home as she had been to get out of the house.

When she arrived home and there was no post, she was absurdly disappointed.

Tony's homework sessions did not get any easier. The 'long suffering Mr. Reed' as she now called him to herself, had even written out paragraphs with gaps for Tony to fill in and make a story. He thought of words and phrases, but was painstakingly slow to write them down.

At last she joined Jennifer, Simon and George in the lounge. 'It's a wonder Mr. Reed doesn't have a nervous breakdown, I feel exhausted after one page of homework with Tony.'

'Remind me not to be a primary teacher' said Simon. 'I'm going to make first and second years go on long cross country runs. That's what you'll do next term Jenny, when the weather's cooler. You'll have to run past our house.'

'I don't care, that's what we're going to do on our camp.'

'I've got some news for Simon' said her father. 'Greek George is giving the Italian lad a holiday and about time too. So if you want to fill in during the Easter holiday son, grab the chance before he gives it to someone else. You'll have to go on the bus the days I'm having off and it will be hard work, but it's a chance to earn and save some money. Don't take it if you think it will interfere with your studying.'

'I'm not going to study during the Easter holidays. How much is he going to pay me?'

'The same as the other lad, the going rate, but it's not as if we're going to take your keep, like we would if you were working full time.'

'Okay Dad, thanks; maybe I'll save up for a drum kit instead of a guitar.'

---o0o---

Jennifer persuaded her mother she only needed a couple of bags for the camp, not a large suitcase. Her father still insisted she have a lift to the school, but promised not to stay and see her off. Melissa was already waiting, so she pecked his cheek and scrambled out of the car.

'The coach isn't even here yet' he laughed.

Maria and Catherine from their class arrived and Maria's parents hugged and kissed her as if she was leaving home for ever. Melissa's father suddenly appeared at her side.

'Your parents not staying to see you off Jenny?'

She blushed. 'I've been away from home before.'

'So you can look after Liss if she's homesick.'

'Dad… I'm thirteen.'

A slight girl rushed up to greet her. 'Jenny, I didn't know you were coming; I've only seen you once in school, maybe we'll be in the same dormitory.'

Jennifer introduced her. 'This is Maiya, we used to go swimming at Bayswater in the summer; her brother's a friend of Simon's.' She felt quite proud to know someone the others hadn't met.

When they arrived, the campsite looked rugged; wooden buildings were scattered over the site, which sloped steeply. They assembled in the hall to hear rules; *don't wander off or go on the trampolines by yourself*…

Miss Thompson introduced the other leaders, another Phys. Ed. teacher and her husband and some young men and women who were university students. She turned to a piece of paper.

'Dormitory lists; your dorm will also be your team, so that makes five teams with eight girls in each. I've put you with your friends, but also with girls from other classes so you can get to know each other. If someone is ill during the night or there is an emergency, come and tell us straight away, otherwise we don't want to see you till breakfast. Ten minutes to find your hut and dump your stuff, then we'll sit out here and eat our picnic. Did any girl forget her sandwiches?'

Maiya stood up, embarrassed.

'Hands up anyone whose mother gave them too much lunch.'

Jennifer's hand shot up first, followed quickly by Maria's; importantly they each handed the other girl a sandwich, plus a banana and an apple.

'Well done, two points for C team. When you take your bags down to the huts, vote for a team leader; no one eats till I have five names.'

Melissa, Jennifer, Maria and Catherine stood between the metal bunk beds looking at the four girls from 1-5. Ten minutes was a short time for eight people to reach an agreement. On the way down the dusty path they had decided it should be Catherine, or at least Catherine had persuaded them it should be her, as her family went camping in the bush. But the 1-5 girls did not agree, even when Christine pointed out that her class was higher than theirs. Melissa looked at her watch.

'Three minutes left; how about we choose the leader and you can pick which bunks you want?'

'A whole week without parents' said one girl, as they sat on logs eating their lunch.

'And no annoying brothers' added Jennifer.

'The only thing I'll miss is television,' said another 'what are we going to do in the evenings Miss?'

'You won't have time to miss telly, you'll all be tired and we'll have quizzes, games and a concert on the last night. Each team is going to do an act, so start thinking now.'

After lunch they went for a walk led by the teacher's husband, to familiarise themselves with the landscape. Miss Thompson brought up the rear. One girl attached herself to a university student, Jennifer heard her telling the young woman that she didn't know anyone at the camp. Jennifer thought it very brave of her to come.

Jennifer quickly realised this was not going to be like one of the twins' treks through Tonydale. The man was setting a brisk pace and Miss Thompson did not allow anyone to slack. Living in flat Glendale, none of the girls were used to climbing up hills.

'Girls, this is nothing compared with what we're going to do this week' said Miss Thompson, ignoring their complaints. 'No stopping till we get to the top.'

Jennifer was glad it was now autumn; not like English autumn, just not as hot as summer. At the top they sat on huge boulders and Jennifer drank cordial out of the plastic bottle with the shoulder strap she usually took for school lunches. The air was fresh and smelt of Eucalyptus.

'Can we go down now?' asked one girl.

'No,' said the teacher's husband 'there's a track to follow through those trees, then we come down on the other side of the camp. Put your hands up if you can give me one fact about the Darling Ranges.'

Jennifer's hand hovered as she tried to think, hoping to get another point.

'They aren't hills, they're an escarpment,' said a 1-9 girl 'the edge of the great plateau.'

Jennifer knew that, she just hadn't remembered the words. Then she shot her hand up. 'They have some of the oldest rocks in the whole world?'

'Well done.'

She was thankful for the random pieces of information, gleaned from the school library books, that her father came out with on outings.

As they set off again her legs began to ache; family walks in the National Park were limited by how far the twins could walk, if their mother might get tired or whether they were likely to get lost; a constant, but not unreasonable worry of her mother.

Just when she thought they would never go down, the campsite came into view again, but the downward path was steeper and wound between rocks and prickly bushes. They were glad Miss Thompson announced free time until dinner. Jennifer and Melissa went to the dorm to unpack. Some of the other girls were lying on their bunks to recover. Jennifer let Melissa choose the top bunk as she had never slept in a bunk bed. Seeing some girls unpack she noticed they had brought more clothes than her; more clothes than she actually possessed.

Supper smelt like English school dinners, but with a lovely mixture of wood smoke. On the long tables were aluminium jugs of water and plates of bread. The meal was some sort of stew with carrots and potatoes; the plates were passed down the table and passed back to be stacked when empty. Pudding was sponge and custard. Afterwards they played charades, had a quiz, then drunk hot chocolate. It was a thrill to think they had already done lots of things and it was still only the first day. Jennifer knew she was going to have a wonderful week.

'Two minutes each in the shower' Miss Thompson was saying.

It was dark outside and the shower block was grey and musty with concrete floors. They gripped their sponge bags and towels and couldn't find anywhere to hang their clothes and keep them dry. The girls who had brought their pyjamas with them regretted it.

'Come along girls, you'll have to be quicker than this every evening or you'll never get any sleep.'

Catherine had brought a torch, a reason to be glad they had chosen her as leader. She led them back to their hut, which they all agreed was the furthest away from the toilets. It was chilly now and they struggled to take off their clothes and get into pyjamas; there had been no time to get dried. The beds had rough sheets and old grey blankets. Jennifer would tell her father it was like being in the army. She looked up at the black and grey striped mattress that poked through the springs of Melissa's bunk, her bed felt thin and lumpy. There was lots of creaking and giggling as they tried to get comfortable. Jennifer's pillow nudged the windowsill, which smelt dusty and the sheet wouldn't pull up far enough. But the chatting soon faded as everyone was tired.

Jennifer woke up in the dark feeling cold, the first time she had felt cold in Australia. Snuggling under the blanket did not help; the cold was seeping up through the thin mattress. Now fully awake, she needed to go to the toilet and was sure she would never remember the way in the dark. She was relieved when Catherine started clambering down from her bunk, waking some of the others; their leader switched on the torch and led a procession to the toilet block. Back in the dorm they put on jumpers and socks; Jennifer regretted not bringing more warm clothes, she had not expected to need them.

In the morning Catherine declared she would ask for extra blankets. Breakfast appeared to be leftover stew ladled onto toast. After breakfast they were to have dorm inspection and Catherine put her hand up. Miss Thompson agreed to her request and they filed to a store shed to be given musty blankets. In the dormitory Catherine ordered them to put the blanket under the bottom sheet.

'Keeping warm from underneath, first rule of camping' she declared.

Outside it was raining, but not enough to deter the leaders from setting off on the morning walk. They went out of the camp gate and down the road, before turning onto a track which led over a creek; they had to try and cross without getting their feet wet. Jennifer was enjoying herself; years of jumping over the ditch in the recreation ground had made her nimble.

Every afternoon would be trampolining lessons. As they gathered round in their shorts and T-shirts, there were more rules. As you waited your turn, you had to stand guard round the sides to make sure no one fell off.

When it was finally her turn Jennifer understood why no one was doing it properly. She felt wobbly and even standing still on the yellow cross in the centre proved impossible. Her turn was over too quickly, followed by another long wait. An hour passed, then teams C and D had to make way for the others; but team games with the university students turned out to be far more fun than Phys Ed at school.

The second night was far more comfortable and warm and the next thing Jennifer knew, Catherine was waking her up; she didn't want their team to be late for breakfast and lose points. Breakfast was mince on toast; she couldn't wait to tell her mother what strange meals they had.

The morning activity was a treasure hunt, but the only treasure was a bar of chocolate for the team back first with the right answers. Teams of four to find their way with a map and list of clues; four was a good number, one person to stay with an injured girl and two to stay together and go for help.

Catherine was convinced their team would win and led them out of the gate at a brisk pace, till Melissa pointed out that if they went too fast they might go in the wrong direction or miss a clue. She was proved right when she spotted the sign on a gate, missed by two teams in front who diverged in different directions. One of the male students sprinted urgently after a team.

'See, now we know not to go that way' grinned Melissa.

'Good thing my mother can't see us,' said Jennifer 'she would worry we'd get lost and never be seen again.'

By the fifth clue the campsite should have come into sight.

'Wrong track, back track' said Catherine.

The others moaned and they could not decide which way to go. Miss Thompson suddenly appeared and dropped several hints. There was a time limit at which moment you had to give up and head straight back to camp. Catherine looked at her watch and sighed.

'Two more clues to go, but we'd better head back.'

'But we don't know the way' worried Maria.

'Just follow me.'

They arrived back to see the 1-5 girls sitting munching chocolate and looking smug.

'At least our dorm won' declared Catherine.

The other girls gave them a few squares of chocolate. Jennifer was grateful, she was starving hungry and relieved to be back. Other teams straggled in claiming to be dying of exhaustion, but one team was still missing.

'I bet they'll have to get mounted police to search' said Catherine.

'They'll be fine,' said the teacher's husband 'the map only covered a small area.'

But ten minutes later, after consultation with Miss Thompson, he set off at a brisk walk.

'Cook's got lunch ready, go to the dining hall everybody.'

'Miss, what if one of them's got a broken ankle?'

'Then two girls will soon be back to tell us, but I'm sure they are fine.'

Jennifer looked around the dining hall and realised it was Maiya's team who were missing, she felt somehow responsible and tried to recall when they had last seen her team. At that moment the four girls walked in looking very chirpy.

'We thought you were lost' said Miss Thompson.

'We were,' said Maiya 'so we decided to find a road and we got a lift from a nice woman who knew where the camp was.'

'Miss, we'll have to search for your husband now' said Catherine to the other teacher.

'No, he'll have run round the whole route in half an hour.'

That afternoon the trampoline seemed more stable; cautiously Jennifer bent her knees and tried a small jump and then a higher one. At her next turn she managed a star jump.

'Good,' said Miss Thompson 'you can try a seat drop next.'

Her turn came round quickly, some of the girls had retreated to their bunks to recover from the treasure hunt. Melissa and Maiya were already doing seat drops and Jennifer's confidence quickly grew; it was such a wonderful sensation, she wished she could jump up and down all afternoon. When it was their turn to play team games Jennifer found her legs would not work properly back on the ground; her muscles were feeling the effects of the hike and the trampoline.

'Half hour's rest before dinner; you'd better start planning your act for the concert, if you haven't already.'

In the dormitory they all had different ideas. Jennifer had an idea, but couldn't get a word in edgeways. Two girls wanted to sing, Maria wanted them all to dance and the others said 'yuk'. Melissa suggested a play.

'A play about going on a treasure hunt and getting lost' said Jennifer.

'But we find some real treasure' added Catherine.

'No, we find a hiker with a broken ankle and rescue him' said Melissa.

'…and he turns out to be very rich and rewards us for saving his life.'

Friday afternoon came round too quickly; in the last lesson on the trampoline Jennifer was doing front drops and managed a somersault with the teacher's help. Melissa, Maiya and a few others were rolling over as if they had done it all their lives. Jennifer was sure she needed only one more day to master that skill, but in the morning they had to go home.

Team C gathered behind their hut for a last secret rehearsal before the evening meal. Now it seemed as if they had known the 1-5 girls for ever.

'I don't want to go home tomorrow' sighed Melissa.

'Nor me,' said Jennifer 'I wish we were staying another week.'

'We could hide and not go home, stay here for ever' said another girl.

'What would we eat?' said Maria. 'There aren't any shops nearby.'

'Live off the land, Catherine would know…what do you eat when you go camping?'

'We take all our food with us.'

C Team did a very good impression of hiking wearily round and round and getting lost. The teachers laughed. Melissa played the millionaire's wife lost with the broken ankle, how she got there was not explained. She was carried away rather awkwardly then returned to grant them all their wishes; new trampolines, horses or a visit to England to see The Beatles.

When the coach arrived back at the school the next day parents emerged from their cars. Jennifer's father was alone, but chatting to another father. After a week with young adults, when he turned to greet her, she was surprised how old and gaunt he looked.

Chapter Twenty Three   Autumn 1965

When Jennifer arrived back with George, her first words were 'I didn't want to come home.' Her second words were 'Isn't it quiet here?'

'The twins have gone round to Wayne's house and Simon's working' said Helen.

'Your mother's made your favourite cake, we can sit and have lunch without the boys interrupting and you can tell us all about the camp.'

Helen had been looking forward to Jennifer's return; she had realised how much of a companion her daughter had become since coming to Australia. Jennifer's return had also been another target Helen had set herself; when things would seem brighter, when she would start feeling positive. She had enjoyed the Easter school holidays, or at least the days George had taken off, the days they had taken the twins out.

'Look, we had a post card from Uncle John and Aunty Yvonne; they've been up in Geraldton, three hundred miles away.'

Helen had been disappointed when their friends went away; she had hoped to invite them over for a nice lunch. Easter was another occasion that felt flat without her parents coming to visit or taking Easter eggs over to Dennis' children. It was the first Easter Sunday they had not taken the children to church, making her spirits even lower.

Jennifer was studying the note at the bottom of the card.

Sheba doing well, expecting happy event end of April.

'I told you they would be born on April 30th. Mr. and Mrs. Murphy have a phone; we could go to the phone box on May 1st and ask if they've been born.'

George sighed. 'How long did you say puppies have to stay with their mother?'

'Eight to nine weeks.'

'That gives Uncle John plenty of time to tell us they've arrived safely.'

'Yes, but I want to know how many there are and what colours.'

When the twins came back they were impressed with Jennifer's tales of bush walks, but were more eager to describe their visit to Wayne's house.

'His Mum and Dad don't call him Wayne, they call him 'Bluey' cos he's got red hair, why do they call him that?'

'I think it's a joke' said George.

'Jenny, we went to the zoo and saw a real kangaroo and we had a ride on the little train.'

'Oh, I wanted to go to the zoo.'

'You can't do everything' said Helen, irritated.

'That means we can go again and take Jenny… and Wine' said Tony.

323

'…and see the wabally wallabies' said Peter, sending his brother into fits of laughter.

George had one more family outing planned before they went back to school, The Old Mill at South Perth. 'A little piece of history, we can imagine what it was like for the early settlers.'

Simon was complaining. 'It's my one day off, I've been working all holidays.'

'I know, we've hardly seen you; all the more reason to come out with us.'

Helen thought the mill a dear little building.

Inside, George started reading to the children. 'Built in 1835 to grind flour…'

'That's not very old,' said Simon 'St. Stephen's church was nearly nine hundred years old.'

'It is old for Perth and built to last, with solid stone walls.'

Helen started reading about early women settlers. 'It must have been unbearable wearing those long heavy dresses in summer, you should be glad you can wear shorts Jenny.'

The twins soon got bored inside and wanted to run around outside.

'Where are we going to next Dad?'

'I'm not going to be rushed away,' said Helen 'I like it here, peaceful and quaint.'

She liked going out to different places and new sights; with the cooler weather they could look forward to some pleasant outings. The city, King's Park, the river, the hills; there was no doubt that Perth was a delightful place to live and with such a small population you could turn up anywhere and it was never crowded. George came and put his arm round her as they looked across the river back to the city.

'Over six months now, no regrets?'

'No... I miss everyone of course.'

'I don't, perhaps I might in a couple of years. You don't get lonely at home do you? It's not like back in England, when I had to leave home early and get back late. Now we're all home for tea and you have your outings with Yvonne.'

Helen was tempted to say that had only happened twice, but she just squeezed his hand. He was right; she saw more of him at home and it was good he didn't have to commute.

That evening they realised Tony still had not completed his one piece of homework; a story of something he had done in the holidays. He had chosen the zoo and talked enthusiastically, until he opened his exercise book. She and George faced a struggle of wits and tears out of all proportion to the small task at hand and Helen felt her spirits sink.

The next morning the twins set off happily, much to her relief; they were treading a fine line between getting Tony to work harder and putting him off school altogether. She looked forward to getting the housework and washing done and sitting down for a peaceful lunch with her Woman's Weekly. She and George had read all the school library books and were looking forward to a new selection.

The doorbell made her jump and the magazine dropped to the floor; she must have dozed off. She was surprised to see Yvonne on the doorstep. For a moment she thought she had come to announce the arrival of the puppies.

'I didn't know if you'd be in, I've got the car today and I felt like a drive.'

'Come in, ignore the mess, I was just enjoying a quiet lunch now they're back at school.'

'The place looks pretty tidy to me' Yvonne laughed. 'I haven't done a thing. I had some errands in Perth, a coffee in Coles, then I couldn't face going home to housework. I'm trying to get everyone trained to do their own bedrooms and help with the housework on Saturday mornings.'

'Sounds like a good idea, now you're working.'

'You should try it with your lot, you're looking a bit tired.'

'Am I?' Helen was dismayed. 'They all do some jobs at the weekend.'

'…and you've lost weight.'

'I'm hardly like Twiggy, but six months without chocolate is having an effect.'

'So everything's alright?'

'Of course.'

It was an automatic response, to always say you were fine when people asked how you were. How could she explain what was the matter when she didn't know herself?

'Lots of women get depressed sometimes.'

'Oh I'm not depressed, everything's going well.' Now she was annoyed. When Yvonne had appeared she had anticipated a good chat and a laugh, not an interrogation.

'But you're bound to feel a bit low this far down the line, after all the excitement of emigrating and now you're stuck out here…' Was that how Yvonne saw Glendale? Was that how she saw Glendale? '…and George being so bloody positive all the time.'

For a moment Helen felt defensive, but then she started to laugh; it was a long time since she had laughed properly.

'Well someone has to be… it wasn't that exciting where we lived, but at least I saw people I knew every day, at least I saw people…'

'There's nothing wrong with having a moan, but there's a difference between having an off day and being depressed.'

'You always seem to take everything in your stride.'

'Not always; when I had Trish it was more terrifying than anything I'd faced during the war. I realised what it was going to mean never having my mother or sister around. I couldn't explain to John.'

'What did you do?'

'Muddled along; the first few months passed in a daze. Looking back I realise John was more of a help than I gave him credit for. He was so laid back, reckoned babies were no different from lambs and there were some ewes who didn't know what they were doing, had to be helped. It takes anyone a while to settle in and it's always easier for the kids and husbands, they've got school and work. You should do something you want to do, not worry about them; learn to drive, start a new hobby.'

'That's part of the trouble, I have no idea what I want to do... let's have another cup of tea and a large piece of cake before the children get home.'

Helen sat back down and changed the subject, she'd had enough self-analysing. 'So what's Mrs. Murphy like.'

Yvonne leaned forward, eager for a good gossip. 'Ten years older than him apparently, not that she looks it; treats him like a kid, but then don't most wives. Or I should say she treats him like one of the dogs, but she does love her dogs. We had a nice time when they came round for dinner, haven't found out where they met. She's quite refined, but got a sense of humour, you would need that to be married to Bill.'

'Is John really going to buy the whole litter?'

'I'm not getting involved, but the Murphys have promised Jenny can have first pick.'

When they heard George's car draw up Yvonne looked at the clock.

'It's okay, he's early shift today.'

'This is a surprise' said George, coming into the lounge. 'Where's John?

'I am allowed out without him, he's off doing errands in the ute. He's talking of changing his job again.'

'Oh why's that?'

'He doesn't need a reason. We had a good time in Geraldton; Terri did some more horse riding and wants to move to the country and John reckons he could set up his own business in a country town. Trish couldn't wait to get back to her friends and her Beach Boy records.'

Yvonne stayed long enough to greet the children and give Jennifer an update on Sheba's health. As they waved her off, a battered Holden screeched to a halt outside their house. Simon emerged from the back seat, dismayed to see his whole family on the veranda. The car horn tooted loudly as the driver pulled sharply away.

'What on earth are you doing in that car?' said George.

'I told you Paul's brother's got a car.'

'How old is he?'

'Seventeen, he's got his licence.'

'I can't imagine how he passed his test, you'd better not go out with him again.'

'Dad, he's my mate, he's going to lead our band and when we go to play he can drive us around.'

'Not in that car.'

---o0o---

School felt different in the second term. They were no longer new, but there was the prospect of new lessons; dressmaking, hockey and cross country races. In Jennifer's mind the first year girls were now divided into two groups; those who had been to the camp and those who had not. Now when she walked down corridors, fellow campers would greet her or wave from the other side of the quadrangle. The other classes were no longer an anonymous mass, they each had an identity; 1-5 their team mates, 1-4 and 1-6 had been the winning team D at the end of the camp and 1-7 Maiya's class.

When they lined up outside the dressmaking room they wondered how it could take a whole term to make an apron for cooking. It didn't sound much fun, but it had to be better then doing laundry.

'Samples,' whispered Melissa 'how boring is that?'

No one would be starting on their apron until they had practised seams and hems on sample material and no one would go near a machine till they had proved they were adept at tacking.

'Why does our tacking have to be neat if we have to pull it all out again?' moaned another girl.

Jennifer found it easy, or so she thought till Mrs. Butcher said her stitches were too uneven and not straight. When Mrs Butcher wasn't looking, Melissa got her ruler out of her bag and made a show of measuring each stitch. The other girls stifled giggles.

The second half of the lesson was an introduction to the machines, half were treadle and electric machines sat on large tables. There would be no sewing until they had learnt how to thread them, not an easy task.

Jennifer had made a shoe bag on her aunt's electric machine, but that had already been threaded; now she battled with the mysteries of spools and how to make the bottom thread surface. By the end of the lesson she was still puzzled, but the teacher checked the machine and nodded; Melissa had threaded it for her. Her friend had helped a few of the girls, but she was not going to reveal to Mrs. Butcher that her mother had already taught her many sewing skills.

When they walked across the oval that afternoon, Simon and Paul were standing on the corner of the road, their ties undone and their bags slung on the ground. Seeing her brother from a distance, she realised he looked more grown up since her return from camp. Close up he smelt of sweat and had large hands like her father. Paul wasn't scary any more since he had been round their house and she was used to his scarred face. Her friends had been impressed with his guitar at the birthday party. He didn't have any sisters and he was always polite to her.

'Jenny, tell Mum I'll be late for tea, we're having a band practice.'

'But you're not allowed to be late on school nights' she protested.

Her words were ignored as a now familiar car pulled up; it was Paul's brother. The two boys jumped in as the girls tried to get a glimpse of the older boy, before he drew sharply away from the kerb.

Jennifer was now left with a dilemma; her father wouldn't be pleased if Simon was home late and would be angry if he knew Simon had gone in the car.

'Don't tell them about the car, just say Simon might be a little bit late' reasoned Melissa.

When Jennifer got home she found the twins in the kitchen making themselves misshapen sandwiches with a sharp knife.

'Where's Mum?'

'Asleep in bed, don't wake her up, you could cook tea for a surprise.'

Jennifer frowned. Yesterday her mother had been very cheerful when Aunty Yvonne was visiting and Jennifer thought she must be feeling better.

Now looking at the unwashed dishes, she wondered if she did have a serious illness. Nicola had told them little about her mother's death, except that she always seemed to be asleep in bed; then one day she came home from school and her mother had gone to hospital and never came back. An untidy kitchen was normal in Melissa's house, but not in theirs. She peeped in the fridge, it looked bare. The fish mournay recipe had seemed complicated, besides, they had no fish and Jennifer wasn't sure where you bought it from.

In England there had been a fishmongers in the high street where her mother shopped. In the school holidays she would go with her, the fishmonger would say *Good morning Mrs. Palmer, I've got a nice piece of haddock or do you fancy plaice today?*

On the wet slab the fish would lie with their blank eyes, oblivious to the chatter as other housewives came in the shop and the fishmonger made them laugh.

At 'Tom The Cheap Grocer' no one knew her mother; at the Greek shop they were very friendly, but their lollies were not as nice as the four for a penny selection in the little sweet shop. There was no newsagent like the one that sold 'Bunty' and 'Girl' comic and where they knew all her family because Simon was their newspaper boy. Now the milkman delivered their bread, because there was no baker.

If she closed her eyes she could remember the smell of new bread and next door the cobbler; his tiny shop smelt of new leather, polish and the slight burning of the grinder. The cobbler wore a brown overall and always remembered which shoes were your Mum's or Dad's, even though the shelves were full of other people's shoes.

Christine used to do imitations of their mothers walking to the shops and bumping into neighbours.

Good morning Mrs. Brown, how's your husband... did you hear Mrs. Green's in hospital...

Christine reckoned it took her mother two hours to get to the shops. Jennifer wondered if her mother missed her trips to the high street. Probably not, mothers always complained about shopping; like housework it was 'never ending'. At least here her father often took her to the shops in the car.

Jennifer closed the fridge guiltily; they weren't supposed to leave the door open and let the heat in. Maybe her mother hadn't been shopping today, maybe after all those years of 'never ending' shopping she had decided not to do anymore, ever.

'Jenny, are you home already?'

Her mother looked crumpled; glancing at the plates and glasses on the table and then at the clock she frowned.

'Sorry, I thought I'd have a little nap after lunch. I can't believe I didn't wake up.'

'I was going to make tea for you.'

'I hadn't decided what to have, I was going to see what they had at the shops… oh look it's raining now.'

Jennifer was worried, it was a strange afternoon; her mother always knew what they were going to have for tea. They must think of something before her father came home, because he had to have a 'proper meal' after working hard all day.

'Let's have a cupboard supper, that's what Melissa makes when her mother's not well, or busy. You just get everything and mix it up together.'

Before her mother could object, Jennifer ferreted around the good stock of tins and packets; in this Australian kitchen there was room to store up for emergencies. She found two tins of spam, two tins of baked beans and got the solitary egg out of the fridge.

'Spam fritters, we had them for lunch at camp, show me how to make the batter and I can beat it up. We could have bread; at camp we had bread with every meal.'

Jennifer completely forgot to tell her that Simon would be late, but luckily he arrived on foot at the same time as her father.

'That smells nice, nothing like a good old fashioned meal, see Simon, Jenny's always willing to give your mother a hand.'

May arrived with no news of the puppies. One afternoon Jennifer arrived home to find her mother in the lounge with a woman she had never met before.

'Jenny, this is Mrs. Driscoll from next door; we just met coming back from the shops.'

'Hello dear, I've seen you and your brothers playing, I wondered how many children lived here. I don't know how I haven't met your mother before, but I stay indoors during the hot weather.'

She had the broadest Australian accent Jennifer had heard and a very lined face.

'Do you like your new house?' Jennifer wasn't sure what else to say.

'Yes, we've never had a brand new house before, we thought we'd try city life, but I haven't been brave enough to go to Perth yet.'

'Do you drive?' asked her mother.

'Back home, since I was young, but I'm too nervous of the traffic here.'

'The buses are good if you want to go to Victoria Park or Perth…you could come with me when I'm going.'

'Are you sure you wouldn't mind, I've never been on a bus… I'm the new kid in town Jenny, it's like starting school all over again. Right I've go to get back and start cooking tea, my husband finishes work early.'

On the third of May a letter was waiting for Jennifer when she got home from school it was from Uncle John and Aunty Yvonne.

'Mum the puppies have arrived, can we go over at the weekend? They won't tell me anything about them, so it will be a surprise, but Mrs. Murphy says I can go and look at them while they're tiny.'

'Your father's working on Saturday, then on Sunday we're going to visit that new church.'

'But we can go afterwards.'

'What about our Sunday lunch?'

'We could go to King's Park for lunch on the way; it would be a nice treat for you.'

'We can't afford to eat out very often love, you know that, see what Dad says.'

'But I have to writer back to them so they know we're coming.'

'Nine puppies' said Uncle John, when they arrived on Sunday afternoon. 'Good old Drongo, would you believe it, Bill found him on the front door step the morning they were born, how did he know? We thought we'd lost him again. Sheba's a very good mum, though that's made Mrs Murphy all the more annoyed that she isn't being a good mum to pedigrees. Anyway, you can borrow Trish's bike and Terri will take you round there, can't have too many people disturbing her. You two girls do exactly what Mrs. Murphy tells you, Sheba mustn't get nervous.'

Jennifer was nervous, she wondered how cross Mrs. Murphy still was.

'It's down hill on the way there and up hill on the way back' said Terri.

Shyly they knocked on the front door. Mrs. Murphy opened it and smiled in the way of adults not used to children.

'Strictly no touching, Sheba's very sensitive and she doesn't know you.'

They tip-toed in behind her; the hall looked very posh and they caught a glimpse through the door of the lounge, which seemed to be full of china ornaments. They walked through the kitchen which was quite gloomy, then came to a half door like a stable. Two black Labradors came up, wagging their tails.

'No dogs allowed past this point' explained the woman. She opened the half door and the dogs greeted the children. 'Mother and daughter,

Sheba's no relation, I bought her for new blood last year.'

'She hasn't brought the new blood we were expecting' a man's voice laughed. Mr. Murphy had suddenly appeared.

In the laundry there was another half door and on the other side was a cosy room.

'Madam Sheba's apartment' he quipped.

'Stand behind the door and look, as long as you're quiet' said his wife.

Little fluffy blind balls were snuggled up to the big yellow dog, lying on her side on a blanket. She looked up, then protectively licked the puppies. Jennifer was thrilled, but hardly dare breathe under the gaze of Mrs. Murphy. She couldn't count them, but they were every colour, black, Drongo brown, gold, beige and white. After a while they were beckoned away.

'Do you know how many males and females?' Jennifer asked shyly.

'Four females, but one of the males is the runt of the litter, we might have to have him put down if nature doesn't take its course.'

Jennifer was dismayed, it hadn't occurred to her that could happen; she couldn't bear to think of Sheba loosing one of her puppies.

Chapter Twenty Four   New Faces

Drongo was strutting round proudly with a big grin on his face; or that's how it appeared to Helen. John looked equally smug.

'You would think he'd just become a grandfather' said Yvonne.

John laughed. 'Hey George, Drongo's got the right idea; he visited the puppies once and hasn't been near the place since.'

'We wanted to see the puppies' complained Peter again.

'You might scare Sheba; then she'd eat all the puppies' warned his older brother.

'Simon…' frowned his mother.

'It's true, my friend in England had white mice and they disturbed a new mother; the next time they looked she'd eaten the insides out of each baby.'

'Yuk' said Tony. 'Uncle John, Sheba won't eat them will she?'

'Of course not, she's got more sense than a mouse, probably got more brains than some people.'

'Is it okay if I go now Dad?' said Simon.

'Yes, but keep an eye on the time.'

'Don't forget to check if I'm right about the car' he called, as the fly screen door banged behind him.

'If you could look under the bonnet of the car before we go John, Helen's worried we're going to break down.'

'Where's Simon off to, I thought he'd want to be under the bonnet.'

'Going to look up a couple of friends from his old school; the only way to bribe him to come to church with us was the promise of steak and chips in Kings Park and a lift over here.'

'So what was this church like?' asked Yvonne.

'It smelt funny and the vicar was swinging a ball on a chain' said Peter.

'It was very high church,' explained Helen 'not what we're used to, but the people were quite friendly. George saw the nice building when he was out driving and thought I would like it.'

'High or low, all the same to me,' said John 'you get hypocrites in all of them.'

'John….' said Yvonne.

'Everyone's entitled to their opinions.'

'I think it's good they're trying to find a nice church and a Sunday school for the twins.'

'We haven't tried very hard so far' said George. 'I don't think Helen's going to find anywhere that matches up to St. Stephen's. Who was that woman you were chatting to?'

'She was very friendly; they were Anglo Catholics back home, so that church suits them. Her sister lives near us and goes to a nice family church where they make a point of welcoming people new in the area. She gave me her address and assured me her sister would be delighted if I dropped in; they haven't been out here long.'

'That would be good,' said Yvonne 'you should encourage Helen to get out of the house more George.'

Helen was irritated and wished she hadn't mentioned the sister. She didn't need to be 'got out'; she knew now she could do it herself. Yvonne's visit had given her a wake up call, but that had not been enough. When the children came home to find her asleep and the fridge empty, it had frightened her; somehow a whole day had disappeared. She was appalled at the thought of being one of those mothers who have nervous breakdowns or go to the doctors for tranquilizers.

'Actually, I'm going out tomorrow to help our new next door neighbour. They've come up from the country and she hasn't even ventured onto a bus, let alone to Perth.'

'Where are they from?'

'Oh dear, can't remember, something ending in 'gin' or 'din'; hundreds of miles away. They're semi-retired from the farm, left their son to run it; her husband's got some medical condition that requires regular tests at the hospital. He works, so it can't be that serious. They have a car, but she won't drive up here.'

The twins were getting restless and Drongo had retreated into the back yard to escape them.

'Come on boys, let's go and look at your Dad's car.'

341

'Yes, all you boys go outside and play' said Yvonne. 'When the girls get back we'll have some scones and cakes.' She sighed with relief when they all trooped outside. 'That should keep him occupied for a while. What's wrong with the car?'

'Goodness knows, it's making a funny noise. George and Simon looked at it, but I'm not sure they knew what they were looking at.'

'John's still on about setting up his own car business, but we've been through this before.'

'He'd never be short of customers, everyone has a car here.'

'But you have to have premises, you have to work long hours to get started and you have to have a good head for business. I don't want to be lumbered with all the paperwork just when I'm getting back into nursing.'

'I don't blame you, I remember how hard Dennis' wife had to work when they were starting out. Though neither of them seems to do much work at all these days; they're off on a holiday abroad next week, Lake Como, Italy. Can you imagine? I've never even been to the Isle of Wight.'

Yvonne laughed 'You've come a lot further than Italy.'

'All the way across the world, but I'll never go to Scotland or France now.'

Terri and Jennifer arrived back red faced and thirsty after the long cycle up the hill; gulping down glasses of water they talked excitedly.

'Dad, can we really keep one of Drongo's sons' asked Terri.

'I want a girl,' said Jennifer 'then we could breed dogs. Dad can build an extension like Mrs Murphy's got and I'd look after them so they wouldn't be any trouble.'

'Talking of dogs,' said Helen 'guess who I had a letter from yesterday? Liquorice's 'Mummy'. She's invited me to her Tupperware party.'

She didn't add that she was urged to bring friends along.

When Thelma Driscoll knocked on the fly screen door on Monday morning, Helen was still washing the dishes; her neighbour was obviously worried about missing the bus. She was dressed very smartly, complete with hat and gloves. If Perth had not caught up with the sixties, Helen realised people from the country were bound to seem old fashioned.

'I'll be ready in five minutes.' She hesitated, would the older woman need more time to walk to the bus stop? The summer heat had slowed Helen's pace of walking and it was hard to put an age to her new neighbour. 'Come and see the rest of the house while I get my handbag.' She would leave the dishes in soak, getting out of the house was the important thing.

'It's like mine only the other way round. How many bedrooms do you have?'

'Four, we had to stretch ourselves to the limit to afford it, but half the point of coming out here was to get a decent size house.'

'We've got three, like most of the houses we looked at.'

'The other thing we love is having the two toilets, one in the bathroom and one next to the laundry, such a luxury.'

'No wonder your house goes back further than mine.'

'Do you want to see the rest?' She suddenly remembered the unmade beds. 'On second thoughts, we'd better be on our way to the bus stop.'

'Goodness, don't you walk fast Helen.'

'Oh sorry, habit; years of rushing around. Do you like walking?'

'I guess I'm not used to it.'

'Oh, I thought living out in the country you'd have to walk miles on those big farms.'

'No, much too far or too hot to walk; I had my garden, that was my favourite place.'

The bus arrived as soon as they got to the stop and Helen was glad to see it was the cheerful driver today, as Thelma cautiously stepped on board. She had the correct fare to hand, not wanting to leave anything to chance and chose a seat by the window.

'When Bob drove us into town I was too worried about getting lost to appreciate the view; doesn't the river look lovely.'

Arriving at St. George's Terrace Thelma thanked the driver.

'Sorry I couldn't provide better weather' he motioned to the rain that had started.

'Farmers never complain about rain.'

'I never thought I'd be glad to see it,' said Helen 'but after that hot summer… I guess I'll have to get back into the habit of being prepared for rain. Did you say you need to go to the bank first?'

'Yes, then you can show me the best shops to buy things for the house, if that's okay.'

'I shall enjoy that; I miss shopping, now we've got everything we need.'

It seemed it would be a good day, lots of shopping without having to spend any money.

For Thelma, being in the department stores was like Christmas. She insisted on treating Helen to lunch in Coles' upstairs restaurant and admired the wood panelled Ladies' Rest Room.

'I'm really enjoying my day out, thank you Helen. I wouldn't have dared go on that escalator by myself.'

'I'm used to them, working in London; some of the underground stations had escalators about three times that height.'

'I want to hear all about London.'

They walked back from the bus stop laden with shopping. Thelma wanted everything new and modern to go with the house.

'What will Bob say when he sees all this shopping?'

'Not a lot, but then he never says much anyway. The house on the farm has been in his family for generations, so he let me choose this one and I'm going to enjoy it.'

Helen helped her into the house; she had thought of their house as still new, but Thelma's home looked so white and shiny, she realised grubby fingers and dirty feet were taking their toll at her home. There was not much in her neighbour's lounge except a new suite of furniture and a large television standing proudly in the corner.

'That's Bob's baby, we never had one before, now he's glued to it, even the children's programmes.'

After a day of catching up with housework Helen decided she must visit the sister from the family church. She didn't want it to be an opportunity she let slip. The route in the map book looked simple, though how far up the long road she would have to go she couldn't guess. She counted the blocks so it would be easy to find her turning on the way back.

The house was similar to theirs with an equally unsuccessful front lawn. A young woman answered the door with a toddler on her hips.

'Cathy?'

'Yes, come in, my sister phoned, I'm glad you found us alright. Mind the toys and the mess.'

A baby was sitting in a high chair in the kitchen.

'Oh this brings back memories. Is it just the two children you have?'

'No, another one in Grade Two; can you believe it, I was pregnant when we came out here. I wasn't pregnant when we applied and we were planning to have another baby in Australia, but not quite so soon.'

'Goodness, how did you cope with babies and emigrating?'

'I certainly would not have come without my big sister out here already. That's why we had the phone put on. We didn't want to live in her pockets, but I didn't want to be in a new suburb not knowing anyone and not able to contact her. I'll put the kettle on and you can tell me all about your family.'

The toddler was on the floor now and both little ones stared disconcertingly at Helen; she was out of practice with this age group, but she was glad she had come round. Cathy was easy to chat to; she had come from a completely different part of London, a more well to do area and their paths would never have crossed in England, but just being migrants and mothers gave them plenty in common.

'Now here's the leaflet about our church; you know it's not C of E? It sounds silly now, in the sixties and on the other side of the world, but my parents strongly disapproved of me marrying someone who's a Baptist.'

'So is this a Baptist church?'

'No, it is non-conformist though. We have a lovely family service and I'm sure your teenage son will like the youth group, a couple of the boys play guitar.'

'We'll see you on Sunday morning then' said Helen as Cathy showed her out and the toddler gave a shy little wave.

---oOo---

Hockey lived up to Jennifer's expectations; netball was the most boring game in Junior School and she had longed to progress to hockey. She still envied Christine her grammar school hockey skirt, as they ran around in their shapeless gingham tunics and bloomers, but at last here they were in pairs learning how to 'bully'. Hockey one, hockey two, bang the sticks together, hockey three, try to hit the ball; she missed each time, but the clunk of the hockey sticks was satisfying.

Jennifer did not understand the rules and they were beaten by the 1-9 team, but it was still fun tearing up and down the pitch.Simon had chosen hockey; he figured he was more likely to get on that team than for Australian Rules Football; he did not understand the rules for Australian football, though he claimed he couldn't be bothered to learn them. Jennifer felt elevated to be playing the same sport as her big brother.

At home time she caught up with her younger brothers; they were watching a bulldozer and other machinery.

'Jenny, you're not allowed to go near, that man told us off, they're making the new road.'

When they got home their mother was pleased to hear the sandy track would become a road at last and the boys had a new game to play; they took their toy bulldozer and dumper truck out to the back garden.

By the next morning, dumper trucks were bringing heaps of gravel and the twins dallied on the way to school, reluctant to miss any action. It was exciting watching the trucks' base tip, the gate swing open and the gravel slide out noisily, spreading a cloud of dust. Jennifer was annoyed; she wanted to be early, but felt too responsible to walk off and let them be late for school. They weren't little anymore, too independent now to do what she told them. She ended up rushing across the quadrangle and being last in through the form room door.

'Jenny, I thought you weren't coming' whispered Melissa.

So far neither girl had missed a day's school.

In dressmaking class they were ready to sew their samples on the machines. On the electric machine Jennifer's foot was having trouble connecting with her hands and brain. As soon as she pressed the pedal her sample sped through, leaving a crooked row of stitches. She was convinced the treadle would be easier, but the problem was the opposite, as her feet went forwards and backwards on the plate, so did the sewing. The girls on the other three treadles

349

worked steadily; their samples edged out smoothly. Jennifer was relieved when the siren went.

'Does every girl now know how to use both types of machines?' said Mrs. Butcher.

Jennifer kept silent.

Melissa came home with Jennifer to inspect the progress of the road. There was now a truck with a vat of boiling bitumen and she looked around for her brothers.

'Jenny, we're up here.'

They were both perched in a flame tree.

'Haven't you kids got a home to go to?' the workmen were saying to some other boys.

'Come down, let's go.'

'Can't we wait till they pour it on?'

When they got home, their mother asked as usual for lunch boxes to wash and Tony's homework book. He realised he had forgotten his bag.

'Did you have it when you left school?' She went through the usual lost property routine.

He nodded.

'I bet it's buried in the road by now' said Peter.

'Maybe you left it hanging in the tree' said Melissa.

'Jenny, go back with him and find it.'

'Do I have to? They're supposed to be detectives.'

'The more pairs of eyes the better.'

'Can Jenny come round my house and watch television? We could look for it on the way.'

'I'll come straight back after 'Komotion' pleaded her daughter.

The girls had discovered a new pop programme; it was so good Jennifer wanted to suggest to her parents it was time to get a television, but daren't mention it until the puppy was safely acquired. They urged the boys to hurry; they didn't want to miss their programme.

'If I don't find my bag, I won't have to do my homework' said Tony.

'If we don't find your bag, Mum and Dad will be cross and you won't have anything to take your lunch in.'

She was hoping the men would have finished, but it was even busier, with a huge road roller flattening out the bitumen. It was too noisy and she was too shy to explain to the workmen why they were lingering again.

Peter found the bag and she urged them to go straight home, but they were fascinated with the roller. Jennifer imagined explaining to her parents that Tony had been flattened like a cartoon character; but in cartoons they always got up again. The girls set off at a brisk walk, Jennifer turning to make sure the boys were walking in the opposite direction. Melissa laughed at the idea of Tony being pressed into the bitumen for ever.

'There's always an adventure going on in your family.'

At Melissa's house all was peaceful. She poked her head round the door of the sewing room and offered to make her mother a cup of tea.

'Good, we can have the lounge to ourselves and turn the telly up loud.'

She came back from the kitchen with drinks and chocolate. For half an hour young men and women mimed and danced to American and English pop hits.

'Has Simon seen this?'

'Yes, he watches it at Paul's house; they reckon they're going to be on it next year.'

'Cross country tomorrow' warned Melissa as she said goodbye to her friend.

'I bet we do better than the girls who didn't go on camp and I bet we beat 1-9.'

She had never won a race on sports day, but perhaps she would be the first one back tomorrow.

Jennifer's hopes were dashed the next day. Her mother had explained her periods could be irregular to start with and she must always go to school prepared, with 'STs' in her bag, but she had almost convinced herself she would not have another period for at least a year.

At morning recess she discovered the blood with dismay. She was worried about the uncomfortable belt and sanitary towel staying in place when they had to run. At camp Catherine had told the story of her sister's friend, who had got up from a lesson with blood all over her dress and had died of embarrassment; although she hadn't actually died, like the poor person in another girl's story.

1-9 streaked out in front and Catherine urged them to catch up. Jennifer knew from Simon's advice it was better to start slowly and steadily. Much of the route was through Tonydale, but some of the girls reckoned they knew a short cut. Melissa had no desire to win and she and Jennifer got back to find Catherine had arrived first.

Jennifer had been instructed to meet the twins and make sure they brought their bags home and didn't get tar over their shoes. The new road was now black and shiny and joined the intersection. They were surprised to see their father coming towards them.

'I was home early, thought I'd come and have a look. This reminds me of when I was the twins' age. Granny's house was brand new; we were one of the first in the street to move in. Dennis and I loved watching the houses being built and the roads made, it was all fields then. Your grandfather was pleased to have a garden and your grandmother was delighted to have an inside toilet.'

When they got home Mrs. Driscoll was having a cup of tea with their mother. The two women were planning a trip to Victoria Park the next day. Their new neighbour made every trip sound like a big adventure, which was strange, because Jennifer thought it must be more adventurous out in the bush.

'Oh your twins are so adorable, look at their lovely pink cheeks.' When Simon walked in she said 'Aren't you tall? I'd never have guessed you're not yet sixteen.' He blushed. '…and you do look like a Beatle, is Ringo your favourite?'

'No… John' he said indignantly.

'Your mother said you want to play the drums, so I thought it must be Ringo' she replied, keen to show she was up to date with the pop scene.

At tea time Simon did impressions of Mrs. Driscoll that made Jennifer laugh. 'Oh Hilen, yoor so brive going on the iscalitors and foinding yoor wiy raond Peerth.'

'Simon, don't ever let Mrs Driscoll hear you talking like that, she would be hurt' said his mother.

'Yes remember we're the foreigners here' added his father.

'I know, but I bet she does imitations of us to 'Bub'.

On Sunday they set off to walk to the new church.

'What's it called?' said Simon.

'I told you, it's called 'The New Church', it's a nice building, I went round there yesterday and it's not far.

'Don't kick the sand boys, keep your shoes clean.'

'Doesn't look like a church' said Simon.

'It's modern,' countered Jennifer 'everything's new in Perth.'

Inside, everything was different from a normal church. The walls were light with ordinary windows and the pews were plain beige wood. There was no altar, just a table with a white cloth and Jennifer couldn't find a kneeler. At St. Stephen's they always knelt down and prayed when they first got there; she wasn't sure why or what you were supposed to pray about. A young woman in front turned round and asked if they were new. Jennifer nodded and the woman smiled.

'You'll like Pastor Roberts.'

A man in a smart suit suddenly appeared from a door in the front corner and she was surprised when he came to stand at the front. He raised his arms, smiled to reveal shiny teeth and said good morning to everyone. Then he looked directly at the Palmers.

'…and we welcome a new family to our church, the Palmers.'

How did he know their names?

'Would you like to introduce yourselves?'

Jennifer was embarrassed, her parents looked uncomfortable and Simon was sinking as low as possible in the pew; but the twins stood stiffly to attention. Everyone laughed when Peter told them he was half an hour older than Tony. His brother introduced the rest of the family and they sat down obediently when Pastor Roberts nodded.

A young man sat at an electric organ and everybody picked up blue books and heartily sung a hymn Jennifer had never heard before. When it was time to pray there were no prayer books and everyone perched on the edge of their pews and bowed their heads. Simon took the opportunity to make faces at his brothers while their parents had their eyes closed.

For the second hymn a teenage boy walked to the front with a guitar. Helen smiled encouragingly at Simon, but Jennifer caught his eye and nearly giggled. The guitarist had short hair plastered down with hair cream. This meant he was square, irredeemably square. For Simon all things and all people were either Fab or Square, mostly they were square.

After praying for a few people they didn't know, the Prime Minister and the 'trouble in Vietnam', a woman set up an easel at the front with large sheets of paper pegged to it. Pastor Roberts produced some large wax crayons and her father frowned at her mother. When the pastor asked for two volunteers and looked directly at the twins, their arms shot up and they stood on tip toe.

'Who likes drawing?' he asked, turning to Tony.

Jennifer wondered if he could read boys' minds.

It seemed both boys had listened well in Sunday school and scripture classes at St. Stephen's; they answered all his questions correctly and their parents beamed proudly. Tony was then allowed to draw; Simon grinned as he drew a lurid picture of a man lying in pools of blood, with stick men walking by. He then drew another upright figure with a yellow halo and Peter wrote 'The Good Samaritan' underneath.

Jennifer thought they had got away without having a sermon, but babies and toddlers were gathered to the back of the church by several ladies and Pastor Roberts prayed silently and prepared himself to speak to the adults. Jennifer turned back to see a cosy circle of chairs and a colourful collection of toys.

'That's Cathy' whispered her mother, pointing to a young woman in the centre of the crèche with her arms full of babies.

As Pastor Roberts talked about the modern relevance of the Good Samaritan and Jennifer wondered guiltily if she had ever passed by on the other side, the occasional toddler would escape, but the pastor just smiled benignly.

Afterwards, a man with a beard, carrying a toddler, introduced himself as Trevor, Cathy's husband and swept them next door into the church hall.

'I'll introduce you to a couple of the lads from the youth group' he said to Simon, who had been looking round for an escape route.

Cathy pointed to a large hatch and told the twins to go and get cordial and biscuits, then turned to Jennifer.

'I'll introduce you to a couple of the girls who go to Girl's Brigade, your mother said you were interested in joining.'

Jennifer had no idea what Girl's Brigade was, let alone that she wanted to join. As she was led away to the other side of the hall, she could see her parents standing chatting to the pastor with cups of tea in their hands. The same green china they had at St. Stephen's church hall, the same green china that appeared everywhere that grown ups had cups of tea.

Chapter Twenty Five New Church

The only thing the 'New Church' had in common with St. Stephen's was the green 'Beryl' china, Helen mused as they chatted to Pastor Roberts. The beef would be late in the oven, but she was enjoying meeting people who were genuinely friendly and welcoming. Even Simon would be pleased to have lads his own age to talk to.

'This was the old church,' the pastor was saying, 'so when we built the new church we had a ready made hall and just added the kitchen.'

'It's a lot smarter than the hall at our old church; they're still fund raising for a new hall that the junior school can use as well.'

'Our buildings were an answer to prayer, or rather many prayers; every time we thought progress would halt, along would come an architect or a builder, or an electrician to join the congregation.'

'God helps those who help themselves' said George.

'...so can I put you down on the crèche roster Helen?'

They were already on first name terms it seemed.

'I'm rather out of practice with little ones...'

'I'm sure it will all come back to you, after bringing up four lovely children.'

Helen looked around to see if there was a Mrs. Pastor or any little pastors; he read her mind.

'Come in the kitchen and meet Muriel, my wonderful wife.'

Muriel and another lady were wiping up and wiping down, after what looked like a major catering operation. They looked so joyful, Helen wouldn't have been surprised if they had broken into a Sunday School chorus.

'Your twins won't know our boys,' said Muriel 'they go to Glenmore Primary, that's nearer to us.'

Her husband had magically summoned four identical boys who filed politely into the kitchen. They came in four different sizes, though obviously close in age and they all had their fair hair in a crew cut.

'Barber's every fortnight,' said the pastor 'sensible and hygienic in this climate and much easier for their mother, no Beatles in our house.'

'Have you told Helen about the Ladies' Fellowship?' said his wife.

'Not yet, but she's signed up for the crèche. George, we don't forget the chaps; we have a men's breakfast first Saturday of each month.'

'I have to work some Saturdays...'

'I'm sure you'll find it a worthwhile experience.'

Outside at last, Simon had found some girls from his school to chat to and George sent

Jennifer to find the twins. He whipped out his packet of cigarettes.

'George' Helen whispered urgently, as two cigarettes headed for his lips.

'Don't you want one? I was going to have one before, but I couldn't find an ashtray in the hall.'

'Wait till we're on the way home, they don't believe in smoking… or drinking.'

George chuckled. 'Where did they get that from? They didn't have cigarettes in Biblical times and Jesus turned water into wine.' They set off down the road with the twins skipping along in front and Jennifer and Simon trailing behind. 'That was an interesting experience.' He inhaled with relish, now they were out of sight of the church. 'I suppose he fancies himself as Billy Graham.'

'Nothing wrong with being sincere and everyone was so welcoming; it's bound to be different to what we're used to.'

'The twins certainly enjoyed it, if you really like it we'll go there. It would be good for Simon to meet some nice young people.'

When Helen went out to the back yard to call the twins for the late lunch, she was surprised to see three heads bob up from behind the largest gum tree.

'Patricia… I thought you were in Sydney.'

'Hello Aunty Helen, we just got back yesterday, can I stay in your garden while you have your lunch?'

'Have you had your lunch, does your mother know you're here?'

'Yes, she said I could come round while she unpacks.'

'Pat's going to join our detective agency' said Peter, not at all surprised the little girl had suddenly appeared when she was supposed to be two thousand miles away.

Over lunch the family discussed the latest events. Patricia was in the twins' bedroom reading the old 'Eagle' annuals they had brought out from England.

'Apart from that one postcard, I haven't heard a word from Valerie; I couldn't write back, there was no address. You could go round and see how Caroline is, Jenny.'

'Do I have to? I hope she's not going to be in my class.'

'They really are a feckless bunch,' said George 'you would have thought they would have come back during the Easter holidays, so the girls were ready for the beginning of term.'

'We don't know what happened; perhaps Mike lost his 'wonderful' job.'

'You can invite Aunty Valerie to the Tupperware party' said Jennifer.

'Good idea, I'm sure Barbara only invited me to make up numbers. Thelma's keen to come, I suppose even a Tupperware party is preferable to an evening at home with Bob and the telly.'

On Monday afternoon Helen decided she would go round to visit Valerie; she was curious and quite looking forward to seeing her again. She had forgotten how much she talked, more so now there was so much to relate.

'I meant to write when we had a permanent address, but things were so hectic. Of course, Sydney's a real city, not old fashioned like Perth…'

They were onto their second cup of tea and Helen had still not gathered how or why they had come back.

'…so when we heard our tenants wanted to go back to England, we realised how much we missed Perth.'

Helen tried to get a word in edgeways. 'Do you think you'll feel more settled now? I went through a bit of a down patch, it felt as if nothing was real, I knew we couldn't go back; I didn't want to go back… you have to make an effort for it to feel like home.'

'Exactly what Mike says; we have to make the best of it now.'

'How did you get on with the schools this morning?'

'Patricia's in your Peter's class, grade four and five, she needs the stimulation of the older children, she can easily do grade five work. We asked if Caroline could be in Jenny's class, but the headmaster said she had originally been put in 1-5 and that space had not been filled.'

Helen was relieved on Jennifer's behalf. 'There are some nice girls in 1-5, Jennifer shared a dormitory with them on camp. Oh I mustn't forget to ask, I know it's short notice, but do you want to go to a Tupperware party on Thursday evening?'

'Oh that should be a laugh, I'll give you a lift, Mike won't need the car.'

When Helen arrived at the Ladies' Fellowship she was embarrassed to find that everyone had brought a 'plate'. Cathy reassured her; visitors and first timers weren't expected to bring anything.

'I'm always baking at home, they eat it as fast as I cook it; especially Simon. At least the food basics seem to be very cheap here.'

'Yes, we find the everyday things very reasonable, just as well; Trevor doesn't earn a lot and we stretched ourselves to buy the house. Now I'd better introduce you to everyone.'

Some of the women had brought sewing and knitting and there was a large cardboard box they were putting clothes and toys in.

'We're making and collecting for the Aboriginal children at the mission' said one of the women.

Helen suddenly realised she had never given a thought to the original inhabitants of Australia; no one had mentioned them as far as she could recall.

'I'm ashamed to say I know very little about the Aborigines.'

'Most Australians know very little about them,' said Cathy 'especially in the cities.'

'If they have lived on this continent always, they must know much better than white

Australians how to live on the land, why do they need any help?'

As soon as she spoke, she realised from the expression on a couple of faces, it should have been evident to her that the Aborigine children needed the Christian help of 'The New Church'. She decided to keep silent till she knew more.

Cathy smiled at her. 'I'm sure they didn't need any help till we came along and interfered; when I say we, I mean the English, that's what the first settlers were' she added hastily, lest any Australians were offended.

'Alcohol was their downfall,' said another woman 'they can't cope with it.'

'The downfall of many people' said another.

'It is thought that medically speaking, as a race who have never used alcohol, their bodies are unable to deal with it' said Cathy. 'I don't know if that has been proved scientifically, but either way they should be helped not blamed.'

'I think it's time we had a cup of tea and cake' said an elderly genial lady.

When Helen, Valerie and Thelma arrived for the Tupperware party, Rover greeted Helen enthusiastically

'Oh, he remembers… you must be Helen; I'm Barbara, Rover's 'Mummy'. Thank you so much for looking after my baby… I always tell everyone I've got three boys.'

Helen resolved that their puppy would never be her baby, nor would she be its 'Mummy'. She introduced her friends.

365

'Welcome everybody; I've never had a Tupperware party before.'

In the lounge an assortment of chairs had been squeezed in and there were at least half a dozen women. Helen was relieved, the more the merrier when it came to the pressure to buy something. The Tupperware lady was English and turned out to be one of those people who had found Tupperware to be a life changing experience. Helen imagined her talking about little else, even when off duty; she was already mentally composing a letter to Joyce.

'….and take the lid off and you have a cereal bowl for breakfast…'

Helen had not been paying attention; absorbed in guessing who was English and who Australian. She wondered when they were going to get a cup of tea.

'I'll put the kettle on while you ladies give your orders….'

'Well done Thelma, winning the quiz,' said Valerie 'at least it was someone from our 'team'. Let's go in the kitchen and see if she needs any help, I'm dying for a cuppa.'

There was a little group asking earnest questions about sizes and lids.

'If you don't want a whole set of something Helen, we could share the order. If you don't want eight beakers or ten bowls, we could divvy up later.'

'Good idea, but we'd better work out what we want secretly, in case we're not allowed to do that.'

'I don't think it's illegal' Valerie laughed. 'How about you Thelma?'

'Oh I'm going to order lots of stuff, I wish they'd had these things when I was first married.'

'You should have a party; like she said, you get a hostess gift and a discount, depending how many orders are taken.'

'I'm not sure about that Valerie.'

The woman had been pressing the guests to sign up for a party; if Thelma had a party it would take the pressure off she and Valerie to have one, but she felt responsible for her neighbour.

'Would Bob mind?'

'No, I could send him off to the pub, George could take him out for a drink.'

'...and Mike, it would be good for the blokes to get to know each other.'

Helen remained silent. Valerie always seemed to end up organising everyone's lives for them.

There was no holding Thelma back when they returned to the lounge; as other ladies completed their orders and took their cups of tea, she sat down with the order form and declared her wish to have a party.

The Tupperware lady was almost ecstatic at such enthusiasm; a customer ordering items she hadn't realised she needed till that evening.

Helen and her two friends helped wash up after the other guests left; then had another cup of tea after the Tupperware lady left. Thelma seemed in no hurry to go home.

'Will Bob wonder where you are?' said Helen.

'No, he won't notice I'm not back till the white dot disappears from the middle of the television screen' she laughed.

Barbara wanted to hear all about Drongo and Sheba's puppies.

Thelma didn't think much of their attitude to dogs. 'Kelpies are working dogs Helen, are you sure that's what you want, they belong on a farm.'

'I gather working was not what Drongo wanted to do, that's why the farmer was going to shoot him.'

'Oh, that's dreadful' cried Barbara.

'Every creature has to pull their weight on the farm' said Thelma.

When they finally got home George had been worried. She hugged him.

'I was beginning to think I might never see my home again, but it was fun going out. Thelma's going to have a party. A few weeks ago I hardly new anybody, now the calendar's quite full.' She hugged him again affectionately. 'You have been patient, putting up with me all these weeks.'

By June, they understood what everyone meant by 'real winter rain'. It would come unexpectedly, heavier than any English rain, soaking the children if they were caught on the way home from school. The local boys went to school barefoot, carrying their shoes to keep them dry.

Indoors in the evenings it got chilly and they were glad to have a fireplace. John helped George construct a grate and they collected wood from the bush around them. The wood smoke had a unique smell that Helen would forever associate with the house beginning to feel like a proper home.

In the backyard George and Simon built a kennel so the new puppy would have shade and a retreat from the twins when it was outside. Also, Helen had told the family, so it would know it was a dog.

Excitement was mounting in the family as the twins' birthday loomed and the time grew closer to choose the puppy.

---oOo---

Jennifer liked to leave for school early, before Caroline came slouching up the road. At least she wasn't in the same class, though she felt sorry for her, arriving in the middle of the school year. Caroline was not the only new person in first year; every few weeks a new English boy or girl would arrive. Migrants were moving into the new homes near Melissa and new houses were being built further up Smith Street. At weekends the girls went exploring on their bikes, tip toeing into the skeleton buildings if no one was around, walking by waist high walls, imagining the finished houses.

Three weeks to go till they could choose the puppy. They had not seen them again; Mrs. Murphy had made it clear that they would be busy and would not expect to see the Palmers until the big day. Jennifer was worried that no arrangements had been made; they had not seen Terri's family either. Melissa was still trying to persuade her parents to let her have a puppy, though Jennifer's father warned her not to involve other people; it was up to Mr. and Mrs. Murphy what they did with the puppies.

'Are you going to Girl's Brigade this evening Jenny? …Tony come and eat your breakfast or you'll be late… Have you asked Caroline if she wants to come?'

Jennifer finished her drink of milk. 'Yes, it is fun and they're going to go real camping like Guides.' In England she had longed to 'fly up' to Girl Guides so she could go camping; she also wanted to wear the impressive leather belt and buckle that went with the uniform and coveted the light blue airtex T-shirt Christine' older sister wore for summer outdoor activities. 'I don't have to ask Caroline do I?'

'Aunty Valerie said she would love to come.'

Jennifer laughed 'That doesn't mean Caroline wants to come.'

Her mother veered between urging Jennifer to be nice to Caroline and sympathising with her daughter.

'You could mention it and hope she doesn't come' she smiled.

Jennifer didn't see Caroline at school, nor did she go out of her way to find her. That evening, playing games in the church hall with the other girls, she decided she would join Girl's Brigade; the leaders were young and enthusiastic and though she only knew one girl from school, the others were friendly.

They were all looking forward to Sunday morning; the whole congregation was going to Crawley Beach for a picnic, instead of church. The most important reason was for two grownups to be baptised in the Swan River; just like Jesus was baptised in the River Jordan by John the Baptist.

On Sunday morning it was chilly by the river and the sky was cloudy; Jennifer wondered what would happen if it rained. In the Bible it never seemed to rain, that was why they had flat roofs. Her father didn't agree with everything Pastor Roberts did, but her mother said at least they were doing something they would never have done in England. That was her father's favourite saying 'We wouldn't have been doing this in England!'

The man and woman were dressed in white robes and so were Father Roberts and his young assistant. They waded out into the water just deep enough to be 'fully immersed'. If the water felt cold they showed no sign. Miraculously, as Pastor Roberts blessed the river, the clouds broke and rays of sunlight shone through.

371

She wondered if the whole river was now Holy, like the water in the font at St Stephen's, like the Holy water Melissa dipped her fingers in at her church before she crossed herself.

Simon nudged her, behind them a photographer had appeared. 'Bet he's from the newspaper. Come to see if God's going to come down from the clouds and speak to us.'

Jennifer shivered, God could do that if he wanted to, but it would be scary if he did. Her parents were motioning Simon to be quiet and she forced herself to look up at the sky and then down to the river.

Pastor Roberts laid his hand on the woman's head; then he and the helper supported her shoulders and let her slip backwards under the water. Jennifer wondered if she was allowed to hold her nose so the water didn't go up. They repeated the action with the man, then they all waded slowly back; through their wet gowns you could see they all had their bathers on underneath.

Some people held out towels and the congregation welcomed them as if they had never met them before; this was because they were now 'new people'.

'Can we do that' said Peter.

'No, you've already been baptised' said her father.

'But we don't remember and that wasn't in the river' said Tony.

Their mother had gone overboard with the picnic; as everyone had been exhorted to share what they brought, she didn't want the Palmers to look less than generous. The sharing also gave Simon an excuse not to sit with his family.

The boy who played the guitar came to speak to them politely and thanked Helen for the homemade cake. Jennifer was pleased he talked to her as well, not treating her like a child.

'What a nice polite lad' said her father, when the boy left to make sure his granny was okay. 'Does he go to your school Jenny?'

'No, Simon says he's an apprentice, something to do with metal.'

'Well it's good to learn a trade, but he could be a musician, he can certainly play that guitar… better than Simon's friend, all he does is strum a few chords.'

Jennifer giggled, but looked round guiltily, hoping Simon hadn't heard.

'That's why Simon wants to learn the drums, he thinks it will be easier than the guitar' she confided to her parents.

Other people came over to talk to them. Grownups always asked how school was and what your favourite subjects were.

'Painting and English… painting is the most fun, but I'm not that good, English I get good marks and I like Science when we have the Bunsen burners…'

'Has anyone blown up the lab yet?' chuckled one man.

Grownups always said that and thought it was a huge joke.

Jennifer didn't add that dressmaking was her worst subject. She couldn't get the hang of the treadle machines and devised tactics to avoid them. Her apron was progressing slowly; Melissa had finished hers and was bored.

At home time on Monday, Jennifer and Melissa stood chatting on the edge of the oval with some of the other girls; they wanted to hear about the river baptism. When Simon and Paul came strolling towards them she wondered if her brother would say hello so she would be proud, or if he would ignore her and she would have to pretend not to notice him. Before that moment arrived Paul's brother drew up in his car.

'Hey Jenny, do you two want a lift?' asked Paul.

Before she could say 'no thanks' Melissa had said 'yes please.'

'Come on Jenny, your parents won't mind if you're with your brother' said her friend.

They found themselves in the back seat with a grumpy Simon. She couldn't explain to Melissa, with the brothers listening, that her parents would not approve of she or Simon being in the car.

'We could take them to see our rehearsal studio' said Simon.

Jennifer thought this was a ploy to make sure they went nowhere near Smith Street. She felt sick with guilt; her mother would assume she had gone to Melissa's or Maria's. The brother drove carefully, but fast and they seemed to be going a long way up a bush road. At last they drew up at a derelict weatherboard house with ramshackle stables; there was no sign of a studio, but she felt a thrill of adventure.

'Is it haunted?' said Melissa.

'Only by our dead granny' said Paul.

'He's just kidding,' said his brother 'Dad said we could use this place until he sells it, he doesn't like us practising at home, nor do the neighbours.'

Jennifer was not allowed to go off to strange places by herself; sometimes it was exciting having a big brother. The property smelt of wood smoke, fresh winter grass and old cars; there were several small paddocks and rusty fences. A large shed was where they practised.

'If you want to look inside you have to be careful,' said the big brother 'there's broken glass and sharp nails sticking out.'

'Yeah, Dad will kill me if you cut yourself' said Simon.

The girls tiptoed in and the boys brought two guitars from the car boot.

Simon's drums turned out not to be the musical sort, but when he beat the metal drums and paint tins with wooden sticks the girls were impressed. He had a good rhythm and the brothers played in time with him.

'I haven't heard that one on Komotion' said Melissa.

'You might one day,' said Paul 'I wrote it.'

'Has it got any words?' asked Jennifer.

'I'm still writing them…'

His brother started singing a Beatles song.

'Oh you've got a really good voice' said Melissa.

'He's the lead singer,' said Paul 'but his friend's got a good voice as well.'

'I think you will be famous' said Jennifer. She wanted to please her brother, but she also believed what she was saying.

'Come on, we'd better go,' he said, 'take Melissa home first, then you can drop me and Jenny at the shops.' He looked at both girls seriously. 'First you have to take the oath of secrecy; no one knows where this place is.'

Jennifer nodded earnestly and Melissa crossed herself.

When they arrived at the shops Simon bought her a bottle of coke and a Violet Crumble', she wondered if it was bribery.

'Don't mention the car, Mum and Dad would only worry, but they don't need to, he is a good driver.'

It was easy for him to say that, but what if her mother asked what she had been doing? They walked back in silence.

As they approached their house they were surprised to see their mother, Aunty Valerie and Caroline standing on the veranda looking worried.

'Have you seen Patricia and the boys?'

Jennifer was scared they would have to reveal where they had been. She thought quickly.

'I bet I know where they are, in the swamp, Simon and I will go and look for them.'

Simon was too grown up to want to know where 'Tonymarsh' and 'Peterbog' were; only she knew where they played. If they didn't find them they really might be lost. She led her brother down the track that had been dry and sandy in summer, then ducked under paper bark trees into a squelchy paddock. Simon looked genuinely worried and Jennifer felt a stab of fear as she wondered if something really had happened to them.

'Jenny, Simon, Pat fell in the bog and we had to rescue her.'

Three muddy children came tramping towards them. They weren't supposed to play in their school uniforms, but hopefully the two mums would just be relieved to see them.

Simon pulled off his jumper and put it on Patricia.

'Hyperthermia' he said importantly. 'Do you want a piggy back Pat?'

She squealed with excitement, thoroughly enjoying the adventure.

'Oh thank you Simon' said Aunty Valerie, practically kissing him.

Jennifer mused resentfully that he wouldn't have found them without her.

When Patricia had been showered, dressed in some of Jennifer's clothes and taken home, their mother questioned the boys.

'Why did you take poor Patricia down there, you're very lucky Aunty Valerie wasn't cross with you.'

'But it was her idea,' said Peter 'then she fell in when we told her not to go that far.'

'..and she would have drowned if we hadn't rescued her' added Tony.

'Thank goodness Jenny knew where to find you, it's getting dark already.'

'Will Pat get 'hi po thurm ia' asked Peter.

'No, I think she's tougher than you two boys put together, but I don't know what your father's going to say.'

Simon winked at Jennifer.

Her mother had had enough worries for one day and Jennifer was relieved there would not be a chance to tell her about their afternoon.

Chapter Twenty Six   Parties

'I hope they weren't trying to baptise her.'

'What?' George raised his head from the newspaper.

'At the swamp, marsh, whatever the boys call it.'

'Oh… Patricia in the bog, perhaps we'd better have a look over there; I thought it was their imagination, but if we keep having these heavy rains it could get deep.'

'I wonder if she's alright? Valerie won't be speaking to me.'

'Wouldn't that be a good thing?'

'It's nice to see Simon being responsible.'

'…and getting on well with Jenny.'

She smiled. 'Girls mature quicker, mentally; she's catching him up. They've got more in common now, same school, pop music.'

'So… you have a busy week.'

'Thelma's worried she won't have enough guests at her Tupperware party and I'm worried we'll have too many at the birthday party.'

'Joe's wife and his sister are coming to Thelma's, though he'll kill me if they spend too much.'

'It will be nice to meet them, I hope it won't be boring for them, they must be quite young.'

'How many boys have Tony and Peter invited?'

'I daren't even count, that's the trouble with them being in separate classes. Then they'll be Pastor Robert's boys, Cathy's eldest and according to Valerie, Barbara's two sons, though I don't recall inviting them.'

'Barbara?'

'You know, Rover's 'mummy'; she and Val are quite pally now. She has the car quite often so she can go out and about visiting.'

'Good, at least she's not round here all the time. Anyway, the whole day will have to be planned with military efficiency. Do you remember last year's party?'

'I'm not likely to forget; the rain and that boy who kept jumping on the beds.'

'Plenty of games, plenty of food, then everyone home.'

'Are you ready for your coffee?'

'Yes, did Tony finish his arithmetic?'

'Simon helped him; he's very good with them when he wants to be.'

Thelma's Tupperware party turned out to be livelier than they expected. Joe's wife and sister admired her bright modern home and Thelma quickly introduced them to the two Australian ladies she had met at Tom the Cheap's. Valerie brought two English neighbours and Barbara came with a car load of women. The Tupperware Lady had to readjust her display to fit everyone in the lounge.

Valerie greeted Helen effusively. 'I hope George wasn't cross with the boys, Patricia told me it was her idea.'

She turned to the packed room. 'Helen's Simon rescued our Patricia from drowning, it's very dangerous over in those marshes.'

The Italian ladies looked concerned and Valerie's neighbour said 'I didn't know we had marshes in Glendale, it's not exactly Exmoor is it?'

'Oh, I'm sure they're not...' Helen tried to get a word in.

'Helen and I thought something had happened to the children, we were so worried, you never know these days, even in Glendale there could be some funny men around.'

'There was that little girl that went missing near us, just before we left England,' said her neighbour 'never found a trace of her...'

The Tupperware lady was getting restless; the conversation would be hard to steer back to plastic bowls.

'I'm sure Patricia wouldn't go wandering off by herself, she is sensible.'

'Yes like your Jenny, she's a good girl, Helen never has any worries.'

'We're very lucky; if she's late home from school I know she'll be at Melissa's or one of their other friends.' Helen caught Thelma's eye. '...That's enough of me chattering on...'

The Tupperware lady launched into her welcoming speech before anyone else could interrupt.

Helen helped Thelma in the kitchen.

'Phew… it's going well.'

'Yes, I think everyone is going to buy something. What time is Bob coming home?'

'I suppose it depends how much beer Mike got in; it was nice of him to invite them.'

Helen wondered how the three men were getting on; it would be the first time they had met Mike; even Bob and George had only said hello to each other.

Back in the lounge they realised they were missing some juicy gossip from Valerie's neighbours.

'Wife swapping?' said Valerie.

'Not car keys thrown on the coffee table, though maybe they did after we left, we didn't stay long enough to find out. One of the wives was sitting canoodling on the lap of someone else's husband and in another corner…'

'Is that what happens at English parties?' said Thelma.

'No' said Helen hastily.

'Perhaps I could swap Bob for a younger model' she laughed.

'I would have gladly lent out my husband,' said the other woman 'if there had been anything better on offer!'

Everyone was laughing and the Tupperware lady was having trouble concentrating on her order forms. Helen was relieved that the ladies from the church fellowship had not been able to come.

When she got home George was already in.

'What was your evening like?'

'Quiet, we had a couple of drinks and watched telly; Bob doesn't say much and Mike sent Caroline to bed early; said he was going to watch what he wanted to for a change. I left before Bob, said I had to get up early.'

'Our evening wasn't quiet.' She hugged him. 'I don't think I'll swap you.'

'Where was the party?' he asked, after she'd described the 'wife swapping'.

'Palmer Street, would you believe.

'Perhaps we'll get invited; if they throw their car keys in the middle I might get a newer model car and wife!'

Friday was the twins' birthday, Saturday was the party. Helen found Monday and Friday to be the worst mornings to get the boys off to school; on Monday they had to get back into routine and by Friday they were tired.

They would have their presents after tea, when everybody was home.

'Don't invite any more children to the party' she warned, as they set off down the road.

After much thought she and George had chosen one present each, with added money sent from England. A choice they hoped would suit the boys whether they were in detective or explorer mood. The boys had changed their minds every day as to what they would like, interspersed with pleas for one or even two of Sheba's puppies. Helen had put her foot down, one set of twins had been enough, one puppy would be enough to cope with. They promised them a puppy for their tenth birthdays; if they behaved all year and helped Jenny withy her dog.

That evening the presents were greeted with delight; a camera for Tony and a science set for Peter, including a large magnifying glass. They soon swapped.

Three pm to five pm had seemed a civilised period for the party, but not all the guests adhered to Helen and George's schedule. Wayne arrived at 2pm with his uninvited younger brother and other boys from school started arriving soon after; several children asked Thelma if she was the twins' granny, but she took it in good part. Muriel arrived at three pm precisely with her four boys smartly dressed in white shirts and bow ties. Her husband was looking forward to writing his sermon in peace and she declared the boys would behave better if she wasn't there.

Helen didn't recognise Patricia, she was wearing a frilly pink dress and mohair cardigan. She had brought another girl from their class, at Valerie's instigation, so she wouldn't be the only girl.

Simon had acquired a teacher's whistle from somewhere; if he was forced to be at home for the party, he had decided he and Jennifer would be in charge of games. Pass the parcel and pin the tail on the donkey were declared too babyish for nine year olds and twins provided an ideal opportunity for team games.

The sky was clear; the party could stay outside. Helen still could not remember all the names of the Roberts boys, let alone which was which. They had names unfamiliar to her, such as Ashley and Lee. The eldest had new teeth too large for his mouth and another had no front teeth, but the two younger with their baby teeth could not be told apart. Barbara's two sons looked huge next to the little boys, but Simon and George soon had ages and sizes shared equally between Tony and Peter's teams.

The other girl took to the little boy on her team and looked after him with maternal pride, but on Tony's team Patricia was too busy trying to win and Jenny had to comfort the other little brother. He sat on Helen's lap for a couple of the more hectic races.

At four pm precisely George declared it was time for tea and made them line up, with the youngest at the front of the queue. In the kitchen Helen and Thelma handed out Tupperware plates, bowls and beakers. The children helped themselves to food then sat on the blankets outside. Simon and Jennifer went around pouring Coca Cola and cordial into their beakers. Peter managed to jog Patricia so she spilled Coca Cola onto her dress.

At four fifty pm Helen brought the birthday cake out. Last year the boys had not been able to blow sixteen candles out at once; this time they blew all eighteen candles out. The other children were suitably impressed. It was five o'clock by the time last children left; Wayne and his brother had to be persuaded to go home.

Helen and George collapsed in the lounge with a cup of tea while the boys sat on the floor excitedly investigating their presents; sensible small gifts, some shared, some identical; most classmates brought one present for the relevant twin. In England Helen had known all the parents and always told them not to worry about bringing presents to the party. The gifts were mainly little cars, colouring books and paperbacks, but it amounted to quite a collection, which they were already swapping round.

'That's it till next year, thank goodness' said George.

---oOo---

When Jennifer came home from school on Monday afternoon there was a letter waiting for her with Mrs. Murphy's name on the back; she opened it excitedly and read it carefully. Finally she handed it to her mother.

'This is more complicated than when that lady at church adopted a baby.'

'It is important to make sure the puppy settles in properly.' Jennifer felt nobody in her family was taking the imminent arrival seriously. Mrs. Murphy stressed that only she and her father should come to collect the puppy, as it must be kept calm on the journey. 'Dad's not working on Saturday is he?'

'Only in the morning, you're not expected till three thirty.'

At tea time Jennifer wanted to discuss puppies, but Simon was talking about drums again.

'It's not even the end of June yet,' said their father 'we haven't recovered from Peter and Tony's birthday, it's another three months till yours.'

Melissa and Jennifer had kept their promise and not breathed a word about their visit to the practice shed, but at home Jennifer could talk about drums. Simon wanted her on his side, she was the only one who understood drum kits; she had seen them on Top of the Pops and Ready Steady Go, two English programmes they both missed.

'You could start a skiffle group they used whatever they could find.'

'Mum, that's so square, we're going to be a proper band.'

'I hope Paul sings better than he plays the guitar' laughed their father.

Simon didn't rise to the bait. 'No one will notice him at the back; his brother and the other bloke can really sing and play. They were in another band, but they wanted to start their own; that's why I want to get some proper drums, before they find another drummer.'

'I expect you'll get some birthday money from England, like the others.'

'If they send it early I could add it to the money I've saved from work and you could give me my birthday money early…'

'Look in the weekend paper, they always have lots of advertisements; maybe a failed rock group will be selling their kit' said his father.

'I think Simon will make a good drummer.' Their mother added a note of encouragement. 'He's got natural rhythm, look how he loved rock and roll when he was a little boy.'

'…and he was good at the Twist' said Jennifer.

'Just because we didn't have the same opportunities George… we should encourage him.'

'…when I was your age there was a war on…' Simon did one of his imitations of his father.

'Your mother's right, at least you're doing the sensible thing and getting yourself a proper career first; music's a good hobby, like that clever lad at church.'

'Give me oil in my lamp…' Simon did a falsetto rendition of one of the choruses from church.

On Saturday morning Melissa turned up on her bike; she wanted to show Jennifer the new shopping parade near her house.

'Good idea Jenny, better than you wandering restlessly round the house; we'll have lunch at twelve thirty. You can report back on what the shops are like, maybe they'll be near enough for me to walk.'

A ten minute ride took the girls to the shops, Jennifer was impressed. There was a large shop like Woolworths in England and a little supermarket. The shops had a frenetic Saturday morning feel and many women wore rollers in their hair, covered by scarves or nets.

'Why are they going around like that?' said Jennifer.

'They're getting ready to go out tonight, Saturday night their husbands have to take them out, or they'll be grumpy all week.'

'Where do they go?'

'I'm not sure, Perth I suppose, Dad says there's nowhere to go out around here.'

'My Mum never wears rollers.'

'Her hair must be naturally wavy then.'

Jennifer had never given much thought to her mother's hair; it was just brown and ordinary. 'Dad doesn't take her out on Saturdays anyway, except last week. Joe's brother's got a new Italian Restaurant; Dad said they deserved a night out after the birthday party the weekend before. They didn't just have spaghetti, they had all sorts of things they had never tasted before and they were delicious; lucky things.'

There was also a pet shop with a few budgies in cages and bags of hay. The girls breathed in the exquisite smell of new leather as they examined the dog collars and leads, then they sniffed the huge tub of dog biscuits.

'Christine and I ate some of her dog's biscuits once.'

'Not the hard bone shaped ones' said Melissa.

'Not Boneo, Winnalot, little brown biscuits, out of the box, not from his bowl' she giggled.

The shop owner frowned at them, as they showed no sign of buying anything.

'Let's go exploring,' said Melissa 'you've got nearly an hour. Follow me, it's a secret destination.'

Jennifer loved going exploring with Melissa on her bike; though they were both new in the area, her friend had a good sense of direction and always found her way back. Now Melissa was streaking up a quiet road that was beginning to look familiar and Jennifer was worried, but all she could do was pedal fast to keep up.

A few minutes later Melissa squealed her brakes; they were outside Paul's granny's old house and the practice shed.

'I thought it was further away than this' said Jennifer, putting one foot on the ground, but unwilling to get off her bike.

'I think Paul's brother took us the long way round and a different way back. Boys like driving around in their cars, like my cousin. Dad and I came this way the other day and I recognised it.'

'You didn't tell him you'd been here?'

'No fear, at least you were with your brother, I'm not allowed to go in cars with boys.'

'We can't stay; we're not supposed to come here.'

'We're allowed to cycle on a public road, it's a free country; anyway, their car's not here. Let's go down that track and have a look round the back.'

At the same time as they heard a familiar banging from the shed, Jennifer spotted Simon's bike propped up against another. They wheeled their bikes hastily to the road, jumped on and pedalled furiously away. When they were nearly back at the shops they dismounted, Jennifer's legs were shaking, but they couldn't stop giggling.

'I feel like a burglar' said Jennifer.

'It's not as if we were trespassing, they couldn't have seen us.'

The journey to the Murphy's house seemed to take for ever; when they drew up outside it was three thirty five and Jennifer looked nervously at her watch.

'I'm sure she hasn't sold all the puppies in the last five minutes' said her father.

The front door opened and Mrs. Murphy came out to show them through a side gate. In the back yard were two large runs and no flowers or lawn. The two black Labradors were in one run and the puppies in another.

'Sheba's inside, I've been gradually keeping them apart.'

'Will she know one is missing?' said Jennifer. It seemed sneaky.

'Oh yes, but she'll be busy with the others.' She handed her father a huge box to put in the car. 'There's a puppy collar and lead, the puppy food they're on, a blanket that smells of Sheba and the phone number of a good vet in Victoria Park.'

'I hope we won't need that' he said.

'Have you and Mrs Palmer decided on the sex?'

'…not really.'

'Good, Jennifer's not going to choose the puppy…' For a moment Jennifer felt a stab of disappointment. 'I'm sure the puppy will choose you; when you go in, sit quietly on that log and let them investigate you. Breeders look out for an alert dog, bright eyes, one that responds quickly if you call.'

The puppies were much larger than she had expected; eight of them. She didn't like to ask what had happened to the runt of the litter. They were all so cute she wanted to take them all; chocolate brown, black with white markings, black all over, brown with white paws and face, yellow… some with floppy ears like Sheba and others with pricked ears like Drongo.

'Have you got buyers for the rest?' asked her father.

'Your friend John still reckons he's going to buy the lot; I told him they are staying here, I like to interview new owners, they may not be pedigrees, but they're an excellent litter and they deserve good homes.'

'Quite right, I'm sure Jenny will look after her puppy very well, she's read all the books.'

'You realise the whole family has to be involved in the care?'

'Oh yes, we're all looking forward to having the first Australian in the family' he quipped.

She didn't laugh, but before she could speak again a cheerful voice called out.

'You must be Gip, pleased to meet you, I'm Bill. Hello again Jenny, they're a fine bunch aren't they?' He pumped her father's hand vigorously. 'I'm trying to persuade the Missus to let me keep one, a real dog to go out bush with me.'

Finally Mrs. Murphy declared it was time for Jennifer to go in the pen. The puppies all came up to her, snuffling with their cold wet noses, their little tails wagging. The yellow one with pricked ears jumped up at her knees.

'Looks like a dingo pup,' said Mr. Murphy 'though I reckon he'll grow bigger than a dingo, look at the size of those paws.'

Jennifer decided he should be called Dingo; he did have a glint in his eye, he was the one she wanted, but would Mrs. Murphy deem him to have chosen her?

'Excellent choice, I had a feeling it might be him, what do you think Mr. Palmer?'

'He seems to have taken a liking to Jenny.'

'Shall I call him Dingo?'

'Have you remembered how to pick puppies up properly?' Mrs. Murphy had not finished giving out instructions.

Jennifer nervously carried Dingo to the car; he wriggled strongly and she was scared she would drop him.

Chapter Twenty Seven   Dingo

'Dingo son of Drongo?' laughed Simon as he yanked open the car door, just catching the puppy in time as it tried to escape.

The dog was bigger than Helen had expected.

'Don't let go of him,' said George 'he nearly took over the steering wheel on the Causeway, so much for us keeping the journey calm for him.'

Helen went ahead and made sure the door to the lounge was closed; then shut the back door as soon as they were inside. Dingo looked relieved to be put down before the twins pulled him out of Simon's arms. The puppy tottered around sniffing everything and everyone; then stood still.

'Look, he's doing a wee' said Tony in delight.

'Toilet training's your department Jenny' said Simon.

'Mrs. Murphy says the garden will be too big for him, we have to make a run.'

'Bill gave me a spare roll of wire, come on Simon, we'll fence in the terrace and lawn before it gets dark, then it will be safe to let him out.'

'Not my new mop Jenny, use those old cloths… boys keep the door closed, we don't want him going beyond the kitchen and laundry.'

As Helen finished getting tea ready, Dingo helped Jennifer unpack the box and put his blanket in the cardboard tray George had brought back from work.

'Do you like him Mum?'

'Oh he's adorable; I was expecting something brown and scruffy, but his fur is like velvet.'

They sat at the table with their meal and watched through the doorway as Dingo licked his bowl clean, then curled up in his box. They dropped their voices to a whisper.

He didn't sleep for long; by the time Helen and George were washing up and the twins were in the shower, Dingo was rushing around investigating.

'Please can I have him in my room?' said Jennifer. 'In his box, just so he won't be alone?'

'No, we don't want him ending up in our beds like Rover; he has to learn the laundry is his room.'

Jennifer spent all evening cleaning up after him and taking him outside every half hour. 'Don't forget I can't come to church tomorrow, I have to stay here looking after him.'

'…and don't forget Jenny, you are going to get up in the middle of the night if he cries' said Helen. 'You get to bed now; Dingo doesn't seem to be tired, we'll tuck him up.'

'At least he shows up in the dark' said George, as they put him out before they went to bed.

'He doesn't seem to be doing anything.'

'I suppose it takes a while to get the idea, but at least puppies are quicker than human babies. Come on Dingo, bedtime.'

'The whole house is quiet, even Simon's turned his radio off' said George, sliding over to Helen's side of the bed. 'No reason why we can't…'

He was interrupted by a piteous whining. There was no sound of Jennifer getting up.

'We'd better see to him George, before he wakes everyone up.'

When they opened the laundry door the puppy greeted them enthusiastically. Behind him was strewn the newspaper they had laid neatly on the floor.

Helen picked him up, intending to put him firmly back in his box. His little round belly felt warm and he snuggled up against her shoulder.

'I thought you weren't going to treat him like a baby.'

'But he is a baby,' said Helen 'a little baby who's missing his mother. Perhaps Jenny was right; he should be beside her bed, like a real baby.'

'Real babies wear nappies, he has to stay in the laundry till he's house trained.'

Reluctantly she put him back in the box and reassured him; they closed the laundry door.

'Now we know he's fine, we can ignore him if he cries again.'

They were woken up again at one in the morning; this time they heard Jennifer padding out of her room.

When the alarm went off, Helen got up to put the kettle on. The laundry door was open and there was no sign of Dingo. She peeped in Jennifer's door; the puppy's head was poking out from the blanket, resting on Jennifer's pillow.

'Where's young Jennifer this morning?' said Pastor Roberts, as they gathered in the church hall after the service. Helen described the new arrival. 'Ashley will be jealous, he's been begging for a dog, but it wouldn't be fair to expect Muriel to take on a dog as well as the boys, when I'm so busy.'

'Yes, I'm wondering what we've let ourselves in for.'

'Oh has the puppy arrived?' said Cathy, overhearing the conversation. 'Can I come round and see him; would that be too much trouble with the babies?'

'No. I'll be glad of company if I'm stuck at home puppy sitting; come round and have a sandwich tomorrow, before you have to go and pick Sally up from school. Jennifer is following the breeder's rules exactly; twenty four hours getting used to his family, before we start 'socialising' him. I've got a feeling Dingo's going to be more trouble than my babies were.'

'Not as bad as doing the crèche?'

'I'm out of practice, I feel quite exhausted.'

'That little baby always cries, not your fault. Next week you're on tea duty; then you get a few Sunday's off, as long as no one goes sick.'

'Helen, thanks for helping with the crèche.' Muriel excused herself from another group and came over. 'My boys haven't stopped talking about your birthday party; sounds as if Simon was brilliant at organising the games. What a pity he doesn't want to join the youth group or be a junior leader in Boys Brigade.'

'I quite agree, but wait till yours are teenagers. I have to tread on eggshells keeping the peace between George and Simon. The trouble is, we didn't have teenagers in our day; I suppose we'll be experts by the time the twins are that age. At least we've managed to get him to church, but he's old enough to be out at work, as he keeps pointing out, we have to let him make decisions for himself.'

'We are praying for him' said Pastor Roberts.

Helen could find no answer to that, she felt rather miffed. Just because Simon didn't want to go to Boys Brigade it hardly meant he had gone astray. She looked around to make sure Simon wasn't listening near by.

He wasn't, he was outside chatting to a couple of the young girls.

'I'll see you at home' he said, as she and George came out of the hall.

'Cigarette?' said George as they turned the corner.

'Yes, just what I need after that crèche.'

'Do the other ladies know you smoke' he grinned.

'Well not exactly, but perhaps I should be a little rebellious. After all, we aren't signed up members of their church and Pastor Roberts can be rather sanctimonious.'

'I'm going to the men's breakfast next Saturday, I thought you'd be pleased; can't expect Simon to join in if I don't set an example.'

'That's good; give you a chance to get to know the other men better, some of the older Dads might have a few hints on bringing up teenagers.'

'We're doing quite a good job aren't we?'

On Monday morning Helen persuaded Jennifer that Dingo would be fine and the children reluctantly trooped off to school. Soon after there was a torrential downpour of rain; they had been caught out again by the weather. It had looked fine and she had not reminded them to take their raincoats.

Dingo thought she was doing her chores for his entertainment; in the laundry he played in the bundle of dirty washing on the floor. By the time the first load was ready, the sun had come out and the sky was clear; only the wet ground and the fresh air signs that it had rained. When she hauled the dripping sheets onto the rotary hoist Dingo leapt away as drops fell on his nose. She was thankful for the run as Dingo scampered round the patch of sand and grass that passed for a lawn. The rest of the back yard was as wild as the day they had moved in and she wanted the puppy where she could see him.

Tidying up the lounge she saw the postman put something blue in the letter box, hopefully an aerogramme. Dingo had fallen asleep in his box, the laundry door was closed; it was safe to go out and collect the mail. A bill and two aerogrammes, a good moment to have a well earned cup of coffee. She crept around as she did when the babies were having their naps.

One letter was from her mother, the other from her sister; dutifully she opened her mother's first. She was concerned as she read the first line.

I'm afraid I have to tell you some news that could come as a shock. Reg has asked your sister to marry him.

Helen paused to take in the news announced in such a strange way.

Of course at first we were delighted, but what we didn't know was that Reg is divorced. This means they will not be able to marry in church, not only that, we are now wondering what sort of person he really is; he seemed such a nice man.

The garden is looking a picture... Mrs. Green next door is having an operation... you remember Mr. Pritchard at church, he's got a slipped disc, he can hardly move...

Helen almost laughed at the abrupt change to other news in which she had no interest. Squeezed in at the end was a PS; a plea for her to write to her sister with advice. She sliced open her sister's letter.

...I hope to post this before Mum and Dad write to you; they have over reacted to our news;

what news? I hear you ask. Reg and I have decided to get married. Of course I've known all along that he was divorced. I hadn't told anyone else, because it wasn't anyone else's business and I wanted Mum and Dad to get to know him first. We only want a quiet little wedding in a registry office at our ages; so the church thing is not an issue.

With you all over there I wouldn't want a big do anyway; can you imagine our sister-in-law as a matron of honour or our poor little niece as a bridesmaid? Now that you have made the big break away from the narrow confines, I'm sure you'll understand. Anyway, before this aerogramme runs out I must ask if you can drop a line to Mother and Father and reassure them.

Was that how her sister saw their migration? Helen heard the doorbell and put the letters down. A frantic yapping was coming from the laundry.

She rushed to let Cathy in while Dingo was still safely shut in, but the front veranda was an insurmountable obstacle to her splendid silver cross pram.

'Can I come round the back way? The baby's fast asleep.'

'Of course; give me a couple of minutes to pick up the puppy and negotiate a path for you.'

When the pram was safely installed in the hall, Cathy sat in the kitchen with her little girl on her lap. Dingo sat on Helen's lap, regarding the toddler with fascination.

'Thanks, can't leave the baby outside in case we get another one of those downpours.'

'…and I suppose in summer it's too hot to leave them in the garden.'

'People don't seem to put their babies out in the garden here or take them out for a walk.'

'How do they do their shopping?'

'In the car; they don't take the baby out just for fresh air or to show it off; because of the heat I guess, but I insisted the pram was shipped out.'

'I'll put Dingo down and get the kettle on.'

The little girl was keen to play with Dingo.

'How was the baby's second night?'

'Dreadful, nobody got any sleep, but I can't bear to look into those soulful eyes when we shut the laundry door. We might have to weaken and let Jenny have him in her room. Anyway, I'm glad I've got someone to tell my news, my sister's getting married.'

'Oh congratulations… that is good news isn't it?' Helen explained the situation. 'Well what do you know about this Reg, not nearly forty or something is he?'

Helen laughed. 'George is forty.'

'Yes, but he's not thinking of having a baby.'

'I don't know if they want to have children, I hadn't thought of that. My sister's seven years younger than me, so there's no reason why they shouldn't… Do you think she sees this as her last chance?'

'It's 1965; do women still worry about being left on the shelf?'

'Yes, I must get 'with it', of course you've been to university, seen more of life than me; you can take a broader view than my poor parents.'

'I still believe marriage is for life.'

'No, I can't imagine being married to someone who was with someone else before.'

'Not brand new' Cathy laughed. 'But widows and widowers marry again. Perhaps it wasn't even Reg's fault the marriage didn't work. Nobody should be condemned to stay in a miserable marriage or spend the rest of their life alone. Whatever you write back in your letters, you will have to be tactful.'

'This is the first big family event that we are going to miss; I assumed that my parents would be okay with my sister at home.'

'If they accept the situation, they'll have a new son-in-law to look after them.'

---o0o---

Jennifer rushed Melissa out of school, anxious to get home to see Dingo and show him off to her friend. They went round the back, but the run was empty; opening the back door, there was no sign of him in the laundry or kitchen. In the lounge her mother was sitting in the arm chair with the puppy asleep on her lap.

'Oh hello girls, the baby's tired, he's been playing with Cathy's toddler all afternoon.' Jennifer stroked his head with her finger and he opened one eye. Melissa admired his wet brown nose and they examined his paws with their soft brown pads. 'Did you get wet this morning? Dingo didn't want to go outside.'

'No, we just missed it.' At the sound of the fly screen rattling, Dingo's ears pricked up. 'Here's Daddy.' Jennifer scooped him up to greet her father.

'Has he been a good boy? Did you manage to stay awake at school after that horrendous night?'

'Of course and I'm sure he's going to be fine tonight.'

'Joe and I got caught in that downpour this morning, it was so heavy we couldn't see where we were going, had to stop the van.'

'We had some letters this morning,' said her mother 'you'd better read them while I put the kettle on… I'm sure they were on the coffee table, maybe Dingo knocked them on the floor, or Cathy's little one moved them.'

Still clasping Dingo, Jennifer looked around the room; then behind the chair she spotted a scrap of blue. She held up a chewed piece of aerogramme.

'Oh dear, it would have to be the letter with important news' said her mother.

But her father laughed. 'Aerogrammes weren't on Mrs. Murphy's diet instructions.'

'Dad…' Jennifer was more worried about Dingo's health than the letters.

'So what was the important news?'

'I'll tell you later George, isn't it time you took the puppy outside Jenny?'

Jennifer wondered what the news could be, but knew better than to ask in front of visitors. It was probably about money or someone having an operation.

The girls played with Dingo on the grass and praised him when he went to the toilet.

'Mrs. Murphy hasn't got homes for all the puppies; Dad's got her phone number, you can give it to your Dad. She'll have to sell them soon, they have to get used to humans while they're still young.'

Melissa sighed 'I'm sure if we went to see the puppies Mum would fall in love with them, if they're all as sweet as Dingo.'

Jennifer hoped it would be a while before her brothers turned up. The twins had gone to Wayne's house and she had persuaded Simon not to bring his friends round yet; the thought of his large noisy mates clumping round the house was scary when the puppy was so delicate. Simon had retorted that his friends would not be interested in seeing a puppy and he had hockey practice anyway. According to Simon, he was well on his way to becoming captain of the team. Jennifer was still trying to get to grips with the rules.

The peace didn't last for long; Patricia appeared with Caroline trailing behind. Dingo greeted them like long lost friends.

'Mum says we can have one of the puppies' said Caroline.

'Mrs. Murphy's very fussy about who she sells them to' Jennifer couldn't resist saying.

Melissa stifled a giggle. 'They might all be gone' she added.

'Can we take him for a walk?' asked Caroline.

'No, he's too young; we have to get him used to his puppy lead and collar first.' Jennifer thought perhaps it would be a good idea if they had a dog of their own; otherwise they would always be coming round to see Dingo. 'I could write down Mrs. Murphy's phone number for you…'

At tea time they sat and watched Dingo eat his puppy supper, then curl up in his box.

'He has had a busy day' said her mother.

'How many people have you given Mrs. Murphy's phone number to?' said her father. 'It was only for us to call if we had problems.'

'Only Melissa and Caroline.'

'Oh dear, I wonder what Mrs. Murphy will make of Valerie?' said her mother. 'Do you think John will have one of the puppies George?'

'We could take Dingo over to see his Daddy and his brother' said Jennifer. 'When he's learnt to walk on the lead, then we can get him used to the car. Can I have him in my room tonight?'

'Perhaps, after last night, your father needs his sleep.'

'We all need our sleep' he said.

'I'll put newspaper all over my floor and take him out every time he wakes up.'

'Okay, as long as you're up in time, your mother has enough trouble getting everyone off to school.'

'I'm not any trouble, nor is Simon,' she added loyally 'it's only the twins.

'It's Tony not me' retorted Peter.

Jennifer went to bed without any prompting.

'Not on the bed remember, I don't want to be washing bedding every day.'

Dingo settled down in his box, looking very pleased with himself. When she woke up during the night he seemed to be on top of the blanket beside her, she couldn't work out how the little puppy had climbed up.

In the morning she was up before anyone and outside in the rain with Dingo while it was barely light. She crept around tidying up her bedroom, wiping up wet footprints in the kitchen and laid the table for breakfast; then mopped up the laundry after the puppy knocked over his water bowl, by which time her father was up and shaving, so she put the kettle on.

'This is very impressive; will you be doing this every morning?'

'Yes, I'm going to get up early now I've got a dog. Can you bring some more boxes home from work; then he can have two beds.'

'Yes, but when I make him a proper box it's going in the laundry.'

She went over and put her arms round his waist. 'Thank you for getting me a puppy.'

At breakfast the twins pleaded to bring Wayne round to see the puppy.

'That's fair Jenny, your friends had their turn yesterday.'

'I didn't ask Caroline to come round... I suppose I won't be able to go round to Melissa's to watch 'Komotion', I'll have to come straight home every day.'

'Yes you will, I can't look after him and cook tea.'

Simon appeared in the kitchen looking wet.

'It's pouring, no one brought the paper in; shall I put it in the oven?'

'Yes please,' said his mother 'it should be dry by the time I get a chance to read it.'

As he unrolled the paper and tried to flatten it out, he peered closer at the bottom corner.

'Read it later, come and have breakfast otherwise you'll be late, was it anything important?'

'Nothing... I'm going now.'

'But you can't go without anything to eat...' He had gone out the door before she finished her sentence. 'What's the matter with your brother Jenny?'

'I don't know, he's been quite cheerful for the last couple of days.'

Jennifer left after the twins, kissing Dingo on his forehead as her mother held him firmly. 'Now be a good boy for Mummy.'

'I'm not his mummy, if you want to be his mummy, that's fine.'

She giggled. 'You've got four boys now.'

At school the day passed slowly; Jennifer hoped Dingo wasn't missing her, or worse, had forgotten about her.

'How long would a day seem to a puppy?'

'A week' suggested Melissa. 'One dog year equals seven human years. Dad might phone Mrs. Murphy when he's at work. I shouldn't have told them about Dingo chewing the letters, Mum's worried a dog would chew her dressmaking material.'

'We've got too much homework tonight' grumbled Maria.

'...and I've got to cook tea as Mum is trying to finish that wedding dress.'

'I didn't do any homework at the weekend' added Jennifer. 'I'm sure Simon never does any homework.'

'He doesn't need to,' said Cathy 'he's brainy.'

'How do you know?'

'My sister said.'

Jennifer felt proud.

At home her mother was surprisingly cheerful, considering the mess in the laundry. 'Dingo's got his own towel now, it's so wet outside and he's so near the ground I have to dry him every time he's been out. Did you see Simon?'

'No, but I often don't anyway.'

'We've got bubble and squeak for tea; we're running out of food, but I don't like to leave him to dash up to the shops.'

Simon turned up just as tea was being served, he looked different. Her father looked at the clock.

'Everything okay?' asked her mother.

'Did you read the newspaper?'

'Oh, it's still in the oven, I've been so busy with the dog and just using the frying pan…'

'Paul's brother got killed in a car accident.'

For a moment Jennifer couldn't take in what he was saying.

'It's on the front page of the newspaper, only small, I didn't know if I'd read it right this morning.

I went round Paul's house, but I didn't knock, I didn't know what you're supposed to do. Then his uncle came out and said *Don't you know what's happened, Paul won't be coming to school today.*

When I got to school only a few others had seen it.'

Her father retrieved the curled yellow newspaper and read the small paragraph out.

'A *seventeen year old driver was killed instantly and his passenger seriously injured in a collision yesterday…* every other day there seems to be one of these in the paper.'

'Poor Paul and his parents' said her mother.

'It's no surprise, the way he drove.'

'Dad, you don't even know if it was his fault.'

'I know, I'm sorry for your friend and Paul, but it's a good thing I told you not to go in his car.'

Jennifer didn't dare look at her brother; she felt her face go red. They could have both been killed, she felt even more guilty about the car ride day.

'I wonder what we can do to help' her mother was saying.

'We don't know them Helen, they've got family; we can't intrude.'

Jennifer had never known anyone who had died; only her grandfather, but she didn't remember that, Simon probably did. Dingo had retreated to his bed as if he knew something was wrong.

'One tiny paragraph in the paper,' sighed her mother 'such a waste of a young life.'

At school the next morning Jennifer whispered the news to Melissa.

'That's creepy, we mustn't ever tell our parents we were in that car; do you think Simon will tell?'

'No way, I bet Dad won't even let him learn to drive now.'

'I'll have to go to the church in secret and light a candle for him; I can't believe it's happened.'

'Can I come, would I be allowed to?' Jennifer knew Pastor Roberts disapproved of

anything involving candles and the Roman
Catholic Church. That would have to be another
secret.

Chapter Twenty Eight   Letters

'Where do you think they'll live?'

'Who?' mumbled George into the pillow.

'Reg and my sister of course.'

'That's not our problem, especially at this time of the night. Perhaps your sister will discover the realities of a mortgage. Have you written to her yet?'

'I was going to write this evening, but by the time we had all that upset with Tony's homework… and I wanted to have a chance to talk to Simon.'

'He doesn't want to talk, we shouldn't press him.'

'His poor parents; that could be us in a few years time.'

'Helen, don't even think like that. It won't be because I'll teach Simon to drive myself, make sure he's sensible.'

'That doesn't account for other drivers on the road.'

'He could drown or be knocked off his bike; we can't worry about what might happen. How do you think my mother coped during the war?'

'I can well imagine how awful it must have been for her… I wish we'd talked more to them.'

'Who?'

'All the parents, your father before he died and before we left England we should have made more time to discuss the past with your mother,

413

Mum and Dad; shown we appreciated them, now we know how hard it is being parents. We'll never have the chance now.'

The next morning Helen was about to put pen to paper when Thelma turned up. Dingo greeted her enthusiastically.

'I couldn't resist coming round to see him, oh the posty's been.'

'Can I leave Dingo shut in the kitchen with you? I don't want him to get out the front door. I have to check in case it's something important.'

There was one aerogramme in the post box and she was surprised to see her brother's address on it.

'We are honoured, he doesn't often write. Dingo's not making a nuisance of himself is he?'

'No, we've made friends already. You read your letter before you put the kettle on.'

'…That's good, he likes Reg and thinks he will liven up the family, whatever that means. He was very good when my sister-in-law was in hospital. I didn't know she had been… and my niece adores him. Under the circumstances, what circumstances… he's urging them to get on with it, book the registry office and he'll treat the whole family to lunch afterwards.'

'Sounds like it's all sorted then.'

'I hope he's talked to Mum and Dad and reassured them.'

'Life goes on Helen, they can sort themselves out without you being there.'

'Yes, that's what George says; I think he's relieved we're not there… sorry, I'm prattling on and I haven't even heard how your family are.'

'But I like hearing all about your English 'relis'. Nothing much to tell about ours; it's the same as with you; we thought they wouldn't cope with the farm by themselves, but they have. Bob's got a week off, we've given them time to settle down, now we can go and visit. I can't see them wanting to come up here yet.'

Dear Mum and Dad,

We were thrilled to hear the news, I'm sure Reg will make a wonderful son-in-law and I shall write to say how pleased we are for them, though sad we can't be there. I was surprised to get a letter from my brother, but if he approves of Reg he must be a good bloke. As we are not the Royal Family I'm sure it's okay to marry a divorced man.

Helen paused over her letter, was that last phrase too flippant?

At least you will have more space… Unless they hadn't got anywhere to live and Reg was going to move in with them, surely not… instead she wrote

I look forward to hearing all about their plans.

The puppy is gorgeous and we have all fallen in love with him, even though he is more trouble than a baby, though I suppose I've

415

forgotten what it was like when the twins were babies.

She was running out of space and crammed in the last few words.

It's not till your own family are growing up that you fully appreciate your parents...

With all my love, Helen.

Dingo was curled up asleep, now would have been a good time to pop to the shops, but she was determined to dash off aerogrammes to her brother and sister as well.

I have written to mother and father and I'm sure they'll come round. If you know this is what you want that's all that matters. I want to hear all your plans, where will you go for your honeymoon?

'Now Dingo, be a good boy, I'm just going to post the letters and go to the shops. Jenny will soon be home.'

He looked reproachfully at her. When did she start having conversations with the dog, she wondered.

'That was a nice meal' said George.

'Bit of a mish mash, you're lucky to get any tea. No sooner had I posted the letters to England than the heavens opened. I dashed into the Greek shop and decided not to bother with Tom the Cheap. They thought it was funny that in summer I'm too hot and in winter too wet.'

'I'm off tomorrow; I'll puppy sit while you got to ladies' fellowship, you can take as long as you like at the shops on the way back.'

'Thankyou Dad,' said Jenny 'I'm sure Dingo will be on his best behaviour.'

Helen met Cathy on the way to the church.

'Do you want to push the pram?'

'Yes please, it's years since I did this.'

The toddler sat on the pram seat staring solemnly at Helen.

'It's good they like the crèche.'

'Yes, I'd go mad stuck at home; when we're there at least I know I can pop next door if one of them cries. It's our turn next meeting. How's your baby?'

'Not potty trained yet and I could have done without this wet weather and I'm sure Jenny's been letting him sleep on her bed, but apart from that...'

She didn't mention Paul's brother. Young mothers should enjoy the baby stage without worrying about all the things that could happen when they were grown up.

But after the short Bible Study and prayers, the talk over tea and cakes turned to the terrible accident. It had happened near one woman's house and a couple of the long term residents knew the family.

'Bunch of tearaways that family and they let the grandmother's property go to wrack and ruin after she died.'

'But his younger brother is a friend of Simon's and he has always seemed very nice,' put in Helen 'and the mother's not very well apparently.'

'The mother's an alcoholic' whispered another.

'I suppose that might explain why Paul has to get his own meals… what about the father?

'Works up North most of the time.'

'So she probably hasn't had an easy life, poor woman.'

'And we should be praying for the family, not judging them' added Cathy.

When Helen arrived home she was glad to see George and Simon sitting together at the kitchen table; Simon was cuddling Dingo.

'I did what you suggested… not wagging the last lesson, I mean me and a couple of the others went round to Paul's. That's the first time I've met his Dad. He thanked us for coming so it wasn't as bad as I was expecting. Paul was okay.'

'I don't suppose it's really sunk in yet. How's his mother?'

'I don't know, she was lying resting. We didn't stay long, we didn't know what to say.'

'You went, that's the main thing.'

'The boy that got injured, was someone we don't know, not the one in the group. Do you think they'll still want to have a group?'

---o0o---

In the changing rooms at lunchtime, Jennifer was practising crossing herself; Melissa giggled every time she got it the wrong way round.

'If I think how I do it, I get muddled as well.'

On the way to the science room one of the fourth year girls Simon knew pointed to Jennifer and a teacher strode over.

'Are you Simon Palmer's sister?' Her stomach knotted, she was unused to being addressed by teachers outside the classroom and she could not imagine why he would want to talk to her. 'Is he crook?'

'No, he left for school before me; we never have any days off sick' she added.

'I know, it's unusual for him, he had an important piece of work to hand in. Tell him he can have an extension as long as he hands it in before school tomorrow.'

'Yes Sir.'

'Are you as clever as your brother?'

Jennifer was about to shake her head, but Melissa said 'Yes she is.'

In the science room Jennifer worried about what could have happened.

'I saw him go out the door with his school bag full; where would he go?'

'Jennifer Palmer, if you want to be a vet, you will have to learn a lot of science' said Mr. Holloway 'and you can't do that if you're talking.'

She quickly bent her head over her exercise book.

'Why does he think I want to be a vet?' she asked the others as they left the classroom.

'He assumes all girls want to be vets, nurses or air hostesses' giggled Christine. '…and you have pictures of dogs on your exercise book.'

'I know where Simon might be,' whispered Melissa 'is Paul back at school?'

'I don't know, Simon won't talk about it.'

After school they went straight round to Melissa's church. She assured Jennifer that if she dipped her fingers in the holy water and crossed herself, anyone in the church would assume she was a Catholic.

At first the church did not look as strange as Jennifer expected, but as her eyes became accustomed to the gloom she could see Mary dressed in blue looking down at her and a graphic wooden carving of Jesus on the cross. When they did the Ten Commandments in Scripture lessons at Saint Stephen's she had always wondered what the graven images were, that they weren't allowed to worship. She didn't dare look at any statues in case she accidentally prayed to an idol. Melissa led her to a metal stand beneath another statue, where small white candles flickered.

'Light one and pray for Paul's brother and his family' Melissa whispered.

Outside, they discussed Simon.

'If he's home when you get there, don't say anything to your parents and tell him in secret about his homework.'

'But what if he's not there?'

'Come straight round to my house on your bike, then we'll go to Paul's granny's property.'

In the back yard her mother was bringing in the washing and Dingo rushed to greet her.

'At least I got the clothes dry today.'

'Is Simon home yet?'

'No.'

It wouldn't be telling tales if Simon hadn't told her to keep a secret and something might have happened to him. She told her mother about the teacher.

'He certainly didn't come back home, surely he wouldn't play truant?'

'I could go out on my bike to some of the places he hangs round with his friends.'

'Oh thanks Jenny… I won't mention it to Dad till Simon's had a chance to explain.'

When the girls arrived at the old house there was no sign of the boys' bikes. Jennifer was nervous. The big shed was empty and they crept up to the house and stood looking at the fly screen door hanging off its hinges. They could smell cigarette smoke.

'It won't hurt to peep in' said Melissa.

'There must be someone else in there.'

'If it's an old tramp, we'll run out and jump on our bikes.'

As they nudged open the wooden door they saw Simon and Paul sitting at an old table smoking. The boys turned round in surprise when they heard the door creak.

'Jen, what are you doing here?'

'We've come to stop you getting into trouble' she tried to explain. 'I won't tell Mum where you are, or that you were smoking.'

Neither boy spoke. Melissa gazed round at the cobwebs and grimy windows and shuddered.

'I hope there aren't any red back spiders.'

Now they were here, Jennifer wondered if it had been a good idea. She had no idea what else to say to her brother and she was too embarrassed to look at Paul.

'We've already taken the oath,' said Melissa 'we won't tell anyone.'

'Now you are here Jenny, you can tell Mum I won't be home for tea, I'm having it at Paul's.'

'But it's a school night.'

'I'm not a kid. Look, Paul's staying here.'

'You mean living here?'

'Yeah, why not.'

She looked at Paul, but he didn't seem to be listening. 'What about his parents' she whispered.

'They're not bothered' Paul suddenly spoke.

'We could bring you food and supplies' Melissa's eyes lit up with the prospect of the adventure.

Jennifer knew her mother would not like Simon eating somewhere as dirty as this.

'I brought some food from home this morning,' said Simon 'just a few tins Mum won't notice are missing.'

'Yes she will.'

'...and Paul's got plenty of money, his Dad always gives him loads when he comes back.'

Jennifer looked at her watch.

'We're going now,' said Melissa 'if you need anything you can give Jenny a secret message at home.'

The girls cycled quickly away and didn't stop till they reached the corner where their ways parted.

'It's hardly a secret,' said Jennifer 'Paul's family will just guess where he is and go round and look. If he doesn't go home they will be worried in case he's got killed as well.'

'Maybe they've gone mad with grief' suggested her friend.

At home Jennifer's mother was looking flustered in the kitchen and the twins were dancing round.

'Jenny, Dingo's done a pooh in the lounge and you have to clear it up.'

'It's only just happened; I didn't want to let dinner burn.'

Jennifer scooped up Dingo and took him to see his mess, wondering why he had chosen the carpet and not the floorboards round the edge. She deposited him in the garden and fetched the emergency cleaning things they now kept in the laundry.

'Did you see Simon' asked her mother when Jennifer returned to the kitchen.

'Yes, he's going to have tea with Paul.'

'Oh dear, surely Paul's family won't want visitors.'

'I think they are going to get fish and chips and eat them in the kitchen and not disturb his parents.' She was perturbed how easy it was to make up a plausible story, but it wasn't really lying, she hadn't said which kitchen.

When the twins were in bed and her parents were sitting in the lounge smoking and casting worried glances at the clock, Simon strolled in the front door with his empty school bag and a guitar case slung over his shoulder. Her mother had not mentioned the school absence to her father.

'Sorry I'm late.'

'That's okay son, it's good you're looking after Paul.'

'He gave me his guitar; it's okay Mum, he wants me to have it, he's got his brother's now and that's a much better one. We'll still be able to keep our group going.'

'You can take it along to youth group, that nice lad can help you learn properly' said their mother.

Jennifer waited for her brother to make some sarcastic comment, but he was being careful to stay on the right side of his parents.

'Okay, I will... probably soon be better than him.'

'Perhaps you'll be another Hank Marvin,' said their father, 'you used to love Cliff Richard and the Shadows before the Beatles came along.'

'The twins aren't to touch the guitar though.'

By the time Jennifer was taking Dingo out in the yard before they went to bed, Simon was in the kitchen raiding the fridge for a huge snack.

'Is Paul really going to sleep there?' she whispered.

'Of course. Don't come tomorrow, maybe at the weekend.'

On Friday morning Melissa had news. 'My prayer was answered.'

Jennifer was puzzled.

'When we lit the candles yesterday, I prayed to St. Francis, he loved animals. When I got home again yesterday Dad said he'd rung Mrs. Murphy. She has a shy puppy who would suit a family without children.'

Jennifer wondered if Saint Francis had a direct line to Mrs. Murphy 'But...'

'I'm not a child am I,' said her friend 'Mary wasn't much older than me when she had Jesus.'

Jennifer was astonished. 'How do you know?'

'About the puppy?'

'No, how old Mary was.'

'Quick, everyone's lining up and we haven't even opened our lockers.'

'Did Simon come home; did he go to school today?' Melissa whispered from her desk.

Jennifer nodded. 'He wants us to go to the house at the weekend.'

At lunchtime Melissa insisted they take a circuitous route to the canteen, to try and spot Simon and make sure he was at school. They spied him in the queue for hot pies, but there was no sign of Paul. They retreated to the first year girls' quadrangle.

Caroline trailed out of school with Jennifer and Melissa. She overheard them talking about Melissa's puppy before they realised she was behind them.

'Dad's going to get an Alsatian' she said.

Melissa set off for home, keen to help her mother now she had agreed to a dog. As Caroline and Jennifer turned the corner into Smith Street, she knew something was wrong. There was a lot of noise and dust and Patricia and the twins were running back up the road towards them.

'Jenny, Caro, they're knocking down Tonydale.'

It was true; bulldozers and diggers were ripping up the bush opposite their house.

At tea time Simon and his father both arrived just as her mother was serving up.

'I see we're going to get some new neighbours' said their father cheerfully.

'But Dad,' cried the twins 'we didn't want them to chop down Tonydale.'

'Boys, we always knew they would be building more new houses in our street, at least we should have a nice new footpath.'

'I've got some exciting news' said their mother trying to change the subject.

'So have I' said Jennifer.

'Me as well,' said their father 'shall I go first? Guess what we're getting at the weekend? It's large and square.'

'A television?' said Peter excitedly.

'No, a new shed for the back yard, not exactly new, Uncle John found a nice old widow who wants to get rid of it from her yard. He's borrowing the ute and Simon can come and help us take it down and reassemble it here.' Jennifer's brothers didn't look impressed. 'It will be much bigger then our tiny shed in England. I can get a proper workbench and teach you boys woodwork.'

'Can we make a tree house?' asked Tony.

'Yes, but you'd better learn how to make small things first.'

'What was your news Mum?' Jennifer couldn't think what it could be.

'Your aunty's going to get married.'

'At her age,' said Simon 'and who to?'

'Reg of course, Uncle Reg he'll be now.'

This news didn't seem as exciting as Jennifer's. 'Melissa's going to get Dingo's brother' she announced, waiting for a reaction.

But the twins were talking about tree houses, her mother and father about the wedding and Simon was silent.

She realised her mother was speaking to her. 'So you don't mind not being a bridesmaid? I know it's sad we won't be there.'

'I don't want to be a bridesmaid and I don't feel sad at all.'

Epilogue October 1965

Helen stood on the terrace; it was still strange to think of October as spring. Really there were only two seasons in Perth; summer, hot and dry and winter, cool and wet. Her small collection of exotic shrubs, refreshed by the winter rain, looked as if they would produce some flowers. Confining gardening ambitions to her little corner by the terrace and the front garden had been a sensible decision. The end half of the back yard still looked the same, with its gum trees and black boys. Only Dingo and the twins ventured to the back fence. George's huge shed was used more as the twins' castle, but he did have his work bench. The shed would provide much needed shade for her little plot in the summer and she would ask Yvonne's advice on growing some bougainvillea to trail over it.

She wasn't looking forward to the barbeque season starting, but George and Simon were proud of the huge brick barbeque they had built. Even if they burnt the meat it didn't matter, as long as George enjoyed cooking. The party to celebrate their first year in Australia had taken on a life of its own, but all the ladies were bringing a plate and Helen only had to make cups of tea; or at least that's what her husband claimed.

George came out, eager to light the fire; all last evening he had been debating how long the fire might take to be ready for cooking.

'If we get eating underway early the families with young children can leave sooner' he said hopefully.

'Yes, it would be nice to get a chance to talk properly to John and Yvonne later in the evening.'

'Oh I forgot to tell you, I saw John in Vic Park yesterday, I told them to come early so we had a chance to chat.'

'Oh, I better go and get changed.'

'You look fine to me.'

'George, these are my housework clothes.'

'Yvonne could take a look at Tony's hand.'

'I still think we should have taken him to the doctors.'

'Every carpenter has to take a few bangs and cuts.'

'Perhaps you should lock the shed when you're not here.'

'No, they have to learn to be responsible and do as they're told. They know which tools they must only use under supervision. When Simon was that age, you only had to tell him once.'

'We've probably forgotten what he was like when he was nine' she laughed. 'The worse the twins' behaviour, the rosier your memories of Simon.'

'Mr. Reed isn't going to be pleased on Monday when he finds out Tony can't write with his bandaged hand.'

'I wonder how many people Simon's invited, he wasn't very forthcoming. Let's hope the party cheers him up. I can understand Paul's father taking him off to Queensland, but it was very sudden.'

'He's got other friends and he's bound to find boys who want to join a group. I'm more worried about his school work, the time he spends with that guitar. If he doesn't get good results at the end of this term he'll use that as an excuse to leave school.'

As Helen got changed, Dingo's barking announced the arrival of the Charles family. It would be their first meeting with Dingo's brother.

Helen came out of the back door to see a black shape bolt down the garden.

'He's just as stupid as his father,' said John 'or maybe it's the bad influence.'

'It's probably why he was the last left of the litter,' sighed Yvonne 'no one else wanted him; I don't know why I let myself get talked into keeping him.'

Banjo was jet black, but had the same Kelpie look and pricked ears as Drongo.

'Look at that, Drongo has finally decided to be a sheep dog.'

The brown dog was busy rounding up his two sons.

'Do you think Banjo knows Dingo is his brother?' said Jennifer.

'Goodness knows; if it has four legs he likes playing with it.'

'Melissa might bring her dog, he's called Major; he looks just like Drongo.'

Helen was beginning to regret being persuaded by Jennifer that it was Dingo's party as well and he should have guests.

'Dad, can I tell them our news' said Terri.

'Bad news' added Trish.

'Yes, we're off to Geraldton' said their father.

'For Christmas?'

'No, to live' said Yvonne.

Helen could not tell how her friend regarded the news, but John was obviously excited.

'Time for a change; last day of school we're off, going in to business with those friends up there.'

'Jenny, I'm going to get a horse, you can come and stay.'

'We wanted to get settled before Trish starts her exam year. You girls will soon make friends, look how well Simon and Jenny have got on.'

'What about my surfing?' complained Trish.

'Same ocean up there.'

'Dad... the beaches aren't the same.'

Helen was surprised at their decision to move such a long way from Perth, but didn't want to get involved in a family argument.

'Everyone seems to be on the move; Simon's friend has gone to Brisbane and Valerie and Mike have gone back to Sydney.'

'So soon?' said Yvonne.

'Just as suddenly as last time; it's strange without them, we'll miss young Patricia, she was always round here with the twins.'

'We won't miss Caroline' said Jennifer.

'Or that yapping dog' added her father.

'Thought they were going to get an Alsatian' said Yvonne.

'Valerie fell in love with this young Dachshund, her owners were going back to England, declared she'd always wanted a sausage dog.'

Suddenly George disappeared and returned with a bottle of wine and glasses.

'It's not champagne, but we can still drink a toast to Helen's sister and her future husband. They're probably just getting up now, preparing for the wedding.' He put his arm round Helen. 'I'm sorry you won't be there.'

'We sent a telegram yesterday,' said Helen 'and they'll probably be the only couple in Sussex with kangaroos on their tablecloth and a koala on the key ring for their new front door keys. It's hard to find wedding presents you can send airmail.'

'Sussex, not very near your parents then?' said Yvonne.

'They both wanted to live in the countryside apparently and Mum and Dad are looking for a little bungalow near them. It turns out Mum Dad wanted to move years ago, but with my sister working in London they stayed put. More news, my brother suddenly announced they are going to have another baby in three months time. They're such a private couple; all my sister-in-laws' visits to hospital, we didn't realise she was trying to have another baby.'

'That should give your parents plenty to keep them busy.'

'No wonder Mum said in her last letter she couldn't believe a whole year had gone by. Sometimes it feels to me as if we've been here for years.'

'Uncle John, have you seen our tree house' said Tony.

'I wondered what that amazing construction was.'

'It's not finished yet.'

'Goodness knows what they've scrounged from the building site across the road' said George.

'They're not going to be as big as your house' said John.

'Nor will they be on a quarter acre block, or as well built. They cleared all the bush, piled yellow sand on the land and put the foundations on top.'

'I miss our bush outlook and the twins were upset' said Helen. 'We still have all that empty land next door, but for how long?'

'If you want bush, there's plenty more out there' said John.

'Yes, we are going to plan some camping, now the puppy's settled in 'said George.

Helen had hoped he had forgotten about camping.

As guests started arriving Helen found having a party easier than she thought it would be; it was just a matter of introducing each new arrival to another person they might have something in common with and leaving them to it.

'Cathy, this is Joe from work and his wife, they're expecting another baby soon… Muriel, Thelma and Bob our next door neighbours, they're going to be grandparents at Christmas… Trish, come and meet Simon's friends…'

When everyone had managed to get some food, Helen's main worry, she had a chance to wander and listen in to the conversations. The new English family renting Valerie and Mike's house seemed friendly and Helen hoped she would get a chance to chat to them. Simon was talking to John.

'So if I go to university I can have long holidays and plenty of time for my group to practise.'

'You'll have to study hard as well, you'll be up against lads from private schools and the best brains in the state; it won't be like Glendale High. But if you work hard next year and get on a good course you can choose any career you like; have the chances me and your Dad didn't.'

'Yeah, but at least you and Dad had some excitement in the war.'

A few beers had made John mellow.

'Is that what he told you?'

'No, he's never told us anything about the war.'

'I won't pretend there weren't good times and we had plenty of laughs, but we had some bad times as well and our best mate got killed. It was your Dad who saved my life…'

434

'Really... in a battle? Tell me what happened.'

Helen moved on, she felt she was intruding. George was talking to Melissa's mother.

'Back in England I'd be getting up in the dark and coming home in the dark on the train... yes I have much more time at home.'

'Helen, are you enjoying your party, have you had anything to eat yet?'

'Oh Thelma, I've hardly spoken to you all afternoon. I haven't had any meat yet, I was more worried if everyone else would survive George's cooking. You will stay for coffee after all the families have gone?'

'Six coffees Helen? Trish and Terri are impressed with Simon's guitar,' said Yvonne 'or at least Trish is impressed with Simon's mates.'

'Yes, the boys have got quite an audience with Jennifer and her friends' said Helen. 'Thank goodness Simon turned the record player off. At least it's a pleasant evening for them to stay out on the terrace.'

In the lounge the six adults relaxed. Bob sat quietly in the corner and Thelma praised George's barbeque skills, out of politeness Helen thought.

'This time last year,' said George, 'we had been in Australia less than twenty four hours and had no idea where we would live; though thanks to John and Yvonne we didn't have to go to a migrant camp. I know we haven't seen much of the rest of Western Australia, but there's plenty of time for that. We've got our house and good neighbours, Jenny's got her dog and half the family have learnt to swim. I'm sure Helen would agree we've all settled in well and as someone said on our first day here, the first ten years are the worst!'

The End

About the Author

I have been writing frantically for ten years; taking it seriously when I joined a weekly writing group. When our tutor urged me to write a novel, two very different themes were suggested.

'What happened to Emma, whose fate was literally left hanging in the air at the end of a short story?' Emma became my first and longest novel 'Brief Encounters of the Third Kind'.

The other suggestion was to write about our family emigration to Australia. 'Quarter Acre Block', my second novel, is not autobiographical, but is inspired by our family's experiences and the Australians and other migrants we met and became friends with. My mother was a great help filling in the details of what migration was like from the parents' point of view, though the Palmer family and their relatives bear no resemblance to my family.

I have continued to write short stories, novellas and novels. Writing has propelled me into the ether; becoming a self published Indie Author has involved a steep learning curve. As fast as we authors learn to connect with readers and writers, some new form of social media arrives. Writing and real life come first, in that order, but social media can be fun if you are selective; I enjoy writers' forums, reading and writing blogs and reviewing books.

It is at this point, at the end of the book, that lots of writers beg the dear reader to write a review. I would not dream of suggesting that, I just hope you enjoyed the novel, but if you do happen to be on line with a few minutes to spare, wander over to the Amazon site where you downloaded the e-book or ordered the paperback in the first place and write a couple of sentences to tell other readers why you might recommend it. If you have any questions or comments you will find my e-mail address at my website.

You are welcome to visit my website
www.ccsidewriter.co.uk
Read about the other books I have published.
Catch up with my regular Beachwriter's Blog illustrated in colour.
Enjoy Fiction Focus.
Dip into Travel Notes from a Small Island.
Try the picture quiz.

ooo000ooo

I have published four novels and four story collections on Amazon Kindle.
The collections are all now available in paperback.
Visit my Amazon Author page.
https://www.amazon.co.uk/Janet-Gogerty/e/B00A8FWDMU

ooo000ooo

You can find me on Facebook here.
https://www.facebook.com/Beachwriter/

ooo000ooo

I am one of the authors at Goodreads
where I write a regular blog 'Sandscript' and
also review books.
www.goodreads.com

ooo000ooo

I also scribble a little as Tidalscribe on
Wordpress.com
https://wordpress.com/posts/tidalscribe.wordpress.com